FRACTURED KARMA

BREWER BROTHERS SERIES, BOOK TWO

NANCY STRAIGHT

Book formatting by Jeff at Indie Formatting Services

ACKNOWLEDGEMENTS:

As I finished this story, there were many people I needed to thank. Erin Fisher, Tammie Zimmerman, Jaime Radalyac, Kim Haddix, Shannon Hannah, and Pamela Marden – thank you all for your unwavering support! I feel blessed to know you.

To Charles Young, Melissa Balentine and Rebecca Ufkes: Your support means the world to me. No author could ever be more fortunate than I – to have three of the best beta readers and friends on the planet.

To all the book bloggers who have supported me since I started this career a few years ago, "Thank you," is inadequate. I have never met a group of people who are more giving of their time. Your willingness to take a chance on my work has humbled me from the beginning, and I grow more grateful every time I discover a new one of you in the blogosphere. Your passion inspires me every day. Thank you for doing what you do for me and for all the other independent authors out there.

Linda Brant, can you believe this is number nine? I love that you make me find forgotten coffee tables in trunks. Thank you for your patience and one day, I promise to learn where commas actually go.

To my sons, Alex and Zack, I am blessed to have two of the coolest sons in the world. You are the reason that my books have happy endings – you are both responsible for helping me to see the silver lining in every situation.

Finally, Toby, thanks for the encouragement to chase my dreams. I am the luckiest wife/mom/author I know.

All my love,
Nancy

FRACTURED KARMA

CHAPTER 1

Four years ago – Mark Brewer, age 18

My breath looked like smoke in the crisp night air. I had walked this street during the day: when the sun was up, it was choked with commuter cars and city buses. Men in suits pushed their way into office buildings. Ladies carried oversized handbags. Street vendors offered everything from tours of the old town to Rolex knock-offs. The evening was a different story – almost a different town. The rush of all the people diminished after six p.m., with the street nearly barren by nine. This time of night, the only inhabitants were the people who had nowhere else to go.

A parking lot set tucked behind two office buildings. It was used as the overflow for the Four Seasons. Lifting a car from the hotel's garage was a rookie mistake: cameras everywhere, a manned exit with key card access, and too many people who could be witnesses. I had known others who boosted cars from the hotel's garage – none ever stayed free long after. This secluded lot was only used on the weekends, and even then, only after their main garage was full.

Lenny told me from day one, "Don't get passionate about a car, Mark. It's just a ride. It's a thrill. It's a test of skills," but I knew in some cases a stolen car was bragging rights. As I looked at the cherry red Ferrari – I wanted it. I wanted to squeeze the leather wrapped wheel between my fingers. I wanted to feel the G-force when I stepped on the gas pedal, and more than anything else, I wanted to hear the grumble of an angry engine catapulting me through city streets. I'd been lurking in the shadows eyeing it for over an hour. I needed to make a decision. If I delayed much longer, I'd run the risk of a valet picking it up to return it to its owner.

I crept a few feet closer to it while watching a valet who had brought in a dark Mercedes SUV. He wore a white button-down shirt, black pants, and a sissy black vest just like all of the others. If I had done my homework, I would be wearing the same uniform to reduce suspicion if anyone saw me in the lot. I didn't. I was walking down the nearly abandoned street when I saw the car pull in. I followed it like a baby duck following its mother.

My attention was pulled away for a second as the Mercedes chimed good-bye to the valet who had just dropped her off. Once the chime sounded, that was his cue; he sprinted through the alley, around the corner, and down the block back to the Four Seasons.

The red Ferrari stood alone, glistening in the moonlight and casting the car's shadow on the asphalt. No other cars flanked it. It had been parked off by itself so no doors could ding the pristine automobile. I took another look around the lot: no watchful surveillance systems with remote viewers were positioned anywhere. No one stood between the car and me.

I heard Lenny's warning in my head, "Don't get passionate about a car. Passion makes you stupid." How could someone look at this work of art and not feel passionate? I walked through two rows of cars, zig zagging from row to row. I reasoned that if I were to be seen, I wouldn't look like a moth attacking a headlight. As I approached, I walked around the car, studying each contour, allowing my fingertips to caress her.

I slid my hand into the back pocket of my jeans to pull out a Slim Jim. There were lots of ways to unlock cars, but this slim strip of flexible metal worked on every car I'd ever tried. I had barely pulled it out of my pocket when I saw the headlights of an approaching car through the alleyway. I squatted down immediately and ran to the cover of the row of cars I had emerged from.

Parking was getting tight in the little lot. A white Lincoln Navigator emerged from the alley, then pulled into the parking spot next to the black Mercedes which had just been dropped off. This valet was different than the last: he, too, saw the Ferrari I was fixated on. The valet wore the same uniform as the last one had, but his hair was longer in shaggy ringlets. The Ferrari was like a beacon to him as soon as he exited the Navigator.

I had staked out this lot several times but had never jacked one from here before. I routinely had to fill orders, and this was a good place to look for high-end rides, but even without a surveillance system, the constant coming and going of valets made it a harder target. One of the things I noted was that few, if any, of the valets paid any attention to the luxury they drove. This was the first valet who seemed to have any appreciation for his job. I watched as this valet allowed his fingers to run along the Ferrari, just as mine had – he felt the power. His hand slid over the contours of the car from the headlights, along the hood, over the roof, all the way to the taillights.

Another set of headlights appeared through the mouth of the alleyway. The valet snapped out of the trance the Ferrari had put him into and jammed his hand into his pocket. He trotted over to the mouth of the alley and waved a hello to the arriving valet as he returned to his post at the hotel.

This was stupid. There was too much traffic tonight. This latest one made it three valets in less than five minutes. I wasn't lifting a Honda – someone would miss this one. I'd have maybe ten minutes before someone noticed it was no longer in the lot. Assuming I could successfully remove the anti-theft systems to keep the satellites from locating me, every cop in a ten-mile radius would be hunting for me on the streets. Could I get it to Lenny in ten minutes? If I could, would he take it off my hands?

People who had cars like these were one of two: either they were loaded legitimately and every cop in town would trip over himself to make sure their property was returned, or they were on the other side of the law and every slime ball in the city would be on the lookout for me. Neither option was good if I got caught before I could get her to Lenny.

Lenny would be ticked off at me if he saw me right now. Or maybe he'd say that I finally had bragging rights. No one in his crew had ever lifted a car like this. This wasn't California: a Ferrari in Kansas City stuck out like a wind-turbine in a cornfield. When I'd first gotten to the city, it was Lenny who taught me all he knew about hotwiring, tricking the new anti-theft devices, even ripping out the GPS transmitters. Before I'd met Lenny, I'd never even driven a car. Do-gooders might consider Lenny someone who exploited kids, but they could only make those observations because they'd never been alone in a big city.

Lenny gave each of us some skills. So long as he could find a buyer, he paid a decent price for any car we brought to him. Some of the kids had worked for Lenny for years. Others came by, made some quick cash, and hit the road again.

When I got to Kansas City, all I had was four changes of clothes, a single pair of shoes and thirty dollars. He found me sleeping in the back seat of a totaled Nissan Maxima at a salvage yard that he owned. Peering into his face from the back seat of the car, I was sure he was going to run me off. Lenny tossed me a blanket and a business card, told me to keep warm and to come see him in the morning.

The first day I worked for him, I walked away with two hundred dollars. The end of my first week, I had a grand in my pocket and an apartment to sleep in. Lenny took care of his crew. I had been fifteen when I started. Lenny taught me more than just how to steal cars; he taught me about manners, about dressing well to throw off suspicion, about looking someone in the eye when they spoke.

I took a deep breath, confident that I was alone in the parking lot: now or never. I stood up, walked to the glistening beautiful red rocket in front of me. I slid the Slim Jim down through the gap between the window and the metal part of the door. The door unlocked as easily as if I'd pushed the unlock button from the inside. When I pulled the door's handle, the audible alarm rang out loud. I reached down under the dash and had it disabled in less than five seconds. I stood up like a prairie dog to see if the sound had made someone appear – it hadn't.

I pulled the lever from the inside, lifted the hood, and disconnected the relay to the GPS tracker. From my coat pocket, I grabbed a pen and paper, wrote down the serial number, closed the hood, and scurried back to the shadows where I had been crouched down for the last hour. I phoned Lenny, who picked up on the second ring as I blurted out, "I've got a Ferrari. Can you check the VIN?"

Lenny's angry voice shouted, "A Ferrari? Are you nuts? Wherever you are, get outta there." That was just like Lenny, always worried I was going to get busted. Lenny preferred to fill orders. He didn't want us stealing cars he couldn't move quickly.

When he had an order to fill, he always gave the riskiest jobs to the guys he wasn't attached to on his crew. Those jobs paid the best, but I had to force my way onto those crews. I grinned into the phone, "You're telling me that if I bring it to your shop, you won't give me ten large for it?"

Barking his answer back, "How am I supposed to move that?"

Ignoring his question, I said, "Just run the VIN so I know who I'm stealing from."

Lenny sighed heavy into the phone, "Fine. Read it to me."

I read Lenny the Vehicle ID Number, watching the alleyway in case another set of headlights emerged. The seconds ticked slowly. Finally he came back on the line, "You're in luck. Registered to a Reginald Black."

"Reggie Black? The tight end here in town?"

"Looks like it."

I had hit the jackpot. Sports figures were almost always legitimate with their finances. If I took this car, I'd only have to contend with the police; a posse of criminals wouldn't be after me. Reggie would turn it into his insurance company, and by the time he got his check, this ride would have a new VIN and title and be untraceable. Elated, I asked, "So, fifteen minutes. You'll take it off my hands?"

He blew out another heavy sigh, "You get busted, I don't know you."

"I'm not going to get busted. Fifteen minutes, okay?"

"You disabled the tracking?"

I rolled my eyes. He must have thought I woke up on the stupid side of the bed. "Yes. It's already disconnected and smashed."

Another sigh echoed through the phone, "Take it to the Second Street shop. I'll tell them you're coming."

Trying not to sound like a kid who'd just got a later bedtime, I shouted, "You're the best!" I was committed. This was the first time I'd driven a car that cost more than most houses. In fifteen minutes, I'd have ten thousand dollars in my pocket, and bragging rights for the next decade.

I'd never asked Lenny any details about how he moved the cars he got, but I knew he had a guy on the inside at the Department of Motor Vehicles who could create a VIN for any car. All I had to do was drive it three miles on a Saturday night.

I eased into the car, sat in the soft leather seat, crossed the wires to override the ignition circuit, and felt the engine grumble to life. Easing the car out of the lot, I spied a set of headlights at the mouth of the alley. I flashed my headlights, letting the other driver know I was coming through. The driver attempting to enter through the narrow alley held tight at the entrance to give me plenty of room to get past.

I was sweating bullets as I approached the large SUV. The valet couldn't see me through the windshield; my lights were aimed in at him. He had no reason to believe I was a thief. I wished I had planned this better, wearing the same dorky uniform all these guys were sporting – it was too late for that now. It was dark and with any luck he wouldn't see any more than a glimpse of me as I passed him.

At the point where my headlights were no longer shining directly on him, I gave it some gas and accelerated out of the mouth of the alleyway and onto the street. The light at the end of the block was green – it was my lucky day. I made a right at the next block, then a left at the following intersection. My eyes were trained on the rearview mirror – no one followed me.

Five minutes into my fifteen-minute drive, I breezed through a yellow light near the industrial district. Lenny pounded it into us that most thieves were caught because they were scared and drew attention to themselves. As I sped through the yellow light, I silently chastised myself. I had barely cleared the intersection when cherries were flashing at me from behind. Damn! My heart began picking up speed in my chest: I could punch it and be going 60 mph in less than three seconds. No way could a patrol car catch me. But could I outrun his radio? I felt my grin spread wide – yes, I was pretty sure I could outrun his radio, too.

I turned off the headlights and stomped my foot to the floor, sped around the first corner I came to, and took another right as soon as I hit a second intersection. The red lights were nowhere in sight when I tucked in behind a warehouse and stopped the car. With the headlights off, I pushed the dimmer button on the dash to try to blackout the interior, too. I held my breath as if the act of filling my lungs were somehow a signal fire for police.

A squad car eased past the street where I was parked in the shadows, his spotlight shined directly on me – busted. I slammed the car into reverse as the tires squealed away from the cop whose face just registered that he had found me. I turned my headlights on, shoved the car into first and was headed for the main street. My head swung wildly from left to right, looking for a place to dump the car if I couldn't shake this guy in the next thirty seconds.

I got on the throttle and was ready to spin around a corner when a second squad car blocked my egress and a third car in pursuit was closing in. Lenny's words played in my head, "You get caught, I don't know you."

CHAPTER 2

The third squad drove up the narrow alley toward me. There was nowhere to go. I was trapped. Where had all the police cars come from? I flung the door open, ready to make a run for it. One of the policeman shouted, "Freeze," as I launched myself out of the car. A warning shot was fired into the air. The cops in this part of town didn't play – I stopped. Anywhere else, and an unarmed criminal wouldn't catch any lead, but the industrial district of Kansas City was a different story. I wasn't going to risk it.

A few kids in Lenny's crew had taken a bullet for a couple hundred bucks – I wasn't one of them. My hands shot into the air and I froze. Even if I got off of grand theft, Lenny didn't let anyone stay on his crew once they got pinched. He didn't want anyone with a record leading cops back to him. I had a plan for that and believed even after getting busted I'd be able to stay.

From behind me, a slow confident voice said, "Good evening, Son. Keep your hands where I can see them."

I did as I was told. There was no getting out of this one. When I had sprinted from the car, I should have kept running. I might have been able to outrun them, but I was definitely in stun-gun range now. A cop used a stun-gun on me once at a concert that got out of hand. *That* was not an experience I wanted again anytime soon.

Caught red-handed. I was going to jail. The only thing I had on me that incriminated anyone else was my phone. I couldn't take the chance of the police getting it and tracing it to Lenny. A few years ago, just stepping on it was enough to make sure the police couldn't get anything from it. The way they did forensics now, they'd be able to pull up all of my history by just getting my phone number. It was a disposable, so all they could get from it was the numbers I had called. But that was enough. My only chance was to keep them from finding it. I decided to hide it where they'd never think to look.

As I was frisked by a young cop, I yelled, "Hey! Where the hell are you grabbing?" I turned around quickly, grabbed hold of his jacket with both my fists. When I did, two other guns pointed at me. I let go of his jacket as I slid my cell into the outside pocket of his winter coat.

I stuck my hands in the air pretending to be surprised that two of his closest friends were willing to shoot me on the spot. Trying to play it off, I said, "Easy, Sunshine, I didn't like you getting fresh with me."

I looked around, trying to find an escape route. One of the guns trained on me lowered. The cop asked, "Mark? Mark Brewer, is that you?"

I looked at him. I squinted a little when recognition flooded over me. I hadn't seen him since I was fifteen. "Chad?"

Chad motioned to the other two officers to lower their weapons. "Easy. I know this guy." He turned toward me, holstering his own gun. "What are you doing in this car?"

"Didn't you read about me in *Forbes*? I'm a bazillionaire now. The boys at Hastings House would be proud, right?"

Hastings House was the group home where the two of us had lived. Chad had been my roommate. He motioned to the other cops who had lowered their guns, but were standing at the ready. "Hey, can you guys give me a minute?"

Both the cops looked at each other skeptically, but the younger one now holding my cell phone answered Chad, "Sure."

Both of the cops who had been ready to fill me full of lead holstered their guns. The two walked back toward a squad car, which was easily thirty feet away, while Chad stood in front of me. Surprised that he could call them all off so quickly, I asked, "What are you? Super cop?"

Irritation seeped into his voice. "Never mind what I am. Tell me what's going on. Now. The truth."

"Isn't there some law about self-incrimination?"

He shook his head at me. "Damn it, Mark. This is stolen, isn't it?"

Playing innocent, I answered, "I don't know what you're talking about."

Chad lowered his voice. The other two officers were watching us, but Chad's voice was so quiet they wouldn't be able to hear a word. "Look, I owe you, but I can't help you if you don't level with me."

He owed me? What did he think he owed me for? Angrily he barked, "Whose car is this?"

I knew, but I wasn't about to let on that I knew. I kept my mouth shut.

"C'mere." Chad motioned for me to sit in his squad car – not in the back where the criminals sat, but in the front seat next to him. He typed in the license plate on his computer. As if I couldn't read, he pointed at the screen and said, "Reginald Black. I suppose you're going to tell me he asked you to take it out for a car wash?"

I kept quiet. He had me. I went into damage control mode. So long as he didn't get any information from me on Lenny, the only thing I was looking at was jail time. Lenny had been good to me, but my life wouldn't be worth a twenty-five cent pack of gum if he were implicated in this.

Chad looked at me earnestly, and said, "I can make this go away."

He had to be screwing with me. "Why would you do that?"

Chad pursed his lips together and looked away from me, focusing his attention outside the driver's side window. "I'm where I am today because of you. I make this go away and we're even."

I didn't know what the heck he was talking about. Chad was going to let me off of grand theft auto when he'd caught me red-handed with two other cops as witnesses? What did he think he owed me for? Disbelief seeped through my words, "You're serious?"

"Yeah. I am. Stay here." Chad got out of the car, and walked over to where the other police officers stood. He talked to them for a couple minutes, then returned to the squad car where I sat. Without even looking in my direction, he barked, "Buckle up."

I looked at him sideways. "You're really letting me off?"

"I said, buckle up."

Not sure what to make of what he was doing, I pressed my luck a little more, "Hey, my phone is in the outside pocket of that cop who frisked me. You think I could get it back?"

Chad rolled his eyes, but went back to where the two cops were a second time. When he returned, he sat back in the driver's seat and tossed my phone at me. I grabbed the seatbelt, locked it in place, then asked, "Chad, what's going on?"

He eased the car out of the alleyway. "All three of us went to the academy together. They're calling it in. A suspicious vehicle was found in the alley. They're going to have it towed to the impound lot then clear the recorders on their dashboard cameras. Once the owner reports it stolen, he'll get it back."

"That's it? You're letting me off?"

"Buy a lottery ticket. It's your lucky day." It didn't add up. Why was he letting me off? After living on my own for the last three years, if I'd learned anything it was that no one did something for nothing – no one. Chad eased his squad car to a stop several blocks away. His gaze was fixed on something out in front of us through the windshield. His voice was low when he asked, "You remember the last day you were at Hastings House?"

The day I ran away was a pretty shitty day. Shitty enough that every time I started to have a decent day, the memory came rushing back in to remind me how truly worthless I was. "What about it?"

Instead of glancing at me, he pivoted his whole body, looking at me as if he didn't believe me. "You don't remember what you did right before you took off?"

I had left Hastings House three years ago, when I was fifteen, but the memory was so fresh it could have happened yesterday. I had seen Mom in a minivan sitting at a red light while I was huddled inside a bus stop. I hadn't seen her since

I was six years old, but I recognized her right away. She looked great, not even remotely like she had looked the day the social workers came and took Davey and me from her. Her hair was in a fancy style, she wore nice clothes, and drove a minivan that looked brand new.

I was so excited to see her that I pushed my way out of the Plexiglas enclosure and nearly crawled through her window from the street corner. A little boy voice escaped me when I shouted, "Mommy!" Mom looked directly at me. She knew who she was looking at because her eyes grew to the size of quarters as she stared at one of the sons she had thrown away. She put her foot on the gas and sped away before the light had even turned green.

The red of the signal light invaded my thoughts, and everything I saw from then on bore a red tint. Fury poured from my insides out. I went back to the group home to gather my things. I didn't eat dinner, I didn't check out, I just left. Trying to shake the memory of seeing Mom, I answered, "Sure. I remember it."

"So, you know why I'm doing this."

I didn't have a clue. Whatever had happened was going to let me beat a grand theft auto charge; I played along pretending I knew what he was talking about. "That was a long time ago."

Chad grabbed my forearm tightly, "It feels like yesterday. You never let me thank you. None of us ever got to thank you."

Thank me? Chad had been short and skinny; lots of the guys gave him a hard time. Back then his hair was longer, his nose looked like it was too large, and acne had peppered most of his face. His hair was cropped close to his scalp now; it looked like his face had grown or his nose shrunk, and he must have made friends with a dermatologist. I was fifteen when I left and he was three years older than I was. He was one of the few boys who didn't seem to belong there. Chad should have aged out of the home, but he was in his senior year of high school, so the state agreed to let him stay until he had his diploma.

He took a lot of razzing from the other residents. Chad talked about college, how he wanted to go into criminal justice – looking at him right now, I guess he wasn't blowing smoke back then. There was a reason I wasn't living in Hollywood. I couldn't act, so I came clean and told him, "Look, I appreciate what you just did for me. I'm not sure why you did it, but thanks."

"You're not sure why? I'd be dead if it weren't for you."

Dead? I racked my brain trying to remember the day, but other than Mom in her speed-racer minivan, I came up empty. A smart guy would have said, "You're welcome," and been done with it. But something about the way Chad looked at me – it felt like a whole chunk of my memory was just gone. "What are you talking about?"

Chad shook his head. "Does Clint Michaels ring a bell?"

Clint "Monsters" rang a bell. The only people who called him "Michaels" were the counselors who were charged with making sure we didn't kill each other. He and I were in several of the same group therapy sessions together. Clint had been a thug from the time he was two and only got worse each year after. We all had to share things about ourselves; his stories made me cringe.

He belonged in juvenile detention rather than a group home, but the state could never find enough evidence to prosecute for anything he was charged with. Clint and I had had a run-in early on; he shoved me into a wall and I broke his nose in the rec room. After that, he gave me plenty of room. "Sure, I remember Clint. Why?"

"You told him if he came within a foot of me you were going to slice him from his neck to his crotch."

That brought a grin to my face – I was a punk back then. The group home was full of testosterone. That sounded like a threat I would have made. "Well, I never cut him. I would have remembered that."

Chad looked at me, disbelief coloring his features. "You really don't remember."

I had blocked out most of my childhood. I remembered a few things from when I was really young, but I was eleven when I heard my brother Davey had died. From eleven until fifteen, I didn't remember much of anything. I could name the places where I had lived, and I remembered a few people from back then, but trying to recall events during those four years was next to impossible. I'm sure if I went to a shrink, he'd tell me it was some sort of a coping mechanism. I didn't care what it was. I just knew those four years of my life were a black hole I had to crawl out of.

Chad interrupted my thoughts, "You and I were roommates."

That much I did remember. We weren't friends, but he was one of the few guys who I was sure wouldn't jump me in my sleep for a pack of cigarettes or steal anything I neglected to lock up. Chad waited for me to say something – I didn't. He continued, "You hadn't said more than ten words to me in the three months we lived together. You walked in while Clint was beating the shit out of me."

I tried to remember the day. Other than seeing Mom, I didn't remember anything. I remember Clint being at Hastings House because he was always either whaling on someone or threatening to do it.

Chad turned away from me, his gaze fixed on the windshield in front of him. "You had this wild look in your eye when you walked in. You yanked him off of me by the back of his neck and punched him in the face. You told Clint you'd cut him from his neck to his crotch, then carve him into little pieces and drop him in the river if he ever laid a hand on me or any of the other boys whose parents didn't want them."

I didn't remember it. As mad as I was at Mom that day, anything was possible. He kept talking. "Clint said something, I don't remember what, I guess because I was bleeding like crazy. You told him, 'I'll be watching you. You lay a hand on one of these boys, I'll kill you myself. Test me to see if I'm kidding. I've got nothing to lose. Try me.'" Chad smiled, then added, "I'd never seen Clint back down from anything. You scared him. It's not like you and I were friends; you sort of scared me, too."

I didn't remember any of the incident Chad had just described. That seemed like a pretty big deal for me to have blocked it out. I wondered if maybe someone else had done it. Chad was watching me for a reaction, then added, "I watched you throw your stuff into a bag. You walked to the bathroom, got a wet washcloth and tossed it at me saying, 'If he comes after you again, tell him I'll be back. Clean yourself up. Watch your back.'"

When he was done with his trip down memory lane, I asked, "Seriously? That's it? That's why you're letting me off for stealing the Ferrari?" I didn't want to sound ungrateful, but it didn't make sense.

"Yeah. You took off that night, but Clint didn't bother me or anyone else after that day. It sort of became an inside joke. Every time he threatened someone, they would say, 'Don't make me call Mark.' He always backed down."

A little more dismissively than I had intended to sound, "It doesn't seem like that big of a deal."

"You don't get it. No one, anywhere, anytime in my life, ever stuck up for me. When he was beating the crap out of me, I was sort of wishing he'd kill me. It wasn't until you stepped in and stopped it that I thought maybe someone thought my life was worth saving. You made me want to help others who needed it. You're the reason I'm a cop."

"You're not a very good one if you're letting me go."

Chad laughed, not a snicker but a belly-laugh. "Everyone needs a break. You were facing prison time if I'd have taken you in and booked you. Not county lockup, not a fine, but hard-core prison. Maybe my letting you go will change your life the way you changed mine."

I shook my head, "Yeah, I don't think the uniform would fit me."

"You don't have to be a cop to make a difference. You see things. You know things. I'm sure you've seen drug dealers pushing to kids on the street. I bet it turns your stomach the same way it does mine."

It did, but I wasn't about to let on that it bothered me. I tried to pretend like I didn't care. "Survival of the fittest."

Chad shook his head at me. "If you believed that, Clint would have killed me that day."

What was he asking me to do? He kept staring at me like I was going to put on a cape and save the youth of America from bullies. "I'm just one guy."

"Me, too. But I make a difference every day. You could, too."

Well, wasn't he the happy little infomercial? "Keep telling yourself that. You say drugs are the problem? You guys only go after the lowlifes who sell them. You won't make a dent in anything unless you go after the source."

Chad nodded. "You're right. Help me figure out who the source is, so I can arrest him."

More offended than I should have been, I flinched away from him. "I'm not a snitch."

"No, you're not a snitch. But you are in the perfect position to conduct surveillance. I'm not asking for info on car theft rings, chop shops, prostitution, illegal gambling – I'm only asking for you to pay attention and point me in the right direction on who's filling this town with drugs. Tell me where the dealers get their product."

My eyes narrowed on Chad, "I'm not following. You pick and choose the criminals you want?"

"No. A criminal is a criminal, but there are worse things out there than stealing cars. You beat a grand theft rap by ditching a car tonight. That's got to be good for your reputation on the street. Am I right?"

He was right. That was huge, especially since Lenny knew it was coming. When I didn't show, he would automatically think I got busted. Once he found out that I had ditched the car instead of risking his operation, word would spread like wildfire. "Yeah, maybe. So what are you asking me to do?"

"You have great survival instincts. I couldn't care less about a car that some insurance company would be willing to write a check for. What I do care about is drug dealers, their suppliers, meth labs that can take out whole city blocks, and what the connections are to the drug cartels."

I had always assumed Davey's death was drug-related. My little brother was dead, but no one was ever able to tell me how he died or any of the circumstances surrounding his death. I'd never gotten a straight answer. Nine year olds don't just die. Foster kids always got the shaft. No one cared about us, at least no more than the monthly check the state gave out. Drug dealers and gangs targeted foster kids; I'd had a couple try to recruit me while I was in middle school. I wasn't ready to jump in with both feet, but my curiosity was piqued. "So what are you asking me to do?"

Chad slapped my back like we were old friends. I eyed my shoulder where he had slapped me then looked at him with that "I can't believe you just did that" look. He ignored my near-glare and asked, "Do you know Johnny Corozzo?"

I felt my stomach tighten from just hearing his name. He couldn't be serious. "Not personally. I know who he is. Everybody does."

"He's got a pretty sophisticated drug ring that no one has been able to penetrate. Not even the feds can get close to him. He's too good. He's got eyes and ears everywhere. I need someone on the inside who isn't on any rolls."

"You want me to infiltrate one of the most influential criminal organizations in the Midwest, for sure the biggest in Kansas City, and give you information on their operations? Clint must have beat your head pretty hard that day."

"Johnny supplies every dealer in the surrounding states. Find out how he does it. Tell me how I can catch him in the act, and I'll arrest him."

"That's suicide. What makes you think I'd want any part of this?"

"Because you have no reason to do what's right, yet you still did."

I shook my head at the absurdity of his reasoning. "If Clint was beating you that badly, anyone would have done the same thing. I'm not a poster child for good choices."

Dismissive of my answer, he countered, "There's a lot better money in drugs than in cars, but look where I found you tonight."

"Forget prison, I could get shot. You're a cop. You infiltrate them."

"There are lots of cops on his payroll, but they're there to fix records and lose evidence. Even if I could get to one of the cops I suspect to be on the take, Johnny's too smart ever to let any of them in on how it all works. No, it's got to be someone outside of law enforcement."

Shaking my head at the absurdity of his idea, "What makes you think I'd help with this?"

"I'm guessing you may already be on the wrong side of the law." He grinned, "Let's face it, no one's first offense is a Ferrari. You are smart enough not to take it unless you have a means to unload it. Either you are already connected, or you're an idiot."

"I'm an idiot if I consider this." I stared out the window for a minute, considering whether I should just bolt out of the car and forget this conversation ever took place. Chad didn't press me; he just sat in the driver's seat fiddling with the steering wheel. Irritated with myself that I would even contemplate such a buffoon move, "So, if I were willing to help, I'm not saying I am, what's in it for me?"

Chad shrugged his shoulders. "Nothing. If you screw up and get caught by Johnny, I'm pretty sure you'll be killed."

Self-preservation shivers shimmied up my arms. My body was telling me to open the door and get out of the car: walk away, put my head down, and forget this night ever happened. Chad and I may have shared a room together as teenagers, but no way was I putting my life on the line for some delusion he had about stopping drugs. I'd rather he busted me for the car.

If Chad took me to jail, Lenny might kick me off of his crew. I could be stuck holding a stupid piece of cardboard on the side of the road begging for money. I didn't want to come right out and tell Chad he was a moron, because if he really was planning to let me go, at least I wouldn't be diving in between cars for loose change. "That isn't much of an incentive. You got a lot of people you've made this deal with?"

"No. And I don't make a habit of destroying evidence and letting car thieves go. But if you get me the information I need on Johnny, you'll be crippling one of the biggest illegal drug rings in the Midwest. There were boys in the home we grew up in that were used up and thrown out. Eddie and Collin were both killed within a year of leaving Hastings House. Remember Nathan? He's in prison for dealing. Wouldn't you want to give kids like us better odds?"

Yeah, I did. I never cared one way or the other for Eddie, Collin or Nathan, but an image of Megan flashed in my head. I squinted my eyes closed to try to make her haunting features go away. I never knew Megan's last name. No matter how I tried to stay focused on Chad, my mind drifted to my first night in Kansas City.

CHAPTER 3

Seven years ago – Mark Brewer, age 15

She found me huddled next to a building just a few blocks from here. It was freezing that night; I tried to stay warm but couldn't shake the chill from my body. Megan was my age, pretty, but just another throw away. Her voice hadn't taken on that "tough-street" sound most of the other kids had; hers was young and sweet.

Crouched low to the ground, my arms wrapped tightly around my legs while I tried to use my knees for a pillow. It felt like more of a medieval torture position, but it was the only way to keep me off of the frigid cement. Initially, I had leaned against an office building behind me, but the structure's cement was just as cold as the sidewalk, so I stayed in my uncomfortable squatted position. I had dozed in and out of consciousness.

My legs shook – either from the strain of squatting or the wind biting through my jeans. I didn't have a winter coat, a blanket, or even a scarf; I wore only a light jacket over a t-shirt. I had left Hastings House without a plan. I hitchhiked to the city with no idea where I would go or what I would do once I got here. Before the sun had set, I dug through a bunch of trashcans looking for newspaper and cardboard I could put on the ground to try to insulate me from the cold.

Initially I had avoided the eyes of people who had passed by, sure that one would notice me and send me back to Hastings House. When I could no longer feel my fingers and my toes, I started to believe I might die from exposure. I finally swallowed my pride and asked a stranger for help – he pretended not to hear me. Another guy dressed in a suit, bundled up in a long thick wool coat as a scarf hung loosely off of his shoulders, swaggered toward me. I waved at him trying to ask for help – he glared at me. No one could see me, or rather, they chose not to see me that night.

The cold tore clear through to my bones. Despite my squatted position, my body wanted to sleep, even if it meant I would never wake again. It was Megan's sweet voice that pulled me from my frigid haze. She leaned down close to my ear, "You're new here. I'm Megan." My first thought when I heard her voice was that she was an angel – I quickly dismissed the possibility. Never having spent any time in church, the idea that an angel had come to my aid seemed absurd.

I lifted my head off of my knees and looked up into a set of pale blue eyes. Strands of her blonde hair hung down from under her raspberry-colored stocking cap. Megan was a willow of a girl, her skin so fair she could have been a Geisha girl. Megan held out her hand to me. "C'mon, I'll take you to a place where you can crash tonight." Hers was delicate and warm as I wrapped numb fingers around her hand. She helped me to my feet. I had difficulty keeping up as she led the way down the street, my legs stiff from squatting.

"When did you get here?" I didn't answer her as I followed her like a puppy – one who no one wanted. Megan turned to see me trailing a few steps behind her; she slowed her pace, "How old are you?" My shoulders shrugged. I didn't want her to know I was fifteen since I looked old for my age and could pass for eighteen. Her eyes remained fixed on mine, waiting for an answer as I plodded along a couple of steps behind her. A sharp gust of wind blew through an alley as we crossed in front of it. My body would have collapsed had she not reached out and held me on my feet. I wanted to go back to my perch on the cardboard to escape the arctic wind.

"Have you had anything to eat?" My stomach growled at her words and I shook my head. Megan must have decided I was incapable of speech because she stopped asking me questions and began to tell me about herself. "I've been here for four months. It was warmer when I got here. You picked a bad time of year to show up. When it's warm out, there are a lot more of us around. I lived at my aunt's house in Missouri. Couldn't take all the lectures about the devil inside me, so I left." She smiled an easy smile that thawed my insides. "It's not so bad here."

Megan led me out of the industrial area where I had been and into a run-down residential neighborhood. Decent houses with their sidewalks shoveled peppered the street, but there were nearly as many dark houses with broken windows and forgotten trash bags lining their porches. Hearing her words over the howling wind was hard, but she kept rattling on. After what felt like miles, we reached an overgrown hedge in front of a house with boards covering all the windows on the first floor. She pointed toward the back yard where a well-worn path cut through the snow. Hundreds of footprints created mini ice-covered craters on the path to the back of the house.

She did her best Vanna White and gave me a bright smile. "This is it. It isn't much, but it's better than the street." She led me to the back of the house where a bowed-out wooden door stood ajar. Megan opened the door and I followed her in. The place was dark, but as my eyes adjusted to the shadows, there were people everywhere. Not adults, but kids.

Sleeping bags were scattered along the walls. Low voices murmured to each other as we walked past. One corner looked like it must have belonged to the mayor of the place. Next to him stood a little table with a battery operated camping light, a stack of comic books, and a plastic cooler. Jugs of water were stacked neatly beside his table. Several kids were lounging next to the "mayor" wrapped up in sleeping bags. The house didn't have electricity or heat and likely not running water. I had entered the group home from hell.

Megan led me up the steps to the second floor. The hallway was pitch-black; I could just make out doorways stretching along both sides from the faint light peeking out from under them. When Megan opened the second door on the right, two people sat bundled up near a window. Megan introduced me to the two figures, "This is Leon and Evan." I couldn't make out either of their features; they both looked eerie – the only light in the room came in from the window without curtains or shades, washing their faces in silvery light.

All three looked at me with curious eyes. I muttered, "Mark." Megan pulled out half a sandwich wrapped in a napkin from her pocket and offered it to me.

I didn't feel right taking her food. She must have read my apprehension because she said, "Go ahead, I already ate the other half. You need it more than I do." I devoured it in two bites. It tasted a little like cheese and peanut butter. I wasn't a fan of cheese or peanut butter, but at that point a pickle and onion sandwich would have been delicious. She reached into a pile of clothes, pulled out a heavy wool coat and offered it to me. I gratefully took it, just as fast as I had taken the sandwich. She turned toward the guy on the left side of the window, "Leon, where did all the extra blankets go?"

A slow southern drawl answered. "Chesty found a thirteen year old girl at the waffle house tonight. I gave her the spare blanket, the yellow coat and your pillow. We need to hit the Goodwill again soon."

Megan sighed. "I have a run in the morning. Can you go before everything gets picked over?"

Leon shrugged, "Yeah. They're getting smarter though. They've been emptying the bins outside before they close up at night."

Megan reached in her pocket and pulled out some wadded up money. "Buy some if you have to. I saw the weather forecast – supposed to be cold like this all week." Megan turned to me. "We don't have much, but we have more than most."

Leon took the money and shoved it in his pocket. "Personal shopper, I'll add that to my resume."

Megan smiled at him. "Better than a prostitute." She must have had the eyes of a bat; even in the dark she saw my eyes grow wide. In a reassuring way she offered, "Don't worry. No one's going to sell you as a sex slave. Most everyone here is okay. Leon, Evan and I have this room. You can stay with us. Someone has to be in the room all the time or we'll come back and everything will be gone. Can you stay here tomorrow when Leon makes a run to Goodwill?"

It wasn't like I had anywhere else to go. "Uh, yeah. What do I do if someone tries to come in?"

Evan spoke up with a heavy New York accent, "You tell them to get out and keep their meat hooks off our stuff."

Megan eased a little closer. "I can get you a job with me and Evan – it pays twenty bucks a day. Evan and I will be working tomorrow morning. Leon usually stays here while we're gone."

Evan answered for me. "If three of us are working, we could have pizza every night." After being in foster care and group homes and never having more than a few dollars in my pocket, twenty a day seemed huge. I eagerly nodded my agreement.

None of the three asked anything about me, and neither Evan nor Leon volunteered information about themselves the way Megan had while we walked here. We settled in for the night. Evan, Leon and Megan all tucked into their sleeping bags. I leaned up against a wall and covered myself with the coat she had given me. Shivers rocked me as my body began to thaw, and I mashed my teeth together to keep them from chattering. Evan fell asleep first, his breathing slow and heavy. Leon only lasted a few minutes longer than Evan.

I hadn't realized Megan was watching me until she climbed out of her sleeping bag and held it open for me. "Here, you need to get warm." I shook my head at her offer. "Go on. You need to warm up or you'll never be able to sleep."

"No. I'm fine. This coat is great."

"Yeah, that coat would be great if you weren't close to freezing. Give me the coat, you take my sleeping bag." She held her still warm sleeping bag out to me.

If it weren't for her bringing me here, I'd still be on that street corner. No matter how badly I wanted to crawl inside, I shook my head. "No. I'm okay. I'll warm up soon."

When she understood I was drawing the line at her generosity and refused to take her sleeping bag, she offered, "We could see if we could both fit?"

Any other night, in any other circumstance, my hormones would have taken over, but this wasn't any other circumstance. I wanted the shivers to go away. Reluctantly I nodded. Megan climbed in first and held it open for me to get in behind her. When I did, she reached down to the bottom and zipped it up tight.

I folded up the wool coat and propped it under my head for a pillow. Megan's back faced me. My arms were awkwardly crossed in front of me; she reached behind her and pulled my left arm out, using my bicep for a pillow. Without any more coaxing, I draped my right arm over her body.

I had never held a girl against me before. I knew our sleeping arrangement wasn't an invitation for anything other than sharing body heat, but it felt good – really good. Warmth radiated off of her and I soaked it in. My jaw relaxed, my teeth no longer threatening to chatter. She whispered, "Better than the street?"

My arms tightened on her, "Much better." I wasn't a touchy-feely person, despite the thousands of hours of mandatory group therapy I had been subjected to – but there was something about Megan. She had saved my life and did it for no reason other than she saw another kid in trouble. She gave me a coat, which may seem trivial to most, but to someone who had nearly frozen to death – it was a lifeline. She had given me a safe place to stay and offered to get me a job, yet Megan hadn't asked for anything in return. Where I came from no one did something for nothing.

I tried to figure out what her angle might be. She already had two guys hanging around; it wasn't like she needed protection. I didn't have anything to offer, why was she helping me? Megan must have sensed my unease, because she said, "I don't miss it."

"Miss what?"

"Home." Megan angled around so she could see me. "I don't know why you're here. Whatever your reason for leaving home, you're safe now. We take care of each other. Get some sleep. Tomorrow will be better, I promise."

Her words shattered my defenses. I wanted to tell her everything: how Mom had given me up, Missouri had taken my little brother away, I'd been bounced from one home to another, the whole awful story of my life. I struggled to find the words, but none would come. Instead I gripped her tighter with both arms savoring the girl who had saved my life and promised tomorrow would be better.

She may have been just as starved for human affection as I was because when I gripped her more tightly with my arms, she wrapped her arms around mine and squeezed. We lay together holding each other for a long time, no words, just the comfort two people could offer each other. Evan's quiet snores grew in volume, my eyes got heavy, and I felt Megan's grip slack around my arms as she drifted off to sleep.

All the things I longed to tell her could wait. I didn't need to spill my guts tonight, because I had found so much in Megan. For the first time in my life, I trusted someone.

I felt a rush of cool air the next morning as she climbed out of the sleeping bag. I started to follow her when she whispered, "No, stay warm. Evan and I have to go. We'll be back in a few hours."

I don't know what made me do it, but I reached up around the back of her neck pulling her back toward me. Even in the morning haze there were so many things I wanted to tell her. I was grateful she had saved me last night. I wanted her to know I'd find a way to pay her back. The only words that would form were, "Thank you."

She answered me with a beautiful smile. "We'll be back soon. Evan and I will bring a pizza for lunch. Get some rest." She pressed a soft kiss on my forehead and zipped up her coat.

I hadn't meant to, but I did fall asleep after she and Evan tiptoed out the door. Leon shook me awake to tell me he was leaving sometime later. Their sleeping bags and pillows were piled up against the wall behind me. I sat in that second floor bedroom all morning and well into the afternoon. When Leon came back, he had two garbage bags full of coats, blankets and pillows. Leon's southern drawl was a welcomed sound after the hours of isolation, "I went to Goodwill, the Salvation Army Thrift Store, and even hit a church rummage sale on Ninth."

He was pulling items out of the bags and putting them into piles. Coats, bedding, and clothes. He tossed me a package of thick wool hunting socks, "Here, put these over the other socks you're wearing." I did as I was told and couldn't believe the difference.

Leaving him to sort through his purchases and to watch everyone's things, I cautiously began exploring the house. Not many kids were here during the day, but those who stayed were watching treasured belongings for others just like I had done. Megan and Evan weren't back when darkness started to fall. Leon, in his southern twang said more to himself than to me, "They aren't normally gone this long." Nervousness was clear as he glanced at the door each time we heard footsteps in the hallway.

She said they would be back by lunch. Just after the remaining light from the day disappeared from the sky, Evan burst through the door and shut it hard behind him. Leon and I had been sitting quietly, so Evan's abrupt arrival startled us both. "Hey, where's Megan?" I was glad Leon had asked the question. I hadn't left the house all day and my stomach was so empty it hurt. Beyond the hunger, I missed her – I had this idea that even though there were blankets and pillows now, maybe she and I could share her sleeping bag again.

Evan's head snapped from side-to-side, looking wildly around the room. When he was sure it was just the three of us in the room, he came at me and grabbed me by the neck of my t-shirt, "You need to go."

I shoved him away from me. He landed hard against the wall. Was it because she had shared her sleeping bag with me last night? Was he jealous? I had spent all day waiting for her and now he tells me I have to go? Echoing Leon's question, I asked, "Where's Megan?"

Barely more than a murmur, Evan answered, "Got herself killed."

The hunger I had been feeling disappeared as the hairs on my neck danced to attention. "Killed? When?"

"This morning." Evan tossed a bag of chips and some snack cakes on the floor to Leon and me. "She was late on a delivery. When she showed up the guy was insane. The guys we work for are paranoid. When she was late, he decided she must have been talking to the cops. She said she had a friend who needed a job," Evan's eyes glared at me, "she told them his name was Mark."

His words hung in the air for an awkward minute before he continued. "The guy capped her on the street then told me to find you. He's convinced whoever this Mark is, he's a police plant or a snitch; they told me to bring you to them."

I only followed about half of what he had said. "Megan's dead?"

"Yeah. Now get out. Take whatever you want, but if they come looking for you – you can't be here. If they find me with you and I haven't turned you over – it's my ass."

None of this was making sense. Who was *they* and why were *they* after me? "Capped? Because she was late delivering what?" I knew the answer before the words were out of me. Megan was a drug mule. She was one of the faceless masses who moved drugs around the city – she was expendable.

Evan glared at me. "One of the local dealers. That's how she and I met. He hired her because she had that "girl-next-door" face. She stuck out in a couple of the neighborhoods where she delivered, but every time she ran into the police, they were stepping all over themselves to help her. A few times, the police gave her a ride out of the bad neighborhoods."

Megan's angelic face was burned into my memory for all time. I had spent almost no time with her. She shouldn't have been more than a single blip in my life, but no matter how hard I tried, I couldn't forget her. She was the first kind stranger I had ever met. There was no reason for her to help me, but she did.

Shaking off the image of Megan, I answered Chad, "I don't have a death wish." He didn't respond, instead he just kept staring at me. His eyes were a bright blue, just like Megan's. It was as if she were asking for my help through Chad. A heavy sigh escaped as I asked, "What exactly do you need?"

"I've got a plan, sort of a plan, it's more of an idea. We've got a couple of sweet cars in the impound lot. If you lifted one from police impound that's a ballsy move - it would get you noticed. Johnny brings people into his organization based on their street credentials. The rest is up to you. If he takes the bait – you'll be able to insert yourself into his operation. When you have enough evidence to arrest him, we bring him and his whole organization down."

"Johnny doesn't move stolen cars. If he did, I'd know."

"No, but he pays attention to criminals with good instincts. You stealing from the police department is exactly the type of move he'd be interested in."

"And if I get caught, I'm dead."

"Right." Chad smiled a toothy grin and added, "And if you get busted doing anything for him, I may not be able to make the charges go away."

Shaking my head at the absurdity of his plan, "Chad, this is by far the worst offer I've ever heard."

His smile didn't wane. "Are you in?"

"What're you paying?"

"Nothing. If I file for CI pay, there would be a paper trail. That's the last thing you want." I knew snitches on the street who were confidential informants. They got paid more if the quality of the information they were giving was worth it. Chad was asking me to infiltrate Johnny Corozzo's organization yet wasn't offering a nickel in return. Chad offered, "But when we bust him, I might be able to score a spot in witness protection for you."

"It seems like you're going about this the wrong way. Every snitch I've ever heard of got recruited after they were already in a position to sell information. You're recruiting me to do this with no guarantee that I'll ever be able to get into the organization."

Chad motioned behind us. "That Ferrari stunt you just pulled will have people tossing your name around town for a while. You follow that up with taking a car out of the police impound lot and everyone will be talking about you. You take it from there."

I saw where this was going. "Yeah, you put a tracking device on it, I take it to the chop shop, then you bust everyone in sight. Pass."

Chad's voice lowered to an angry growl, "I couldn't care less about a stolen car. That's what insurance companies are for. I want the drugs to stop. I want the murders to stop. I want to send a message to every half-wit who is cooking meth in his kitchen that they aren't welcome in Kansas City. The best way to send that message is to take Corozzo down."

"So if Johnny finds out you and I are BFF's – I'm dead." Chad stopped looking at me, as his fingers twiddled with one of the knobs on his dashboard. "If I try to weasel my way into his organization and he finds out it's a set up – I'm dead. If I'm successful getting into his organization and get busted doing anything illegal – I go down without your help. Assuming I can get in his organization, feed you the info you need, and you can prosecute, the best I can hope for is a new identity?"

"Yeah, it's a good deal, right?" Chad grinned sheepishly.

"It's the worst deal in the history of deals. I think I'd rather get arrested for boosting the car."

CHAPTER 4

Present day – Mark Brewer, age 22

That was how I got started. I was sort of a confidential informant, well, not really because I didn't get paid. Absent the cash, that was how Chad handled me. We would go weeks without talking. Chad never initiated contact; we agreed it was too dangerous, but I kept him in the loop on everything I learned about Johnny's drugs. Chad always waited for me to contact him. He had no way of knowing if I was really on the level or if I was as corrupt as the scum he had me snuggling up to, but for some reason, he believed he could trust me.

He kept records of each of our conversations. In the event a wide net was ever cast on Johnny's organization, I'd have Chad in my corner to make sure I didn't go down with them. The more I learned about Johnny, the more I believed he'd never go down for anything.

Chad wasn't a detective, but he wasn't a beat cop, either. Chad didn't have a partner. When I pointed out that he didn't fit the typical mold, he was vague about how he fit into the police force. He seemed to work on every task force Kansas City had. Sometimes it was drugs, sometimes prostitution, other times it was stolen goods. The only guidance he ever gave me was to get close to Johnny, learn his operation, then report back on how it could be exploited.

Chad and I weren't pals, at least we didn't hang out on the weekends. We didn't socialize. As far as I knew the only thing we had in common was that growing up, neither of us had known of anyone who cared whether we lived or died. He was a cop, and I was much more comfortable on the other side of the law. It had taken me four years, but I was finally in a position to gather the kind of data Chad wanted from me.

Chad was working some sting trying to find truckloads of stolen electronics. I knew who was behind it. I knew where the trailers were parked with the goods. I knew who he could call to buy wholesale for twenty cents on the dollar – but that wasn't our deal. I didn't take issue with someone making an honest living being a thief. My issue was with drug dealers preying on and poisoning kids. I never offered Chad any information on anything criminal that wasn't attached to Johnny's drugs.

I was walking toward my apartment when Ronnie shouted from a street corner, "Lenny's looking for you."

Damn it. I was supposed to have checked in with Lenny earlier today. I had been scouring parking garages looking for a BMW and lost track of time. I had made it on to Johnny's payroll two years ago, but I still moonlighted for Lenny when he had to fill an order. "Did he say what he wanted?"

Ronnie leaned up against the pole anchoring the traffic signal on the corner. Ronnie counterfeited tickets for every event in town. He sold them for thirty cents on the dollar for general admission; sold out shows he did for face value. Ronnie's tickets were impossible to tell from the authentic ones, and everyone looking for tickets knew this was his corner. He wore a white striped button-down shirt, black dress slacks and loafers. Ronnie had unbuttoned his shirt one button too many, and was flashing his over-hairy chest at everyone who passed by. His fingers scratched his chest, as he answered, "Says Johnny Corozzo came by his place looking for you."

My whole body tensed. Johnny didn't know who I was. I was too far down his food chain. "Corozzo? Did Lenny say what he wanted?"

"I ain't a messaging service. Go ask Lenny."

This could be very good or very bad news. Johnny Corozzo was into all things business. Although on his payroll, I was just a tourist; I wasn't on the inside. I had never spoken to Johnny directly. Some of his businesses were legitimate, others. . . weren't. Corozzo's was a popular bistro where reservations were booked three months in advance; I didn't have any waiter skills. Johnny had a used car lot where only high-end imports took residence; I wasn't a car salesman, either. The first day I worked for Lenny, he had pointed out Johnny's car lot and warned me never to steal from Johnny.

To make good on my agreement with Chad, I did whatever I could to get a job working in Johnny's network. One of Johnny's not-so-legal businesses included nearly every bookie in town reporting to him. I started my career in Johnny's organization there. Working with the bookies didn't pay as well as the money I made on Lenny's crew, but I had to start somewhere. Lenny let me pick up jobs stealing cars a few times per month to supplement my income after taking the pay cut to work with the bookies.

Chad caught me with the Ferrari when I was eighteen. It took two years to get into Johnny's organization, moving cash around for the bookies. After ten months of delivering envelopes of cash around the city, a shooting happened at a convenience store. That shooting resulted in an opening for a low-level position in his drug operations. I jumped at it.

It was nearly identical to my previous job, except money wasn't being moved around. I worked with the mules who moved drugs and delivered cash to me, but I never had enough intelligence in advance to tip Chad off on much of anything. That's not to say Chad wasn't there when I needed him – he delivered a big helping of Karma exactly when I asked for it.

Evan, who I hadn't seen since I was fifteen, was one of the mules who worked for me when I took over. My second day on the job, I was introduced to him. I hadn't recognized Evan, and I couldn't understand the strange look on his face. I called him on it and all he said was, "We met a few years ago. I'm glad you didn't freeze after you left the house."

Those few words brought our first meeting back to me in living color. I hadn't gotten any of the details of what had happened to Megan at the time, but this time, given my position, he was more than willing to fill me in on what had happened. The dealer who killed her was still dealing for Johnny – his name was Valentine. Street level drug dealers got busted regularly. None ever had any interaction with anyone higher than me, most rarely interacted with anyone other than the carriers. A drug dealer going to jail was of little consequence to the organization as a whole.

Once Evan told me Valentine was the one who had gunned Megan down, it was my turn for a little payback. I called Chad, told him when Valentine would have the most stash, Chad swooped in and busted him. Valentine would never be tried for Megan's murder, but he already had two felony convictions for distributing drugs, so this bust made him a three-time loser and got him twenty to life. Karma's a bitch.

Before I took the job, mules were treated as expendable. Either they did what they were told, when they were told to do it, or they stopped breathing. I took a more hands-on approach. No drugs moved to any of the dealers without my say so. Every dealer in town knew if they had a problem with one of my carriers, they took it up with me or they would answer to me. I wasn't giving Chad anywhere near the level of intelligence as he had hoped for, but there was something about taking care of the kids who delivered the drugs that I liked.

Megan may have died over nothing, but no one else would share her fate so long as I was in this position. About the only thing I had learned since taking my new position was that Johnny was tight with one of the cartels in Mexico. His biggest shipments lately were super-meth. The Mexicans were trying to destroy their competition, so they sold their product cheap – really cheap. Johnny's dealers were undercutting the local meth lab prices by half, and the quality was better than anyone had ever seen before. I was getting closer to learning how he moved so much product undetected for years and the source of this new super-charged product

When Ronnie told me Johnny was looking for me, my first thought was Chad. He was always careful to keep my name out of any reports, but I couldn't imagine why Johnny would go to Lenny about me. Lenny had been my mentor when I first moved to Kansas City. He took me under his wing, but the things

Lenny had helped me with were isolated to stealing cars and getting them into his chop shops. Since I began working for Johnny, I'd done very few jobs for Lenny.

"Thanks, Ronnie."

I walked the three blocks to Lenny's bar. All the windows were blacked out on the front, so was the glass front door. I took my usual stool in the corner, which gave me the perfect vantage point to see the whole place. Lenny shot a nod my way to let me know he knew I was here, but didn't come over right away. He finished whatever conversation he was involved in, grabbed a glass out of the freezer the way I liked it, and delivered a double-shot of Crown Royal to me. He glanced to his left, then his right, his eyes landing on me when he was sure there were no prying ears. "You got no family, am I right?"

I furrowed my brows at him. "You know I don't."

"That's good. You got nothing to lose. You tell Johnny no."

"No? What're you talking about?"

"Tell Johnny you aren't interested in his offer. Walk away, Kid."

"What're you talking about Lenny? I'm already working for Johnny."

"Johnny wants to promote you. He stopped by to ask if I had any reason to think you untrustworthy. He's looking for someone without a record. Someone who can do drops for him."

A promotion? This was what I'd been working towards for the last two years. I forced the muscles on my face to stay slack, so my face wouldn't betray me with the elation I was feeling. Drops meant I would know when drugs were coming in and with enough notice that Chad could do something about them. "What did you tell him?"

"I didn't tell him anything. I told him you were better at cars than drugs." Lenny dropped his voice, "The last few guys who had this job didn't end up so well."

"You're like the mother I never had, Lenny. Why the question about my family?"

Lenny's voice dipped low. "You know Jorge?"

"Sort of. Short guy, walks with a limp. He runs numbers for Johnny."

"Yeah. Jorge wanted out of the organization a few years ago. Right about the time his wife had their third. He didn't used to walk with a limp." Lenny paused to let that sink in for a few seconds. "His wife convinced him to quit Johnny. Jorge told Johnny he wanted out. The same day Jorge gave Johnny his notice, his oldest boy never came home from school."

"What?! Johnny had his son kidnapped? What happened?"

"Jorge reconsidered his options – told Johnny he wouldn't leave. His son was found in a park the next day. He was alive, but the kid was missing a finger when they found him. A few days later Jorge had an 'accident.' He's had that limp ever since. Johnny looks decent on the outside, but he isn't someone whose inner circle you want to be a part of. Tell him you don't want the promotion, Kid."

"I'm already working for him. You know that."

"You're directing his mules – not much of a sentence if you're caught. There's a big difference between sending drugs to dealers and working drops from the Mexicans. Tell him you don't want it."

Lenny was the closest thing to a parent I'd ever had. I didn't spend holidays with him or anything, but I knew he cared. I wasn't doing this for me. I had seen kids used, wadded up and thrown away my whole life. I had seen addicts of all ages so strung out they'd sell their own kids for a fix. If Lenny was right and I had a shot of moving up in Johnny's drug operations, I was one step closer to doing what I'd set out to do with Chad. My voice wavered, not for the reason Lenny thought. "A promotion's a promotion."

Lenny grabbed my arm, "No, it's not. Turn this one down. Stay where you are. You don't need to climb this ladder. If he gives you any crap, come back to my crew – I'll give you choice of any order I need to fill."

I wished that I could have told Lenny the truth. If I did, he'd have no choice but to tell Johnny I was working with the cops. No one crossed Johnny. Ever. If Lenny knew what I was up to and didn't report it up, he'd be forfeiting his life in the process. Doing my best to sound like the cocky kid Lenny believed me to be, I answered, "There's got to be better money than what I'm making now."

"It's an honest living, Mark. You got a nice apartment. You drive fancy cars. You wear nice clothes. I've seen you with plenty of ladies. You're doing okay for yourself. You're in a position that if you decided to go legit, you could. That's a luxury you'll never have again if you take this job."

His comment, "It's an honest living," made me smile. There *was* honor among thieves. My position in Johnny's organization was honorable: I didn't hurt anybody, and as far as Lenny was concerned, I was as honest as a cashier at Wal-Mart. I patted his arm, much more gently than he had grabbed mine just minutes before. "Going legit isn't in the cards for me. This is what I know."

Lenny's voice was low, "It doesn't mean it's the only thing out there."

"How would you know? You've been doing this type of work your whole life."

Lenny lowered his voice to barely more than a whisper. "No. I did a lot that I'm not proud of. You got your whole life ahead of you kid. You're smart. Use your head."

"Thanks for worrying, but don't. I've got this covered."

Lenny shook his head. It looked like he wanted to say something else, but he just handed me a slip of paper with an address on it. Lenny didn't say another word, nor did he look me in the eye. Lenny walked back to his perch behind the bar with a defeated look on his face. In that moment I wanted to come clean, tell him everything. The disappointment in his face stung, but I was too close to what I'd been working for. I left the bar and walked to the address on the slip of paper.

Lenny was right: Johnny had been polling references all day. Two of my mid-level bosses left voicemails to tell me Johnny was looking at me for a big promotion – he had asked them both about me. From what they told me, Johnny had heard nothing but that I was an honest criminal. I was someone who could be counted on to get the job done, regardless of what the job might be. One told me Johnny had had one of his contacts pull my police record – I was squeaky clean. For someone like me who wasn't born into this life, but worked my way up to the position I was in, my record had impressed him.

The address was to Johnny's high-end used car dealership. I had carefully avoided the lot from the time I first started working for Lenny. The car on the far corner was a sleek black BMW M3, next to it a Mercedes SUV, then a Jaguar: nothing in the lot screamed "Used." One of the other things absent were the tacky windshield numbers sported at other dealerships. Everything about the place seemed to whisper tasteful elegance. I made my way to a receptionist sitting behind an elevated desk. Before I could tell her who I was, she said, "Mr. Brewer, I'll let Mr. Corozzo know you are here. Please have a seat."

My butt had hardly touched the chair when she said, "Mr. Corozzo is ready for you. He is down this hallway, last door on the left." I looked to where she was pointing. A highly polished white marble floor spread out before me. I hadn't been nervous until I saw the gloss on the floor. My feet felt heavy as Lenny's warning echoed in my head. My pace slowed as I soaked in every detail: the geometric pattern of the floor, the opaque glass walls, posh Italian leather furniture in each of the offices, the smell of a fresh linen air freshener in the air. When I found myself standing in front of the last door on the left, it was cracked open.

Johnny sat behind an enormous mahogany desk with intricate designs that looked hand carved. I had seen Johnny before, but never up close. He was overweight, but had a polished look about him. He wasn't tall or short, standing somewhere near five foot ten inches. His eyebrows either grew perfectly, or he had them waxed, because there were two, and they seemed to form in an angry slant. Johnny had dark hair slicked back with grays sprinkled in, giving him a formidable distinguished look. He wore a gray suit and a black dress shirt without a tie.

Johnny pointed at a black Ferrari outside his window. In a throaty voice, he asked, "You ever driven a car like this?"

My heart began beating like a hammer in my chest. Had he somehow found out about my deal with Chad? "Once. A red one."

He raised his eyebrows, turning the angry slant to an angry question. "Working for Lenny?"

"I was sort of freelancing that night. Lenny was going to take it off my hands, but some cop started following me, so I ditched it."

The slant of his eyebrows grew in height. "You ditched a paycheck because a cop followed you?"

"I wasn't working with a crew that night. I didn't want to take a chance."

Johnny nodded. "I heard that about you. Everyone says you have good instincts. They all tell me I can trust you. Are *they* right?"

I shrugged my shoulders. "If I were you, I wouldn't trust anyone."

"I don't." An awkward silence hung in the air as he looked me up and down. "I see what Lenny saw in you."

Clueless as to what he was referring to, I stayed quiet but glanced at my shoes. Most guys my age wore athletic shoes, I wore leather loafers. I didn't have an abundance of clothes, but what I wore fit well and didn't show wear marks. I wore button-down shirts and blue jeans nearly every day. This look allowed me to blend in with working stiffs, but didn't make me stand out like a virgin in a whorehouse when I worked on the street. If he were commenting on my wardrobe, that was one thing, but he seemed to be paying little attention to my clothes – instead, he continued to stare directly at my face.

When it was obvious I didn't plan to respond, he asked, "You know what I see in you?"

"No." I quickly added, "Sir."

"You don't get rattled. You heard I was asking about you today?"

"Yeah. Lenny told me first, then Lance and Gerry both called to say you were checking references."

He nodded. "If I told you that I told all three not to mention to you that I had called, and I'm going to have to have a chat with them for betraying my confidence, what would you say to that?"

I considered his question for a minute, but didn't react to it. When my eyes met his, I accused, "I'd say you were lying to me." His eyebrows furrowed, nearly touching this time, but he said nothing, so I clarified, "None of those three would say a word to me if you had told them to keep quiet."

His stoic expression morphed into a comfortable smile. "Smart boy."

He handed me the title to the Ferrari, an "In-transit" plate, and an address. "I want you to go to a car dealership in Lincoln, Nebraska and trade this in on a blue Ford Escape."

I didn't know Johnny well enough to know when he was kidding or if he would even kid with someone so far beneath him in the organization. Rule was never to question the boss. But this was such a ludicrous task, I had to ask, "Seriously? Is this a joke?"

"I never joke about cars. When you go to do the trade, ask for Larry. He's a salesman who has given me excellent deals in the past. I trust him. Understand?"

"Sure. You want me to go now?"

"We aren't at my bistro, so I'm not cooking you dinner. I'll expect you back here with my SUV tomorrow night." He handed me a business card with only a phone number on it, "If you run into any problems, you'll call me."

He was serious. He had just given me his phone number. No one had Johnny's number – no one. At least no one I had ever met. A Ferrari for an Escape? Something wasn't right. I knew better than to ask him any questions. Instead, I looked at the date written on the plate and the title, and answered, "Of course."

"Tomorrow night. You'll be back by six."

"I will. How much do you want for your car?"

"Larry will make you a fair offer. I trust him." His words felt wrong. He had admitted just minutes ago that he didn't trust anyone. He must have some idea of what he wanted for his car. Why wouldn't he tell me what was acceptable?

The entire drive north I wondered if this was some sort of a test. No one trades a car like this for a little SUV. I was sure he had tagged me for a promotion in his drug operations – I hadn't expected for my promotion to be to one of his legitimate businesses. Chad wouldn't be very happy to learn I'd left my position in the drug business to move cars. I wasn't complaining, but I wondered what I had gotten myself into. Had Lenny gotten it wrong? Had I just been demoted?

Everyone who told me of Johnny's inquiries told me I was being promoted, but I couldn't figure out how moving cars was a promotion. Every car on Johnny's lot was high-end. Maybe he didn't trust his cars to just anyone?

Lincoln was only three hours away from Kansas City, so leaving at 8:00 a.m. guaranteed I'd be back well before Johnny's deadline. When I arrived in Lincoln, it took almost no time to locate the dealership. I pulled into the parking lot just after 11:00 a.m. and asked for Larry. He came outside, let out a hearty whistle, put his hands on his hips, and said, "I think I've got just the thing for you."

He must have expected me because he didn't ask me any of the normal questions. Was I looking to trade? How much did I want payments to be? How much did I owe on my trade? It was a bonus that he hadn't asked me any of those, because I wouldn't have had a clue on how to respond.

Larry led me to a blue Ford Escape without me even mentioning that was what I was in the market for. He had definitely been expecting me. Even used, the Ferrari was worth well over one hundred thousand dollars. Larry motioned for me to come into his office and wrote up a trade agreement, where he valued the Ferrari at thirty-five thousand dollars, and sold his vehicle for the same. This didn't feel right.

The last thing I wanted was for Johnny to think I'd been taken. I fidgeted in my chair, my knee bounced like a jackhammer as panic washed over me. I was only a few hours on the job, and I was already in over my head. No one in their right mind would take this deal. Hesitantly, I looked around the crowded dealership, then asked, "You're sure that's the best you can do?"

Larry smiled and answered me jovially. "First time jitters, huh? No problemo, take your time. Would you like a pop? I can get you one while you're thinking it over."

A pop? What was up with this guy? Why was he so happy? What would Johnny do if I returned without the SUV? How could I get close to his operation if I royally screwed up my very first job? My voice was unsteady, "Uh, hey, look, this isn't my car. I was told to do this trade and you'd give me a fair offer. I'm not an expert," that was debatable, "but this car is worth more than thirty-five."

Without an ounce of offence in his voice, Larry answered, "I know. You see cars like these on Ebay and on-line auctions go for waaaaaay more than thirty-five thousand. I agree." He pasted a sad look on his face, "But reality is that there isn't much demand for a fine automobile like this in Nebraska. I mean, who would drive something like this in the snow? No, sorry. This one could sit on our lot for months. Go ahead. Take your time. No rush."

Who did he think he was kidding? He could have this posted on Ebay and sold today and ship it anywhere in the world. Dealerships did that all the time, so did car thieves.

Furrowing my brow, I was sure I could make twice what he was offering on Craig's List or Ebay. Hell, I could take it back to Lenny and get better than thirty-five if I told him it was Johnny's car. If I got Johnny more money than his contact was willing to value the trade, I could give Larry thirty-five thousand cash, then give the rest to Johnny and bring him his new Escape.

It seemed like a win-win and a good way to build trust with Johnny. The only stipulation Johnny said was that I needed to be back by six p.m. If I were to get a fair market for his Ferrari, I would need at least a day, maybe two. Not wanting to screw up I said, "Let me make a call."

"Okey dokey, but sometimes asking for clarification when instructions were already clear can be a bad thing." His words stopped me short. Despite his freakishly happy demeanor, Larry had a point. Johnny told me he trusted Larry. If this was all he was going to offer and Johnny didn't like it, I wouldn't be the one dealing with Johnny's wrath.

My heart pounded hard against my chest. This Larry guy was right – Johnny wasn't someone to call to ask for clarification of simple instructions. People who didn't do exactly what they were told didn't last long. Lenny had told me as much yesterday. I wouldn't rock the boat; I'd do as I was told. Following his instructions to the letter would prove that he could trust me. The more Johnny trusted me, the quicker I could be moved back to his drug operations. "Okay. Where do I sign?"

Within fifteen minutes we had effectively traded cars. Larry was all smiles as he walked me out to the Escape and pressed the key into my palm. "Hey, I didn't catch your name."

Strange. I had just signed a ton of paperwork. I pointed at the paper in his hand, "Mark Brewer."

In a whisper he chastised, "Seriously? You used your own name?"

Not technically my identity, but it was my name. "I wasn't told to use anyone else's."

Larry's smile grew. "It's nice to have someone with some skin in the game. See you in a couple weeks."

Skin in the game? What was he talking about? Two weeks? I knew not to ask questions, but this purchase continued to get stranger as it went forward. I wasn't sure if I had unloaded a hot car or just purchased one, but either way, I was now knee-deep in some sort of criminal activity, and the dollar value was large enough that the IRS could track it. It didn't have anything to do with drugs, so Chad wouldn't be much help if I were busted. I was no closer to finding out how Johnny moved his drugs, and I might have just put myself on an FBI watch list in the process.

A different thought occurred to me. If Johnny had put me in his car operations, maybe he wanted me to learn the ropes before he gave me any kind of senior position in his drug operations. A monkey could have made this vehicle trade, but it wasn't a monkey – it was me.

Three hours later I was standing in front of Johnny's desk. It was five p.m., a full hour earlier than the deadline he had given me. Johnny was elated. He took the keys from me, hung them on a hook behind his desk and placed the paperwork I handed him in a vanilla folder. As he returned to his chair, Johnny slipped the folder into a desk drawer and asked, "No problems?"

"Uh, not really." The information was in the folder he had just slid into his drawer, but he hadn't looked at any of the paperwork, so I wanted Johnny to know that he didn't get much for his Ferrari. "Larry did an even trade. He only gave me thirty-five thousand for your Ferrari. That seemed really low."

Johnny's eyebrows pinched together, "You didn't try to get a higher price from anyone else?"

My eye muscles flexed. That was exactly what I had wanted to do. I stammered, "N-no. I followed your instructions." My heart lurched, then sped out of control. I was an idiot. Nervously I pointed at the door. "I'll go back right now and have a chat with him." My legs felt like rubber bands underneath the weight of Johnny's stare.

Johnny smiled, not a grin, but a wide smile. "No. I like a man who follows orders, even when they don't make sense. Here," Johnny reached into the narrow drawer in front of his gaping girth and tossed me a sealed white envelope. "You're in the big leagues now. Don't forget who put you here. Come back on Wednesday."

I had been dismissed. Confusion had to have shown on my face. He was okay with thirty-five grand for the Ferrari? I didn't wait around to see if he would change his mind. I was in my car, and off of his used car lot before I opened the envelope. He had given me $2000 in cash. That was a lot considering it was one day's work, and I had only gotten thirty-five grand for his car.

I returned on Wednesday just as he had instructed. From that minute on, I was in. I moved cars between dealerships, always delivering a high dollar import and trading it even money for a new domestic car, typically three runs per week. I delivered to Lincoln, Nebraska; Des Moines, Iowa; even went as far north as Green Bay, Wisconsin and several cities in between. Each time I returned with a new car, I was handed an envelope full of cash.

At first I believed I was actually working for his car business, but it didn't take a genius to figure out this was how he was moving drugs from one location to another. There was a set salesperson at each dealership who "sold" me a new car. We never exchanged money. Before I departed with one of Johnny's cars, he told me what type of car he wanted me to return with. At each dealership, a vehicle was waiting for me when I arrived. Driving the high-end cars around was a perk that I could get used to.

The new cars I purchased were filled with drugs. Payment for the drugs was the value of the vehicle I traded. From my perspective, I had never expected to drive a Viper, Lotus, Aston Martin, or any of the other high-end vehicles he sent me to cities with. No dealer trades came under police scrutiny because money didn't change hands. The secondary market for cars was all over the place: fair-market value was set by the buyer, so the whole operation flew under the radar. Each salesperson bought the trade from their dealership at cost and sold it over the Internet, pocketing the profits. All of the new cars I purchased ended up on his used car lot, so no one was the wiser.

I kept a spreadsheet file of dates, locations, times, names, and when I was sure I had enough to put Johnny and his team away for good, I set up a meeting with Chad. Chad was thrilled, but told me to keep doing what I was doing. He planned to set up a sting, but because I was crossing state lines, he needed to bring in the feds. Chad's only advice to me was, "Don't do anything to bring attention to yourself. Keep your file safe."

Chad gave me a USB storage device that looked like a grocery store loyalty card. It was plastic with some crazy design on the front advertising organic produce. I stored the card in a covered flap inside my wallet. If someone knew what they were looking for, finding it wouldn't be a problem, but if anyone dug through my wallet, I doubted they would give it a second glance.

CHAPTER 5

Months after I began "trading" Johnny's cars, I realized the job was harder than I thought it would be. Not the part where I was moving cars – a moron could do that part. It was hard because I was now part of Johnny's inner circle. It was easy to forget his role in the drug trade.

When Christmas came around, he chartered a jet and took everyone to an A-list-only restaurant in Manhattan for Christmas Eve dinner, then made sure everyone was back before midnight so they were home for Christmas morning with their kids. Johnny knew I didn't have any family, so he insisted I spend Christmas at his home because he didn't want me to be alone on the holiday.

Before Johnny, Lenny was the person to care where I spent Christmas. Growing up, Christmas was fun in the group home, only because there was usually a single ticked-off staff member watching us who didn't care what we did. Waking up Christmas morning to the squeals of Johnny's two daughters redefined the holiday for me.

One of the older guys in his circle, Oscar, was diagnosed with cancer; Johnny pulled some strings to get him into the Mayo Clinic the next day. Rather than have Oscar stay up there for treatment, Johnny flew a specialist in from Rochester, Minnesota to see him three times per week. No expense was spared. Everyone in his circle was family; none were family by blood, but each would have gladly laid their life down for him.

There were six in his inner circle, including Johnny, and he included the five of us in everything: visits to be paid to unions, confrontations with small time trouble-makers encroaching on his enterprise, even open discussions on super-meth. Oscar, despite his illness, oversaw Johnny's muscle and clean-up crew, Felix was responsible for the car dealership and distribution of drugs, Jorge ran numbers and worked the bookies, and Spencer worked with the prostitutes. Johnny kept us in the loop on his legitimate businesses, but we had little interaction with the people who worked the casino, sports complex, sports bar or bistro.

There didn't seem to be any specific pecking order. Oscar was Johnny's right hand. Everyone but me had worked for Johnny for decades. Lenny had been good to me; he treated everyone on his crew well. Johnny was different. Those of us in his inner circle were denied nothing. We drove nice cars, we had more money than we could spend, and Johnny took a genuine interest in each of us.

A meeting had just dispersed. Johnny excused the others and said, "Mark, stick around for a minute." I wasn't worried; Johnny held someone back nearly every meeting. The first couple times he did it, I was nervous, but I had been in the circle for over three months and was feeling more comfortable around everyone each day. He gestured for me to take one of the leather chairs near a coffee table. "You are doing well. We haven't had any problems at the remote dealerships since you took over the trades."

I probably should have told him thanks for the compliment, but I still believed that a moron could have done my job. I nodded in acknowledgement, but didn't say anything. "So, where do you see yourself in ten years, Mark?"

I had purposely never planned my future, not because I had a death wish, but I had never seen myself living very long. I didn't have dreams like most people. I didn't want a family. Anytime I found a lady looking for anything permanent – I went the other way. I didn't want to retire to somewhere quiet, or have a nine-to-five job like I watched on television. I wanted a big life in the here and now.

Johnny delivered on that, and when the police took him down, I didn't figure I'd live many days afterwards. I had already lived more than a decade longer than my little brother. It had been my job to keep him safe – I had failed. I wasn't sure if I believed in life after death. If there were something after, I wondered how I would ever explain to Davey how I had failed him in life.

My fingers slid over the soft Italian leather chair where I sat. I looked Johnny square in the eye, and told him, "Dead."

My answer took him off-guard. Not the response he had expected. He leaned in, his dark eyes narrowed on me. "What? No ambition? You don't see yourself growing with my operation?"

I shook my head. "Plenty of ambition. But I don't ever expect to have wrinkles. Besides, no one will miss me when I'm gone anyway." Johnny eased back, a soft chuckle escaped. My answer had been serious, but something about Johnny's reaction forced me to give him a smile.

"No one will miss you? You're young." He shook his head as if dismissing the notion. "You have your whole life ahead of you. You'll find a girl who will change your perspective. You'll start a family of your own."

After three months of seeing Johnny at least three days a week, we were sort of close. I knew about his freak allergy to wool, about his hatred of venison, I even knew he couldn't swim. It was getting harder to picture him as the enemy. Although I would never admit it to Chad, there was something about Johnny that was endearing – nobody had handed Johnny anything, he had made this life for himself on his own.

There were times I wanted to call Chad and tell him the deal was off; most of Johnny's businesses were legitimate. I reasoned that if Johnny weren't bringing in the drugs, someone else would. Then I would wander into the back of the garage and watch Eddie taking the new car delivery apart to retrieve the bags of meth hidden inside. Johnny moved drugs for a Mexican cartel, laundering the money he made on the drugs through his other businesses. He was rich while people hooked on his product died. I felt Johnny's eyes boring into my head as he waited for my answer.

I shook my head, "Not interested in starting a family or finding a girl. I've done more living in the last twenty-two years than most people have in a lifetime. When my time's up, it's up."

Johnny's gaze narrowed as his fingers dug into the leather on the chair where he sat. "That's a pretty pragmatic take on life."

"Not pragmatic. Realistic." The guilt that I felt for turning evidence on Johnny weighed heavier every day. He didn't respond, just leaned back in his chair studying me. He was unaware of my dealings with Chad, yet his gaze made me squirm. "You asked. I've got no reason to lie to you."

"You plan to be buried in the next ten years?"

"I haven't pre-paid for my funeral or anything, but I live my life without regrets, my own moral compass, I guess. I'll never wake up some morning and say 'I wish I had. . .' I like what I'm doing. But I'm not an animal; I won't live in a cage. If one day my luck doesn't hold and I get busted. . ." My voice trailed off.

"What? You're saying you'd take a cop's bullet before you'd do a couple years behind bars?"

It wasn't a bullet from the cops that would end my life; it would be one of his after he learned I had betrayed him. "Bullets are quick. Like I said, I'm not an animal, and I don't have regrets."

He rubbed the side of his face hard with his hand. "I want you on the security detail for my family. The pay's better. I need someone like you looking out for my girls. Your job is to put their lives above yours – can you do that?"

The pay was better? I was stuffing pillows in my closet with money I couldn't spend now. What did he think I'd do with more money? I didn't want to be moved off of his drug operations – that would defeat me having worked my way up to where I was. Going to security was a demotion. Had I just said something seriously wrong? I had met both his daughters at Christmas; I knew both were escorted with armed guards everywhere they went. A person like Johnny had enemies no matter where he was. This wasn't an offer I could decline, but it put a serious kink in my plan with Chad. "Whatever you want, Johnny. But I like what I'm doing now."

He reached across the little coffee table and grabbed my jaw in his hand. "It is an honor that I would entrust you with the lives of my children."

Surprised by the tenacity of his grip on my face, my first reaction was to shake it free – I didn't. I looked into his angry stare and answered, "I won't let you down."

Johnny released his grip on my jaw, leaned in closer, and placed his hand on my shoulder. "My enemies know my weakness. If anything were to happen to my girls, it would destroy me."

I swallowed. "I understand." Doing my best to keep the snarkiness out of my voice, I asked, "When do I report for babysitting duty?"

Johnny slapped my cheek – hard. "You won't be babysitting. You'll step in front of any knife thrust at them, any bullet fired in their direction, and you'll gut anyone you believe to be a threat. You'll protect my girls with your life."

"I got it. You can trust me." My mind raced. Four years, four stinking years of doing everything possible to get the information on drugs, and I was moved to a glorified babysitter position. I would be out of the loop. I had just been bounced from Johnny's inner circle. Chad would be as frustrated as I was.

"You start tonight. First, I need you to run an errand for me." He grabbed a pen and scrawled a message on a piece of paper. Somewhere in Johnny's past he may have gone to medical school, because I couldn't understand a single word he had written on the piece of paper. He handed the slip to me. "Take this to Oscar." Delivering a message wasn't something I typically did. Johnny had plenty of messengers available at the snap of a finger, but I didn't question him.

After studying it for five full minutes in the car, I had concluded not only was it sloppy handwriting, it was not written in English. Johnny spoke several languages; it shouldn't have surprised me that he wrote in something other than English. After delivering the slip of paper to Oscar, he looked up at me from his desk. He only uttered, "Impressive. Felix will be furious, but I'll pass the word."

"What word?" I didn't want to let on that I had no idea what Johnny had written.

"About the change in the organization. Congratulations. Enjoy your new duties."

That's what Johnny had written? He wanted Oscar to know I was a babysitter? Great. It probably said something like: *Mark has a death wish. I don't want him moving my drugs*. Oscar was Johnny's right hand, so one of his duties must have included the organizational structure. "What's Felix going to be pissed about?"

Oscar shared a broad smile. "I believe he was hoping for this position." Oscar picked up his phone and began dialing. He nodded at me in a wordless goodbye. As I walked back to my car, I was seriously confused: Felix wanted to babysit? I'd trade with him in a heartbeat, but it wasn't like I had that option.

Johnny said I started tonight. I went back to my apartment to change clothes and grab an overnight bag. When I opened the door, my apartment was empty. It looked like I had been robbed – a single envelope sat on the floor just inside the door. The envelope had my name scrawled across the front, inside was a note with an address I was to go to. I sprinted to my closet where I kept the money-stuffed pillows – they were gone, too.

I called Chad to tell him of the development. He told me to keep doing what I was doing, but warned me not to take the phone I called him with there. With my apartment stripped, I didn't have a safe place to keep it. It was a disposable, so I tossed it in a garbage can on the street outside my apartment before I went to Johnny's.

I made a detour before going to the estate – Lenny would know what to make of my new position. I stopped by Lenny's bar, but before I walked inside, I saw Kerry approaching on the sidewalk. Kerry may have had a woman's name, but there was nothing feminine about him. He was responsible for taking care of the mules who transported drugs around the city; he reported to me. I figured I'd better let him know I planned to recommend him to Johnny to take over my job.

Kerry was in his early forties, dark skinned, with hair cropped close to his scalp, and he dressed like he was upper management. I'd rarely seen Kerry wear anything other than a shirt and a tie – today was no exception. Blood dripped down from a split lip while dried blood droplets stained his previously pristine white collar on his shirt.

Kerry's head was down so he didn't see me walking toward him. When Johnny gave me my new assignment, Kerry was the person who I first thought of to take my job working the remote dealerships. I asked, "Kerry, what the hell happened?"

He looked up when I said his name, and flinched when he saw me just twenty feet away. After he got right up to me, he answered, "One of the dealers thought he was shorted today. I went to try to straighten it out. He didn't want to talk."

A dealer did this to him? "Who?"

"Chuck Brown. Higher than a kite. I should have known better. Should have waited."

Kerry never asked for my help with anything and he wasn't asking now, but Chuck needed a reminder of how the food chain worked. "C'mon, let's go see Chuck."

Kerry shook his head. "I got this, Mark. No big deal. I'll talk to him after he comes back down."

This wasn't up for discussion. A dealer being high was no excuse for hitting Kerry. "We see him now."

Kerry knew not to argue with me and led me to where Chuck lived just a few blocks away. The house had an upscale brown brick front. Chuck resided as an upstairs tenant of the duplex. The house was in a nice neighborhood – not exactly what I had expected. Kerry's lip was no longer bleeding when we climbed the steps and my knuckle rapped on the door.

The door cracked open as an eyeball stared through the opening. The door swung open, as Chuck's face registered the surprise of me standing at his door. "Mark, hi, I wasn't expecting you. Uh, come in."

I dispensed with any niceties. Pointing to Kerry who stood two stair steps down from me, "You do that to Kerry?"

Chuck's demeanor registered fear. His eyes widened, he took a step back from the doorway, and his head bowed. "I didn't. . .shit, I. . ." Chuck trailed off.

"You didn't? You calling Kerry a liar? He says you sucker punched him when he was trying to work things out with you about a delivery you said was short."

Chuck's eyes wouldn't meet mine. "I took a swing. I didn't mean to hit him. I'm sorry, Mark."

"Not good enough. No one lays a hand on one of my men." The door was open but I shoved it hard against the wall anyway. The door's handle planted itself in the drywall. I launched myself forward, my fist connected hard with his jaw. Chuck fell into the wall behind him and slid to the floor. Chuck came up to a kneeling position, refused to meet my eyes and wouldn't stand up in front of me. I told him, "Get up."

Sweat peppered Chuck's brow. "Mark, I'm sorry." His eyes darted to Kerry, "It'll never happen again. Kerry, I'm sorry. It was a mistake. I swear I didn't mean to hit you."

I lifted Chuck from the floor where he still kneeled in front of me; he was like dead weight and refused to stand up, preferring instead to stay on the floor. I shouted again, "Get up!"

Kerry's arm squeezed my shoulder from behind while I tried to force Chuck to his feet. "Mark, c'mon. He got the message. Let him be." I had seen too many men jumped in alleyways and nearly killed by dirty fights. As big as Kansas City was, it was a small town for the criminal element – everyone knew I wouldn't kick a man on the ground. Chuck's strategy of staying down was his way of protecting himself.

I took my eyes off of the remorseful Chuck to look at Kerry. "You're going to let him off that easy? How are you going to kiss your wife goodnight, Kerry?"

Kerry snickered. "She'll understand. C'mon. Chuck made a mistake. He won't make it again."

I glared back at Chuck who still refused to stand but was vigorously nodding in agreement with Kerry. Since I was going to be out of the picture, I needed word on the street to be clear that no one in my old organization was to be screwed with for any reason. "I hear one whisper that you disrespect one of my employees again, I'll beat you so bad they'll be looking for your dental records to ID you. You understand?"

"I do. I won't. I swear it was a mistake, Mark."

Looking back at Kerry, he nodded that my point was made. I turned and walked back down the steps. Kerry was exactly two steps behind me all the way until we got to the sidewalk. We stood there, Kerry grinned back at me, "I didn't need you to do that, Boss. I had it covered."

"I know you did. Listen, I'm taking a new spot in the organization. I'll be working at Johnny's place starting tomorrow. I need someone to take my spot at the dealership. Up for a promotion?"

Kerry shook his head, "No, thanks. I like what I'm doing just fine."

"Dealing with dealer scum? C'mon, you've done your time in the trenches. It's about time you had a job with an office for you to wear all those ties to."

Kerry didn't hesitate, "No. I like working with the carriers. Most of the time it goes like clock-work; tonight was an anomaly. I'll keep doing what I'm doing." He glanced back at the brick duplex, "Thanks for that. Chuck really didn't mean anything by it. If I were quicker, I would have gotten out of the way of his fist. Let me know who I'm working for."

CHAPTER 6

When I arrived at the metal gate of the address, two men with Uzi's stood tall. The one on the driver's side of my car checked a list of names, found mine on the list, and waved me through. I had been to the estate several times, but usually I was in a car with Johnny. I hadn't paid much attention to the exterior those times.

The main house was as big as any mansion I had ever seen – it was an architect's dream with all different angles and geometric shapes built into the structure. It featured a white stucco finish, expansive windows on all sides, and a perfectly manicured lawn spread out in all directions. The driveway was well lit. Two different armed men on ATVs rode beside my car as I drove up the driveway and pointed me toward a path to the left of the main house. I hadn't received this type of welcome on Christmas Eve because I was with Johnny and riding in one of his bullet-proof SUVs.

I drove where I was directed, knowing full-well they would put a bullet in my head if I varied so much as an inch in the wrong direction. When Johnny told me he wanted me on his daughters' security detail, I believed I'd be one of many, but it never occurred to me how many people provided security for his family.

I parked my car in front of a large maple tree and was guided toward a cottage that sat just behind the main house. The cottage was likely guest quarters at some point, but as I stepped through the front door, it was clear that this structure's purpose was not to house guests. There were twenty-four monitors lined up along a wall, with one man sitting in a chair watching all of them. He glanced toward the door, saw me standing at the entryway, and jumped to his feet.

"Mr. Brewer, welcome to the Ops Center. I'm Zane."

"The Ops Center?"

"Uh, yeah, that's what we call this place." He motioned to the monitors on the wall. "We have forty-eight live video feeds. These twenty-four monitors can display individually or collectively." Zane wore the same uniform as the men I had seen with the automatic weapons when I arrived: dark pants, a dark shirt and black boots. He looked to be about my age, but had a military air about him. It may have been the short hair – something screamed special operations.

Zane clicked a mouse a few times, and the image which had been on the lower left screen expanded to display across all twenty-four screens. He clicked a few more times and the images went back to individual monitors. A few more clicks then the monitors split in half and all forty-eight video feeds were on the wall.

I was not a technological wizard – at least not unless we were defeating anti-theft devices on cars. "Impressive. How do you keep track of them all?"

"Based on the family's schedule mostly. This time of night everyone is inside, so we spend more time watching the cameras in the common areas. Our focus is wherever the girls are."

Attempting to sound like I knew something about personal security, I asked, "Are there any blind spots on the property?"

Zane answered confidently, "None."

Another man in the same clothes as Zane wore appeared in the room. I hadn't heard him enter, so when he cleared his throat behind me, I hadn't expected him. I wheeled around to see a man who was easily six inches shorter than me standing just three feet away. Without meaning to, I asked, "Where'd you come from?"

He was pleased with his stealth. He ignored my question, "Nice to meet you, Mr. Brewer. I'm Collin. Zane, pull up the stations." Zane whizzed back on the mouse and the video feeds which had been present disappeared, and a schematic of the property stretched across the screens. There were nine little red dots. Collin explained, "Each dot represents a post. Each post is monitored by two guards." He tossed me a handheld radio, "Keep this on you at all times. Each member of the guard has been notified of your arrival. I'd recommend going to each post to introduce yourself. Change over happens at 0600, 1400, and 2200."

That was six a.m., two p.m. and ten p.m. – I hated military time. This was going to suck. I should have never shot my mouth off to Johnny. Eight hours standing a post, hoping like hell nothing bad happened, but bored to tears if it didn't. "When do I go on?"

"You're always on the clock, Boss."

"I get that. But do I have a set post or partner I'm supposed to work with?"

Collin glanced at Zane, then back to me. "Mr. Brewer, you are the head of security. We were notified by Mr. Corozzo this evening. We all report to you."

Head of security? What the hell did I know about security? "There must be some sort of mistake. Johnny told me he wanted me guarding his daughters."

"No mistake. Everyone guards his daughters. We all report to you." He pointed toward a large binder, "You might want to read this. It's our SOP."

"SOP?"

"Standard Operating Procedures: anything you need to know is in there. If you want to make any changes, just let me know."

Still not making sense of what Collin had told me, "Who was head of security before Johnny appointed me?"

Both Zane and Collin's gazes went straight to the floor. Collin answered without looking in my direction, "There was an incident this morning. Annabelle, the youngest, insisted on taking her dog for a walk. A team went with her. Some photos were taken off the property by a guy in a car. The team chased the car down on foot and radioed the incident in to our driving patrol, but we didn't catch the photographer. Mr. Corozzo was. . .angry."

"He fired the head of security? Because a guy took photographs of Annabelle?"

Collin's eyes still refused to meet mine, "Uh, yeah. Maverick was fired."

From his hesitation, the fact that neither of the two men would look me in the eye, and the way my question elicited fear in both of them – I knew much more than a simple pink slip had happened to the previous head of security. "Guess I'd better get familiar with the binder."

I spent three full months on the estate. I learned the entire family's routines. His daughters, Annabelle and Anastasia, were ten and seventeen – each was a handful in her own way. Annabelle was strong-willed and kept every single guard on their toes – she routinely wanted to do things that took her off of the estate: to the mall, to the park, to Chuck E Cheese, all of which were a security nightmare. If told no, she was quick to say, "If I tell Daddy you were mean to me, you will be in trouble." That single sentence spoken from her little mouth was enough to make beads of sweat form on a grown man's head.

Anastasia was worse. She was seventeen and looked twenty-two. Anastasia was an insatiable flirt, and, on more than one occasion, I had to direct her to put more clothes on or send a guard for a cold shower. Most of the guards on the team were young; we hired them after a four or six year stint in the military – which put each one in the category of "should-know-better," but reality was, she didn't look seventeen, and they were pretty young, too.

My first week on the job, Annabelle decided she wanted someone to play with her. She took out the board game *Clue*. I got a call from station two that Annabelle was demanding three players be sent to her playroom. It seemed like a reasonable request and was far better than trying to accommodate any of her off-property demands. I sent Mike, Ryan, and Jason. Mike had come out of the Marine Corps, Ryan and Jason the Army. I smiled to myself after I had directed them to the playroom – I bet none of the three trained killers expected their responsibilities to include board games. Mike radioed me as soon as the three showed up.

"Boss, Annabelle's got a knife, a rope, a trophy and I don't know what else. She wants to play *Clue* for real."

Rolling my eyes at the absurdity of the idea. "Give her the radio, Mike."

"Annabelle, it's Mark. Mike, Ryan and Jason are there to play *Clue* on the game board. You are not to play with any real props, understand?"

Her high-pitched response crackled through the radio. "But we have a hall, a dining room, a pool and a spa. We can use my room for the observatory. I think Mike did it with a rope in the theater."

Shaking my head at the radio, "No, Annabelle. If you want to play, Mike, Ryan and Jason will play with you, but only with the board game. You are not to play with any weapons or leave your playroom. Do you understand?"

A whiney voice crackled on the radio, "But Daddy said I could."

"No, he didn't. Your dad is at work. Give Mike the weapons, and the four of you stay in your playroom."

Just as Annabelle went into full melt-down mode, my radio buzzed to life from station three. I tried to get Kevin to tell me what was wrong, but he would only say that he needed to be relieved. Kevin had been a Navy Seal and was someone who never complained about anything – if he needed to be relieved there was a problem. I sprinted the three hundred yards from the Ops Center to where station three was by the pool. Before I could ask them what was wrong, the younger of the two, said, "Anastasia just went into the Jacuzzi." His eyes darted to the ground, "She wasn't wearing a swimsuit. If Mr. Corozzo hears any of us saw her like that, he'll take a hot poker to our eyes. We didn't look, I swear, Boss."

I got on the radio and asked the housekeepers to send a bathrobe out to the Jacuzzi. Before they could respond to my request, Mike got on the radio and said, "Boss, Annabelle's still got a butcher knife. How do you copy?"

Housekeeping responded, "Towels with the bathrobe?"

"Yes. A towel and a bathrobe."

A panicked voice cut on the radio. "She's got a rope, and she's putting it around Ryan's neck."

A third voice crackled on the radio. "Boss, the video feed on camera eleven just went out."

Chaos – my life was a circus. I was impressed with the calm I heard in my voice as I responded to all three calls for help. "Housekeeping: take the bathrobe and towel to the Jacuzzi. Let Anastasia know I'm notifying her father that she is not following the dress code, and boarding school looks like a safe bet. Ops Center: call the security company who installed the video surveillance system and tell them they have one hour to get a technician out here. Have one of the roving guards take a post where camera eleven sees until the technician gets the feed fixed. Mike: take the rope off of Ryan's neck. Tell Annabelle if she plays with one piece that didn't come out of the *Clue* box, her trip to the zoo on Sunday is cancelled."

Most days I stayed on the estate. Occasionally, Johnny had business which required a team from the house to accompany him. Those were the only times I was off the premises. When my apartment was packed up, my furniture had been put in a storage unit; all of my personal belongings waited for me in my quarters on the estate. I lived in the master suite of the converted guesthouse, so the Ops Center had easy access to me twenty-four hours per day.

The kitchen was stocked, and meals were cooked for the entire staff all day long. The cook published the next week's menu a full week in advance. If someone didn't like what was to be served, they had the option for an alternate meal.

I had lived in the same apartment since I was fifteen. It wasn't anything to look at; it was just a place to stay. My accommodations at Johnny's estate felt more like a five-star hotel. Marble lined every surface in the bathroom, the bedroom had its own sitting room with furniture and a king-sized bed in front of floor to ceiling windows. The night I arrived, housekeeping told me I could decorate it any way I chose – I couldn't imagine what needed to be changed.

Behind the guesthouse was the barracks. Having so many on staff with some form of experience in the military, this was what they all called it. If it had been my responsibility to name it, I would have called it an apartment complex. It, too, was full of amenities, and each staff member had his own studio apartment and private bathroom.

I may have been on the clock all the time, but when the girls didn't act up, there was time for whatever I wanted to do. There were two tennis courts, a bowling alley, two basketball courts – one was indoors and doubled as a racket-ball court, a gym packed with equipment, and a heated swimming pool that was half outside and half inside the house. There was a media room in the guesthouse that the security team used, but I was also permitted use of the one in the main house whenever I wanted. There were more options for downtime than I had ever imagined.

I worried that Chad may have thought the worst since he hadn't heard from me, but since some of the world's most sophisticated surveillance systems were in use, I didn't want to take the chance for a phone call or email. Nothing was private here.

After my day from hell had calmed down: Anastasia was fully clothed watching movies in the media room, Annabelle had decided to skip *Clue* and was playing with her nanny, and the video feed had been restored, I opted to relax in the Ops Center to wait for the next set of emergencies to come up. Johnny wandered in and caught me with my feet up. I scrambled off of the sofa, but he didn't seem to give my break a second thought. "Mark, you're doing an excellent job." It was the first time I had seen Johnny in the guest-house.

Johnny and I met several times a day in the main house, but in the three months since I had arrived, he hadn't ventured out to the little house. He wore a dark suit, white shirt, and white tie – not an ensemble I would have chosen, but it looked good on him.

"Thanks, Johnny."

"I've got a problem I need you to help me out with."

"Sure, just name it."

Johnny looked toward Zane who was in his usual position watching video feeds. Taking Johnny's lead, I stood up and the two of us walked outside the front door. Johnny asked, "You remember Haden?"

Haden was another who was promoted up from Lenny's crew. He and I had picked up a few Mercedes to fill an overseas order for Lenny just before I began working for Johnny four years ago. "Sure – from Lenny's crew."

"Haden died this morning."

Died? Haden was a couple years older than I was. "Natural causes?"

"If a cop fires a bullet into your head, you're naturally going to die."

"Damn, I hadn't heard. What happened?"

"He took over your old job and was reckless. I have to shut down the Sioux Falls operation. The dealership is compromised."

My heart sped up. Was Chad finally going after Johnny's operation? I hadn't contacted Chad. Had he hurried the sting because I had fallen off the map?

Feeling Johnny's eyes on me, I asked, "What do you need me to do?"

"You're taking over."

"Taking over? You want me shuttling cars again?"

Johnny motioned for me to take a seat on a little wooden bench. The bench was one of my favorite perches on slow days; it gave a clear view of the estate all the way past the main house. "I don't know how much of the operation was compromised. All the dealerships know you. Word travels fast. They're all nervous, so I can't put a new guy in. They all trust you. Instead of just the trading aspect, I want you running the books for the organization, as well. Too many hands can be a problem. Right now, there are a handful of people in my organization who know the drop schedules. When you take back your old job, all of the Cartel operations are yours."

That had been Felix's responsibility. He coordinated all the schedules with the remote dealerships. Felix and I were never tight, and he would not be pleased with me taking over some of his responsibility. But it wasn't a popularity contest. Johnny was promoting me. I would finally have access to all the info Chad needed. It wouldn't take any time at all to halt seventy-five percent of the drugs coming into the Midwest. A pang of guilt echoed through my body. Johnny completely trusted me.

I had made the most of my position as head of security. I had met every visitor who was permitted entry to the estate during my tenure. I had modified the SOP so that the head of security was provided a copy of all the visitor logs electronically at the end of every day, including dates, times, and names of everyone who had any ties to Johnny. No one batted an eye when I made the change, and the USB device where I had copied each of the daily files was tucked away in my wallet. I had hoped for a day where I could hand over the files to Chad when I was off-site, but thus far I hadn't been able to.

If I were being replaced as head of security, I wouldn't continue to get updates, but I had three full months' worth of daily reports plus archived visitor records in my wallet that I could give to Chad the next time we met. That pang of guilt morphed into a morsel of fear when I realized my own prophecy from my conversation with Johnny just months ago was going to come true. I had told him I expected to be dead in ten years. Once I turned over all the information I had been collecting to Chad, not even witness protection would be able to bury me deep enough to make it to my next birthday.

CHAPTER 7

I had moved off of Johnny's estate and hoped to move back into my old apartment, but it had been rented to someone else. The property manager who had rented me my other apartment said she had several vacancies; just not the one I had lived in since I was fifteen. I had never seen a hearse with a trailer; I wouldn't be able to take my money with me, so a better apartment seemed like a good plan.

I had enjoyed the amenities at Johnny's estate and decided it was time for an upgrade. The property manager showed me a penthouse apartment in a renovated building downtown: the building was elegant, had a great location, had its own indoor swimming pool, gym, parking garage, and a doorman. I was ready to sign the lease before she even opened the door to show me the apartment; I unstuffed part of one of my pillows and had a new home the same day.

It wasn't long before I was trading vehicles all over the Midwest again. Lincoln was one of my least favorite cities to travel to: limited choices for decent meals, no nightlife for anyone other than college students, and the hotel choices were poor at best. I was to meet Larry from the car dealership at ten a.m. tomorrow. To meet Larry on time, I would have had to be on the road to Lincoln by six-thirty a.m. Since I had shed the head of security detail, I'd gotten back into my routine of not being up early. Rather than rise before dawn, I chose to drive up today to make the trade tomorrow. I found myself at a hole-in-the wall bar: Bank Shot. There were no worthwhile clubs in the area, and even if there were, I couldn't imagine who would go to them on a Tuesday night.

I had always been an observer, so going to bars was something I mildly enjoyed. That's what gave me my edge. I watched people interact, studying them, trying to anticipate what their reactions might be before they made them. I had heard the best and the most socially inept pick-up lines. I saw a person gamble away his life savings on a hunch. Bars were an observer's paradise. Tonight was no different.

Teddy was here. He, too, had been on Johnny's crew, but after Haden was killed a couple weeks ago, Teddy quit. People didn't quit Johnny. Either they got pinched and went down for whatever they got caught doing, or they were in the dirt for breaking a rule – I didn't know any that had ever retired.

Teddy didn't see me as I propped myself against the wall. Johnny would want to know I had seen him tonight. I had no loyalty to Teddy. He and I ran in the same circles, but he was more of a minion. It concerned me that Teddy miraculously happened to be in the middle of farm country, in a sleepy city where I routinely traded cars for Johnny.

Teddy was too far down in the organization to know about this part of the operation. He was merely hired muscle who had reported to Oscar, one of many Johnny kept on staff to intimidate whoever needed it. Looking at him, the average guy wouldn't expect Teddy to be hired muscle, but the guy was ruthless with a knife.

I'd never seen any of his handiwork up close, but Johnny had once told me there was something that wasn't right about Teddy. Listening to stories of his carvings in people he was trying to drive a point home with, I had to agree. He had once carved the word "snitch" into the forearm of a bookie who moonlighted as a confidential informant for the police.

A brunette waitress pulled me out of my daze when she said, "You want another, Hun?"

My gaze flashed to her. She wore blue jeans and a tight Bank Shot t-shirt. She wasn't unattractive, but I hated a woman who chewed gum, and her mouth smacked while she waited for me to answer.

"Sure." She took my empty glass without asking what was in it. Either she had a decent memory or she had the snout of a bloodhound. My eyes rested back on Teddy playing pool with a very tall, thin, young man. The two shared many of the same features: dark hair, overgrown dark eyebrows, similar noses. I guessed the two were related. The longer I watched them, the more confident I became in my conclusion. Both had the same stance over the pool table and leaned on their sticks the same way while watching the other take his shot.

The gum-chewing waitress returned and handed me my Jack and Coke. Not incredibly impressive, as she merely had to select the correct whiskey, but I gave her ten dollars and told her to keep the change anyway.

Pulling my cell phone out of my jacket, I considered calling Oscar, but knowing this was his final week of radiation treatment, I decided to call Johnny. He picked it up immediately, "What's wrong?" Since Haden had been killed, he seemed more jumpy than he had been the last time I traded cars for him.

I rarely called Johnny, and he knew I was on a run to Lincoln. Johnny was confident that if I got caught, I wouldn't take him down with me, but he was just as confident I wouldn't go down without a fight. Sending in a clean-up crew if one of my trades went badly was not an idea he relished. It had taken him years to get this operation set up, and now all the dealerships were in an uproar after Haden. Up until a couple weeks ago, he hadn't had any incidents – Haden got sloppy. "Nothing's wrong. I just saw an old employee in Lincoln, and I thought you might want to know."

"Who?"

"Teddy McAlister is here."

"Teddy?" Johnny grumbled, "What's he doing there?"

"I'm not sure. I haven't talked to him. I thought you'd want to know."

"Who's he with?"

"No one I've seen before, maybe a relative. They're playing a game of pool in a bar. What do you want me to do? Do you think he knows about the drop tomorrow?"

Johnny hesitated then answered, "If he knows what's good for him, he won't know. Tell him I said hello. Ask him what he's doing there."

"So you think it's a coincidence that he's here?"

"I don't like it. Watch him. Call me back after you have a chat with him." Johnny hung up.

If Teddy had gone rogue and was working as an informant for the police, they would have him holed up in a motel somewhere. They wouldn't have taken the chance of letting me see him. I continued watching him as two ladies wandered up to the pool table where Teddy and the lanky guy were playing. I didn't know where these two had come from, but neither looked like any farmer's daughter I had ever seen.

The shorter of the two initiated a conversation with Teddy, while the taller girl held back. The one talking to Teddy made my breath hitch – she looked like Megan. Her skin was light and her features angelic – I shook off the feeling. The Megan look-alike wore a green halter top, cut low, showing her cleavage to any who wanted a peek. It was tied behind her neck, and a second thin scrap of fabric tied across her back. The color contrasted against her milky white skin. She wore a short, and I mean barely-covering-her-ass short, black skirt. Every contour of her body was visible, and every guy in the place was getting an eyeful. She had these black leather boots on that looked to be on loan from a strip club. They had sky-high heels and climbed over her knees. A tiny patch of muscular leg showed between the top of her boot and hem of her skirt. Her hair was long, blonde, and straight, flowing halfway down her back.

I shook off the feeling. It wasn't her. It couldn't be her. Megan was gone. Damn. What could this girl possibly see in Teddy? She dwarfed him. Was there a shortage of men in this town? I took a look at her friend who had just introduced herself to the younger, taller version of Teddy. She, too, wore an outfit that made my pants a little tighter than I liked in public. The tall brunette wore half a black sweater. Her abs were tight, and I was pretty sure I could wrap both my hands completely around her waist. The taller version of Teddy was mesmerized by the brunette. It looked like he might swallow his tongue – douche.

Now wasn't the time to approach Teddy. Instead, I leaned against the wall watching the two ladies. They began playing pool with Teddy and the other guy. I wasn't alone; as I looked around the dark bar, eyes from all over the room were watching table four.

The blonde wearing the green halter top played hostess and introduced everybody. "That should be easy to remember, Teddy and Tony," as she gestured to Teddy and his taller companion, then she introduced the brunette, "This is my friend, Candy."

I did my best not to be obvious, but I don't think I could have pried my eyes off of them with a crow bar. I tried to tell myself I just needed an opening to talk to Teddy like Johnny told me to, but reality was, this was a much better view than the one from my hotel room – I didn't mind waiting.

The two girls had moves on the table - the first game went quickly. The blonde won with no effort. I had never seen Megan play pool, but something told me she would have been great. I couldn't hear the chatter between Teddy and the blonde, but he was liking the view as she leaned in close to him. These two had to be working girls. I'd never had a problem with prostitution; I knew several of the ladies who worked for Johnny. I was just never a guy to pay for it. The four chatted like old friends. Maybe it really was a coincidence that he happened to be in Lincoln the night before I had a scheduled trade.

Candy had been watching the pool table, but she must have felt my eyes on her because she looked up from the table and stared right at me. Her hand raised in a wave. A weird pit formed in my stomach. I didn't wave back; no one stood behind me, so her gesture had been directed my way. Her expression baffled me, as if she were nearly giddy to see me. She looked over at me several times over the course of five more games.

As I studied the dynamics of the table, it looked like the four had money riding on it. So this was their game. The ladies weren't prostitutes – they were pool hustlers. Nice. That's something you don't see every day. The girls won the last game and Teddy looked seriously torqued. I had seen him wear the same look at Lenny's – it was right before he busted a beer bottle on the bar and went after some low-life like he was going to slice the guy's jugular.

I liked the blonde and the brunette's necks just as they were. I was about to step forward to let Teddy see me when I heard him shout, "I'm not paying this bitch." I smirked. I was right – he *had* been hustled. An exchange I couldn't hear took place, then he stormed away from the table, leaving Tony and the two ladies. Candy shot me a look like she was drowning and needed a life preserver. I didn't have a clue why, and stranger still, I didn't know why I started walking toward her.

Teddy returned to the table with a pile of twenties that he tossed at the blonde: they all floated to the floor. She squatted down to gather them. Teddy spat, "Go ahead, Honey, you can stay down there if you are looking for some more cash."

Something about the way he said it turned my stomach. I wasn't one to interfere in anything that wasn't my business, so no one was more surprised than I was when I stood at the corner of the table and said, "Teddy, you sneaky son-of-a-bitch, I thought that was you. Just got beat by a girl? Careful, your rep may never recover."

Teddy turned toward me, his face paled. Seeing me in this moment seemed to scare the shit out of him. The surprised look on his face calmed me, marginally, because he obviously was unaware I was in town. That meant he was unaware of the drug trade operations, too. His presence was just a coincidence.

Candy looked gratefully at me. She was smoking hot halfway across the room, but up close she was stunning. The blonde finished picking up the money from the floor, and when she stood up, I wanted to rub my eyes. She could have been Megan's twin. I turned away from her before it could get any more awkward, focusing instead on Candy. "Ladies, if you're done with Teddy, I need to talk to him for a minute."

The blonde closed her clutch that was now jammed with Teddy's money and answered, "Sure. We were just leaving."

Teddy flinched. I liked watching the slime ball squirm. "I saw you toss her winnings at her. You weren't disrespecting the ladies, were you?" The Megan look-alike began walking toward the door, but Candy stood in place staring in my direction. I got the feeling she was interested.

Teddy floundered, but remembered who he was talking to. "No. Of course not, Boss. Just wrapping up a friendly game."

"That's what I thought." I would be up this way a couple times per month; either lady would be decent company. The way Candy had been staring at me like I was a big hunk of chocolate cake, I decided to introduce myself. "I'm Mark. I'm sorry we couldn't meet under better circumstances. Can you stick around for a drink?" I was rarely in the same city two weeks in a row, but I had already worked out the trade schedule for the month and knew I'd be in Lincoln again next week.

Her expression changed. I had thought she was really into me, but she looked – confused. She took my hand and said, "It's nice to meet you, too, Mark. I'm Candy."

I glanced toward Teddy who was whole-heartedly scared. Teddy could keep squirming; my attention staying focused on Candy. I liked the idea that he believed Johnny had sent me up this way to find him – I was sure hundreds of possible scenarios were scrolling through his head. I repeated my offer, "A drink?"

"Um, no thanks. Libby and I were just leaving."

Disappointment I wasn't expecting ebbed at me. It wasn't often that I was turned down. Then again, I wasn't in Kansas City. No one knew me here, other than Teddy cowering a few feet away. She was into me; if she weren't, she wouldn't have been staring at me the whole time she was hustling Teddy. I figured I'd give her another chance. "My loss. I'll be here next Tuesday night. Maybe I'll see you then."

"Maybe. I don't usually go out on Tuesdays, but I'll try." She turned toward Libby and asked, "Ready?"

My pride was wounded. Maybe? She couldn't be serious. She might as well have said, "If I can't think of anything better to do." Women came onto me all the time. She said, "Maybe." I tried not to let the irritation creep into my voice when I responded, "I've got some business with Teddy. I hope you two lovely ladies have a good evening."

The two walked away without another word. I turned toward Teddy who looked as if he were concerned to see me but was preoccupied as he watched the two ladies walk toward the door. He stammered, "Hey, Mark, it's great to see you. I, um, need to be somewhere right now. Will you be here in a half hour?"

Not believing my ears, I asked, "Really? You want me to wait for you?"

He raised both his hands in the air as if I were holding a gun. "It's not like that. I swear, Mark. I had a previous engagement. Thirty minutes tops, I'll meet you right back here." His eyes continued darting toward the door, which had just closed behind Candy and Libby.

Suspiciously I asked, "What do you need to do for thirty minutes?"

"It's important. Here," he motioned for Tony to come toward us, "Tony will buy you a drink." He shoved Tony forward, "He's my brother. I wouldn't leave you with him if I weren't coming back."

Teddy looked like his skin would melt from his body if I held him here another few seconds. "I don't need entertainment. I'm sure *we* can trust you to return." Purposely accentuating "we" had the desired response. Teddy cringed. I gave him a dismissive gesture with my hand, "Go on. Run along. I'll be here for another thirty minutes." He was several strides toward the door when I called to him, "Teddy, we will have a chat tonight."

"I'll be right back, Boss. I promise." He bolted for the door.

Tony sized me up. I'd never seen the kid before. Almost bashfully, he asked, "You want to play a game?"

My phone rang before I could answer him. It was Johnny. I held up a finger to Tony as I took Johnny's call, "Hey."

"What happened?"

"He had to run an errand. He and I are going to have a chat when he comes back."

Johnny's voice was loud enough I had to pull the phone away from my ear. "An errand? You let him out of your sight?"

My eyes glanced toward Tony standing just feet away. "He'll be back."

"I don't like it."

"Me, either. I'll know how much he knows when he returns." Tony was straining to hear my half of the conversation. I wasn't discreet. A man should know if his life's going to be cut short, especially if he's related to a moron. "So, if he knows, you want me to get rid of him or are you going to send a clean-up crew?" Tony had his back to me racking the pool balls as I saw my words made his posture tense.

"Just find out what he knows and call me back."

As promised, Teddy was back in less than thirty minutes. Tony blended into the background at first, then excused himself entirely. From what little time I had spent with him, Tony seemed like a good kid. My guess was his record was so clean he'd never even been issued a parking ticket. After Tony left, I turned to Teddy and asked, "What are you doing up here?"

"Started a new enterprise, outside of Johnny's stomping ground. I haven't seen my kid-brother in ten years. Figured it was time to reconnect."

"Strange place to turn over a new leaf. How'd you end up in Lincoln?"

"My brother moved here to go to the university, then he decided to stay. He lives here. I moved up here a couple weeks ago."

I could usually tell when someone was handing me a line of crap. Teddy seemed to be telling the truth, but to be sure I reminded him, "You didn't give Johnny much notice."

Teddy pursed his lips together. "I got no beef with Johnny. He was good to me. I just needed to strike out on my own. I'm all my kid-brother's got left – our parents are gone."

Grey walked through the bar making his way toward us, and all the pieces snapped into place. Teddy had been hired muscle for Johnny whenever he needed it. Grey was the next rung up the ladder, not as in a chain of command within the organization, but when muscle wasn't enough to persuade someone to do what Johnny wanted, Grey was called in.

Grey strutted over toward me as if we were old friends. He was on Johnny's payroll, but his services were rarely required. He could easily have relocated and no one would have been the wiser – Grey was a one-man clean-up crew. Grey smiled widely, "Good to see you, Boss. Haven't heard from Oscar this week. Must be quiet in Kansas City."

"Does he know you're up here?"

Grey looked indifferent. "I don't normally check in. I get a call. I grab my cleaning bucket. No call, no bucket."

"Cleaning bucket" was a nice visual, but his cleaning supplies typically consisted of a handgun, a silencer, and a shovel. Grey was what everyone called him. I'm not sure if it's a name his parents gave him or one Johnny assigned to him before I joined the organization. I can remember when I was still new, Johnny said, "When I tell you to do something, it's like reading the newspaper – it's black and white. No ambiguity. No room for interpretation. You do what you're told and I'll take care of you. Always work on something that is black or white, because you don't want to operate in the gray area." I wasn't the only one he had given this little speech to. Grey Blair worked in the gray area – he wasn't muscle; he was a killer.

Still addressing Grey, I said, "Imagine Johnny's surprise when Teddy left town. Word on the street is he quit."

Grey didn't deny anything. "We both made Johnny a lot of money. We're not muscling in on his action. The two of us," Grey's fingers motioned between the two men, "we wanted to branch out. This town looks good. If Oscar needs me to clean up anything, all he has to do is call."

"So that's it. Teddy left on good terms, and you're at the ready if Johnny needs you?"

"Until I hear otherwise. I always did good by Johnny; Oscar can call me anytime day or night. If he has a mess he needs me to take care of, I'll take care of it."

"What type of operation are you two setting up in Lincoln?"

This was the first time Grey's eyes left mine; they landed on Teddy. Teddy stood up straighter. "Nothin' much. There's some college students here who like to bet. We're going to give them some better options."

"College students? That's chump change."

"Maybe. But it's good to get 'em young. They don't stay students forever. Once they're fine upstanding citizens, they're still going to like to bet; they will just have more money to do it."

"And you need Grey helping you?"

"He'll do clean-up if I need it. For now he's extra muscle."

Neither of the two knew about Johnny's operation up here, and from what they described, none of their new enterprises would be taking money out of Johnny's pocket. As long as they stayed out of my way, neither was much of a concern for me.

"What about the two girls I saw you playing pool with tonight?"

Teddy all but shouted, "They're cheats! Both of 'em! They're going to get a visit from Grey later."

Grey flinched and my eyes grew wide. We were in public. Teddy had just shot his mouth off in front of at least twenty people. If anything happened to either Libby or Candy, there were plenty of witnesses who had just heard the threat. My voice lowered so only the two of them could hear me. "You think that's wise? I thought you were setting up shop. Bad idea to start out making enemies with the locals."

"No one cheats me and gets away with it," Teddy spat. "That's a message I want broadcast loud and clear. I don't care how short their skirts are."

I looked at Grey, quietly warning him, "If you do this – you are on your own. Johnny won't make this go away if you get caught."

Confidently, Grey answered, "I've never been pinched. I'm not worried."

I picked up the cue ball off of the table and rotated it in my hand. I didn't want some stupid police task force looking for criminals before tomorrow when I had the chance to do the trade. "Neither better end up in the morgue while I'm still in town. You hear me?"

Teddy said, "Right, Boss. Grey's just going to warn them about the hazards of cheating. No one's going to be in a body bag."

"Fair enough." I set the cue ball back on the table. "Always a pleasure, boys."

CHAPTER 8

Thursday

This morning had been a complete waste of time. I should be in Kansas City instead of this sleepy little city. If I were home, I could be at Lenny's bar, listening to an endless string of "good ol' days" stories. Lenny retired decades ago, well, retired from his earlier profession. He had been a lot like Grey when he was younger. He worked for one of the "families" in Chicago. The family he worked for was removed from power.

Johnny wasn't part of the mob, at least not like the families on the east coast or Las Vegas. Johnny was all business, he was organized, and his source of revenue was crime, but it wasn't like the stories Lenny told me about from back in the day. When Lenny's employer was gunned down and a new family took over, he chose to start over in a new city. Almost no one sharing his profession lived to retirement. Those who did normally spent their last years in a ten-by-ten cage.

Lenny could have retired to the Bahamas, Mexico, hell, he could have gone anywhere he wanted. He reinvented himself and created one of the most effective chop shops east of Los Angeles. He took me under his wing while I was just a kid, before I was legally old enough to drive. He didn't knock heads or prey on anyone, and everyone shared in the wealth. Lenny was like the father I never had.

My phone rang: I looked at the number and recognized it as Felix. Felix was in Johnny's inner circle, too – he and I weren't all that tight. Assuming it was a routine check-in because I was late with a delivery, I accepted the call. "Yeah."

Felix's nasally voice asked, "What's the hold up? You were due back yesterday."

Frustration ebbed my words, "The salesman called in sick again. No trade today."

"Sick? Did you tell him you were coming?"

"No moron. I showed up with a cake and balloons and planned to surprise him." Now that my irritation with the situation was obvious, I added, "He knew I was coming."

"He doesn't like to wait." The "he" referred to was Johnny. Felix was a professional; he rarely used names on the phone – none of us did. No names was a precaution along with disposable cells and code names for the cities where trades were made. Lincoln, Nebraska was "Grandma's House."

"Yeah, me neither."

Felix asked, "What should I tell him?"

My first trade after my hiatus as head of security, and, of course, the numbnut at the dealership doesn't come to work for two days. "Tell him I'm working on it."

"So tomorrow?"

"I talked to the salesman this morning when he let me know he was taking another sick day. If I can trade tomorrow, I'll be back tomorrow night."

"Don't pull my chain. You'll be here tomorrow night?"

Felix wouldn't have called me unless Johnny was concerned. Rather than spell it out for him with big purple crayons telling him I had no control over whether the salesman was going to take another day off, I confirmed, "Tomorrow night."

Felix hung up. This was the aspect of my job that I hated. My reputation was tied to scumbags who I wouldn't trust with the responsibility of caring for a plant. "Scumbag" may be a little harsh. Larry was the same guy I had my first trade with after Johnny had promoted me. Every time before this one, he had been reliable.

From the urgency in his voice this morning when he called me, Larry was just as anxious as I was for the trade. He gave me a sob story about not being able to leave his girlfriend in the hospital. I had cut him some slack because I had traded with Larry lots of times. This was the first time his reliability had come into question.

This was to be a simple trade. I bring up a vehicle with clean tags and trade it for a new vehicle. Everything was legitimate. There was no reason for anyone to suspect anything. Larry had the perfect set-up at the dealership. He was a salesperson, and as far as I knew, he worked with a single technician. There were no dark alleyway trades, just a new vehicle purchase once or twice per month. The vehicle I purchased was worth about thirty thousand dollars, but held closer to a quarter million in street value of drugs. Johnny paid twenty cents on the street value dollar, but he did it with car equity.

When Larry and I spoke last Saturday, he chose Wednesday for our trade. I made the necessary arrangements and arrived on Tuesday night. Wednesday morning I got to the dealership to find Larry wasn't there. After poking around for a few minutes, one of the other salespeople told me Larry had called in sick and offered to help me. I declined. At ten a.m. on the dot, the time when we should have been making the trade, my phone rang. Larry called me to tell me we needed to reschedule. This morning at eight, he phoned me again.

Nothing seemed out of the ordinary. I had checked his story and even went so far as to do surveillance at the hospital his girlfriend was in. When I had checked, he was indeed sitting in a waiting room.

I killed time cruising around the little city. There were plenty of places to stop for a drink, but none of them had the energy I gravitated to. The town was full of a bunch of college kids and working stiffs. I liked the anonymity of a bigger city, the possibilities for entertainment. Other than finding Teddy here a couple nights ago, there had been no excitement whatsoever.

I worked out, watched television, and got a bite to eat. Sitting in the hotel was grating on my nerves. I decided to go out for a while – I wasn't surprised when I pulled into the parking lot of the same place I'd been a couple nights ago: Bank Shot. It wasn't great, but the drinks were cheap and the music was decent. Tuesday night had been thoroughly entertaining, so I figured I'd try my luck again. I eased into the parking lot and shut off my car. It was a habit to watch for any telltale signs before entering. There were no surveillance vans or unmarked police sedans hiding in the shadows. Either of those two indicators were a warning to steer clear.

As I slid out of my car, I was a little surprised to see a familiar face. It was the same brunette I had met on Tuesday night; Teddy had kept his word about not putting her in the morgue. I had offered to buy her a drink, but she turned me down. I smiled to myself: girls like persistence. What was her name? Carey. . .Cassie. . . no, I continued to focus – Candy, that was it.

Watching her a second longer, something seemed off. Single females usually travelled in packs. She was alone in the parking lot, looking at cars. Was she looking to boost one? If she were a car thief and a pool hustler, I had just met the girl of my dreams. I watched Candy for nearly a minute; she seemed to be waffling about whether to go inside. Whatever internal argument she was having, she made her decision and started toward the bar's door.

Candy wore jeans and tall boots; a turtleneck sweater peeked out of the top of her coat – not at all the same way she had been dressed a couple nights ago. Her outfit Tuesday night had been memorable: a short skirt, tall boots, and half a sweater – it looked like she was on the prowl. Tonight she was sporting soccer mom clothes.

Just before she got to the door, I called, "Well, if it isn't my favorite eye Candy."

She wheeled around with a glare. Had I screwed up her name? No. She told me her name was Candy. Maybe that was a nickname? Once her eyes took me in, I saw the recognition register on her face. I must have made an impression because she offered a warm smile and said, "Geeze, you scared me. All done working for the day?"

She strode over to me confidently, as if we were old friends. "I'm always working." I met her halfway through the parking lot and stopped just a few feet from her. She gazed at the distance between us and took a tentative step closer to me. I liked a girl who knew what she wanted. Maybe being stuck here an extra couple days wouldn't be a total loss.

Her face was flawless: ivory skin, rosy cheeks from the cold, not caked with makeup. I liked the way she wore her hair better the other night, hanging loose around her face. It was pulled back in a librarian's braid tonight, not unattractive, but somewhat less to my liking. She asked me, "What? Having second thoughts?"

Confused, second thoughts about what? I'd watched her friend and her take money from Teddy and his little brother on a pool table. That was pure entertainment. Teddy had lived on the Kansas side of Kansas City, but we traveled in the same circles. His side of Kansas City was around 150,000 people, the Missouri side was more than twice the size with over 400,000 residents. He had envisioned himself as the ultimate pool hustler, so it was a riot to see two ladies take him for a chunk of change.

Candy was looking at me with inviting eyes, waiting for me to answer. "I have lots of thoughts. Just giving you space so as not to smother you. Glad you don't need time to warm up to me."

"After last night, I think we're past the bashful stage." She rose high on her toes and pressed a kiss on my cheek. My mind whirled to life as I thought of last night. I'd stayed in my motel room watching a game on ESPN – alone. Was she so much of a barfly that her days were all mixed together? I had hardly even talked to her on Tuesday. She and her friend slipped out right after they took Teddy's money. Her lips lingered on my cheek as I realized I didn't care if she couldn't keep her days of the week straight.

My lips found hers. They tasted like grape jelly, soft and inviting. A gentleman would have stopped with a soft answer to the invitation, but being a gentleman was not on my resume. I pressed my lips against hers hard, forcing her mouth open as I slid one hand behind her head and my other hand slid to her back and pulled her body against me. When she answered my call with equal desire, we locked hard in place in the middle of the parking lot. I was known for my control, but in this moment I wanted a quiet dark room. We didn't let loose of each other until a car pulled up and nearly ran us both over.

Her breath was labored. I had no desire to go into the bar anymore. I scanned the city streets around the area hoping to see a motel we could get to before I exploded. Nothing. This was an industrial area, and choices were limited. My motel was a fifteen minute drive from here. I'd take her to the first one we came across. "Where's your car?"

She answered me with the brightest smile, then pointed at Bank Shot's entrance. "We've got time for that later. We're already here. I want to see if Chris has seen anything."

I didn't know who Chris was, and I couldn't have cared less what he'd seen. She took my hand and began walking. She had gone a couple steps before I gripped her hand hard and yanked her back to me. I wanted her like I hadn't wanted anyone in a long time, "We've got time for it now."

I pulled her out of the main traffic area of the parking lot and stepped against her. I felt every inch of her body against mine. I grinded myself into her as my eyes closed and images assaulted me. None of those images included the two of us merely standing in a parking lot in the dead of winter. She smiled at me like this wasn't some run of the mill chance encounter. She pulled her lips away from me and said, "This'll take ten minutes, then we can go back to your place."

Ten minutes and she was going with me to my motel? I could last ten minutes. Hell I could wait twenty, but not much more. I took another look at her and decided I sort of liked her librarian braid. She had looked like she was ready for action the other night, but tonight it was almost as if she were in disguise, a raging sexual beast hidden under the sweater and jeans. I chuckled, "Man, this is a switch. Usually that's my line."

She answered my humor a little defensively when she said, "You say that to a lot of girls?"

No. I'd never had a girl come on this strong to me before, at least not one who wasn't looking for me to shove singles in her underwear. She got a strange look on her face when she asked, "You're not kicking me out, right? I don't want to overstay my welcome, but there isn't much I wouldn't do for another one of your special coffees."

A special coffee? Kicking her out? I was only going to be in town another night. Did she plan to move into my motel room with me? Something wasn't making sense. I eased my body away from hers and asked, "Candy, when did I make you coffee?"

"Sorry, didn't mean to offend you. Hot chocolate with an extra shot of caffeine or whatever you call it."

Thoroughly confused. Hot chocolate? What was she, twelve? Eyeing her cautiously, I asked, "Are you medicated or something?"

"Um, no. Call it whatever you want, but I've got to say that was better than slamming a Red Bull. Breezed through my test without any effort at all this morning."

I took a step back, way back. A great lay was one thing, but this girl was odd; there was something seriously wrong. None of her statements were making sense. She was looking at me with just as much apprehension. She asked, "Did I say something wrong? Hey, if you are sensitive about your secret recipe, I'll keep it on the down low."

My body was all in, but there was something not right with this girl. "I have no idea what you're talking about."

She cocked her head to the side as if she were studying me. I watched her eyes rove over me from my shoes all the way to my face. Her eyes widened when she asked, "Mark?"

Well, at least she knew who I was. It didn't explain all the other odd things she had said, but it made me feel a little better that she wasn't all doped up. Recognition showed through her eyes as words shot at me, "OHMYGOD, it's you. You're here. Holy crap! I didn't know that was you." She paused for a second then added, "I mean, I know your brother."

All images of the two of us wrapped up on a bed disintegrated in that instant. It was as if she had turned a switch in me. Anger from my core bubbled to the surface. Every muscle in my body went rigid. Rage pulsed through my blood stream. Not wanting to lose control on this psycho in public, I answered coolly, "I don't have a brother."

"Dave. Your brother is Dave Brewer."

Anger welled up within me. I saw red. She had no right. My rage seeped out through my hand as I saw her body rise in the air, my hand holding her several feet off the ground. "My brother's dead, you stupid bitch."

I would have killed her. I would have held her dangling in the air until every bit of oxygen had been squeezed out of her. Repressed rage I had held in tight coursed through my body. Images of my little brother flashed through my mind. I was no longer standing in a parking lot; I was with him playing army men in a fort we had made. A voice from behind me brought me back to reality, "You better put her down, friend." One of her feet connected with my leg.

I tossed her aside. Trying to regain control, I put my back to her and walked away. He had been alone in the world. I was his big brother: it was my responsibility to protect him – I had failed. Davey was dead because I hadn't been strong enough to care for us both.

My feet moved away from her, attempting to distance myself from the fury. I went straight to my car. Memories flooded me from all directions. How did she know my brother's name? What kind of game was she playing? How had she found me? Had Teddy put her up to this as a payback for shaking him up the other night? If Teddy was behind this, I'd kill him with my bare hands while his little brother Tony watched.

She launched herself off of the ground and ran straight for my car. I wanted to kill her. I was already in my car's driver's seat when I revved the engine. I envisioned driving straight into her, sending her librarian body sailing high into the air.

She waved her hands at me while she ran straight for my car. I put the car in drive and spun the tires on the ice. It should have been enough to get her to stop in her tracks, but it didn't. She jumped in front of my car while my tires spun on the ice. Easing off of the accelerator, the tires halted as I stared at her through my windshield. She had rattled me. No one had rattled me like this before. No one knew about Davey. My heart hammered hard, the rage refusing to subside. I rolled my window down and warned, "Get out of my way, or I will run you down."

Her face looked frantic as she stammered, "Dave's not dead. Lives here." She drew in a ragged breath. "He told me about you. I told him I saw you here Tuesday night."

It felt as if a bolt of electricity shot through my body. Davey's not dead? He had been dead for more than ten years. Was she trying to play me? What was her angle? A glimmer of hope sparked – I wanted to believe Davey was alive, but that was too much to hope for. I jammed the gear selector into park, opened my door, and stood on shaky legs. "What do you mean he lives here?"

Her voice still sounded strained, but words poured out of her quickly. "He moved here when he was nine. He said you two got separated when he was five. I was supposed to come here with him tonight to try to find you."

I felt dizzy on my feet. Closing the door to my car, I stalked toward her. If this were some sort of a trick, I would kill her. I wouldn't waste time calling Grey in to do it for me. "Davey Brewer. My brother? You're telling me he's alive and he lives here?"

"Yes. He and I have been friends since high school. He restored my car," she pointed toward the backside of the parking lot. "He told me about what happened with the two of you when you were little, how the foster family kept you and gave him back to the state."

My stomach knotted. How could she know about that? Davey was sent back to the state within a couple months of us going into a foster home. I never saw him after our social worker took him away. I studied her face to see if there were an ounce of deception staring at me through her eyes. Her voice was kind when she offered, "I can take you to him. Or give you his phone number. You have no idea how badly he wants to see you."

I couldn't make myself believe it. The state of Missouri had sent a grief counselor to tell me he had been in an accident. Davey wasn't dead? None of this made sense. "He's alive?"

"Uh, yeah. At least he was when I left for school this morning." She smiled at me like this was the funniest thing she'd said all night. I couldn't process it. How could he have been alive all this time? He must be furious with me. My hands were shaking and my legs felt weak. I turned away from her to the serenity of my car, easing back into the driver's seat. She followed me. Her knuckle tapped on the passenger side window. Mechanically, I unlocked the door as she slid into the passenger seat.

She said nothing at first. Her eyes were fixed on me. Questions sailed through my mind: How did he get here? Was he okay? What was he like? How did she know we were brothers? Did he hate me? I couldn't make any of the questions come out.

Her gaze didn't waver. A warmth I hadn't felt since I was in grade school formed in my chest – I wasn't alone. My brother was alive. Visions of football games, ski trips, racetracks: all the things I routinely did alone assaulted me. He was here. I took another look, confirming there was not even an ounce of deception in her. Davey was alive. Trying to keep the warmth from morphing into a giddiness, images of Davey as a child played on a constant loop in my head.

Reality was a cool chill on my skin. What would happen to Davey when Johnny found out about him? Nothing, until Johnny learned I was feeding Chad information. I was the perfect plant because I had no family that could be retaliated against, until now. Grey was right here in Lincoln. What did he say Tuesday night? He was a phone call away. This was bad – horrifically bad. Chad knew everything I knew about Johnny's drug trade. When Chad stormed in with guns blazing, Johnny would know it had been me who gave the cops the information. Johnny would hunt Davey down. Worse, he'd send Grey to hunt Davey down. No.

The thought made me cringe. Instead of asking her anything about where Davey was or what he had been doing for the last ten plus years, I simply told her, "I've got some things I need to take care of. You should go. Don't tell him you saw me tonight."

"What? Are you kidding me? Dave was beyond excited when I told him I met you. He would kill me if I lied to him about seeing you tonight."

Davey had talked to her about me? Did he think I had abandoned him? My pulse was beating erratically; I took a deep breath trying to keep the fear at bay. "Give me some time. I need to tie up some loose ends before I see him again. You said he lives here?"

She pulled out her cell phone and began scrolling through contacts. "Just let me get him on the phone. Five minutes. Please? Just talk to him for five minutes and let him know you're okay."

My heart ached. Davey was alive. I grabbed her hand holding the phone to keep her from calling him. She studied me, and I could tell my reaction made no sense to her. I tried to piece together what had happened. When she saw me tonight, she thought I was Davey. Doing my best to keep her from seeing my fear, I uttered, "So, when you kissed me, you thought. . .you thought I was him?"

"Well, yeah. I don't even know you."

I attempted to play it off. I couldn't let her know how important Davey was to me. If she breathed a word of it to Teddy or Grey, word would get back to Johnny about my brother. Instead I pretended to be disappointed she hadn't come on to me after all. "My loss."

Her voice was quiet when she asked, "Why did you think Dave was dead?"

"It doesn't matter. You're sure it's my brother? People steal dead people's identities all the time."

"He has the same eyes as you. The same cleft chin. Your hair is the same color, too; yours is just a little longer. No, your appearances are too close for you not to be brothers." She paused for a minute as if she wanted to say something else. "He only lives like ten minutes from here. We could go there now."

Every fiber in my being, every cell in my body, every bit of me wanted to scream, "Yes." I swallowed the elation, forcing it to the deep recesses of my mind, steadied my voice, and answered, "No."

"I don't understand. You don't want to see him? He's a great guy. He owns his own repair shop – all custom muscle. I know he wants to see you. He told me about you last night. It almost ripped his heart out to share it with me. Please go there with me."

I needed a new phone so I could call Lenny for advice. I needed to tell Chad this was over – I was out. Davey wouldn't be alive for long if Johnny found out I'd been working with the cops. I turned away from her and looked into the parking lot full of cars. "Not now. Soon. I'll find him."

I motioned for her to get out. My answer was not what she was expecting, but I couldn't tell her why I wouldn't see Davey. I had too many things I needed to fix. She started to reach for the door handle, but stopped and asked, "Hey, before you go, how well do you know Grey and Teddy?"

Was she serious? If she were in tight with Grey or Teddy and told them about Davey, there would be no way for me to keep that information from Johnny. I was screwed. I didn't answer her, so she prodded. "Teddy was one of the two guys that my roommate and I were playing pool with the other night?"

She must have thought me dense. I answered her with a question. "You two hustled Teddy, right?"

"Sort of. I mean, we needed groceries."

Grocery money? She was an idiot. "Bad move."

Her voice pitched high. "You know him? Because the police are looking for them now."

The police? The two had just barely arrived here. Why would the police be looking for them? A small gambling operation shouldn't have elicited any attention from the local police department. I didn't want to let on that I knew much about either of them, especially if she were cooperating with the police on anything.

Johnny would want details. How would I explain to Johnny that Teddy and Grey had already done something to warrant police involvement, while I was in the city. Shit. Things just kept getting worse. Even if I had wanted to answer her question, I couldn't. "You might as well be looking for a ghost. He has more identities than a shark has teeth."

She asked hopefully, "Can you tell me their last names?"

Refusing to give her any information that could put Davey in danger, I simply answered, "Get out." She didn't so much as flinch, so I made myself clear. "Now."

She did as she was told, but from her expression, I knew she didn't understand my reaction. As soon as the passenger side door closed, my car was in motion. I needed to talk to Lenny – this couldn't wait.

CHAPTER 9

Lenny picked up the phone immediately. "You okay?" I hadn't checked in with him in a couple days, but ever since Johnny had moved me up in his organization, I'd go a week or more without talking to Lenny. The urgency in his voice didn't make sense.

"Yeah. No. Shit – I don't know."

"Felix was in here shooting his mouth off earlier. Says you're a couple days late on your delivery. They're looking at sending someone up there to check things out."

That explained the urgency I heard in Lenny's voice. Felix purposely talking loud enough for Lenny to hear was one thing, but if Johnny was sending someone up to check on me – that means there was real concern about my trustworthiness. "Shit. Lenny," it was the first time I had ever used his name on a phone call, and I cringed at my screw up, "you need to keep Felix busy down there." I didn't have any love for Felix, so it didn't bother me that we'd both used his name on this call.

I had never asked Lenny to help me with anything work related. I didn't need to spell it out for him: Lenny knew I was in trouble. Concern colored his voice when he asked, "What have you gotten yourself into?"

"Everything's jacked up. The guy I do the exchanges with hasn't been at work the last couple days. I said I'd be back in Kansas City tomorrow night."

"You better be back tomorrow, or someone's going to be paying you a visit."

My mind was racing. If someone came up looking for me, what if they also paid a visit to Teddy and Grey? This was a small city – it would only be a matter of time before they ran into my brother. If word got out about Davey. . . I cringed at the thought. "It sounds like I need to take a road trip south to let the boss know things are under control. I'll leave now. I'll stop by your place later tonight for a drink. I have some things I want to run past you."

Lenny didn't try to find out what it was I wanted to talk about, and he didn't try to talk me out of my road trip. All he said was, "I'll be looking for you."

It was normally a three-hour drive to Kansas City. I was just entering the city limits at two hours and twenty-five minutes. There was a chance my speed might draw suspicion if I were to be pulled over, but driving a hundred plus miles per hour kept my mind focused on the road and didn't let me overthink everything I had learned. I wanted to talk to Lenny, but I needed to make sure Johnny knew I hadn't flaked out on him. I dialed Johnny's number; he picked up right away. "Where are you?"

"Five minutes from your house. Going to stop by to chat."

Johnny paused for a minute then asked, "We've got a customer waiting on that F-150. Did you already deliver it to the dealership?"

"No. It wasn't ready to be picked up yet. They wanted to detail it before I took it off the lot." I was purposely as cryptic as Johnny was on the phone. This was how we spoke because cell phones were so easily monitored.

His voice was slow and measured when he asked, "Did you start the paperwork for the trade?"

"No. My favorite sales guy called in sick the last couple days. He's supposed to be at work tomorrow."

"So, if you don't have the F-150 I sent you for, what is there to chat about?"

"I got a call from one of the employees at our car lot. It sounded like you were questioning my ability to close the deal. I decided to come back to reassure you that there was a delay, but there was no trouble." That was as plain of English as I could use without telling Johnny that Felix was getting nervous, so I drove three hours to pacify the guy.

"I'll see you in a few minutes."

I pulled up to the gate, but instead of checking the list for my name, James leaned down into the Mercedes, "Hey, Boss, wasn't expecting you tonight."

"Hi, James, here to see Johnny."

His smile wavered. Few people came by the house to see Johnny this time of night. He must have expected I was delivering bad news. James reached over to the wall of the guard shack, pressed the button, and the wide metal gates swung clear for me to enter.

Johnny stood on his front porch as I turned off the ignition. His breath looked steamy in the cool night air. A potted evergreen flanked him on either side of the front door. Johnny held the door for me to pass, then ushered me into his office. He closed both of the large wooden double-doors behind us. I stood by the brown leather sofa, waiting for him to take his seat behind his desk before I sat. He eased into his overstuffed wing-back leather chair and motioned for me to sit, too. "What's going on in Lincoln?"

"Nothing. Nothing at all. Larry and I were supposed to meet yesterday morning. He called in sick yesterday and today."

"You spoke with him?"

"Yes. His girlfriend is in the hospital. He didn't tell me what's wrong with her, only that he needed to stay with her."

Johnny leaned his head back against the chair. His eyes roved to the ceiling when he asked, "You believe him?"

"I didn't at first. Lincoln's not very big. I found the hospital where she's staying – he was in the waiting room just like he told me."

Johnny's eyebrows drew close together, but nothing else on his face gave away any kind of concern. "What did he say when he saw you?"

"He didn't see me. Larry has always been reliable. Once I checked his story out, I went back to the motel."

"So, why are you here? Why aren't you still waiting?"

"Felix called me. He made it sound like you were questioning my ability to make the trade."

Johnny's eyebrows went back to normal. His face remained expressionless. The chair complained as his weight shifted. "So you drove back to put my mind at ease?"

"I did. If you wanted to replace me on this job, I didn't want you to have to go looking for me. The Mercedes for the trade is out front. I'm right here."

My accusation hung in the air before he answered, "You could have called."

"I could have, but with Teddy taking off on you and Haden getting himself shot in Sioux Falls, I didn't want you wondering about my loyalty. It was worth the drive to answer your questions myself."

Johnny sat in his chair staring at me hard – studying me. After what felt like enough time to wash a car, he reached over to the phone on his desk and dialed a number. He didn't make eye contact with me when he spoke, "Mark's here. Everything is fine. No one takes a trip north." He didn't wait for any kind of response from whomever he had called. He hung up.

Johnny's elbows leaned forward on the desk. His demeanor had changed. Coming to see him in person was the right move. "It means a lot to me that you worried I would question your loyalty. I don't. Get back up there and bring me my truck. If Larry needs more time – give it to him."

My heart was hammering in my chest. I hadn't felt it gaining momentum until Johnny told me he trusted me. No one from Johnny's crew would be going to Lincoln to check on me – none would find Davey. Relief crashed over me. Now I just needed to figure out how to keep anyone from finding out about Davey.

I barely remembered leaving Johnny's house. We must have talked about something, but the relief drowned out any conscious thought, and I went on autopilot. I had pulled into a parking space outside of Lenny's bar with little recollection as to how I had arrived there. I walked in and scanned the place quickly; not finding anyone from Johnny's crew on the premises, I went straight to Lenny. He had been in mid-sentence with one of his customers, but I didn't care. "I need to talk to you."

He didn't excuse himself from the conversation or anything. He just set down his glass and motioned toward the back office. I led the way.

As soon as his office door was shut, he said, "Spill it. What's going on?"

Lenny could read me like a book. I glanced around the little room. "Your office clear?"

"No ears. Tell me what's going on." "No ears" meant there were no bugs in the place. Lenny had it swept regularly for listening devices, web cameras, hidden recorders, and who knew what else. Lenny wasn't on anyone's radar, but old habits die hard.

A cheesy grin I wasn't expecting spread across my face. "I got family."

Lenny's smile mirrored mine. "Family? That's great." He made a logical leap and asked, "So, you're going to be a father?"

"What?! No."

Lenny looked confused. "Wait. What family? You patched things up with your mom?"

I had nothing but hate reserved for the woman who had handed Davey and me over to the state. I felt the hard lines in my face form as I answered, "No."

Lenny's eyes searched mine. He knew all about my past; Lenny was the only person I had ever told my life story. "Davey. He's alive. I don't know how, but he's alive and lives in Lincoln."

"But you said Davey died. You talked to him?" This wasn't making any more sense to Lenny than it had to me when Candy told me a few hours ago.

My eyes darted to the desk overflowing with papers. "No. But I met a girl who knows him. She knew all about us. She thought I was him. People used to confuse us as little kids because we looked so much alike. She says she saw me and thought I was him."

Understanding registered on Lenny's face. "That's what's got Felix all worked up?"

"No. No one from Johnny's crew knows. Felix is nervous because the guy I was supposed to get Johnny's latest shipment from flaked." I didn't want to talk about Johnny, Felix, or anything work related. Lenny was my only real friend and the only person I trusted with this information. Excitement poured out of me. "He's not dead. He's been three hours away the whole time."

Lenny opened his drawer, pulled out two glasses and poured. Crown Royal was how he celebrated everything. I preferred mine on ice, but I wasn't about to go out to the bar for ice. As he poured, he asked, "That's great. Why haven't you talked to him?"

"No. Not great. Remember what you told me a couple years ago about having family and what could happen to them if Johnny wanted to keep me in line?"

"That was when you were just starting out. No one's going to lift a finger against you or any of your relatives unless they are told to do it from Johnny himself. You're not at the bottom of the food chain, Mark."

An image of Chad's face flashed in my head. My teeth mashed together. "Yeah, so what if I screw up?"

Lenny narrowed his eyes at me. "Don't screw up."

"Easier said than done. I was a couple days late on a routine trade, and Johnny was ready to send out the search party. I can't have them finding Davey."

"You're planning to hide Davey from Johnny? Bad move."

Although I shared nearly everything with Lenny, I had never let on that I was feeding information to the cops. If Lenny knew I was, he'd understand why I needed to keep Davey buried. When I didn't defend my plan, Lenny asked, "You squared things with Johnny on the late delivery?"

"You think I came down here because I missed you? Yeah, I told Johnny I was late because my contact had an emergency. He called Felix off."

"You bought yourself some time. When are you going to meet Davey?"

I shook my head. "Not while I'm on the clock for Johnny. I'll set something up after Johnny gets his truck."

Lenny nodded approvingly at my decision. "How did this happen? She just walked up to you and said she knew Davey?"

"Pretty close. I met this girl a couple nights ago. Tonight I saw her in a parking lot and she kissed me. When she realized I wasn't Davey, she told me he had been looking for me." That warm feeling from earlier was back. "I've thought he was dead since I was in middle school – I just. . . froze. I remembered what you told me about Johnny and family, so I took off and called you."

Lenny cocked his head to the side. "But you are going to talk to Davey?"

"After I make the trade. I'll go back up to Lincoln tonight, make the trade tomorrow, and have Johnny's truck on the lot before the sun goes down. Once I'm sure everything is calm here, I'll take another trip up to find Davey."

Lenny's enthusiasm diminished, marginally. "You're sure it's your brother. Dead people's IDs are taken all the time."

Exactly the question I had asked Candy. Her certainty convinced me. "I'm sure."

His smile returned. "What can I do to help?"

"Nothing right now. I just wanted you to know."

Lenny did something I never expected. He stood up, walked over to me and put his hand on my shoulder. "You've had a tough life, Kid. If anyone deserves for things to work out, it's you. Tell me if you need anything." His hand squeezed my shoulder, then he walked back to the bar, leaving me with my warm whiskey.

Eyeing the still full glass in front of me, I didn't want to sit in an empty office. I needed to get this trade done. I saw a bunch of official looking papers stacked in a pile on the corner of Lenny's desk, and my mind went to Chad. If I didn't finish what I started, the last four years of my life would have been wasted. In my position now, I had access to everything Chad needed. But finishing what I had set out to do could mean I'd lose Davey forever.

CHAPTER 10

Friday

I got back to Lincoln – late, after two a.m. Being cooped up in the car for another three hours on the return trip, I was full of nervous energy. I had waffled at least every thirty minutes the entire drive back. Part of me wanted to find Davey and tell him how sorry I was that I hadn't searched for him as soon as I was on my own. The other part told me I didn't deserve to have Davey in my life – I was a criminal well before I began working for Johnny. I debated whether I could find him, just to see what kind of a life he led, but stay in the shadows. Three hours' drive coupled with two stops for coffee, I was no closer to a decision than when I had left Lenny's bar.

I tried to find sleep, but the turmoil inside me raged through the night. When the sun began peeking through the curtains of my hotel window, I startled myself awake without realizing I had ever found sleep. Sleep had come in short spurts all night, so I was exhausted. Dreams had been a combination of Johnny,

Felix and Lenny all jumbled up. I shook off the dreams and grabbed my phone. There were no missed calls. I dialed Larry – he picked it up quickly, but spoke in a whisper. "Hey, I'm still not at work."

Frustration ebbed in my voice, "You told me today. We have a buyer who is anxiously awaiting the F-150. How about you go into the office for a couple hours, we do our deal, and I'm out of your hair for a while. I'll reschedule the trade we have set up for next Wednesday, but I need this truck – today."

Larry was broken up, his words pained. "Libby is still in critical condition. I can't leave her."

Libby? That wasn't a common name. I had only ever met one Libby in my life, and that was Tuesday night – the blonde who had been with Candy. Pieces of the puzzle began assembling themselves. Candy and Libby had hustled Teddy and Tony Tuesday night. As soon as the ladies left, Teddy was in a rush to leave, too. Would he have attacked Libby? No, but thirty minutes was more than enough time for Teddy to have followed the girls home and to have called Grey.

Candy told me last night that the police were looking for Teddy and Grey. My stomach cinched tight when I remembered what I had told Teddy and Grey at Bank Shot: that I didn't want either girl in the morgue while I was still in town. If I had known Candy was Davey's girlfriend, I would have told Teddy and Grey to steer clear of both of them. I had let this happen. I could have told Teddy to let the pool game go, to drop it – I didn't. My inaction Tuesday night is why Larry hadn't met me for the trade on Wednesday. It was because of me that his girlfriend was in the hospital.

This deal between Larry and me had to go down – now, before the police tied me to either of these two morons. Remembering the sexy blonde in the green halter top Tuesday night, I pushed her image out of my head and barked, "If she's in critical condition, she won't know you've stepped out for a couple hours." I didn't care that Johnny had said to cut Larry slack. Larry and I weren't pals: I was here to do a business transaction, and I couldn't afford to get sucked into any of this, especially when my ability to see Davey was riding on it.

Larry's voice was low, "Let me get an update from her doctor. I'll call you back right after I talk to him."

Several hours later, Larry finally called to tell me he couldn't leave the hospital again today. Johnny had told me if Larry needed more time, to give it to him. If I leaned on Larry, he might call Johnny, and I'd be in even deeper for not following instructions. Larry's voice was meek as he interrupted my thoughts, "The doctors plan to wake her up tomorrow afternoon. I just need to be here until they do. If you knew her, you'd understand why I can't leave."

I did know her – that was the problem. I may not know her as well as Larry, but I knew who she was. Reluctantly, I agreed. "Fine, but, Larry, tomorrow night. Nine p.m. we do the trade. No more excuses, no more delays. I've been here since Tuesday."

"Thanks, Mark. Nine tomorrow. I promise."

I had a little over twenty-four hours on my hands. I went to the business office of the hotel and began searching for my brother on the internet. I didn't know much about him, but enough that I was pretty sure I could find him with Google's help. I brought up a search engine screen on the browser and typed: David Brewer Lincoln NE automobile repair.

The very first link took me to a white pages hit for *Bodies by Brewer*. I searched around and didn't find a website for the garage. Returning to the same search box, I found a second link and then a third, of testimonials on blogs about the work he had done on cars. It almost looked like a cult-type of following, not religious, but all motor-heads. There were pictures on several of the blogs which included before and after photos of cars he had worked on – I was impressed. He had skills. Even after being separated, we had both gravitated to careers with cars. It was good to see he hadn't gotten his start the way I had. Instead it looked like he was rescuing cars from bone yards and breathing new life into them.

One of the blogs had a picture of Davey with a wide smile leaning over an old red Oldsmobile. I stared at the picture for a long time – dumbstruck by our similarities. Candy was right – we looked like twins. I couldn't remember ever smiling that big. I printed the picture from the website. When the page printed, the web address printed on the bottom of the page. I tore the photo away from the rest of the page that had printed and tossed what was left of the page into the trashcan. Jagged paper edges surrounded the happy candid, but I didn't care. I folded up the small photo and tucked it in my wallet.

By late afternoon I was sick of hanging around the hotel and stalking Davey on the computer. My curiosity only grew each time I learned a little more about who Davey had become. I grabbed my keys, my coat, and headed for the parking lot, the address for his garage scrawled on a tiny piece of paper. I wouldn't go up and introduce myself. I just wanted to see him, or maybe see a piece of his life.

As I approached his garage, I slowed the car nearly to a crawl. I didn't stop, but as I rolled slowly by the place, it looked locked up tight. There were some sweet restorations setting outside, which were mostly covered in snow.

I had considered going back to Bank Shot, but if I ran into Candy again, I wasn't sure I could turn her down if she tried to take me to Davey. I didn't want to screw everything up and meet with him right now. The sun set early this time of year, and it was already getting dark – I needed to get back to the hotel where no one would see me. I went to a drive through, took the food back to my hotel room, and turned on the television.

Saturday morning arrived. My phone was ringing and relief washed over me when I saw Larry's number flash on my phone's screen. I cleared my throat and said, "You ready to do this trade?"

He sounded like a kid who got a second birthday party, "She's awake. She came out of her coma last night. They're still running tests, but the doctor told me he thinks she's going to be okay."

Now I was really out of time. If she knew it was Grey and Teddy who did this to her, and Teddy had ties to Johnny. . . If a real detective did some digging, he would think it suspicious that I was up here during the same time with no viable reason for my trip – at least none I could offer as an alibi. "You never said what happened to her."

I had a pretty good idea, but wanted to know what Larry knew. He stammered, "I'm not sure. She. . .she and her roommate. . . well, Libby plays pool for fun. She sometimes bets on games. Her roommate thinks that someone she beat Tuesday night followed her home from the bar and beat her up."

Frickin' Teddy and Grey. Idiots. Neither one of them had the sense that God gave a gnat. "So the police know who did this?"

"No, at least not their names. Candy, that's Libby's roommate, says she thinks she knows the guy. The police have been here off and on all week. That was part of the reason I wasn't in a hurry to do this trade – I was worried if I went to the office to meet you, it might look suspicious."

Larry was someone Johnny trusted – I guess I knew why. Not wanting to sound like an insensitive bastard, I asked, "So she's fine now?"

"Libby's still in the ICU, but she's awake and talking. The plan is to move her to a regular room in the hospital later this morning. Look, I know you've been patient. I've got keys to the dealership, you still want to meet there at nine tonight?"

Meeting at the dealership after closing could draw suspicion. At this point I needed ten minutes with Larry to do the trade, and get on the road south. "There's an Irish Pub over on Windham Street. Can you bring the truck and the paperwork there instead?"

"Why?"

"To alleviate suspicion. Do you normally go into the dealership after hours to trade a car?"

"No, I guess not. But I've never made a sale over a pint of beer, either." Larry paused as if pondering my suggestion. "Okay, I'll leave here when visiting hours are over, go to the dealership and pick up the truck and the paperwork. I'll meet you at the pub at nine."

When Larry and I hung up, I finally believed things might be okay. We'd make the trade, I'd be headed south by nine-thirty and get the F-150 on the lot just after midnight. I tabled all of my "Davey" enthusiasm for now. Once I got everything smoothed over with Johnny and Felix, I'd figure out how to get back up to see Davey. Just knowing he was alive was enough for now.

My room was paid through Sunday, so for most of the day I watched college games on television. No matter how hard I tried to concentrate on the games, my mind kept returning to Davey. As darkness fell, and there were only a few hours to go before my meeting with Larry, I packed my suitcase and wheeled it to the car. Driving around town, I couldn't help but notice that my car gravitated to the side of town where Davey's garage was. I forced myself to drive away from his neighborhood and to get my mind focused on where it should be: making the trade. Turning toward Windham Street, I watched Davey's neighborhood in my rearview mirror growing farther away. It was time to find a secluded table at the Irish Pub.

I wouldn't be meeting with Larry for a few hours, but now was the perfect time to case the pub where we would meet. Although I'd never done a trade outside of a dealership, I had done this type of work long enough to know simply being punctual wasn't adequate. The pub was a public place: I needed to know who was working, where the exits were, what the crowd was like inside. If things went south, I needed to reduce the chance that the police or anyone else would have an advantage over me. My first inclination was to park several blocks away in case I needed to leave undetected, but since I was trading this Mercedes, it needed to be close enough for Larry to see it.

A small neighborhood grocery store huddled next to the Irish Pub. There was a parking spot directly in front of it. I had considered going a little further down the block, but it was cold; no sense walking any further than I had to. I got out of my car, stood up, and stretched as the frigid air attempted to steal my breath.

As I looked down the street, a woman ran at a dead sprint across the busy street. She was nearly mowed down by several oncoming cars. Her hair was wild, her face registering terror, as she emerged onto my side of the street. When she approached the Irish Pub I was heading to, I was able to get a closer look. The fine hairs on my arm stood at attention. It couldn't be.

It was Candy – the same girl who had told me Davey was alive. She ran toward the pub – the pub where I was to meet Larry in less than two hours. Why did she keep turning up at the most inopportune times? I had scared her Thursday night. After having checked her story, she had been truthful – Davey was alive. I was excited for the reunion with Davey, but I couldn't let any of the players I was working with find out that he lived here. I needed for him to be isolated from my life.

She would be wary of me after the way I had treated her Thursday night. If she saw I intended to go into the pub, she would certainly turn and go the other way. I needed to catch her attention, let her know where I was going. I put on an angry sneer and shouted, "Are you training for a marathon? There are better activities to be had on a Saturday night."

She stopped short. She was close enough that I saw her eyes widen as her long brown hair blew in the cold night air. Her hand had already been on the door handle. She tried to ignore me, turning her attention back to the entrance.

A car horn sounded in the street as I saw Grey Blair giving chase. Frickin' wonderful. Grey was in hot pursuit of Candy. If I ignored him, he might do what I needed done on his own – keep her out of the pub.

During my conversation with Candy the other day, she had told me the police were looking for Grey. I didn't need any police in the area while I was meeting with Larry. Damn it. I looked at my watch. I had time to intervene on her behalf and still have enough time to case the place before my meeting. She seemed to be pretty attached to Davey; if I didn't intervene, she would probably tell him I watched Grey attack her on the street. Instead of turning my back, I threw her a lifeline. "Ah, an interesting way to train for a marathon. Someone chasing you is excellent motivation to push yourself. Don't let me interfere."

I walked back toward my car, assuming she would look for the only safe-haven offered and be at my passenger door in a second. She didn't. Instead, she pulled the handle of the pub, only to have some exiting patrons nearly run her over.

Grey had made it across the street despite a Green Hyundai nearly dismembering him. His voice was full of rage as he bellowed to her, "You'll regret it if you take one more step."

Candy didn't sneak inside the bar, nor did she run to the passenger side of my car. She seemed to be weighing options. She stood her ground and shouted back, "Back off. I'm calling the cops. You lose." I was intrigued – not even one of the options I would have guessed. I'd seen marks many times backed into a corner. Reactions were much the same: bartering for their lives, pleading for absolution, even offering their pursuers money in exchange for letting them live. I had never witnessed a victim act so aggressively and threaten their pursuer.

Her threat worked – he stopped short. Now Grey was considering his options. He was winded; she seemed to be in much better shape than Grey. He placed both his hands on his knees trying to get air as he continued glaring in her direction. He tossed out an empty threat, "No one cheats Teddy and gets away with it." It was a rookie move if I had ever seen one.

Teddy McAlister, aside from applying pressure to whomever Johnny believed needed it, was also a smalltime pool shark. He'd been bounced from most of the legitimate tournaments in Vegas and Atlantic City for fixing games. Teddy's only income now that he had quit Johnny's crew was hustling in bars and his bookie plan he had told me about. I'd seen him play in Kansas City, I had heard of his exploits in Chicago and Omaha; Lincoln, Nebraska seemed a little too small time for him.

Again, Candy didn't back down. "I never cheated Teddy. Neither did Libby. It was a fair game. Ask Teddy's little brother."

Grey wasn't budging, "Teddy says you cheated."

"How did we cheat? And even if we had, Libby's in the hospital right now, and you already got your money back. You nearly gave my neighbor a heart attack. All this over a few hundred dollars is insane." Her back straightened when she added, "Kidnapping just got added to your attempted murder charges. When the cops find you, you're done!"

If that were true, I definitely needed to get both of these two away from the pub. This whole area would be crawling with local law enforcement as well as the federal boys. Shit. Grey was too stupid to understand the implication of her threat. His next comment cemented the fact that he was intellectually inept. "I'm going to make an example out of you. No one messes with Teddy in this town. Others need to know there are repercussions when they cheat him."

She shot back, "I got news for you: Teddy lost fair and square. Word gets out that all of this happened over a few hundred dollars, and he won't be able to show his face anywhere around here. Libby has lots of friends who aren't going to be happy about what the two of you have done."

His smirk returned to a glare. "Are you threatening me?"

I couldn't let this go on. People inside the pub were starting to notice the exchange, as were people on the street. I needed them both out of here. Grey hadn't seen me, so I stepped more fully onto the sidewalk. "She's right. I asked around. Teddy's always been a hot head. He may have led you down a path you didn't need to go."

Grey's aggressive tone morphed into a submissive one the instant he realized I had just interjected myself. "Oh, hey, I didn't know you were still in town." Grey's posture straightened and his glare dissolved when he answered, "This is a favor for Teddy, you understand."

Candy turned toward me but continued speaking to Grey. "So, Grey, why don't you tell Mark how you tried to kill his brother Wednesday morning." Instead of waiting to see my reaction, she turned back toward Grey and accused, "You shot him on my street. You knew that was Mark's little brother, right?"

Rage rocketed through my body. Grey shrunk. His eyes were fixed on me. From the moment I had learned Davey was alive, I vowed not to let our worlds collide. Davey was a normal guy with a normal life. I didn't want anyone in my world to know about him. Remembering the prying eyes in all directions and the fact that I was to meet Larry here in less than two hours, I attempted to keep the fury safely welled up inside me. My fists balled tightly at my side while my tone remained level, "What's she talking about, Grey?"

Grey stammered, "I don't know. I never shot your brother, Mark."

She added hastily, "You shot him all right. Then the cops arrested him for your break-in. Nice. I'm sure Mark doesn't mind in the least that you almost killed his little brother and left him to answer for your breaking and entering charge." As if I were dense and unable to keep up with her charges, Candy turned to me and said, "You thought your brother was dead all those years? This lunatic almost made that a reality."

The fury in me refused to subside. I could kill Grey right now and the world would be a better place. It would remedy several loose ends. I hated loose ends. If Grey knew my brother lived here, there was a possibility others would learn the same. If I took him out, would Candy report it to the police? Who had seen me? I glanced at the windows of the pub: there were several sets of eyes engrossed in our exchange. This was too public.

Grey might have been reading my mind or at least my intentions. He held up both of his hands, "Hey, I didn't kill anybody. I shot at some guy who was chasing me. It was self-defense. He never told me he was your brother. I never would have pulled a gun on your family – never!"

Candy wanted me to kill him – I could see it in her eyes. Almost jovially she answered, “That’s funny? Dave told me that you let him into my house because you thought he was Mark. Maybe you were trying to kill Mark?”

The color drained from Grey’s face as I felt my own cheeks flush. He had tried to kill me? Me? Grey was small time. He knew better. I wanted to end him, here, now. There would be no repercussions if I did. Oscar had plenty of people he could call in for a clean-up if he needed one. Grey was past frightened when he shouted, “That is not what happened!”

Heat spread all the way to my fists. I was known for my ability to compartmentalize. Yet all I wanted in this moment was for Grey to cease to exist. Before I could do something that would put the entire operation in jeopardy, I turned to Candy, “C’mon Candy.” I used every bit of control I could muster and held my hand out to her. “I believe your altercation with Grey is over. I’ll give you a ride to your car.” Looking at Grey, I warned, “You, Teddy and I need to have a chat later, Grey.”

My offer confused her. She didn’t immediately run to me as I had expected. Grey knew his days were numbered. He was backpedaling as fast as he could. “Hey, this situation is something Teddy initiated. You and me,” he wagged his finger wildly between us, “we’re good, right?”

Unamused, I answered, “Funny. This situation,” I made a circle in the air pointing at the three of us, “as of right now, no longer includes Candy. The new players are you, Teddy and I.”

Grey’s eyes were huge when the reality of what I had told him sunk in. “Oh hell, Mark, I’m sorry. Miss Kane never mentioned the two of you were friends.” He looked back at Candy, “Our misunderstanding is over. I hope your roommate has a speedy recovery.”

Ms. Kane? Her name was Candy Kane? What kind of parents would do that to their daughter? Grey began backing away as I held my snicker in, his eyes never leaving mine. Letting him know this was something he needed to make right if he wanted to continue to breathe, I asked, “Medical bills?”

His retreat stopped short, his stupid head moving like a bobble-head doll. “Way ahead of you, Boss. I’ll take care of Miss Merrick,” his eyes glanced back at me, “and any Miss Kane has as a result of my misunderstanding this evening.”

Candy looked like she had been through the wringer. Her mental faculties were sharp, but she was cut and scraped and bruised. Instead of acknowledging his offer, she pressed, "What about Dave? He was shot as part of the same misunderstanding."

The fury I believed was under control nearly let loose at the idea that this scumbag had shot my brother. She said it happened Wednesday, but when I saw her Thursday night she hadn't told me – it must not have been a serious injury. Grey desperately wanted out of this situation, and I hadn't yet decided if he'd get out of it in a body bag or on his own two feet. His answer was the speed of a freight train. "Of course. Yeah. I'll take care of Mr. Brewer, too." He looked humbly at me, "I'll apologize in person. I'll make it right. I swear I will, Mark."

No one from my world could come near Davey. Glaring in his direction, I warned, "I don't want to hear of you or Teddy around Candy or my little brother again. Leave town. You've got two days. If I hear you're still here on Monday, we *will* have another chat."

Grey froze. "Monday? C'mon, Mark."

"Tick tock, Grey. Make sure Teddy gets my message, as well. I would hate to have to deliver it in person on Monday." Proud that I hadn't killed him on the street in front of at least six witnesses, I turned back toward Candy, "Now, how about that ride to your car?"

CHAPTER 11

My final warning to Grey had pleased Candy. It wasn't like me to stick up for the underdog, well, not unless it was a kid who had been thrown away. Hazard of the job, I suppose. I had seldom let my emotions get the better of me; that's why I was ideally suited for the work I did. She stood with her mouth open, an impressive impersonation of a largemouth bass. I used my index and middle finger to close her jaw. As if unable to process what had happened, she asked, "They're not going to be coming after me or Libby anymore, are they?"

The warmth that spread in me was foreign, and I couldn't help but smile at her, "Grey's about as sharp as a marble, but I left little room for misunderstanding. If you see either of them, even at a checkout stand at Target, make sure to glare at them and drop my name."

Her next question surprised me, "So, are you a mob boss or something?"

The mob had been sensationalized by television and movies. Certainly the old families still existed and carried a significant amount of clout, but Johnny wasn't a mob boss in the traditional sense. He was a businessman, a noteworthy one involved in both legal and illegal ventures for sure, but at his core he was a businessman. If I told her of my role in his world, she would likely not understand, and even if she did, an outsider couldn't be trusted with that type of information. My position with the less-than-lawful was a stark contrast to my other persona, too. Answering her in any way could only be dangerous for her and Davey. "Hmmm, I'm in the 'or something' category."

I walked around to the passenger side of my car with Candy in tow. She looked awful. The two previous times I had found her attractive, definitely not someone to go unnoticed. Tonight she had the look of an animal, one who had been pursued to the brink of capture and had only just survived. I held the passenger door for her, gently closed it behind her when she got in, and took my place in the driver's seat. When I started the car, I set the temperature to high and aimed the still warm vents her way.

I felt her eyes studying me. It wasn't unnerving or anything; I was used to others sizing me up. The only part that made it feel strange was that it was normally a man looking me over, attempting to find a weakness of some kind. Her voice was soft when she confessed, "I told Dave I saw you Thursday night – in Bank Shot's parking lot."

I couldn't keep the frustration out of my answer. "I told you to keep that between you and me."

"I'm sorry, especially after what you just did for me out there. But, you have to understand, Dave is really important to me. He's been looking for you forever. Please, can you just talk to him for a few minutes?"

I couldn't afford for Davey to get mixed up in any facet of my life right now. He had beaten the system. He had graduated high school, started his own business, paid taxes; from what I could see he had a girlfriend who was tough as nails. I couldn't take the chance of tarnishing his life – not yet. "I told you I had some loose ends to tie up. I'm unaccustomed to anyone ignoring my instructions."

"Ignoring your instructions? Hey, I don't know what you're mixed up in, and frankly, I don't care. Neither does Dave. I know Dave's been through hell, but he is the most amazing guy. When he told me how he was taken away from the foster family you stayed with, it tore him up. Fifteen years later, he's still torn up.

He doesn't care what's going on in your life: he just wants you in his."

Her words assaulted my defenses. Davey was my little brother. It was my job to protect him. I had failed him fifteen years ago and wanted more than anything to see him again, but meeting him now, while I was in the middle of a job, could only be detrimental for both of us. "Compelling. But, not now."

Candy's look turned to a glare when she answered, "He folds his shirts in six by six squares. His apartment doesn't have a single speck of dust anywhere. His cabinets are full of items that are perfectly organized. There isn't one dirty dish in his whole apartment."

I didn't understand what she was saying. She thought his organizational skills were why I couldn't see him? Her words continued coming out like rapid fire. "From the day he was taken away from you, he tried to do everything perfectly, so he would be sent back. He loves you. I can't tell him I saw you a third time and couldn't convince you to see him. The rejection would crush him."

Rejection? I wouldn't care if Davey were a vagrant who kicked puppies for fun. I wasn't rejecting Davey – I was trying to keep him isolated from my life until I could figure out a way to safely see him. "Candy, as much as I would like to see him again, now is not the right time."

She didn't relent, instead pointing a finger squarely at me. "Fifteen years ago would have been the right time. Hell, eleven years ago when he was almost adopted wouldn't have been bad, either. Or ten years ago when the adoption fell through. Or five years ago when I met him and he didn't have one single friend in the whole school. All of those times were the right time, but now, today, I'm telling you, you don't have a choice. You're going to say 'hi' to your brother if I have to put a knife to your throat and drag you there."

I didn't know whether to laugh or to be completely offended. Candy had just threatened me, in my car, after I had sent Grey and Teddy packing. She rendered me utterly speechless. Candy sat back in her seat, buckled her seatbelt, and pointed toward the corner. "His apartment is on West Eighth Street, so take a right at the end of this block."

I knew where Davey's garage was; I had driven by earlier today. It, too, was on West Eighth Street. I gripped the steering wheel, knowing I couldn't meet him tonight. I spoke without looking in her direction. "Look, I'm a man of my word. As soon as I finish a couple projects, I will find Davey. I'm glad he has a friend who cares about him as much as you do, but now is not the right time for a reunion."

"Five minutes. Give him five minutes. That's a hello, a cell phone number, and a hug." She reached over and squeezed my arm, "He needs those five minutes more than he needs air." Something about her words touched me – deeper than it should have. I would have given anything to talk to Davey for five minutes at any other point in my life – that five minutes could be very dangerous for him right now. When I didn't answer, she added, "I'm not kidding about holding a knife to your throat."

I could see what Davey saw in her. Minutes before she was running for her life – now she was threatening mine. A smile beamed from me. If ever there was a woman worthy of my little brother, I was sitting in a car with her this very second. Five minutes at his place were safer than her hanging out and observing my meeting with Larry. My heartbeat began picking up speed. I nodded, put the car in drive, and took a right at the end of the block as she had instructed.

We drove in the quiet for several minutes. Curiosity got the better of me. If she had a knife, why hadn't she tried to use it on Grey? "Where were you planning to find a knife?"

A shy grin spread on her face. "The way Grey high-tailed it away from you, I'm guessing there's one somewhere in your car."

A nine millimeter under my seat, a twelve gauge in my suitcase in the trunk, but no knife. "Sadly, no. I try not to keep weapons in my car. I admire your tenacity, but you need to be more careful about who you threaten and what you threaten them with. Grey isn't the worst man in the city, and you can't count on me to run interference for you."

"I would have been fine without your help." Laughing at her would have been disrespectful, so I did my best to keep my attention on the road. When I didn't react, she added, "I had outrun him twice. He wouldn't have attacked me in the pub."

"Your spunk is to be commended, but spunk is only worthwhile when backed up with brawn. Don't pick fights you can't win, and never threaten anything when you are unwilling or unable to follow through."

"I was willing to follow through, well, once I located a knife I wouldn't have had any problem threatening you with it. Dave wants you. I gooned things up with him the other night, and I need to make them right."

Her word choice brought another smile to my face. "How does one "goon up" something?"

"I got back from Bank Shot Thursday night, and I didn't tell him I'd seen you. Friday morning when I did, he was upset with me for lying."

I shook my head, "An omission isn't a lie."

Her eyes narrowed on me. "Any form of deception is a lie. You didn't see the hurt in his eyes. He had given me a glimpse of the emptiness in his heart when it comes to you. That's a void I can't fill – only you can."

Her words made my heart do a double-beat in my chest. Davey has a void because of me? Not possible. I had read article after article on the web about him and his restorations. What could I possibly offer him? I was by all respects just a criminal; it didn't matter why I was a criminal – I was. If he knew the real Mark, that void would be filled with disappointment.

It felt as if her eyes were trying to bore into my skull. There was something about Candy. I had never been open with anyone before. Lenny knew me better than most, but driving in the quiet warm car, the words were out before I could stop them. "I'm damaged. What happens when he meets me and he finds out I can't fill that void, either?"

"I don't pretend to know what you two went through, but you are the only one who can fill it. You just proved to me that you care. Geeze, you ran the guy who shot him out of town."

Grey and Teddy would leave. Of that I had no doubt. But who would they tell the reason I sent them packing? I cringed at my recklessness. I would have been better served to call Lenny and ask him to come out of retirement. "Let's keep that bit of information between us, shall we?"

"I thought that would be my opening line, 'Hey, Dave, Mark scared the snot out of my stalker. Can we keep him?'"

"Funny."

She gave directions throughout the drive. When we arrived, I was surprised to see we were at his garage. I thought she was directing me to his apartment.

It was, once again, dark. There were no lights on inside and no cars parked indicating anyone was there. It was late on a Saturday night, and I was a little confused as to why she believed he would still be at work.

She made several phone calls, with no luck. Each time she dialed, I believed it was less likely that I would see Davey this evening. A pressure on my chest began to ease – he wasn't here. His absence would buy me more time to come up with a safer way to meet him.

She hung up with whoever she had talked to and announced, "He might be inside."

I shook my head, "It doesn't look like he's here." Now I'd be able to take her to her car and get back to my preparations with Larry.

"I don't suppose you know how to pick a lock, do you?"

She was relentless. I shook my head, "Not my specialty."

She started to get out of the car, turned back toward me and said, "Don't leave." When I nodded, she bolted toward the front door. Candy began pounding on it: the echo of fists against metal reverberated up the block. She didn't know the meaning of the word *stealth*. When no response came, she grabbed a handful of snow and launched the snowball at one of the second floor windows. The snowball bounced off with a heavy thump. She threw a second one and then a third.

I began to wonder, if Davey were inside, why would he be ignoring her this way? Maybe the two were not as close as she had led me to believe. I eased out of the car to convince her to get back inside. She reached down, picked up a rock from under a bush and launched it at a second floor window. Was she insane? I rushed over to where she stood and grabbed her hand before she could throw a second rock at the window.

The desperation in her eyes was clear. I shook my head and told her, "He's not here. Stop before you break something."

"He's here. I know it. He's upstairs in the dark, all by himself. You didn't see him yesterday. He was angry with me. But that wasn't the worst of it: his heart froze when he learned that the one person he could love with his whole heart didn't want to see him."

My eyes narrowed, "I never said I didn't want to see him. I said the timing was bad."

"I told him, but that's not what he heard." He thought I didn't want to see him? He knew I was in town but wouldn't meet with him. Dammit. Johnny or not, I had to fix this.

I walked back over toward the door. Most people kept a key hidden near their front door for fear they would be locked out: nothing obvious like a potted plant or strategically placed rock. The door itself looked like a relatively new addition. It was the same color as the rest of the building, but didn't look as though it had fifteen coats of paint. Something else about the door caught my eye – whoever had installed it had put it on backwards. The hinges were on the outside of the door. I couldn't let Davey believe I didn't want to see him. "If he isn't inside, you're ready to face a breaking and entering charge?"

Without hesitating, she answered, "He's in there. I know it."

"This is ludicrous." I was sure there would be some tool in the trunk of the car I was driving. Getting us in the garage would be easy. I wasn't convinced he was inside, but I couldn't afford for her to continue trying to break her way in. I dug through the trunk and found a tire iron and a can of lubricant. She wore a confused look as I walked toward the door holding these two items.

"We're fortunate that a moron installed his front door backwards. The hinges are on the outside rather than where they're supposed to be on the inside. This won't be elegant, but it's better than a broken window." I saturated the hinges with the lubricant, then placed the tire iron under the lip of the hinge. Each of the three pins came out with little effort.

As I placed the third pin on the ground, I warned her, "If we go in and he's not there, I'm leaving you to explain to the alarm company why it was so imperative you get inside."

"Deal." She was all smiles. I planted my foot against the door, used my right hand to hold the hinge, and my left to grab the doorknob. When I shoved my foot against it and pulled with my finger tips, the door came free with little noise. I set the door aside, propping it against the wall to the left of where the now gaping hole was. I gestured for Candy to go inside. No alarm sounded. Did that mean we had triggered a silent one or one wasn't installed?

Candy had disappeared inside the darkness. Her voice was shrill as she said,

"It's me! Dave, it's me!" I heard something fall to the cement floor in the garage. As I stood in the reception area, my eyes adjusted to the darkness trying to locate a light switch. My nose was assaulted by the smell of lemons emanating from every surface. The only time I had encountered this odor was when one of Johnny's clean-up crews was sent in. Had someone been killed here?

"Candy? Where have you been?" The voice stopped me short. Older than the last time I had heard it and much like my own – it was Davey. He was right on the other side of the wall.

Candy nearly squealed. "He's here. I found him. Well, he found me, but he's just outside."

Before he could ask who "he" was, I shouted, "I'm not paying for a new door. This was her idea."

In a quiet, almost childlike voice, I heard my name. "Mark?"

Still standing in the dark of the lemony lobby groping for the light switch, I answered, "In the flesh. Why don't you have an alarm system? Did you forget to pay your utility bill or something?"

My fingers finally located the wall switch: bright white light illuminated the little lobby where I stood. I rounded the corner, stepped into the garage, directly in front of Davey. It was like looking into a mirror. He looked just like me: dark hair, dark eyes, but from the size of his chest, he spent a little more time in the gym than I did. Davey ran at me the way he had as a toddler and nearly knocked me off my feet as he grabbed hold of me. He was alive. He was right here. My brother was right here.

There were so many things I wanted to say. It was surreal and thrilling in the same moment. Davey was alive. He wasn't the obstinate five-year-old I remembered – he was a grown man: a living, breathing, walking, talking, bone-crushing adult. The only words that would form were, "Sorry about your door. She was pretty adamant that we were getting inside."

Davey laughed, brushing moisture from his cheeks with the back of his hand. "Her persistence is only rivaled by a pit bull's."

Remembering how she had threatened me with a non-existent knife to make me come see him, I merely smiled and answered, "You have no idea."

Davey motioned to a set of stairs behind a pop machine. "You want to come in?"

I did. I didn't care about the stupid trade with Larry, Johnny, or even my shitty life. Everything else could go to hell – I was with Davey. I didn't want ever to see Johnny again, nor did I want to help Chad bring him down. This was the life I was supposed to have – the one with a brother who had been stolen from me. My mind spun. I couldn't act rashly; if I did, it would be both our necks. Reluctantly, I answered, "Just for a minute. I'm in town on business, and as I tried to explain to Candy, I need to meet with a client tonight."

Before we could go upstairs, Candy motioned toward the lobby, "Um, should one of you put the door back on first?"

"Right. Probably need to keep the riffraff out." I saw a baseball bat lying on the floor. That had to have been the noise I heard when we first arrived. "So, do you always answer the door with a bat at night?"

Davey answered, "I was on the phone with a friend, asking him to come here so I could leave." He turned to Candy while answering me, "I thought Candy had been kidnapped, so I wanted to go back out looking for her. I figured it was neighborhood kids vandalizing the place, and I had planned to scare them off."

She had been kidnapped. She may have been tossing threats at Grey, but if she reported this, the feds would be here within the hour. I didn't have much time, and what I had, I didn't want to waste rehashing details that would only make me want to hunt Grey down. "I'll let her fill you in on her evening. I bumped into her on Windham Street and offered her a ride to her car."

Davey turned to Candy and asked, "Are you okay?"

Candy blushed. "I'm fine. Put the door back on already. It's freezing out." After everything she had gone through, I thought she might have shared some of what had happened to her – she didn't. She must have decided to tell him after I left. We had the door back on in no time. Davey and I climbed the steps to a small apartment. Although I liked Candy, I was pleased she didn't follow us up the stairs. The apartment on the second floor was tiny – I'd call it a studio, but I wasn't sure it was big enough to qualify as one.

Conflicting emotions were running rampant in me: elation that I was sitting just feet away from the brother I thought I had lost more than a decade ago, frustration that our meeting could prove dangerous for him, anger with myself that I had allowed Grey to know the truth about any facet of my life, guilt because I couldn't tell Davey what I was doing in town. His voice cut through all my conflicting emotions when he uttered, "I missed you."

"I've missed you, too. I can't believe you were here the whole time. I thought you were dead." Davey's eyes widened marginally, so I qualified it with, "The state of Missouri told me you died."

His eyes grew wider, "The state told you I was dead? When?"

"When you were like nine. They brought a grief counselor and told me there had been an accident. If I'd have known you were alive, I never would have stopped looking for you."

Goose bumps erupted on my arm – Davey had the same look our father did, at least the hazy image I had clung to of our father. I was really young when Dad left us, but Davey brought my memory flooding in. Davey's expression was puzzled for a second then understanding registered. I had nearly forgotten that look. "That must have been when I moved to Nebraska. A family was going to adopt me, but it fell through after I moved here. When I checked into a group home in Lincoln, a bunch of official paperwork from Missouri arrived saying they were relinquishing custody of me to Nebraska."

I spat, "Relinquishing custody is a far cry from dead."

"Yeah, I know. There were a ton of papers. I saw them in my file once, but it's not like they let me read them. I've looked for you on the internet, I even hired a private detective. There's no record of you after you were fifteen. Where have you been?"

There is no record of me – not anywhere, at least not enough of a record that anyone would be able to find the real *me*. Ever since moving to Kansas City, I have operated on a cash-only basis. I don't have a checking account, savings account, or a credit card. When I started working for Lenny, he insisted I have a driver's license, which seemed absurd since my job description was "car thief." Since Lenny insisted, and he was my sole source of income, it wasn't an optional request.

Another from Lenny's crew gave me some great advice – he told me I needed to stay off the grid. I didn't want anyone from my past to be able to find me. I had a crazy idea that night and decided to scour obituaries across the country for a Mark Brewer. It only took about ten mouse clicks to find a Marcus Brewer from Pittsburg who had died in a car accident several years earlier. My given name on my birth certificate was Mark not Marcus, but it was close enough. I requested a duplicate copy of Marcus's birth certificate and social security card. One of Lenny's guys who worked at the department of motor vehicles hooked me up with the license, so at age fifteen I had a state issued driver's license that said I was thirty-seven.

Once I had legitimate identification, I was able to stop sofa-surfing and get an apartment of my own. I signed the lease on my apartment as Marcus, and all the utilities were included in the rent. I use Marcus's credentials for identification only, I have never even filled out a credit application, and it's not like I claim any of the income I make, so no red flags have gone off with the IRS or Social Security Administration. My license says I'm forty-three now, a far cry from twenty-two, but no one has ever paid much attention to it. Using this identity, if I ever were to be arrested, my real identity would remain squeaky clean.

My fake identity had worked – too well. My own brother hadn't been able to locate me. I didn't want to tell him why he hadn't been able to find me – at least not right now. Instead, I asked, "So, you were never adopted?"

"No. Almost. You?"

"Not a chance. The day the social worker took you, I tried to follow. Margaret and Dewey only kept me for a few weeks after you left."

"What do you mean they only kept you for a few weeks? Where did you go?"

Earnestly, I answered, "I became a difficult placement. Most of my time was in group homes. Every now and again I would get placed with a family, but none of those ever worked out. I struck out on my own just before I turned sixteen."

Doubt registered in Davey's eyes. "Fifteen? You ran away? Why?"

His question caught me off guard. I had told few people anything of substance about my life, but this was an aspect I didn't want to hide from Davey. "Yeah. I saw Mom on the street one afternoon. She was in a minivan at a red light. When I realized it was her, I started waving like crazy. She took one look at me, then drove through the red light to get away from me." I lowered my voice so it wouldn't crack. "Mom didn't want us. Dad left before you could walk. I thought you were dead – I decided I was done playing by the rules. I took off."

"Mark, I'm sorry."

"You're sorry? You didn't do anything wrong."

Davey's voice was solemn, apologetic when he said, "I swear, as soon as I left Margaret and Dewey, I did everything I could to get back." His eyes watered as he confessed, "The foster family I was placed with didn't know what to think. I made my bed every morning, never left a toy out, did my school work as soon as I got home each day. I begged them to take me to see you. They called my case worker lots of times trying to set it up, but she never would."

It felt like he had just sucker-punched me. Davey became the poster child for good behavior, while my foster parents thought I was possessed by Lucifer himself. No words would come. I couldn't even remember half the stuff I pulled trying to get moved away from Margaret and Dewy. "Margaret was a bitch."

He shook his head, and flashed another one of Dad's expressions. There were holes in my childhood memories, but I remembered that same expression when Dad didn't like something Mom said. "I know. I just want you to know that I know I screwed up when I was little."

"You were five, Davey."

His eyes darted to the floor as he pursed his lips together. That was one of Mom's expressions. Did I do that, too? His voice was barely above a whisper. "I'm just really glad you're here. There's so much I want to tell you."

"So spill it. Tell me about you."

Davey looked around the little apartment. "This place is mine, well, I lease it. If the bay doors downstairs didn't give it away – I restore cars. I've had customers from as far away as Montana bring their cars to me. I graduated high school two years ago. I keep thinking I need to go to college for a business degree, but I haven't slowed down long enough to go. One of my high school teachers took me in my senior year; he's my partner here at the garage."

My chest swelled with pride. Despite everything he had gone through, he was okay – better than okay. Davey had created a life for himself – he had a real future. "And Candy? How long have you two been seeing each other?"

Davey's cheeks flushed. "That's pretty recent. I think I've been in love with her since our freshman year of high school, but we've just started seeing each other."

"Really? I ran into her Thursday night in a parking lot, and it didn't seem like you two had just started dating. She knew about everything – you know, Margaret and Dewey. She wanted me to come with her then."

Hurt registered on his face. "Yeah, she told me. She said you didn't want to see me."

Open mouth, insert foot. "That's not what I told her. I said I wanted to see you, but I needed to tie up some loose ends before we met."

His eyes narrowed on me. "What kind of loose ends?"

"I haven't taken care of those things yet. Until I do, I can't spend too much time with you." He was curious: I could see the questions in his eyes, but I couldn't afford to open that can of worms. Before he could ask, I blurted out, "Look, I'm glad things turned out so well for you. More than glad – I'm thrilled. My life is a little different, and I need to keep you isolated from what I do."

"What do you do?"

"It's complicated. Just give me some time, and I promise I'll tell you everything."

"Mark, I don't care if you deliver port-a-johns. I just want to get to know you. I don't want to lose you again."

Me too. Holy shit, me too. "I've got a few things to take care of. Give me a couple weeks. I'll tell you everything once I get a few things worked out on my end."

His voice sounded distant when he asked me, "So, that's it? You're going to take off, and I won't see you until you can fit me into your life?"

"I sound like a douche when you say it like that. Let's just say that I'm in town doing a favor for a friend. It's not the kind of favor I can brag about. Once I do what I promised I would, I'll go back to Kansas City and get a few things taken care of. I'll be back up this way as soon as I can. Deal?"

Davey nodded and the next thirty minutes flew by. He knew more about cars than I did. Lenny would pay someone like Davey big bucks to help him alter stolen cars. Lenny had been like a father to me, but introducing the two of them wouldn't be my best moment. If I learned anything from Davey, it was that despite everything, he had a heart of gold. Everyone's needs seemed to come before his own. He wasn't jaded. He wasn't cynical. *He* wasn't a criminal.

Davey saw me looking at my watch. "I know you've got to go, but are you hungry? I've got a roast and potatoes I can warm up."

Something about his question tickled me. "Very domestic. I'm impressed. No, don't go to any trouble." He opened a kitchen cabinet, and I saw a bag of chips peeking out from behind some soup cans. My mouth watered as a fit of nostalgia washed over me. I plucked the bag out of the cabinet. "I haven't had Wavy Lays in years. Remember how we used to make little ice cream forts in our bowls and used the chips for fences?"

Davey nodded at me, wearing a huge smile. "I'd have to run to the store to get ice cream; you might be stuck with just the chips."

"No ice cream? You have a roast and potatoes, but you don't keep ice cream in the freezer? You aren't as domestic as I believed."

Davey's answer was strained. "I don't eat ice cream."

That was a strange statement. "You don't eat ice cream? You loved ice cream. I used to bribe you with it to get you to make your bed."

"Yeah, I remember." Davey paused for a few seconds before he added, "I haven't eaten ice cream since. . . well, you know."

"Since when?"

"Since our case worker asked me if I wanted to get ice cream, and I followed her out to her car."

I had remembered every detail of that day. I remembered pleading with Dewey and Margaret to keep him. I remembered the case worker's heel on her shoe wobbled. I could still see the bright blue sky with fluffy white clouds that Davey and I had been picking shapes out of. I remembered the day from my perspective, but I had never considered it from his.

He had been taken away, not kicking and screaming: he had climbed into her car to go for ice cream. Our caseworker had turned one of the few joys of his childhood into an awful memory. The next time I see Davey, I'm bringing him a gallon of chocolate chip, and I'm going to watch him eat the entire thing in front of me. I walked over to where he stood and hugged him hard, "It's not your fault. You were just a kid. You've got to let it go."

Although Davey was just as big as I was, and had me by at least twenty pounds of bulk, when he confessed, "I didn't think I'd ever see you again," I felt like we were seven and five all over again.

"I'm sorry it took me so long, little brother. I've got somewhere I need to be, but I promise I'll be back soon."

CHAPTER 12

I arrived at the pub five minutes before I was to meet Larry. I hadn't taken any of my usual precautions: I didn't know where the exits were, I hadn't looked for people who knew me, I hadn't scanned the area for cops. I hated going in blind and wouldn't have adequate time to do any preparations. Every time I began to chastise myself, I heard Davey's voice echo in my mind, "I didn't think I'd ever see you again." Warmth radiated from me, inside out.

A voice called from behind me, "Heidi-ho!"

I would recognize that obnoxiously cheerful voice anywhere – Larry had arrived. I said nothing, but turned in his direction and waited for him to catch up to me on the sidewalk. "Nice to see you. You ready?"

"Nothing like cutting to the chase. Great googily moogily, it's cold. You want to go inside, so we can get started?"

I glanced briefly at the pub brimming with people. I didn't want to go in blind and take the chance I'd put everything I had worked for in jeopardy. Instead I motioned to the Mercedes I had driven the last few days, "Let's do it out here."

"Out here?" My suggestion caused Larry to flounder for a second. "Why outside?"

"Fewer prying eyes. C'mon, we can sit in the trade." Larry reluctantly followed. I understood his concern: he was three days late. He was making good on the trade for Johnny, but Johnny had a reputation. Larry had only ever known me to drop cars, but he knew I worked for Johnny, and when things didn't go smoothly – Johnny wasn't a patient man. Larry's value was tied to his ability to make good in a well-oiled machine. Anyone who put a kink in the process was subject to repercussions.

Since I'd had to make an extra trip to Kansas City to deal with Johnny and Felix's concerns, ultimately putting my integrity into question, I wasn't going to do anything to put Larry's mind at ease. He could worry that I intended to shank him for all I cared.

When we got to the car, Larry's hands were shaking – I doubted it was from the cold. He took the passenger seat. Larry fumbled with the papers in a leather portfolio, and when he wrote in the trade value for the Mercedes, he wrote in seventy-two thousand dollars. My eyes narrowed – what was he doing?

Larry never gave full retail value, not for any car. The money he made on the car traded in was how he got paid for the drugs. In addition to the inflated trade value, he discounted the F-150 I was to drive away with to forty-eight thousand dollars. "Tell Johnny, this one is on me." Larry wrote a check for the balance of the value on the Mercedes, then asked, "We're good?"

The way our arrangement worked was: I brought in a high-dollar used car. Larry or whomever I was trading with lowballed my vehicle's trade-in value. Typically, we targeted for the salesperson to pocket thirty thousand dollars cash. The times when a dealership received a larger shipment of drugs, I traded a more expensive car. Each salesman earned his payment for holding the drugs, packaging them into a legitimate business deal, and handing them over. Once I delivered the new vehicles, which were full of drugs, to Johnny's dealership, Johnny moved them from his dealership to lower level dealers throughout the Midwest. Everyone got a cut. Larry and others like him at the initial dealership took the biggest risk, so they got the biggest cut. I studied Larry – he was doing this shipment free of charge.

Johnny wanted to keep the boys in the dealerships happy. Having him do this trade for free was not part of the plan. Johnny wouldn't like it. "Look, that's a nice gesture, but no one wants you to work for free. Change the value of the trade so you get your cut."

Larry's hand still shook, his voice matched. "It's been a bad week. Tell Johnny the circumstances were beyond my control. Tell him he can still count on me." Larry handed me the check with the paperwork for the trade. "It's a done deal."

After everything this schmuck had put me through, I decided he owed me. If anything, by him not taking his cut, the money I earned might be higher than normal. Larry's willingness to give up his paycheck strengthened what I had already told Johnny last night. I filled in my signatures on the sheet, took the check and stuffed everything into an envelope. I liked that Larry was sweating Johnny's reaction to the delay. I doubted we would ever have a repeat of this week. "Where's it parked?"

"Around the corner on the left side." He handed me the keys. Larry's face was still pale. He must have been counting on the fact that I was going to give him a hard time for the delay – I didn't.

I had already decided to give him a reprieve on the trade we had scheduled for next week. There was a dealer in Fargo I could count on if I needed to move dates. I asked, "So, what's the plan for next week? You want me to reschedule until you can get your personal life in order?"

"No. Everything is fine. My girlfriend is doing much better." Larry, still nervous, did his best to smile.

"So, Wednesday?"

"Yeah. I'll see you Wednesday morning at ten."

I reached for the door handle because our transaction was done. His words stopped me short, "Hey, Mark, I'm sorry."

Niceties weren't part of our routine. There was no "please" or "thank you" – it was just business. I was still on a high from having seen Davey for the first time since I was a kid, but I wasn't about to let Larry think I was okay with his delays. Girlfriend or not, he had responsibilities. "Don't let it happen again. Johnny gave you a bye this time – he's treating it like an anomaly. Don't let his generosity go to your head."

"I won't." Larry reached over and grabbed the top of my arm, as if trying to convey the gravity of the situation. "Some guy broke into my girlfriend's house and beat her within an inch of her life. I swear, I wouldn't have blown you off for any other reason."

A new worry started to take hold. Grey had attacked Larry's girlfriend. Larry's girlfriend was Candy's roommate. Candy was Davey's girlfriend. That had to mean that Larry knew my brother. Davey and I had the same last name and we looked like twins, why had Larry never said anything before? He wasn't stupid; he should have put two and two together. Had he already done that? If he hadn't yet said anything to Johnny, could I count on him to keep quiet? Davey said he and Candy had only been seeing each other for a short time: was it possible Larry had never met Davey?

My two worlds were getting ready to collide in a big way. Grey knew of my brother – it was just a matter of time before Teddy knew, too. Larry was close to my brother's circle of friends – it, too, would only be a matter of time. Either Chad had to pull the trigger quickly and bring Johnny down, or I had to resolve to stay a part of Johnny's organization for the long term.

If Chad pulled the trigger after Johnny learned of Davey. . .I shivered at the thought. Davey was too engrained in this community to ask him to give up everything and start over somewhere fresh. Even if he were willing to do that, he was sort of a celebrity when it came to custom restores – hiding Davey would not be an option.

My face flushed. Inside the plush cabin of the Mercedes, I felt my life crashing in on me. I needed to make contact with Chad, and I needed to make contact tonight. I had weeks if I were lucky, more likely I just had days before all of my choices would suddenly be taken away from me. My internal thoughts created an abnormally long pause in our conversation. I knew Larry was watching me for a reaction as I continued staring through the windshield. "I'm sorry to hear about your girlfriend. I'm glad she's on the mend. I'll see you on Wednesday."

I pulled the door handle and was out of the car before Larry could say anything else. "My suitcase is in the back." Larry went to the trunk to retrieve my suitcase; I removed the handgun from under the driver's seat and shoved it into the waistband of my jeans. Larry wheeled my suitcase onto the curb and offered to bring the F-150 to me – I waved him off. Sticking the envelope in the outside pocket of my bag, the F-150 keys in hand, I made my way down the street to where it was waiting for me.

I remembered where I had seen a Wal-Mart just on the outskirts of town. I ran into the electronics department, purchased a pre-paid cell phone and went back to the truck. Images of Davey at five years old and the twenty-year-old man I had just met continued to assail my thoughts. I typed in Chad's number; my call went to Chad's voicemail. I rarely, if ever, left a message, but this number couldn't be traced to me. The words were out of me in a rush, "Call me back on this number. It's important. Things have changed. You need to make this bust in the next couple days, or we need to call it off."

I dug through the packaging I had thrown onto the passenger seat, found the power cord, and plugged the phone's charger into the dashboard. I placed the cell phone in the cup holder and began driving toward Kansas City. Every few minutes I would pick it up and check to see if the ringer was on, if there were any missed calls, if cellular service was active.

An hour into my drive to Kansas City, the new disposable cell phone rang. I saw Chad's number on the display. I was almost halfway to Kansas City. I put my blinker on for the next exit and accepted Chad's call. Without wasting time on niceties, I asked, "You got my message?"

"I wouldn't be calling this number if I hadn't. Now isn't a good time for the bust."

I barked into the phone. "You better figure out how to make it a good time or I'm out."

"Hold on. We started this together. You're the best-placed person we've ever had. What's got you all worked up?" Chad sounded sincere, as if he really cared about the shit-storm off in the distance.

I gritted my teeth, "Things have changed."

"What things?"

"Look, I'm not getting into it. Either you move forward with the bust now, or you write it off. If you want my help, it's got to go down now."

Chad's voice lowered. "I can't snap my fingers and make an indictment appear. These things can take months."

"I don't have months. You've got more than enough information on the operation. You don't need me anymore. I'm out."

"Slow down, Mark. What's got you so spooked? I thought you were too high in the organization to touch?"

No one is ever too high in the food chain to touch. I may have had a safety net before, but that was gone, or at least it would be gone when Johnny learned I had family he could leverage if I got out of line. "I'm leaving the organization."

Chad's surprise at my statement registered in his voice. "If you do that, every piece of crap you've intimidated the last few years is going to be gunning for you. Tell me what's got you all worked up."

I trusted few people. Chad may have been someone from my past, but he was a cop first and a friend second. Our relationship was out of convenience, and I had little doubt that if things came down to it, he'd hang me out like wet laundry. "I'm done. We hatched our little plan four years ago. You've got everything you need without me. You know how the product is moved and who the players are – you don't need me anymore."

"So, that's it? You're going to blend into the woodwork somewhere? Just quit Johnny?"

"Something like that."

Chad's voice was calm. "The evidence I have implicates you. If you won't testify, you'll go down, too."

I had made a mess of everything. I had given Chad more than enough information on the organization to make charges from drugs to racketeering and anything in between stick. If he wanted to make good on what he set out to do, he didn't need me. "Do what you need to do. I'm out as of today." I hung up the phone. I pulled back onto the interstate, got up to speed and looked in my rearview: there was no one behind me for as far as I could see on the interstate. I rolled the window down and threw the phone onto the pavement, watching it shatter into a hundred pieces.

I pulled into Kansas City just after midnight. Instead of going to my apartment, I detoured to Johnny's used car lot. I used my regular phone and texted Johnny and Felix. "The truck is on the lot. No problems." Tomorrow morning I would see Johnny and tell him I wanted out. I could get ahold of Lenny and ask him to tell Johnny he needed me back on his crew. Lenny would do it. He knew about Davey and would help me distance myself from Johnny.

CHAPTER 13

It was after midnight when I got to my apartment. Again, full of nervous energy – I couldn't talk to Johnny like this. Neither Felix nor Johnny answered my text, so I went to bed. Sleep refused to find me. I wanted to talk to Davey. I needed to put my life in order, and Davey was now part of that life. I sent him a text. "Made it home safe. Glad I saw you tonight. Can't wait to see you again."

Surprisingly, a response came back within seconds. "Ditto."

Those five letters stirred something inside me. I had been closed off, alone for as long as I could remember. I wasn't alone, and as long as I could get out from under Johnny, I'd never be alone again. Davey was alive. I set my phone on my nightstand as the jittery feeling eased. I drifted off to sleep ignoring the nagging feeling about bailing on Chad and the conversation I needed to have with Johnny tomorrow; instead, my mind kept replaying my reunion with Davey.

The next morning I began to take inventory of my apartment. Other than the furniture, I could pack up all my belongings in just a few suitcases. I didn't think

I'd need to go on the run, but if I did, traveling light wouldn't be a problem.

Johnny was up by six every morning; I knew his morning routine from my time working as head of security. I didn't call him ahead of time. It was almost seven when I pulled up to the gate just as I had hundreds of times before. I had rehearsed this conversation with Johnny all night long. I'd tell Johnny to his face that I was through. I wouldn't tell him about Davey; I would tell him I wanted to go back to boosting cars.

I let myself into the house with the key still on my key ring. Johnny was in his office, already showered, in his usual gray suit, reading the news on his iPad. He set the device down on his lap and looked at me. "I wasn't expecting you."

I wiped my palms on my pants. "You got my text that the truck is on the lot?"

He nodded, waiting for me to explain why I was interrupting his morning routine. My back straightened, my eyes fixed on his. "Last week, I was cooling my heels in Nebraska, you know, waiting for Larry to make the trade."

"I remember. I wanted to talk to you about that. Larry has been someone I have worked with for many years. I get that you were frustrated that he delayed your return trip, but leaning on him was not part of the deal." Leaning on him? What was Johnny talking about? I must have looked confused because Johnny clarified, "I appreciate your service. I know you had my best interests at heart, but I don't want any of my dealership contacts working for free."

How had he seen the paperwork already? He couldn't have already gone into the dealership. Would he have sent Felix in to check on it last night after my text? Cautiously, I answered, "Larry did that on his own. He wanted it to be clear that circumstances were beyond his control. He wanted to make it right with you. That didn't have anything to do with me."

"You didn't encourage him?"

"No. That was all Larry. I spent a few more days in Lincoln than I normally would have. Other than Felix getting out of sorts, it wasn't a big deal."

His brows relaxed as he eased back into his chair. "An exciting trip for you. Running into Teddy was a happy accident."

A happy accident? More like a colossal inconvenience. Johnny didn't know that I had muscled Grey and Teddy out of Lincoln. Or did he? If either had decided to return to Kansas City, Johnny would have heard by now. Johnny couldn't have heard about Davey; if he had, he would have told me he wanted to see me this morning. "Yeah, a happy accident. There was this girl who got a little froggy with Teddy."

"Froggy?"

"She hustled him. He didn't take it well."

"Teddy's always been a hot head. Anything I need to send a clean-up crew in to take care of?"

That was exactly the answer I was hoping for. Because Teddy had left Johnny's crew, he was a loose end. Johnny didn't throw ideas out on a whim; this was something he had considered before I had told him about the girl. "No. I took care of it."

His brows rose. That was not what he wanted to hear. I had never worked on a clean-up crew. He had people on his payroll whose sole purpose was to clear out any evidence left behind and to remove the loose ends from the intricate tapestry of his organization. "What did you take care of?"

"Teddy and Grey had planned to set up operations in Lincoln. The girl who hustled Teddy ended up in the hospital. I found out about it and decided it was too close to your other operations. I gave the two of them until Monday to set up somewhere else."

Johnny's eyes narrowed. "They know about the drops in Lincoln?"

"No, at least they gave no indication that they did. Grey put the girl who hustled him in the hospital. He kidnapped her roommate. The roommate got away, but the police were looking for both Teddy and Grey. I decided it was too close to one of our main dealerships, and I didn't need some cop catching them and doing any kind of background check."

"Why didn't you tell me any of this Thursday night?"

"I knew Teddy and Grey were up to something on Thursday, but I didn't learn what it was until last night. When I found out, I sent them both packing." This was very close to the truth. Enough that if I were hooked up to a polygraph, I would be able to pass it.

Johnny stood up, his iPad dropping to the floor as anger seeped in his voice. "Your first call should have been to me!"

Shit. I wiped my palms on my jeans again. "It was late. I took care of it. I'm here telling you now."

Johnny stormed out of the room. Fear washed over me as I felt the fine hairs on my arms jump to attention. His voice boomed down the hall. "You, call Oscar. Tell him I want him here now!" I wasn't sure who *you* was, but I had no doubt from Johnny's tone that someone was frantically dialing the phone.

I hadn't seen Oscar lately. He had been doing chemo three days per week and looked frail the last time we were all in a meeting together. The fact that Johnny was summoning him to the estate could only be bad. I didn't move. My posture was rigid; both hands gripped my knees as beads of sweat formed on my forehead. I sat there watching the clock on the opposite side of the room – Johnny didn't return. The black Roman numerals against an ivory background stood out in stark contrast as I watched the second hand circle them thirty times. Images of Davey intruded on the second hand.

If Oscar sent in a crew, Davey would be one of the loose ends they'd find. My world was crashing in around me, and I hadn't even gotten around to telling Johnny I wanted out. Oscar entered the room: he wore dark slacks and a brilliant white shirt. Oscar had more color in his face than the last time I had seen him. He hadn't lost his snowy white hair from the treatment. Oscar's olive complexion peeked out through the wrinkles and age spots on his face. He held his hand out to me. "Good to see you, Mark. So, tell me what happened in Lincoln the last couple days."

I did as instructed, sharing a "sanitized" version of the events. I purposely left Candy and Libby's names out, referring to them as girls in a bar, but not glossing over the events which Grey and Teddy were responsible for. My final meeting with Grey had been on Windham Street. Rather than telling him too much detail, I synopsized by saying I had intervened when I recognized the girl; the girl told me she had been kidnapped – that's when I knew Teddy and Grey had gone too far.

Oscar studied me for a minute. "What makes you think Teddy and Grey can be tied to Johnny's business ventures?"

"Teddy may be a moron, but I don't trust him. The police were looking for him. If he were arrested, I didn't think it was too much of a stretch to think he might try to deal his way out of it."

Oscar seemed satisfied with my answer. Johnny stomped into the room. He had been furious when he walked out, so I waited for whatever wrath might be shot my way. After Johnny's entrance, I sort of expected to be told to tell the story again. Without asking for a repeat, Johnny turned to Oscar, "What do you recommend?"

"Teddy left. He doesn't have any information which would implicate you. All of his instructions came from me. Grey is still on the payroll. Mark telling them both to leave Lincoln where we could have kept eyes on them is troublesome."

Troublesome? I didn't like where this was going. Oscar's lips narrowed. "Teddy's little brother is in Lincoln. We could apply a little pressure to determine where they have gone."

It wasn't said as a question, more of a suggestion. My stomach felt as if Oscar had just kicked me. Is this the type of discussion the two would have if I screwed something up? An image of Davey flashed brightly in my head. Johnny shook his head. "Let's leave that as a last resort. What about that mess with Frank? Spencer said the Red Skins game didn't make the spread two weeks ago. Frank borrowed money to cover the bets and is behind on payments."

Oscar looked confused. "You want me to call Teddy and ask him to lean on Frank?"

Johnny's face was expressionless. "If he's got nowhere to go, he may come back to do this – a show of good faith. We could invite him to the bistro." Johnny's gaze was angry as his eyes caught mine, "Let him know Mark was not following my instructions when he told the two to leave Lincoln."

All the air in my lungs disappeared. Johnny wanted to talk to Teddy. Grey knew about my little brother. If Grey knew, he would have told Teddy by now. My mind raced; I couldn't let this meeting happen. Willing my lungs to take in air, "Johnny, I've been looking out for your interests for as long as I've been on your payroll. Teddy striking out on his own was bad enough, but if he were to stumble onto our operation in Lincoln, you think he'd have any loyalty to you? I did what I did to protect you."

Johnny's expression stayed angry. "This isn't like you. First you tell Teddy and Grey to leave town. Lincoln is less than three hours from here. We could have kept an eye on both of them. Do you know where they'll go? Because

I don't. Then you lean on Larry who has been instrumental in our Mexican operations for over seven years. If my source finds out that I didn't pay one of the key members of my team, how does that make me look?"

Arguing with Johnny was never an option. His knuckles were balled at his sides and bleaching before my eyes. I awaited the blow that was coming, instead his voice lowered. "I had to shut down Sioux Falls. If Larry gets nervous, I can't replace two dealerships that quickly."

Oscar eased forward. "Johnny, easy. We won't need the dealerships much longer anyway. Everything will be flowing directly from Chihuahua to Overland Park. We were going to shut the dealerships down right after your license is approved." Oscar's words were cryptic. "You put Mark in charge of the Cartel operations. When are you planning to let him in on the long term?"

Something in Johnny's demeanor changed. The rage bubbling below the surface seemed to shut off with a switch. "You're right, Oscar." Johnny motioned to the chairs in front of his desk, "Take a seat. You've never given me a reason to doubt you – although I don't like that you did this without involving Oscar or myself, your logic was sound."

The fear I had been feeling didn't subside. How could Johnny turn his anger on and off like that? It looked like he was ready to slit my throat; in his next breath he was calm and told me to take a seat. I had seen him bottle his anger up and hold it in before, but I had never seen it just evaporate. Johnny was all about protocol; I was sure he wasn't mad about what I'd done, just the fact that I had done it without first clearing it with him or Oscar. Jorge once requested a clean-up team directly from Oscar and cut Johnny out of the loop – Johnny tore into him like a kid on Christmas morning.

Johnny smiled, a broad rich toothy smile – the look unnerved me further. He had my full attention. "The engines are manufactured in Chihuahua, Mexico. From there they go to assembly plants in the United States. In the assembly plants, there is a line that does quality control and product acceptance. We have a person on that team who verifies serial numbers and fails engines. Failed engines go to another line where they are reworked. Those reworked engines carry packages bound for me. They are packed into certain vehicles, but the rework team has no control over which dealership vehicles are sent to. This is about to change."

Making the connection Oscar had eluded to, I asked, "Those failed engines are all going to the Overland Park, Missouri plant, right?"

"You're quick. Before, from the assembly plant we had to keep track of which dealerships received vehicles. We applied for a franchise and were denied two years ago. I reapplied last year and was denied a second time. So rather than submit a third franchise application this year, I contacted the owner of a franchise here in Kansas City and made him an offer." Johnny slapped me on the back. "Corozzo's Cars has a nice ring to it, don't you think?"

"So you'll be able to bring all the vehicles direct from the assembly plant?"

"Every last one."

"What about the people who work at the dealerships you've been working with?"

Oscar cut in. "We haven't told them yet, but since we are setting up a new dealership, we plan to offer each of them attractive relocation packages to move here and work at our dealership."

Johnny continued, "Now that all the engines will be coming into Overland Park, it will be easier for us to purchase the vehicles directly. Less risk for everyone involved. We will be the highest grossing dealership in the Midwest."

Hiding in plain sight. Johnny was an expert at this. He had his hands in everything illegal, but hid behind legitimate businesses. This new dealership would be another legitimate business. Bringing in everyone who had worked for the dealerships to a single location would make things easier for Chad. It also kept all of the activities away from Lincoln. I tried to hide the excitement welling up inside of me. "So, how soon will you be up and operational?"

"We already ordered the sign. We want you to schedule trades from each of our participating dealerships over the next thirty days. You'll pick up all of the product we have left. I've placed an order for eleven Bentleys."

Bentleys? Finding one of those for under two hundred grand was nearly impossible. Johnny was sweetening the last deal for each of the salesmen. In my head I began cycling through the dealerships. Lincoln, Des Moines, Cedar Rapids, Chicago, Green Bay, Madison, Minneapolis, Topeka, Springfield, Fargo – that was only ten. "Eleven, didn't you mean ten?"

Johnny's expression grimaced. "Right. We weren't planning on Haden being compromised. We hadn't intended to shut down Sioux Falls the way we did. I'm going to keep the eleventh for myself."

The plan seemed elaborately simple. It was my job to relay the news to each dealership. If any chose not to move to Missouri, Johnny was going to let them leave the organization without strings. No repercussions.

Having everything here in Kansas City would simplify Chad's bust – he no longer had to bring in the federal authorities to cross state lines. There was a real chance that I could finish what I had started with Chad without Davey ever being discovered. After my call with Chad last night, he would be scrambling to make his case to his leadership; I needed to get word to him that there was no need to look outside the city. Now all I had to worry about was Teddy telling Johnny the real reason why I had run him and Grey out of Lincoln.

After hashing out the schedule with Oscar and Johnny, I left to enjoy a sunny Sunday. I stopped for a bagel and coffee. Sitting outside at a little metal table and chair, I made a call to Chad; his voicemail told me to leave a message. "It's me. There's been a change. Hold off on your indictment. I'll call you in a month with an update."

CHAPTER 14

Lincoln was the first dealership scheduled to close down. It was the closest and would be easiest to get off of the rolls. I drove into town Tuesday afternoon, and my first thought was to see Davey. I had been distracted since Saturday night: wondering about his foster placements, how he had gotten into restoring cars, what sports he had played in school, and hundreds of other random thoughts. My mind kept returning to a single thought – Davey was alive.

When I called, he said he was at the hospital with Candy. He invited me to meet him there. It was an odd suggestion, but I was still so excited to see him again, I would have met him in the sewer system with a rock and a stick if he had asked.

As I approached room 230, I wasn't sure what to expect. I could hear laughter in the hallway as I approached and didn't want to intrude – but one of those laughs was from Davey. I eased stealthily through the metal doorway, eased the blue turquoise curtain aside, and looked apprehensively at the little group.

I had met Libby last Tuesday night at Bank Shot; she was the first to notice me enter the room. She chided, "Candy, if I've told you once, I've told you a thousand times – stop inviting tall, dark and dangerous men to visit until after I have had a shower."

Her words stopped me in mid-stride. Davey's back had been toward me; he turned in my direction, "You came!" I was immediately pulled into a bone-crushing hug, which nearly knocked me off of my feet and toppled us both. Davey let me go, stepped back, and Candy launched herself at me. She wrapped her arms around my neck like we were high school sweethearts who had just reunited. My body went rigid – her affection felt strange.

Candy let me go and beamed. "Mark, this is my roommate, Libby." Libby sat up a little straighter. She was nearly unrecognizable from the girl I had met a week ago. Her skin was pale, her cheeks sunk in, blonde hair was matted and flat hanging around her face. A patch of hair just over her left temple had been shaved and was covered by a white bandage. She sported a black eye, which was in the process of fading to a hideous purple, and I could see a matching bruise peeking out from beneath the neck of her hospital gown.

"Yeah, I remember. We met Tuesday night at Bank Shot."

Libby blushed – I wasn't sure why. She offered a cheeky grin, as her head turned between Davey and me. "You two are like twins." When her eyes finally rested on me, she said, "Candy tells me you came to her rescue Saturday."

I tried to avert my eyes from Libby's stare. Candy hadn't been embellishing when she said Grey had nearly killed her roommate. A small part of me understood why Larry had been drawn to her side, unable to leave the hospital all week. If she looked this bad now, I couldn't imagine what she had looked like Tuesday night. I downplayed the rescue comment. "Naw, I just offered Candy a ride to her car."

One of Libby's eyebrows arched high on her head. It was an almost comical look, and I couldn't stop the snicker at her expression. Her tone was light as she raised her hands as if displaying her body on a game show, "You didn't chase the guy who did this to me out of town?"

My checks warmed. "I may have encouraged him to find a new place to hang his hat."

Her eyes held me in place. The humor evaporated in the room. Libby's four-word answer was spoken quietly, "Thanks. I owe you."

Those words from anyone in my world meant something more, not the plastic coated, disingenuous appreciation for dinner or helping with a flat tire. "*I owe you*" meant someone would step in front of a bullet or grab a knife in mid-air with their chest. In my life, I had only ever spoken those words to Lenny. Gathering myself together, I needed to remember that Candy, Libby and Davey didn't come from my world. Theirs was a world full of ice cream parlors and Frisbee games in the park. They lived in the make-believe world I saw in movies. Her words may have created a stir inside me, but that was on reflex, because I was sure she didn't mean them the way I understood the meaning.

"No big deal." I tried to brush off the words as no more than a typical "thanks." "Really, I just told Teddy that Bank Shot was going to upload a video of you spanking him on the pool table to YouTube. He didn't think his image would ever recover, so he started packing."

Libby laughed at this. Not a demure giggle or a chuckle, but a laugh. It echoed through the room. I didn't live under a rock – I had heard people laugh before, but something about Libby's laugh and her previous statement caught me off-guard, stirring a foreign feeling in me.

She pushed her head back hard against the pillow. "That's right. You were watching the game. If I'd known it was going to be such an assault to his ego, I would have made a fancier shot instead of the quick kill."

Even though her appearance was close to revolting, there was something about her – her energy was magnetic, drawing the three of us in. I silently wondered if she had ever been on a racetrack – not placing bets or cheering on a driver, but behind the wheel with a few hundred horses under the hood. The track was one of the few things I did just for the fun of it – what I did when I needed a release. I'd never met a girl I wanted to spend time with, or date, or hell, get to know better. Romance was for saps, but if Libby was half as good on the track as she was on a pool table, the adrenalin rush would be insane.

An image of Larry flashed in my head. Libby was Larry's girlfriend. Whether I wanted to take her out for an afternoon of high-speeds and sharp turns was irrelevant. My life was complicated enough. I didn't need for Larry to be any closer to my life than he already was – no matter how much fun his girlfriend might be.

Libby told story after story of gut-busting craziness. The brief glimpse of her last week at Bank Shot had been appealing, but after hearing a few of her stories, I was sure there was nothing this girl wouldn't do. She talked about road trips to concerts, skiing in Colorado, ice fishing in Canada, and it was obvious she had shot pool in every bar in a two hundred mile radius. I had come to see Davey, but Libby was infectious.

I looked at my watch, surprised that over an hour had passed since my arrival. I cleared my throat. "Hey, Davey, I've got a business meeting I need to go to. You want to walk me to my car?"

Libby snickered, "Davey?" She looked at my brother, and in a childlike voice said, "It's almost bedtime. Maybe Candy will tuck you in tonight and read you a story."

Davey blushed. I took a look at him, and he really didn't look like a "Davey" anymore. I took the hint and needed to remember he was a grown man. He only hesitated long enough to lean down and give Candy a quick kiss on the cheek. "I'll be back in a few minutes." He wagged his finger at Libby, "No break-out plans while I'm gone."

Davey asked how long I would be in town, when I planned to return, and if I wanted to get together before I left. It warmed me to my core. I played it off like I was just answering questions presented to me, but reality was I wanted to hang out with him, too. "I should be back sometime next week. I'll give you a call when things firm up." Embarrassed that Libby had called me out the way she had, "Hey, sorry about the Davey thing instead of Dave. Old habits."

Davey bumped my shoulder as we walked, "You can call me whatever you want. Don't mind Libby. She doesn't have much of a filter – just says whatever she feels like." We approached the Bentley I would deliver to Larry tomorrow, and Davey let out a whistle that could have stopped a train. "Nice wheels."

"Not mine. My employer has good taste in cars."

"Who do you work for?"

I sidestepped his question. "A car dealer in Kansas City. Hey, I was thinking, when I'm in the area next week, we should do something fun. Any race tracks around here that we can rent some time on?"

Davey's eyes lit up the way a kid's do when he sees a box with wrapping paper. We obviously shared a love for speed. "A couple. Dirt or pavement?"

"Man, I haven't been on a dirt track in ages. Is there one up here?"

"A friend of mine has one out on his farm. It's a half-mile track, but he keeps it covered with a bunch of tarps when he's not using it, so it's pristine even in the wintertime. What were you wanting to race?"

"I've got an old Oldsmobile that I like to tinker with. I'll bring it up next time – it's not pretty, but it is fast."

Davey grinned, "I can lay my hand on a couple of options if you don't want to bring yours up." After seeing his garage on my last trip, I didn't doubt that offer for a second. Closing my car door, I gave him a quick wave as I pulled out of the parking lot. Social time was over – time to get ready for business.

I had already scheduled the trade for Wednesday, but I decided to call Larry and invite him to dinner. I didn't want to spring the news on him at the dealership tomorrow. He would have questions that I couldn't answer in front of his co-workers.

Larry chose a nice restaurant where few others were eating. The hostess seated us at the back of the dining room with the closest people two tables away. The napkins were a burnt orange linen, the glasses crystal, the food – exceptional. We had just finished our entrées when Larry commented, "Pretty strange how things have worked out. Libby should be leaving the hospital in a couple days."

I nearly choked on my food. Larry didn't know I had ever met Libby, nor did he know I had been to her hospital room this afternoon. I didn't know Libby very well – though after spending an hour with her, I can say I was glad she wasn't dead. I smirked at my earlier idea: it would be bad form to invite his girlfriend out to the racetrack the next time I was in town. "I'm glad she's on the mend. Last week must have been tough for you."

Larry's face went slack, as if he had purposely forced his earlier expressions.

"The worst ever. In a small way, and I mean a very small way, I'm thankful for what happened to her. She and I hadn't been together for a while. She needed me last week. Even though she wasn't awake, something told me I needed to be there for her."

Thankful for what had happened to her? Had he seen her? I wondered if he were a sadistic slime-ball beneath all of the happiness he was always showing. Only someone truly pathetic thought a comatose person needed him by her side. It wasn't my place to point out the flaws with his belief. After meeting her, I could see why he would be broken up. "You must care for her a lot to have stayed by her side like that."

A lovesick grin spread over his face. Before he could comment or break into the lyrics of a stupid love song, I interrupted, "Johnny wasn't happy that you did last weekend's trade without taking a payment. He was sure I muscled you into it."

Larry cocked his head to the side; my subject change had caught him off guard. "Huh, hopefully you straightened him out." Without so much as hesitating for a breath of air, Larry commented, "Dave looks a lot like you. Do you see him very often?"

Dangerous tingles rippled over my skin as fear stretched the length of my arms. I had surmised that the two knew each other, but this was the first time Larry acknowledged that he did. "No. Not often. So, you *have* met him. Did you let on that you knew me?"

Larry laughed, "Of course not. He showed up with Candy on Sunday at the hospital. It was the first time I had ever met him – I nearly called him Mark." Larry's expression took on a more serious look. "What does he know about our arrangement?"

"He doesn't know anything about our arrangement. He isn't aware that we know each other unless you told him. I'd like to keep it that way."

Larry's eyes narrowed. "What does he think you do for a living?"

I hated that Larry seemed to be trying to insert himself into my business. "He doesn't know what I do." This conversation needed to get off my brother and back on track. "So, back to Johnny. He's shutting down operations at the remote dealerships and is starting his own dealership in the next month. He asked me to personally offer you employment in Kansas City."

Johnny had held this information very close, because Larry looked just as surprised to hear it as I was when Oscar and Johnny told me their plan. Larry arched his back against the chair, but said nothing. The awkward silence hung in the air between us. Appreciative that he had been stunned silent, and we were no longer on the topic of my brother, I continued. "I know this is sudden, but given what happened in Sioux Falls, he believes you are all at greater risk working at remote dealerships. He believes he can make the move worth your while, financially."

Larry, who was normally obnoxiously happy, sat across from me dumbfounded. His voice lacked the usual joviality, instead leaking out as a mere whisper. "But, my life is here. I don't want to move."

Nodding in as understanding a way as I could, I answered, "Johnny would like for you to think it over, but there is no pressure for you to do anything you don't want to do. He has sent a Bentley up for the trade tomorrow. The Bentley is higher than anything we have traded in a while. He'd like your remaining stock in this trade. You can use the money from this trade to relocate to Kansas City, or you can consider it severance. There are no repercussions if you walk away."

Larry blew out a puff of air, his lips making an audible "pffft" sound. He didn't believe me. Now was my turn to go into convincing mode. "If you want out, you're out. If you want to continue to do what you're doing, he's ready to offer you a permanent position in Kansas City. If you stay here, working for the local dealership, there will be no more trades from Johnny."

His lips formed two tight lines, his eyes staring at the center of the table. After what felt like several minutes, Larry found his voice – it was loud enough that it caught the attention of nearly everyone in the room. "That's it? Seven years of sticking my neck out, and he thinks he can pay me off with one car?"

Wow, not what I was expecting. I was worried about a couple of the guys at remote dealerships and how they would take the news, but Larry hadn't been one of my concerns. I had never heard him utter a cross word or seen him give a sideways glance before today. I looked around the room as all eyes were trained on the two of us.

I motioned with my hands for him to keep his voice down, but Larry was fuming as he spat, "What does Fernando say? This is his operation, not Johnny's." I didn't have a clue who Fernando was, but I was sure I and everyone else in the restaurant were about to find out. "Johnny walked in and made a lot of promises. If I call Fernando and he doesn't know about this, Johnny's going to have one pissed off drug lord to answer to." Silence is golden, but duct tape is silver. I'd settle for silver right now.

Leaning as far across the table as I could, I kept my voice low. "Look, I just found out about this myself. Up until a couple weeks ago, I was security at Johnny's estate. I only came back in the mix because Haden. . . you know."

Larry's nostrils flared as I prepared for him to spout off more information that could get us both arrested. He had somehow gotten his emotions in check while his voice remained an angry growl. "Is that what this is about? Haden wasn't like you. He was reckless. He didn't give notice. He showed up whenever the mood struck him. Not just Sioux Falls, but all the dealerships were having a tough time working with him. Johnny doesn't have to shut us down."

"That's not my call. Or yours. I'd venture so far as to say Fernando might not have much of a say in it either. Be rational. It's safer for Johnny to take deliveries at his own dealership. You want to stay a part of the operation, fine. You want out, you're out. It's your choice."

Larry scowled at me for a long minute. His brows were forced down in angry slants as his eyes held mine. Through gritted teeth, Larry asked, "When does Johnny want my answer?"

"Take your time. The job's ready for you if you ever want it. But there's no pressure."

Larry was angry – significantly more than I had imagined he would be. The other customers in the restaurant had stopped watching our table, so I began to relax. Barely loud enough for me to hear, Larry mumbled, "Wonder what Dave would say if I told him his brother just fired me?"

Larry had just threatened me. My legs stiffened under the table. The muscles in my arms went rigid. "He'd think you were off your meds. You work for the car dealership, remember?"

"Psha." His eyes rolled. "I bet he'd be pretty interested to know what kind of a double-life you're leading."

Up until this moment, I had only been concerned about Johnny, Oscar, Felix or someone from Johnny's organization finding out about Davey. It never occurred to me what Davey would think if he found out what I was doing. This may have been a job I took with the best of intentions, but as angry as Larry was right now – he could do some irreparable damage to my relationship with my brother. I couldn't lose Davey after just finding him again. I refused to let fear of any kind ebb into my voice. Instead I answered with the only words that surfaced, "Mind your manners."

Larry guffawed, "My manners? Who do you think you're dealing with?"

I wiped the corners of my mouth with the napkin, and slowly set it on the plate in front of me. I reached into the inside pocket of my jacket, pulled out my wallet, and took two crisp one-hundred dollar bills out, tucking them under my plate so only the tips stuck out from it. I stood to my full height and walked casually around the table.

When I stood directly beside Larry, I kneeled down next to his chair so I could speak directly into his ear. "I think I'm dealing with a man who is angry and is spouting off words trying to get a reaction from me. I'll tell Johnny you are considering his generous offer."

Larry jerked his head away from me. When he did, I looped my hand around the other side of his head and pulled his ear back in front of my mouth. My volume stayed low, "Dave gets any information about me from you – they'll be fishing you out of the Gulf of Mexico in two by two squares. Understood?"

Dramatic? Maybe. Effective? Definitely. I had never needed to rattle anyone at the dealerships before. No one knew anything about me, other than I was punctual, and I enabled Johnny to make each of the salesmen very wealthy. I released his head from my grasp, and this time Larry eased away from me. I stood up and patted Larry on the shoulder, "I'll see you tomorrow at ten."

Larry nodded, wearing a blank expression on his face. The last thing I needed was for him to burn up the phone lines as soon as I walked out. "Oh, Larry?" His eyes flashed up to mine, fear shining through for the first time this evening, "If I find out you called Johnny or Fernando about this, I will make good on the Gulf of Mexico."

I left the restaurant with Larry sitting stunned at the empty table.

The next morning I arrived promptly at ten a.m. Larry was ready. There was no chit-chat, nor were there any misplaced glares. He filled out the paperwork, handed me the key to another F-150 and walked me out to the vehicle. "Tank's full. Let Johnny know I thought it over, but I'm going to pass."

I cocked my head to the side. "He'll be disappointed."

"Tell him it was my pleasure working for him. I wish him the best with his new dealership, but Lincoln is my home."

"You don't want to take some more time to think it over?"

A slice of fear jetted through his gaze, but he shook his head. "No, Boss. Thank him for his generosity."

The hairs on my arms prickled. Larry had never called me "boss" before. That was a term I only ever heard in Kansas City. Had he phoned Johnny last night after I warned him not to? I needed to know if I was driving into a hornet's nest when I returned today with the truck. "*Boss*? You've always called me *Mark*."

Larry bowed his head as if his shoes were suddenly intriguing. "I didn't realize Johnny was using someone like yourself to shuttle cars. I meant no disrespect last night."

I felt my control begin to waver. Anger bit through my voice when I accused, "You called Johnny?"

"No!" His eyes shot straight up. A muscle flexed on the side of his jaw as I watched a vein in his neck pulse from the strain. He eased a step closer to me, looking around to see if anyone were within earshot. Satisfied that no one was listening, "I called down to an old friend of mine. I told him I was thinking of re-locating, asked if the town had changed much since I worked there."

"Who was your friend?" Fury burned just under the surface. If he had spilled any of this information to someone locally – Johnny would be furious. Not just with Larry, but with me, too.

"Jorge. He told me that if Johnny was letting me walk away, I needed to accept his offer."

Jorge was in Johnny's tight circle of leadership. He was also the one Lenny used as an example when he tried to convince me not to accept Johnny's promotion – Jorge had tried to quit. Johnny didn't let him walk away. "You asked Jorge about me?"

Larry's words stammered, "I-I-I told him you were delivering the message for Johnny. Jorge told me if it came from you, that I could trust it." His eyes darted to the ground again. "Jorge says you're number three from the top. No one makes a move unless you, Oscar or Johnny okay it."

Number three? Not hardly. Johnny liked me, but I wasn't calling shots any more than Jorge was. The rage I had been ready to unleash subsided. Jorge could be trusted. Even if Larry had blabbed about the entire operation, Jorge wouldn't repeat it. I'd have a visit with Jorge this afternoon, but I already knew it was an unnecessary precaution. I nodded and unlocked the truck. "You need anything, give us a call. If you change your mind, there will always be room for you."

I eased the truck out of the lot. Third from the top? How did Jorge figure that? Felix had been around way longer than I had, so had Spencer and Jorge. Edward, Liam and Luke had been around longer, but I reasoned none of them were in Johnny's circle of six. People began to call me "Boss" after I took the job as head of security on Johnny's estate. The name sort of stuck, but it didn't describe my place in the organization.

It was just a nickname because there had to be a chain of command for security, and we rarely used names over the radios. My head began turning things over – no one called me "Boss" before that job, but come to think of it, everyone I worked with in Kansas City except Oscar and Johnny called me that now. The night I had been moved to Johnny's estate, I delivered a message for Johnny to Oscar – he told me he would pass the word on the organizational change. When he said Felix wanted this position, I thought he had meant head of security, but that wasn't it at all.

Oscar's cancer was in remission, but after seeing him at Johnny's on Sunday, he still looked like a strong wind could knock him over. If everyone believed I was three from the top, and Oscar was past due to retire, that made me Johnny's right hand. Pride should have welled up inside me. Instead, my stomach cinched tight. I was twenty-two. Johnny couldn't have meant for me to be that far up in his organization. He had never said anything to me. Could Jorge have gotten it wrong?

Johnny told me I was taking over his cartel operations. Johnny's businesses were separated into three areas: the legitimate businesses, the illegal businesses that laundered their money through the legitimate ones, and Oscar's boys. The legitimate businesses included the bistro, his used car dealership, sort of, a gambling casino on an Indian reservation, a sports bar, and a sports complex. The illegal businesses included prostitution, drugs, and gambling. Oscar's crew had one purpose – it wasn't to make money, but to make sure the other two areas operated smoothly. Johnny's muscle and his clean-up crew worked for Oscar.

The entire drive to Kansas City, I did nothing but turn over the possibilities in my head – both good and bad. I was in a spot where I could help Chad make a dent in the drugs flowing into the Midwest. If anyone learned about Davey, bringing Johnny down would be a death sentence for my brother. If Larry had been right about anything last night – Davey finding out what I did could prove catastrophic, too, but on a whole different level.

Another thought registered: if Jorge were right, and I really was third from the top, I wouldn't be able to quit Johnny. The only way out would be to bring him down completely and to find a way to disappear.

I pulled into the dealership having figured nothing out. The only decision I had made was that after the truck was delivered, I needed to talk to Chad. He needed to know why I had flaked on him Saturday night and where the urgency was coming from. Felix was waiting when I walked into the office to drop off the keys. He looked up from behind his desk. "Right on time. Johnny called: he and Oscar want to see you."

My stomach burned – if this kept up, I'd need to get checked for an ulcer. "Okay. Where are they?"

"At the bistro." Felix looked smug, but he didn't bother to elaborate and tell me why.

I was sick of surprises. "What aren't you telling me?"

Defensively, Felix answered, "Nothing. Just passing on a message."

I eyed him suspiciously. Felix and I had never had any love for one another, but there had always been a mutual respect between us. "You sure there's nothing else?"

Smugly, Felix added, "No. Johnny sounded a little frustrated on the phone is all."

Trying my best to sound disinterested, "Huh, okay. Thanks for the warning."

The bistro was only a couple miles from the dealership. It wouldn't open for the dinner crowd until five, but it was still a strange place for us to meet. Johnny preferred the seclusion of his estate most of the time. I tried to think of anything I had done that would have ticked Johnny off, but other than the possibility of Larry crying to him, I came up empty.

There was a remote chance that Larry had told Jorge about my brother, but after considering that possibility on the drive back – I thought it unlikely. Larry was a smart guy; that information was something he would keep in his back pocket if he ever needed leverage with me. Ulcer or not, this didn't feel right. It wasn't like Johnny to pass a message to me through Felix. If he wanted to meet me at the bistro, why hadn't he just called me?

CHAPTER 15

The bistro's back door was unlocked. I entered through the kitchen to a flurry of activity. The sweet smell of oregano and basil and bread baking hung in the air. Employees were preparing food for the dinner crowd. Desserts were in full swing, soups were stewing in massive pots, and vegetables were being chopped. No one paid any attention to me as I made my way through the pristine kitchen.

I walked into the dining area but saw no one. Reaching for the light switch and illuminating the dark room only proved that it was empty. I turned the lights back off and went to the private dining area at the top of the stairs. This room was reserved for Johnny's guests. Large double doors were propped open. Tasteful art from local artists adorned the walls. In the middle of the room, Johnny and Oscar sat at a table, looking to be in an intense conversation.

Without wanting to intrude, I rapped my knuckle on one of the open doors. Oscar stopped in midsentence; Johnny waved me over. It felt like I was moving in slow motion, as if weights clung to my ankles. I didn't know why. Maybe because it was rare for Johnny to meet with me here, maybe because he had passed the message for me through Felix, or maybe the guilt I was feeling was affecting me more than I wanted it to.

When I approached the table, Johnny nodded at the chair across from him. I followed his wordless instruction and took a seat. My stomach felt wrong, like I had eaten a meal three portions too big. Oscar didn't look at my eyes, instead focusing on the wall behind me. Something was wrong – really wrong.

"Felix said you wanted to see me."

All niceties were dispensed with. Johnny's voice was flat as he asked, "Who are you, Mark?"

Every nerve in my body shot a pulse at once. If it were possible to have a lightning bolt generated inside a body, that had just happened to me. His eyes remained focused on mine as I struggled to find an answer: a sellout, a snitch, a liar. What answer was he looking for? "I don't understand the question, Johnny."

Johnny looked at Oscar and motioned for the old man to speak. Oscar's steely eyes settled on me. Their color changed with his mood: sometimes blue, other times green, occasionally gray. When he was angry, they took on the hard look of gray steel every time. "I spoke to your widow. Hazel had a tough time believing her husband had returned from the grave."

Widow? I didn't even have a girlfriend, how could I have a wife, or. . . a widow? Hazel? Who was she? Oscar's question made no sense. "I'm not following."

Oscar continued, "Another thing I find striking is how little you've aged." A lump formed in my throat. It felt like tight binding had been wrapped around my chest while Oscar continued to pull tighter with each word. "Forty-four? Yet, you don't look a day over twenty-five."

Understanding finally crashed on me. Oscar had dug into my background and learned I was using a dead man's identity. Some of the worry I had felt subsided. "I drink formaldehyde. It's not just for embalming anymore. Excellent preservative."

Johnny's fist landed hard on the table. "Who are you?!"

Doing my best to keep my voice level, "I'm the same guy you hired off of Lenny's crew. I'm the same one you trusted your daughters' safety with. I'm the same man who Fernando knows as your right hand. Nothing's changed." That last bit, dropping Fernando's name, may have been over the top, but I wasn't ready for my own execution and was grasping at whatever might keep me alive.

Johnny leaned over the table, his eyes narrow and his eyebrows forced down in angry slants. "Fernando doesn't know you. Are you working for the cops?"

I laughed. It was the only response that seemed reasonable given the circumstances. "The cops would have created a new ID for me. They wouldn't have issued me a dead guy's."

Oscar watched me the same way a cat watches a bird preparing to take flight. Johnny accused, "No one appears out of thin air. Where did you come from? How old are you? What is your real name?" With each question his anger seemed to increase.

Easing back in my chair, I tried to hide whatever fear might be showing. "I didn't appear out of thin air. I ran away from home – well, if you could call it that. I grew up in Missouri. The state owned me; I moved here when I was fifteen. I'm twenty-two now. My real name is Mark Brewer."

Johnny pounded his fist on the table a second time. "Stop lying to me!"

In a show of respect, I bowed my head. "When I first came to Kansas City, I was fifteen. Lenny offered me a spot on his crew, but he wouldn't hire me unless I had a driver's license. I couldn't get one because I wasn't old enough. I went to the library and started doing searches on people who had died with the same name as mine. I found a Marcus Brewer. I sent off for a duplicate copy of his social security card and birth certificate."

Oscar's lips pursed into a thin line, his eyes narrowed – doubt clouded his face. "You showed up at DMV and they gave you a license? Hazel sent me a picture of her late husband. You look nothing like him."

I shrugged my shoulders, "I looked even less like him when I was fifteen. Lenny has a guy who works on the inside at DMV. That's how Lenny has new VINS made up, so a stolen car becomes clean before it's sold. Lenny hooked me up with his inside guy, and he made sure I got a license."

Neither of the two men spoke for a long minute. Beads of sweat peppered my brow, but I didn't wipe them away. Johnny eased back in his chair, a thin smile forming. "I don't know whether to be in awe of your cunning or furious that you have lied to me every day since I've known you. You can't use a dead man's identification. The IRS pays attention to that, so do insurance companies."

This was the first time, ever, that someone had called me out on my identity. Seven years I'd been a different Mark Brewer and no one was the wiser – at least until today. "I did those types of searches at the library, too. The IRS only looks for certain things, and since I have never used the ID to get credit, and you have never asked me to fill out a tax withholding form, no red flags have gone off with the IRS."

Johnny looked skeptical, so I added, "I lived in the same apartment from the time I was fifteen until I moved onto your estate. After I moved out of your guesthouse, I tried to move back into the same apartment, but it had already been rented. The same property manager I used before rented me a different apartment, but she still lets me pay in cash."

Oscar didn't look convinced. I reached into my back pocket and pulled out my wallet, opening it for them both to examine. "See? No plastic. I don't have a checking account, savings account, or a credit card. I've never paid taxes for anything." The only thing in my wallet was a pile of cash, my driver's license and the little USB drive shaped like a supermarket rewards card. Neither of the men examined my wallet close enough to see I was carrying two years' worth of electronic files carefully camouflaged in plain sight.

Johnny's head cocked to the side. "Everything is paid for in cash?"

"Everything."

Skeptically he asked, "How did you register your car?"

"Technically, it's Lenny's car. He runs it as a business expense for his bar. I give him the cash every month for the payment and insurance; when the registration is due, he tells me what I owe him for the taxes and tags."

Johnny looked at Oscar; clearly, none of this had made sense to them when they had stumbled across it. When Johnny looked back at me, he no longer looked like he was going to bite steel and spit nails. "You stole a dead man's identity, but only use it for what?"

"When I first got my license, I figured I'd get caught like everyone else at some point. Lenny fires anyone from his crew who gets more than a parking ticket. I figured if I did get caught, I could get a new license with my real identity, and he'd let me stay. But since I've never been busted for anything, there was no reason to switch back to my own identity."

Oscar accused, "You're a ghost. You could disappear at any time and there is no trail to follow."

"My license says I'm a ghost. But nothing has changed. I'm still the guy Johnny hired four years ago. I didn't think it was a big deal. I would have told you both if I thought you were interested."

Johnny shook his head, but finally a smirk appeared on his face. "Oscar thinks I am putting too much responsibility on you. He says Felix should be handling the cartel operations."

After everything that had gone down in the last week, I was all for it. Felix taking over the cartel with his dealership responsibilities would be perfect. It would keep me completely under the radar. My eyes darted to Oscar, then returned to Johnny. "Oscar's a smart guy."

Johnny studied me for a minute. "You agree with him?"

I needed to tread lightly. If Johnny thought I wanted him to bounce me back to the minors, they would surely dig further into my past to learn why. "No, but I don't think Oscar's ever given you bad advice. I wouldn't take anything he says lightly." Oscar's head tilted to the side. He started to respond, then chose to keep quiet.

Johnny held his chin with his thumb and index finger. "Everyone is wrong sometime in their life."

"Johnny, I've never given you a reason to question my loyalty. This promotion you gave me is great, but it's not why I'm working for you. If you aren't comfortable and you want Felix to take over – I'll go back to whatever you want me doing. When you think I'm ready, I'll be here." That was a good answer. I didn't sound eager to be demoted, and I didn't insult Johnny or Oscar.

Still rubbing his chin, Johnny commented, "Felix is a bottom feeder. He'll take whatever scraps someone else leaves behind." As if he didn't believe my earlier confession, Johnny asked, "Twenty-two?"

"According to my license, forty-four, but yeah, I'm only twenty-two."

Johnny eyed me more suspiciously. "You came to the city at fifteen. Why?"

"I was in foster care a few hours from here. I needed a change of scenery."

Oscar stood up without a word, walked over to the wine chiller in the corner of the room while Johnny continued to study me. He pulled a bottle and opened it. Oscar set a wine glass in front of each of us and filled all three glasses. It was red wine – not my favorite, but I didn't decline it.

Oscar swished it around for a minute then took a big swig. It was funny, I watched people all the time and wine drinkers usually took sissy sips; Oscar looked like he had just run a marathon and the wine glass was full of ice water. He put the glass in front of himself as his fingers caressed the stem. "I was wrong, Johnny. Mark has given you no reason to question his loyalty. He's telling the truth about Lenny's rule. Lenny fires employees for just speeding tickets. Mark's actions more than make sense – it was a brilliant move for a teenager."

Those few words pulled what felt like an anvil off of my chest. This chat had nothing to do with Larry calling Jorge. In reality, I wondered why Oscar hadn't looked into my past earlier. No one should be in my position without Oscar taking a fine-toothed comb to his background. The fact that neither Oscar nor Johnny had a clue who I really was meant that neither of them knew about Davey, either. It might be just a matter of time before they found out, but for now, Davey was safe.

A new thought assailed me. I could come clean and tell them about Davey now or risk Oscar finding out about him later. If Oscar looked into *my* records, he would learn I grew up in foster care. According to the state of Missouri, I had one sibling who died before I was a teenager. Would he dig any deeper than that? I couldn't care less if he found Mom or Dad. I didn't know if either was still alive, and even if I knew, I wouldn't care to see them.

No. Oscar would need someone to tip him off to learn about Davey. Larry seemed to be keeping quiet. My only loose ends were Grey and Teddy. Had Oscar already reached out to Teddy like he said he was going to?

"So, what about Teddy?" My question threw both men off-guard.

Oscar looked suspicious. "What do you mean?"

"Sunday you had talked about inviting Teddy back into the fold after I told him he needed to stay away from Lincoln."

Oscar resumed rubbing the stem of his wine glass in a slow rhythm. "I haven't contacted him yet. You have a problem with Teddy?"

Now was my chance. "I don't trust him. There are plenty of people who could do the job locally. Bringing Teddy in after he walked away won't look good to the rest of the guys on the crew – like there are no repercussions for leaving."

Oscar asked, "You wouldn't feel more secure with him where we could keep an eye on him?"

"No. A bad apple can spoil a basket. I never liked Teddy. If he comes back after quitting, the message to everyone who works for Johnny could get convoluted."

I couldn't tell if Oscar believed me or not. He stayed quiet. Johnny's demeanor had changed substantially from when I had arrived. He wasn't beating on the table or glaring my way anymore. I'm sure Oscar wasn't done digging, but at least I didn't feel like I was going to be eating a bullet for dinner tonight.

Johnny answered before Oscar could respond, "I agree. We'll wait and see if Teddy resurfaces. For now, take Grey off of your roster, too."

CHAPTER 16

Over the next sixty days, I shut down our operations with each of the remote dealerships. All took the news better than Larry had. About half of the salespeople accepted Johnny's offer and chose to relocate to Kansas City. I hadn't spoken with Chad since the night I met Davey at his garage; the USB drive in my wallet was still tucked safely inside. I had considered calling him to explain why I had changed my mind, but every time I started to dial, I talked myself out of it. I had left a message telling him I would call in a month, but I had never called to tell him about the changes.

Just as Johnny planned, I took over the cartel operations. My role didn't include moving cars full of drugs from the remote cities anymore. It was more of a white-collar business once Johnny's dealership was set up. We received a list of VINs on engines from Chihuahua, Mexico. Each of those engines was bound for Overland Park, Missouri. Johnny had a standing order for ten F-150's each month. Each of those trucks needed minor engine re-work when we received them from the assembly plant prior to going onto our lot. The re-work was limited to removing several kilos of super-meth.

The whole operation was clean. The salespeople who had been at the remote dealerships and came to work for Johnny went back to merely selling cars. None made nearly the money they had made with the drug trade, but all of them remained fiercely loyal to Johnny and pleased to be at his dealership. I knew each of them and said "hello" when I saw them, but none were involved in the seedy aspects anymore, so we had little interaction. Aside from the minor engine re-work on the inbound trucks, Johnny's dealership was completely legitimate.

My job was fluid. Since there were no set hours, it was easy enough to squeeze in a trip to see Davey every week. I tried not to make a pattern of my trips north, for fear that someone in the organization would realize. I was obsessed enough about this that I kept a calendar in my desk with an X on the day of the week I had seen Davey. There was no pattern, just nine days in the last nine weeks that I took a day off. I didn't even call Davey ahead of time; I just waited until I was in Lincoln, pulled my "clean" disposable phone out from under the passenger seat of my car, and told him I was in town.

As I pulled into town, I checked my rearview mirror: no one followed. I arrived at Candy's house and saw Davey's truck parked right behind her Chevelle on the street. Libby's sad little blue Honda was halfway up the street. Libby answered the door, "Good timing. D'you bring the champagne?"

"Hi, Libby, no. What're we celebrating?" I peered into the kitchen and gratefully Larry was nowhere around.

Davey met me inside the kitchen. "I did it. The garage is mine as of this afternoon." After seeing all of his restores setting outside in the ghetto neighborhood where his garage was located, I had joined Candy and his partner Mr. Kravitz in prodding him to find a bigger garage with a fenced in area for security. Maybe it was my knowledge that every one of his restored muscle cars was a sweet ride and could be gone if the right thief stumbled across them.

He made an offer on the new garage a month ago; I had been with him the day he filled out the paperwork with his real estate agent. It was exciting to see his operation expanding; the new garage was enormous compared to his current place. Secretly, I was envious.

Candy peeked from around him, "That's your most exciting news?"

She was a live wire, but she was good for him. His smile stretched from one ear to the other, so I prodded, "You can top buying a new garage? Spill it."

Davey blushed, reached down to Candy's left hand and held it in the air. She wore an engagement ring. I'm not sure why I was surprised; he had moved into the house with Candy and Libby shortly after we reconnected. "Congratulations." I stumbled mentally, unsure what the right response was. Lenny had spent a great deal of time teaching me things other people seemed to come by naturally, but we had never discussed how to congratulate someone on an engagement. Was I supposed to hug her? Should I shake his hand? Was I supposed to ask about details of the proposal?

Libby must have noticed my momentary mental-stutter. She slapped me on the shoulder and said, "Let's go to the store and get some champagne." She reached for her coat then turned to Davey and Candy, "We'll be back in twenty minutes. Don't let dinner burn."

We got into my car and she asked, "You okay?"

"Yeah. Fine."

Conspiratorially she said, "You don't look fine. Not big on engagements?"

"Uh, no. I mean, I don't have strong feelings one way or the other. I'm happy for him."

"Them?"

"What?"

"You're happy for *them*. That's what you meant to say, right?"

I glanced at Libby. She had fully recovered from her injuries, at least the physical ones. The patch near her temple that had been shaved was growing back nicely. I wasn't sure I had the words to tell her what I was feeling. I had never had a girlfriend, not even a real date that I could remember. Sure, I had taken women out for dinner or dancing, concerts, even a couple movies – but nothing ever came of any of them. Davey was my little brother, and he was going to be married.

I felt Libby's eyes on me as I drove. I needed to say something. "Just seems a little sudden. That's all."

"Yeah, for me, too. Before the night Grey beat the crap out of me, neither of us had seen Dave in two years. Now they're inseparable and getting married."

Libby and I had talked lots of times, but our conversations were usually superficial. I purposely kept my distance because she dated Larry, and I didn't need him getting jealous and spilling everything he knew about me to Davey. It was a bit of a balancing act. "So, you think they should slow down?"

"I don't know what to think. Candy's happy, happier than I've ever seen her. Dave's sweet to her. I was glad he moved in with us after the attack; having him around made the house feel safer. I just wasn't expecting. . .well, any of this."

"Yeah. Don't get me wrong: I like Candy. It just seems fast." I pulled into a liquor store. "You want to go in with me?"

"Sure. I need to make sure you don't buy cheap champagne. I don't need a headache at work tomorrow."

I didn't try to be pompous, but having grown up with almost nothing and now having more money than I could spend, I had never been accused of buying anything cheap. My life was full of the best of everything: my car, my apartment, and my hobbies. Why did she think I would skimp on a celebratory bottle of champagne?

We returned to the house, uncorked the bottle, and Libby and I both put our concerns aside that Davey and Candy were moving too fast. This would be our own little secret; neither of us wanted the person we loved to believe we were anything but happy for them.

I spent the night on the sofa. I was up before anyone else in the house. As I tried to tiptoe out the front door and to my car at 5:30, Libby's voice sounded from the stairs. "Where are you off to so early?"

I didn't know anyone else was awake. Her voice stopped me in my tracks. "Morning. I was just headed home. Why are you up already?"

"Work, remember?"

"Right. I'll see you next time I'm up." I reached for the door handle to make my escape.

"It's Saturday, I figured you were up for the weekend."

I had planned my days away from Kansas City not to show a pattern to anyone who knew me. I had been oblivious to the fact that someone with a regular job wouldn't rush back on a Saturday morning, and my departure would look suspicious to Davey, Candy and Libby. "No, I'm sure Dave and Candy have things they'd like to do without me around."

Libby's expression looked disappointed. "They aren't picking out china patterns yet. Dave and Candy are going to go to Mount Crescent this afternoon after I get off work. You want to stick around and go with us?"

Mount Crescent was a close snowboarding, skiing, and tubing resort area. I didn't have any reason to return to Kansas City, other than I didn't want for anyone to know I was gone. "What about your boyfriend?"

"Larry doesn't want to go. C'mon, it'll be fun. We're just going to tube for a couple hours. My doctor cleared me for all activities, and this is our celebratory weekend."

From my other visits, I knew Libby had been cooped up in the house most of the time and was anxious to get back to regular activities. The injuries Grey had inflicted on her were bad, so bad that she had been banned from anything that could re-injure her head. I looked at her wearing khaki pants and a red polo shirt, "Aren't you working this morning?"

"Yeah, six to noon. We are going to go after I get off work." She had a huge duffle bag she carried down the steps. "You can give me a ride to work, so I don't have to leave my car, then the three of you can pick me up this afternoon. We can go straight from there."

It did sound like fun. No one would miss me in Kansas City if I didn't make it back until tonight. "I don't want to intrude. This is something the three of you were going to do."

She tossed her duffle bag to the floor and pleaded with me, "Please. If you don't go, I'll be like a fifth wheel."

It was already April. The place was only open for tubing when it was cold enough to make snow. It might be the last weekend we could go this year and would be fun. "Okay, I'm in."

I dropped Libby at work. Before she got out of my car, she leaned over and kissed my cheek, "Thanks for the ride. I'll see you in a few hours." Libby exited my car and sprinted up to the doors. I sat there on the curb for a few seconds after she disappeared into the building. Why had she kissed me? Is that what people did? I liked being around Davey, Candy and Libby because they were normal, and there were a lot of normal things I had never been exposed to.

My cheek felt warm. It was nice, but confusing. Libby had never kissed me when I left their house on any of my earlier visits. Did she kiss me as a thank-you for dropping her at work? Did it mean anything? No, she was seeing Larry. It hadn't been an invitation; I would have recognized that.

The reason I had never had a girlfriend was I never wanted to get attached to someone just to have her shred me once I began to care. I had never gone on more than a second date with any girl. Libby was different. She wasn't trying to convince me to be her boyfriend, she was. . . well, what was she doing? I saw her whenever I visited Davey. The four of us ate dinner together, we watched movies, we played pool, we even played card games sometimes. We had fun together. Libby was a friend.

That reality was a strange paradigm all on its own. I had few friends, but Libby was one of them. When I returned to the house, Davey was sitting at the table and looked surprised to see me. "I thought you went back to Kansas City."

"Libby invited me to go to Crescent Mountain with you guys this afternoon."

Davey grinned. "She did?"

His accusation hung in the air, and I got a weird feeling. Should I not have accepted? Did he not want me to go with them? "You don't mind if I tag along?"

"Yeah, that's great. I didn't know you could stay, or I would have invited you."

"I dropped her at work. She said we should pick her up, so we can go straight from there."

"Sounds good. You want to go see my new garage?"

I did. Davey and I spent the morning together. I helped him move some of his tools from his existing place to the new one. We made several trips before Candy tracked us down and reminded us work time was over, and we needed to get ready to hit the slopes. We stopped by the house, showered and changed clothes. Davey loaned me some warm clothes. The three of us were waiting for Libby exactly at noon.

Libby burst through the door and ran straight for us. She climbed into the back seat with me. Candy had packed Libby a lunch, which was waiting for her on the seat. She looked inside the bag, then zipped it closed and said, "Thanks,

Candy."

The drive to Mount Crescent went quickly. It was almost an hour away, but time I spent with these three never dragged. I caught myself daydreaming about my life and wishing I could abandon my current life in favor of one here. Libby's hand squeezed my thigh, "Ready?"

The truck had stopped; I hadn't noticed that we arrived. My eyes went to her hand still resting on my leg as heat washed over me. I looked at her face: a dazzling smile greeted my eyes. "Mark, are you okay?"

"Fine." Candy and Davey both climbed out of the front seats and shut their doors. I shook my head, trying to make the haze disappear; still acutely aware that Libby's hand remained on my leg. Trying to offer an explanation, I muttered, "I was zoning."

"I can tell. You must be scared of me showing you up on the slopes." Libby removed her hand, grabbed her duffle bag and launched herself outside. What the hell was wrong with me?

We caught the chair lift up to the top and each did three runs. At the bottom of the hill after our third time, Candy announced, "This is the last one for me, I'm freezing." Davey pulled her in close, burying her face in his chest. I didn't think his attempt to warm her up would buy us more than one more run on the hill.

Libby grabbed my arm, "This time we should race."

"Race? You can't beat me." I had her by eighty pounds: one good push off with my arms and I'd beat her without effort. Despite not finishing high school, I remembered the lab in physical science where we timed objects dropping with different forces applied to them.

Libby challenged, "Loser buys dinner."

She sprinted ahead of me for the chair lift, and got to the lift just before a group of four people who had been in front of us did. As she was being carried through the air on the chair lift, I shouted, "We aren't racing to the top. We're racing to the bottom!"

She waved at me in a teasing way. As I exited the chair lift, Candy and Davey were in the chair behind me. The three of us walked up to where Libby stood waiting her turn to go down. She was smirking and reiterated, "When you buy dinner, McDonald's doesn't count. Plan on something with silverware."

"That's some pretty big talk. What are you, a buck and a quarter soaking wet? You obviously don't understand the basics of gravity. Don't worry, after you buy dinner, I'll spring for ice cream."

Libby and I lined up at the top of the hill; she had removed the nylon wrap from her tube so hers was just a rubber tractor tire. It didn't seem like it would make much of a difference, but I removed mine, too, so after I beat her she couldn't blame the nylon on mine. I sat in my tube with both legs hanging over the side, readying to shove hard with both hands. She took a different approach, lying headfirst on her stomach. She seriously thought she could beat me. Not a surprise, Libby was the most competitive girl I'd ever met, and she was awesome at most things, but not even she could defy the laws of physics.

Davey cheered, "Finally, something Libby's not going to win. Make me proud, Mark."

Candy chimed it, "I wouldn't count on it. Sorry, Mark, Libby never loses." Sounds like it was about time Libby lost at something. I affixed my goggles over my eyes. Candy stood in between our tubes; the people in front of us were already at the bottom of the hill. Candy raised both her arms in the air and said, "On your mark. . . get set. . .go!"

Libby pulled forward with her hands at the same moment I pushed forward with mine. She tucked her head down and shot down the hill like a rocket. Halfway down her tube was sliding so fast it turned sideways – she had no control. Libby's tube was sliding easily twice as fast as mine. I watched helplessly as she neared the bottom and skidded over the thick snow piled to slow tubes down. She crashed hard into the barrier at the bottom of the hill, her tube flying high into the air as it dropped her heavily on her back in a pile of snow. An employee jumped the fence to check on her still body as I raced to the bottom.

Approaching the bottom of the hill, I rolled off my tube while it was still in motion, righted myself, and dashed the thirty feet to where Libby's body lay. I shoved the slope employee out of the way and shouted, "Libby! Libby, are you okay?"

An enormous smile beamed back at me when she said, "I feel like steak tonight, maybe some sautéed mushrooms."

My heart hammered in my chest as her words sunk in. Confident that she wasn't hurt badly, I asked, "Are you okay?" More employees arrived to check on her as she lifted her hand high in the air, wordlessly asking me to help her off of the ground.

"I'm fine. Did you see that? If I'd been wearing wings, I would have flown!"

"Yeah, that's great. You're sure you're not hurt?"

Her smile didn't waver. "Never better."

Davey and Candy had ridden down the hill and both walked up to us; neither looked the least bit concerned that Libby had sailed into the air and landed hard on the ground. Instead, Candy said, "I told you. Libby never loses."

Ignoring Candy's disregard for Libby, I asked, "Did you hit your head? Should we get you checked out?"

Libby laughed, "Not going to get out of dinner that easy. I'm fine, and you're buying."

We all walked back to the truck. When Libby climbed into the cab, a can of cooking spray fell out of her coat and on to the floor. I held it up and asked, "What's this for?"

"To make sure you bought dinner tonight."

"You coated the bottom of your tube with cooking spray? Are you insane? You could have gotten yourself killed!"

Libby laughed. "Killed? A little dramatic, don't you think?"

CHAPTER 17

The more time I spent with Libby, the more cautious I began to be. She had recovered well from her injuries in the last two months. Initially, it was because I didn't want jealousy to flare in Larry and result in him spilling everything he knew about me to Davey.

After a while, I realized it wasn't Larry who worried me. Libby was a basket of bad decisions setting there with a big red bow on it. The girl had no fear. She was up for anything. She and Candy came along with Davey and me on a few of our adventures.

There was something about Libby. In the beginning I had tried to cut her and Candy out of my outings with Davey, partly because I caught myself paying more attention to Libby than I did to my brother. That was a wasted effort, because Davey wanted Candy with him all the time, even more so since they became engaged, and I craved Libby's spontaneity. Everything else in my life was calculated – Libby lived in the moment – every moment.

I had been right the first day I met Libby in the hospital when I thought she would be aggressive on a racetrack. That girl pushed her car to the absolute limits and then really dug in. Davey waved her off of the track after she took a corner so sharp she had two wheels off of the dirt. He reminded her she was supposed to be taking it easy. Libby threw her head back and howled, "All four wheels are still on the car: that *was* taking it easy."

Another trip Candy suggested we hit a bar to play pool. Libby held nothing back, making shots that included jumping balls and double-banks with hardly any effort.

She was a video game master, too. I tried to play a game with her, but I had never played the game before, so my character couldn't keep up with hers. After at least ten times of having to stop and wait for me to catch up, she paused the game, reached over and took the controller out of my hand. Libby flashed a bright smile, and announced, "You suck." I was sort of pissed, but her bravado somehow endeared her to me. Candy was right: Libby excelled at everything she did.

Two weeks ago I had shown up just before a late winter storm blew through. It started with freezing rain, then proceeded to dump five inches of snow on the icy roads, which shut down the interstates. The four of us had stayed up until 2:00 a.m. playing: Apples to Apples, Monopoly Millionaire, and Sequence board games. I felt like a kid again, or hell, maybe like a kid for the first time.

I always slept on the sofa when I stayed the night, which let me ease out of the house before the other three woke up. It was around seven a.m. when the front door creaked open and closed slowly. I wasn't sure who had left for work so early, but decided to look and see if the snowplows had cleared the road so I could head south. All of our cars were still covered with snow on the street, but there was Libby: lying on the front lawn, stretching her arms and legs out wildly beside her.

I leered through the window without a clue as to what she was doing. Davey came up behind me as I watched her through the window, "Yeah, it's like living with an eight year old. She does that every time it snows." Davey turned away from the window and went into the kitchen. I don't know what possessed me to do it, but I took her picture lying in the fresh powder making a snow angel.

Part of me wanted to open the door and tell her to act her age. A bigger part of me wished I had a spare set of clothes so I could go out and join her. She stood up from her snow angel, making two perfect feet marks in front of it. I eased back from the window, careful to be sure that she didn't see me watching her.

A smile formed at the memory as I passed the mile markers along the interstate. Almost a week had passed since the morning she made the snow angel. That was the image I had carried with me all week. The whole drive up to Lincoln, I was ashamed to admit it was Libby I was hoping to see. Davey was fun, and having him in my life was something that two months ago I hadn't even hoped for. But it seemed like anytime I spent more than thirty seconds with Libby, I got this outrageous adrenalin rush just being around her.

As I pulled up in front of the house, I didn't see Davey's truck or Candy's Chevelle outside. I hadn't called first. His truck not at the house meant he was at his garage. I started to pull away from the curb when I decided I could at least say hello to Libby if she were here. I knocked on the door.

Libby answered the door wearing a pair of baggy green sweat pants and a half t-shirt. My legs took a step back from the door on impulse. "Hey, I was looking for Dave. Is he here?"

She held the door with one hand and had a second wrapped around a chili cheese dog with jalapenos on top. What girl ate that for a snack? A small dribble of chili soaked through the bun and onto her hand. She shook her head as her mouth went to her palm to lick the escaping chili. "No. He and Candy went to look at a car. They should be back soon." She held the door open and offered, "C'mon in."

I looked into her bright blue eyes, trying to keep the images of Megan at bay. No matter how hard I tried, it was hard to see Libby and not think of Megan. I stomped the snow off of my boots as she held the door for me to pass. "Can I get you anything? Do you like chili dogs?"

She took an enormous bite after her offer, and I felt like a perve watching her eat it. "Uh, sure. I could eat one. You only live once, right?"

She swallowed, then corrected. "No. You only die once. You live every day."

Her words stopped me short. After spending time with her the last couple months, I knew first hand this was her mantra – this was how she lived her life. "How poetic. Coming from anyone else I'd think that more of a cliché, but you actually believe that." I did a double-take when she turned, and I got a good look at the side of her head. The little patch of scalp that had been shaved at the hospital wasn't visible at all and her hair looked several inches longer, falling halfway down her back.

Libby caught me looking and answered before I had even asked. "Hair extensions. Keeps me from having to answer questions."

She handed me a chili dog, dripping with chili, cheese, onions and jalapenos. When I tried to pick off the jalapenos, she made fun of me, "Too hot for you?"

"There are a lot of things that are too hot for me. Jalapenos are just one of those things." Our eyes locked, and I could have sworn she was purposely flirting with me. Libby didn't flirt, at least not for real; she did it as a strategy when she played pool, but flirting wasn't her thing. She was more apt to arm-wrestle a guy she was interested in. She leaned down and tucked a few dishes into the dishwasher. My eyes followed her of their own accord. Who would have thought green sweat pants could be enticing?

Davey and Candy walked through the door just as I had shoved the last of the chilidog into my mouth. "Hey, I thought that was your Mercedes outside. You're just in time. I need to go pick up a car I bought. Want to give me a ride to my shop so I can get my tow truck?"

Instead of fantasizing about Libby under those baggy green sweat pants, I opted to go help Davey pick up a car that had been living in a barn for the last four decades. When we removed the tarp it had been hiding under, I couldn't help but notice it was the same color as the ugly sweat pants Libby wore.

My next trip to Lincoln was a little earlier than normal. I knew Davey was probably still at his shop, but instead of driving there, I went to the house. I tried to tell myself that it was because I didn't want to bother him while he was working, but that was a lie. I wanted to see Libby.

She answered the door wearing a pair of khaki pants and a red collared shirt – not at all flattering, but an improvement over the green sweatpants she had worn the last time I was here. Libby had to have just gotten home or was ready to leave - this was her work uniform. It was lunchtime, but her hours were never the same two days in a row.

She smiled at me. It looked like she was glad to see me standing there. "I didn't know you were coming over today." Neither Libby, Candy nor Davey ever knew I was coming; I always showed up unannounced like a Jehovah's Witness. She held the door open to let me in.

Before I accepted her invitation to come inside, I said, "Sorry, were you leaving for work?"

"No, I just got home. Dave's still at work."

I looked at my watch as if I didn't realize it was the middle of the day. "Yeah, I got in a little earlier than normal. I didn't want to bother him. When I'm around he doesn't get much work done. I figured I'd stop here and see what you and Candy were doing."

"Candy's at school. I was going to change and go out for a bite to eat. You want to come with me?"

The invitation made my heart swell. The words were out of my mouth before I could stop them. "What about Larry?" My last trip to Lincoln, Larry and I had finally crossed paths at the house. We pretended we didn't know each other and allowed Libby to introduce us.

Her eyes narrowed. "Not that it matters, but we had a fight last night."

My heart began to speed up. *I wasn't here to see Libby. I was here to see Davey. I was just early.* I wasn't happy that Larry could be out of the picture – at least those were the words that kept cycling through my head as I tried to convince myself. "I'm sorry you and Larry had a fight. Are you okay?" That was a normal response. Anyone would ask the same. I wasn't trying to pry.

She shrugged her shoulders. "I'm fine. I'm sure he'll stop by tomorrow with some flowers and a ginormous apology."

"Flowers and an apology? What did he do?" More phrases went on repeat while she decided if she was going to answer me. *Mind your own business. Stay out of it. Don't get involved.*

"Larry's predictable. He has a couple days a month where he's out of sorts. Yesterday was one of his crabby days. From out of nowhere he gets jealous and sort of possessive. I don't do jealous or possessive very well."

Attempting to keep the smirk from forming on my lips, "Noted," was my only response. I could have guessed that without her saying it. Some women live for boyfriends to get jealous and pound their chests like primates – it's what makes them feel loved. Those are usually the ones who have self-esteem issues. If they feel neglected, they flirt in an effort to make their boyfriend jealous. I had watched it in bars more times than I could count. Libby wasn't one of those girls. She didn't need a display of testosterone to know she was desirable.

She smiled, maybe at my short response – I couldn't tell. "I'm getting a bite. You can either go with me or stay here."

"Sure. I could eat." Everyone had to eat, right? It wasn't like I was putting the moves on her. I was just keeping her company. She was going to go out anyway. I was probably saving her from doing something stupid like buying a new handbag.

"Give me five minutes. I'm going to change." Libby darted up the stairs.

I wandered around the cozy living room. I hadn't seen the house in all of its grizzly glory after Libby was attacked, but the first time I came here there was no carpet or padding on the floor in the living room and no couch. Faded red smears had been on the wall from where someone had tried to scrub the blood off. Davey hadn't wanted me to say something colossally stupid, so he pulled me into the dining room and told me that the carpet and sofa had been destroyed during Teddy's attack. I didn't want to correct him and say it had been Grey who broke in, because I didn't want him to know how much I really knew about what had gone on. This was the first trip where I noticed the room looked brand new: new carpeting was installed, the walls were painted a soft beige and new lamps stood on tables.

Libby didn't talk much about the attack. Several times I had caught her standing perfectly still, her arms wrapped around herself tightly. Her blue eyes normally so full of life took on a distant look. I'm not sure how I knew, something about the far off gaze she had; those were the times I knew she was having a flashback. When I saw that look, I did my best to come up with a question about her job, or a shot I had seen her take on a pool table, or any number of other subjects. It wasn't that I was interested in her answers; it was just my way to pull her back to the present and get her away from reliving the attack.

I had sent Teddy and Grey packing because I didn't want either of them near my brother. I wanted my two worlds separate. After getting to know Libby, if the same situation were presented, I doubted I would have let either of them go on their merry way. I loved Davey, and had been satisfied with just removing the potential threat. I saw Libby for an hour or two a week, and I had this animalistic need to seek vengeance for what had been done to her. What did that say about me?

When Libby came back into the room, she was pulling a sweater over her head as she walked into the room. I wanted to rub my eyes. She wore a pair of jeans that fit her – not just fit her, but hugged her every curve. With her arms in the air, the low-rider top of the jeans called to me. She had paired the fantastic jeans with a sweater that was big enough a second person could have crawled in there with her. It was the most hideous thing I had ever seen, a zig zag of obnoxious colors: teal, orange, purple and yellow. I pretended I hadn't had a glimpse of her with the sweater raised, and turned away to look at a picture on the living room wall as if it were the most intriguing thing my eyes had ever seen.

Libby came up behind me. I knew she was there even though her steps were silent. Her perfume was a sweet scent inviting me to turn around, but I continued looking at the picture on the wall, attempting to force the image of her from a second ago out of my head. *She's nobody. Libby's just a pal to hang out with until Davey gets off work. Nothing's going to happen.* Libby covered my eyes with her hands. I felt her body against mine while the crotch of my jeans got seriously tight. I pulled her hands away from my eyes and turned toward her in a smooth, fluid motion. My hands held hers as I looked down into her blue eyes. For a solid two seconds the two of us stood motionless.

She slipped her hands free from mine, then confessed, "I guess it's not much of a surprise if you're expecting me."

"That's the best kind of a surprise." I sounded like a douche. I desperately wished there were a way to rewind and just answer with a smartass response.

The two of us remained in place for a long second. Her eyes were heavy, like she was waiting for me to lean down and kiss her. Libby's lips were enticing: I wondered if they were as soft as they looked. Shaking off the absurd idea, I eased away, walking toward the door, holding it for her. "Grab your coat. You owe me lunch."

Libby followed me down to my car, and I held the passenger door for her. I don't know why I did it. It wasn't something I was in the habit of doing. As she got in, Libby commented, "Damn, I love this car. Larry never drove the same car twice, one of the perks of selling cars. I don't suppose you work for a Mercedes dealership, do you?"

I had carefully avoided questions about my job, never giving any information that was not absolutely necessary. After taking my place in the driver's seat, I pulled away from the curb. I had told Davey I worked at a car dealership in Kansas City; he must have shared it with her. "I do, but I don't get to take demo models home. This one's mine." Technically Lenny's, but I didn't expect her to dig through the glove box for the registration.

As we turned onto the main street, she asked, "What do you do there?"

I deflected her question, "Sales, sort of. You must have had to go into work pretty early this morning if you're already off for the day."

The few women I had spent time with loved it when conversation circled back to them. Libby, once again, proved to be a very different creature. This was my first lie to her: I wasn't a car salesman. "Yeah, I opened the store this morning. So, what kind of sales do you do?"

I needed to get her curiosity off of me. "Primarily business to business sales. Nothing direct to consumers. So, are your hours pretty consistent?"

She was on to me. Half-answers and sketchy responses weren't going to cut it. "No. I work whenever the schedule tells me to work. Sales, sort of? What kind of products do you sell to businesses?"

I didn't like the way the lie felt. Rather than tell her another one, I ignored her question entirely. "Hey, you never told me where you wanted to eat. If I'm driving, does it mean it's my choice?"

She completely ignored my question and pressed me further, "Is what you sell legal?"

My palms were sweating. I lied to everyone. It was what I did. Why did lying to Libby affect me differently? I glanced over at her narrow eyes waiting for my answer.

For some reason I didn't want to lie to Libby. Absurd, really. She was no one to me – my brother's girlfriend's roommate. I could tell her I worked in the pharmaceutical industry, or that I worked for a car dealership, or I could make something up. My answer to her question was irrelevant. The person I was in Kansas City was not the same person I was when I came here to see her – damn, to see Davey, I meant Davey. I couldn't bring myself to lie to her. Instead I pulled into a parking lot for Five Guys. "You didn't choose, so we're eating where I want."

I shut off the car, opened my door and nearly bolted out of it. Libby didn't move. As I made my way to the passenger side door, I glanced at her through the windshield – her expression was stoic, possibly angry. I stood in front of my car, watching her through the windshield. After several seconds, I walked over to her door and opened it, praying she was purposely acting like a prima donna. I opened her door, waiting for her to get out of the car. Standing there with the door open, she looked at me, but made no move to get out. I finally asked, "Are you coming?"

"You didn't answer my question."

"Sure I did. Are you coming in for a burger? Or did you want to go somewhere else?" My heart was beating so fast I was sure she could hear it where she sat.

"Take me home."

"Libby, c'mon, we're already here. My treat: let me buy you a burger."

She repeated the same words, "Take me home." Libby yanked the door out of my hand and closed it hard.

I stood in the parking lot, not sure what to do next. Why did she want to know what I did for a living? How could that possibly be of interest to her? I climbed back into the driver's seat, making no move to start the car. A full minute passed. Libby hadn't said a word since her second demand that I take her home. She didn't look at me; her gaze was fixed on the windshield in front of her. I could see anger boiling just under her skin, but for the life of me, I couldn't understand why.

When the silence got to be too much, I offered, "My job isn't who I am. It's what I do."

Libby turned toward me. Each time she and I had been near each other, she wore this amazing smile, like it was as easy for her to beam at me as it was for her to breathe. As we sat in this parking lot, her lips were in a tight scowl. "Take. Me. Home."

I began driving, but I didn't go back to her house. Something told me that if I couldn't give her an answer she was satisfied with, I would have completely blown my chance with her. I tried to remind myself for the hundredth time: *You're here to see Davey. Libby is with Larry. You can't risk Larry getting jealous. Drop her at the house and go see Davey.* Lincoln wasn't a big city, so after ten minutes, we had covered most of downtown, driven past the capital building, a university's campus and two residential neighborhoods. I didn't want to drop her off. She didn't look at me or ask any more questions. It was as if she weren't even in the car with me.

I stopped at a red light and blew out a loud puff of air. "I used to steal cars for a living. I don't do that anymore." *I'm an idiot.* The words had slid out of me while my eyes were closed. As if I couldn't see her reaction to my confession, maybe she wouldn't have one.

One eye opened halfway. She didn't even look at me. I had never been a person who was bothered by the quiet, but in the car with Libby, the quiet was deafening. I had no idea what possessed me, but I started spewing random facts. "I was really good. I learned most of it on my own. I was never caught. There wasn't any anti-theft I couldn't beat." Libby continued staring out the windshield. My words spilled out faster. "I miss that. I miss everything about it. Keep in mind, I didn't steal Corollas or Minivans – high end only. How jacked up is that? I miss being a car thief. I could see a doctor missing taking care of his patients. Or maybe a train conductor missing trains, but stealing? What kind of person misses being a thief?"

A horn sounded behind me. I had no idea how many green lights we may have sat through. I turned a corner, mainly so that the car which had just honked at me wouldn't have to drive behind me if I went into "la-la land" again. A desolate street lay in front of us. Libby hadn't said a word since we were in the Five Guys parking lot. For some reason, I couldn't stand the quiet. "I ran away from a group home when I was fifteen. I wasn't old enough for a legal job. No one would hire me. I didn't have a lot of options. I had to eat. That's why I started stealing cars."

The silence was killing me. "What do you want from me? Why do you care what I do?"

She reached across the console and put her hand on my arm. The gesture was comforting in a weird way. It wasn't a come-on, or if it were, it didn't feel like one. For the first time, she spoke, "I just want the truth."

"The truth is I've done lots of things I'm not proud of."

She didn't remove her hand from my arm. Instead she gave it a reassuring squeeze. "Pull over into the park over here." Libby motioned to a small parking lot that hugged a little park with a swing set, basketball court and a slide. A few young kids were on the swings. An exhausted mom sat on a park bench.

When the car was parked, I expected her to let loose with a tirade of conclusions she had drawn. I wondered if she planned to storm off and walk back to her house. I even thought she might go into a full-blown "bitch-fest," telling me what a loser she believed me to be. She didn't. "If you are so ashamed of what you do that you can't talk about it – then maybe you need to stop doing it."

I struggled to find an appropriate answer. There wasn't one. She was right. I eased my hands off of the steering wheel and onto my lap. When I turned to meet her gaze, her voice was low and sweet. "Thank you." I was dumbfounded as to what she could possibly be thanking me for. "Candy told me what you did for us. She said you told Grey and Teddy they had to leave town. I don't know who you are or why those two were so scared of you, but I'm glad you did what you did."

"You do know me."

"No. I know who you want me to see. If you were a cardboard cut-out, you would be perfect. You are handsome, funny, you dress nice, and you are someone I'd like to spend some time with. But you're not cardboard. You're a person, and I need to know who you really are."

"I'm twenty-two. I've lived on my own since I was fifteen. I've done things that are less than ideal. Isn't that enough?"

Libby took my hand. "Here's what I know: You were a delinquent. The night Candy and I met Teddy – you scared the shit out of him. You told him to be respectful of me when you didn't know me. You went out of your way to help Candy when it served no purpose for you. You ran Grey and Teddy out of town for what they did to me, but you refused to tell the cops who they were. You are good at the superficial, but if I wanted someone superficial, I'd be with Larry right now. When you are ready to let me in and let me meet the real Mark – then we can talk about something more." She turned away from me, looking out into the sunshine. "I'm going to walk home. It's beautiful out."

I reached for her arm, holding her in place. She looked at my hand, then raised her eyelashes, her blue eyes staring directly at mine. Before I could talk myself out of it, I cupped her jaw and pulled her mouth to mine. Her lips were closed, but I coaxed them into opening. Her breath was minty and sweet. Libby's delicate cheek went to the side of my face as she pulled her lips away from mine. "You're a good kisser, too. See, I learn more about you every day." Her smile diminished, her voice quieter, "Your secret is safe. I won't tell Candy or Dave about your first job."

Libby kissed my cheek, reached for the door handle and walked away, not in a huff or a hurry. She stepped onto the sidewalk, closed her eyes, and lifted her face into the sunshine. I rolled my window down to get a better view. After a few seconds, she glanced over her shoulder, waved and walked off.

Her comment stunned me silent. Why had I confessed all that to her? What made me spill so much about my past. For what? A kiss? Had I officially turned into a love-sick puppy? This wasn't me. Women came on to me. I didn't chase them. I didn't even want a girl. I watched her walk down the sidewalk. The way her hips swayed, I decided it must have been those jeans that made me forget who I was.

Her word earlier stung: *superficial*. Was that supposed to be a slam? She thought I didn't have enough depth? I could be deep. I only took this stupid job with Johnny so I could pay back a dead girl. How's that for deep? How many Megans had Libby met? What had she done to help them? What was she willing to give up? Then it hit me: I was finally where Chad and I both wanted me to be four years ago. I was at a place where I could make a difference when I told Chad the deal was off. She was right; I was only good at the superficial.

I made that deal with Chad before I knew Davey was still alive. If I'd have known, I never would have done something so stupid. I'd still be working on Lenny's crew lifting cars, and I could do whatever I wanted. None of my decisions could have any impact on Davey if I were still working for Lenny.

Lenny warned me about this before Johnny moved me up. He told me to turn it down. Lenny still had a lot of pull. He knew I had found Davey. If anyone knew how I could unscrew my life – he'd know. I'd already given Chad enough information to put me away for twenty to life; but since the operation had changed so much the last couple months, none of it would put a dent in the drugs coming in from Mexico. The whole thing was too big, too sophisticated for a local police department to do anything about.

CHAPTER 18

BAM! I ducked, sure a bullet had been fired at me. I reached under my seat, yanked my handgun free, and sat up quickly, ready to return fire. A little kid, maybe seven or eight, ran up to the side of my car.

"I'm sorry, mister." He picked up his basketball from the ground beside my car. I wasn't sure if he had used a catapult to throw it or if he was creating a new sport – smashball. I lowered my gun to the floor of the driver's seat, willing my heart to ease back out of cardiac range. The kid wore denim overalls, a green t-shirt, and a pair of tennis shoes missing the rubber that had been worn off of the toes. His mother was at my car a few seconds after the child's apology. "Oh my God, I'm so sorry. He dented your car. He didn't mean to do it. I'll pay for the damages."

I took in the woman's horror as her eyes rested on the front fender of my car. Her clothes were clean, but as worn as the kid's shoes. Her hair was tied back in a ponytail that fell mid-way down her back. The dark circles under her eyes weren't covered with make-up. I could almost see the dollar signs scrolling through her head as she looked at my damaged fender.

Here was a mom who needed a cape. Nobody gets circles under their eyes like that unless they have track marks on their arms or are exhausted. She didn't have the gaunt look of a drug user. The mom was at the park with her son, watching him play basketball even when the kid was about two feet too short to have a fighting chance at the hoop. She wasn't screaming at him. She didn't ignore the accident. I was envious. Maybe she didn't know how expensive parts were for a Mercedes, but repairing a dent on any car wasn't cheap, yet she was offering to make good on the accident.

I shook my head at her offer. "It's no big deal. I know a great body guy."

She fumbled in her purse, pulled out a pen and scrawled on a grocery receipt. "Here's my name and address. Have the garage send me a bill. I'm so sorry."

I shook my head and brushed her slip of paper away. "No. I was parked too close to the basketball court. I saw him playing when I pulled up." My attention moved to the boy who looked like he was about to cry, "It's called an accident for a reason. You didn't do it on purpose. Keep working on your jump shot."

The mother stood beside my car, beaming at her son. She asked, "You're sure? I have some money saved up, really, it was our fault."

Her word choice warmed me, "our fault." She wasn't screaming at her son the way moms do in shopping malls. She wasn't belittling the kid. She was acting the way moms are supposed to act.

"No. Keep doing what you're doing. He's a lucky kid." My response confused her, but I didn't make any effort to elaborate, neither did I get out of the car to look at the damage. I wouldn't have cared if the basketball had put a hole in the fender. Financially, I was sure I was in a much better position to pay for it than she was. What I wouldn't have given for that lady to be our mom. I turned on the car and decided to go see Davey.

I wandered into Davey's lobby. He was elbow deep in a car I couldn't even recognize. The engine, seats, dashboard and tires were gone. The body of the car was naked, and he was sanding it, readying it for paint. He cut the power to the sander, lifted his safety glasses and removed his respirator. Davey's eyes lit up when he saw it was me standing a few feet away from him. "Hey, I didn't know you were coming today!"

"I don't want to interrupt. I was in town and thought I'd stop by. I see you're busy."

He shook his head. "Never too busy for you. How long are you here for?"

"A couple hours. I got here a little after noon."

Davey smiled brightly, "Here to see me or Libby?"

My back arched at his accusation. "You. Why would you think I came up here to see Libby?"

"Oh, come on. I've seen your googly eyes looking at her. Go ahead and pretend you don't know what I'm talking about. She worked this morning, so she's probably at the house right now if you want to stop by and see her."

"I came to see you, Moron." He looked at me sideways, and I couldn't help it, "Besides, I already saw her before I came here."

Davey let out a hearty laugh and patted me on the back. "I knew it! Your timing is pretty good. She and Larry had a huge fight last night. He stormed out of the house saying he was done with her." Dave added conspiratorially, "Between you and me, Candy hates Larry."

Even though Davey made it sound like he was letting me in on a secret family recipe, Candy made no bones about her dislike of the guy. She toned it down in front of Libby, but the eye rolls and behind-the-back glares were easy to catch.

Davey prodded, "So what gives? I know she's into you, so ask her out already."

"Like for lunch? Been there, done that."

"You took her to lunch? Where'd you go?"

"Crash and burn, little brother. I got us as far as Five Guys parking lot before I said something to piss her off. I think the dating gods have decided I'm not supposed to have a girlfriend."

"The dating gods? And you called *me* a moron?"

"Yeah, I don't want to talk about it." I pointed to my car out on the street. "I got a dent today from a kid with a basketball. You got time to take a look at it?"

"Hanging out at parks with kids? Practicing for something?"

"What are you, a girl?" Davey's grin was the only answer he gave me. And once his accusation sunk in that I was practicing for future father duties, I spit out, "Bite your tongue."

There was something about Davey, aside from him being my brother. He really believed anything was possible. He saw himself with the white picket fence, the mortgage, the Christmas programs at school, and the little league games. That wasn't even close to what we had had. How can you dream about something that has never existed for you? Maybe that was something Candy offered him. She had grown up in a normal home. Maybe her childhood stories had become his fantasies.

I didn't see any of that for me. Libby was a blast to hang out with. She was funny and sexy, smart and smart-mouthed – someone I enjoyed being around. But I had never seen myself in any kind of a relationship. Sure I'd been with a lot of girls, but none were ever what I would categorize as a girlfriend. Libby was sort of in a category all her own. Nothing frightened her, or if it did, she rarely let it show.

Davey was staring at me like he was waiting for me to lay out a plan on how I was going to win Libby over. "Nothing's up. She's a unicorn."

He stood up straight, eyeing me like I was the one who had grown a horn. "A unicorn? What the hell does that mean?"

"Libby can play pool better than any guy I've ever met. She eats burgers and fries. She doesn't drink diet soda. She can recite every line from every James Bond movie ever made – even the old ones. Libby does what makes herself happy. Girls like her don't exist – she's a unicorn."

Davey's smile grew. "She and Candy are like sisters."

"And you and I are like brothers."

Dave punched me in the arm. "We are brothers, you bonehead."

"Oh, that's right. I keep forgetting."

Davey started for his office, which was preferable because I liked the couch he kept in there rather than standing on the cement floor in the garage. He stopped in the doorway and said, "That reminds me. I had a weird referral yesterday. Said he knew you."

I froze. No one up this way should know me. "Oh yeah. Who was it?"

"His name was Oscar. He brought up a '65 Mustang. It was in pretty decent shape, not nearly as bad as most of the cars I see – all original. He wanted me to gut it and put in a new engine, transmission, air conditioning. Basically, he wanted me to build a new car but leave the old frame around it."

The words came out hoarsely. "You said Oscar? What did he look like?" I didn't need the description; I only knew one Oscar.

"Older guy, white hair, wore a suit. That was the funny thing. He had the car hauled up from Kansas City on a flat bed, but it was one hundred percent drivable." He pointed to the orange-red colored Mustang a few bay doors over. "I don't see many originals that are in as good a shape as his. I tried to talk him out of gutting it, but he wasn't hearing it. The guy drove a new Mercedes, same as yours. Is that someone you work with?"

My heart sank to my stomach. I thought I was so smart. I should have seen it coming. Oscar and Johnny asked me about my real identity. How had they found Davey so quickly? My biggest fear, that my two worlds would collide, was happening right in front of me.

I got up in Davey's face, unable to keep the fear from oozing out of me. "What did he say?"

"Easy. I just told you. What's wrong? You look like you saw a ghost."

"That's it? He said I had sent him to you?"

Davey responded slowly, "Yeah, that's what he said. Are you okay?"

"Fine. Hey, I just remembered, I've got an appointment tomorrow morning. I need to go."

Davey stepped in front of me, blocking my egress. "Mark, stop. What the hell is going on?"

I shook my head. My mind wouldn't allow my mouth to form words. Fear pulsed through me. If Oscar was up yesterday, he must have suspected something for a while. Did he know about Davey the day they had asked me about my identity? No, they couldn't have known. He would have asked me about my brother instead of my widow.

Oscar wanted me to know he'd found Davey – he'd told Davey that I had referred him. I pushed past my brother to get to my car.

Everything seemed to be happening in slow motion. Davey followed me to my car. I tried to close my door, but his beefy hand held it ajar, his voice unsteady as he was trying to figure out what was wrong. "Mark, what is it?" I looked up at him, unable to explain the fear I was sure was on my face. He must have decided I wasn't going to answer. His eyes roved to my fender, "What about your dent? If you give me a few minutes, I can pull it out and do any touch ups the next time you're in town. When are you coming back?"

"I'm not sure. Soon, I hope. I'll call you in a couple days." I started to pull the door out of his grip, but stopped. I didn't know what was waiting for me in Kansas City. If I weren't coming back, I didn't want his last memory of me to be this. I eased out of my car while Davey watched with a dumbfounded look and grabbed him with both arms, hard. "I love you, Davey."

Davey hugged me back. "Come inside and tell me what's going on." Looking into the mirror, which was my brother's face, his eyes pleaded with mine.

I couldn't. There were no words. I stood there holding onto my little brother, the brother I had never expected to have again. My vision clouded. I couldn't lose him again – not to Johnny, not to anyone. "I need to go. I'll be back as soon as I can."

I let go of him, but he kept holding on. I patted his back, offering comfort when I could offer no words of explanation. His words were muffled as he spoke them while he clung to me. "It's bad, right?"

"No." I lied. "It's no big deal. Do a good job on his Mustang." He let go. I tried to avoid his eyes as I opened the door and sat back in my car. Davey watched me. I offered him nothing: no explanation, no reassurance. I pulled out of his little parking lot and glanced in my rearview: Davey hadn't moved. His legs were planted as he watched me drive away.

CHAPTER 19

The drive back to Kansas City was a blur. Finding Oscar was the only thing I could think of doing. Telling Davey that I had referred him was genius on his part. He made sure that I would confront him as soon as I learned of their meeting. Oscar and I were on good terms. If this were no big deal to him, he would have mentioned it. The fact that he didn't scared the shit out of me.

I didn't call first. Oscar worked in an office at Johnny's sports complex. He could have worked anywhere; his duties weren't tied to anything in the building. I had always believed he chose this location because there was relatively little traffic when games weren't going on, but he had his own reserved parking spot right near the front door if there was a game he wanted to see. I walked into Oscar's office; there was no one else around.

Oscar's office had been decorated by whoever had done the other offices. Sports memorabilia peppered the walls: photographs of football teams, a signed helmet in a display case. Red and white walls trimmed with metal gave it an industrial feel. A fake potted plant stood in a corner. His desk was tasteful but not extravagant.

He looked up from the papers on his desk, registering no surprise at seeing me standing in his office unannounced.

"How's it going, Mark? I haven't seen you much the last few weeks. Dealership's numbers are looking good."

Ignoring his compliment on the transition to the local dealership, I wanted him to know I got his message. "I took today off. I just got back from Lincoln."

Oscar leaned back in his chair. "Ah, I see." He gestured to one of the chairs in front of his desk. "Have a seat."

None of the adrenalin in my body had waned from the moment I heard Oscar had been to see Davey. It still pulsed through me like hot embers in my blood. I did as I was told and took a seat in one of the overstuffed leather wingback chairs directly in front of him. "You met Dave." It wasn't a question. It wasn't an accusation. This was merely me stating a fact.

Oscar slid his weathered fingers through his snowy white hair. "I wouldn't have believed it if I hadn't seen it with my own eyes. You've been holding out on us."

I was unsure if he was referring to how much Dave and I looked alike, or the fact that I had a brother I was hiding from Johnny. "I don't know what you're talking about. My brother has nothing to do with what I do for Johnny. There was no reason to introduce you to him."

"You purposely hid him from us. Do you deny it?"

"Hid him? Why would I deny that I have a brother? You met him – he's not exactly someone I'm ashamed of."

"Johnny and I were both under the impression that you had no family. Maybe there is a reason you didn't want us to know he existed?"

I needed to choose my words carefully. I hadn't hidden Davey from them for a long time, just the last couple months. Technically I didn't hide him; I just never mentioned that I'd found him. When I told them both I didn't have any family, at the time, I had thought Davey was dead. "I have a mom somewhere, too. Have you paid her a visit? If not, you should give her a try – I bet she doesn't remember that I was ever in her womb."

Oscar's brows raised, likely trying to determine if I had just slammed him or my mother. So much for choosing my words carefully. I took in a breath and let it out slowly. "I mean, yeah, I found Dave a couple months ago. We were both in foster care from the time we were little. When I was eleven, the state told me he had died. I didn't know they screwed up stuff like that."

"If you thought he was dead, how did you find him?"

Truth. I couldn't afford for Oscar to catch me in a lie – I didn't know how much he knew or where his information had come from. A familiar tingle spread over me, as this was the same thing I had thought when I was talking to Libby earlier today. "I met his girlfriend in a bar. You saw that the two of us look a lot alike. She thought I was Dave. Once she convinced me she was on the level, she introduced us."

"That seems like a pretty fantastic coincidence, or at the very least some exciting news. You didn't share it with anyone here."

I had told Lenny. His advice was to keep Davey a secret. Instead of defending my decision or Lenny's advice, I shrugged my shoulders and answered, "I don't know where your siblings live."

Oscar's eyes narrowed. "Say that again."

I was coming dangerously close to crossing a line. "I said, I don't know if you have any brothers or sisters. If you do, I don't know where they live. It didn't occur to me that you would want to know about mine."

"So, when I brought the fact to your attention that we knew you were using a dead man's identity, you didn't think telling Johnny and me about your brother would have put our mind at ease that you weren't some sort of a plant trying to infiltrate the organization?"

"You really think that?" I didn't wait for his answer. "No. You didn't ask me who my family was. You asked me why my wife thought I was dead. I've never lied to you. Not about this, not about anything."

Oscar studied me for a long minute. "So, all those days you disappear on your days off, is it safe to assume you are in Lincoln?"

My heart hitched. For two years I had been predictable. When I wasn't working, I was still easy to find. That's what this was about. That's why Oscar was looking into my background. He or Johnny must have looked for me and couldn't find me. That's why they started digging. "Yeah. I've been going up there to see him about once a week for the last two months."

Oscar looked less pissed and more curious, "What does he think you do?"

"Nothing."

Oscar's curiosity fled in favor of a frustrated expression. "Nothing? I find that hard to believe."

Defensively, I answered. "I don't know what he thinks. I told him I worked at a car dealership. He never asked for any details, and I never offered any."

Oscar seemed to mull this over. Still leaned back in his chair, his eyes left mine and rested on the ceiling. I started cycling through all the answers I had given him, wondering what he would pull out of his bag of tricks next. Without pulling his gaze from the ceiling above him, he simply offered, "Cincinnati."

I was confused. Oscar's eyes returned to mine. He looked tired, wrinkles hung heavy on his face; gravity was winning the battle with his skin. "I have a brother who lives in Cincinnati, Ohio. He's a school teacher. He should have retired last year, but he's worried if he quits he won't have a reason to get up in the morning and he'll die. I see him twice a year." I didn't know how to respond.

Oscar's expression lightened when he continued, "It isn't a secret. Johnny has to know who your family is. The cops can be ruthless, and they've been known to lean on family members to coerce Johnny's employees. We've seen it a lot over the years. If Johnny knows who is important to you, then he knows who to protect. I've worked for Johnny for a long time. Johnny may not run things in Cincinnati, but you can be sure if a stray bullet were to pierce my brother, there would be repercussions all the way from Kansas City."

Oscar telling me where his brother lived baffled me. His explanation of why Johnny wanted to know about family members was a stark contrast to what Lenny had told me four years ago, but if it were true, it meant I didn't have to worry about something happening to Davey. At least so long as I wasn't helping Chad, Davey would be fine. I sat quietly waiting for him to elaborate. "You do your job. You stay smart. You keep your family in the dark about what you do, but never be afraid to tell Johnny about problems they're having. Johnny has great Karma; he has the innate ability to make problems disappear."

I nodded. Oscar shuffled a few papers around on his desk. I sat there for several minutes waiting to hear what was coming next. But nothing. He pretended I wasn't in the room.

I cleared my throat. When he looked up, all he said was, "This matter is over."

I didn't know what to think. Ever since I learned Davey was still alive, I was sure if Johnny found out about him I'd be putting Davey's life in jeopardy. Had I worried about that for nothing? Lenny warned me about trying to quit Johnny and how he could influence me once he knew I had family. Was that what Oscar did this week? He was making sure that I knew they had dug into my past – that Johnny had leverage on me that he hadn't had last week?

I stood up slowly. Oscar and I had always gotten along okay, so I decided to ask why he didn't see his brother more often. "Hey, Oscar?" He looked up from his papers. "You said you see your brother only twice a year?"

A small grin formed on his lips. He answered my unspoken question. "I would see him more often if he were closer." He set the papers on his desk and leaned back into his chair again. "It's no secret that I was worried Johnny had promoted you too quickly. I was concerned that you were too young to shoulder this type of responsibility. At every turn you have proved me wrong. I'm glad you found your brother. He seems like a good kid."

These words were Oscar's dismissal. As I walked down the cement steps of the sports complex, an enormous weight lifted off of me. No harm would come to Davey if I kept doing what I was doing. Oscar, Johnny, hell, maybe even Felix knew I had a brother – it was going to be fine so long as I didn't quit Johnny's crew. So long as I kept doing what I was doing, I'd be fine and so would Davey.

I walked up to my car. The dent in my fender was more obvious since I was no longer thinking of all the worst scenarios with Johnny and Davey. I needed to have it repaired and didn't know how soon I'd be able to break away and return to Lincoln. No one would expect me at the dealership today – it was almost closing time. If I stopped over now, I could get it in the shop and grab a loaner at the same time. I phoned the receptionist, who patched me into the service department. The Service Department Supervisor came on the line, "What's up, Mark?"

"I had an accident earlier today. I need to drop off my car and pick up another one."

"Okay. What do you want to drive, and I'll have it ready for you."

"Anything's fine. I'll be there in about fifteen minutes."

As I hung up the phone, I glanced in my rearview mirror only to see police lights flashing behind me. What the hell? I looked at the speedometer – I wasn't speeding. There hadn't been any lights or stop signs for the last several blocks that I could have inadvertently driven through. I pulled to the side of the road to let the police car pass me. It tucked in behind my car – not what I needed right now.

Reaching into the glove box, I pulled the leather pouch where I kept the car's registration and proof of insurance. I took out my driver's license and lowered my window. When I looked up at the cop who had pulled me over, I froze – my hand hanging in midair.

Chad stood beside my door. I started to offer my paperwork to him, but stopped. He gestured for me to give it to him. "Hand it over in case someone is watching."

I didn't. "Why did you pull me over?"

"I wanted to know if you were okay."

Yeah, I bet. "I'm fine. I told you, the deal's off."

"Can we meet somewhere? Just to talk."

I growled, "No. Chad, I'm out."

"Nothing's changed. I'm still going after Johnny. I'll do it with your help or without it."

"Fine. Do it without my help. Are you done?"

"No. We're not done. What's going on? You told me about the remote dealerships. We've had surveillance on them for the last couple weeks. There is no action. Half of those salespeople don't even work there anymore; the ones that do aren't doing any tricked-out trades like you described."

"Things have changed. You waited too long to act on the information I gave you. I told you – I'm out. If you aren't going to arrest me, I'm leaving."

"Mark, look, I've got ATF and the FBI involved. We're coming up with big goose eggs. I need your help or this is going to get shut down."

Relief spread through me. So long as they couldn't do anything with the information I gave him, Davey would be safe. "You had your chance. You didn't act when you needed to. Either give me a ticket or leave me alone."

Chad put both hands on my window. "This isn't you, Mark. Look, I know you're way up in the organization now. Just meet with me. I promise it'll be somewhere safe."

Through gritted teeth, I answered, "You're not listening. I'm out."

Chad's voice hardened. "Either help me or you're going down with him. I've got enough to put you away for a long time. I don't want to do that."

He looked like the scared kid I remembered – it didn't match the tough words he had just spewed at me. The reason I agreed to help him didn't hold water anymore. When he had let me off the grand theft charge, I didn't have a reason not to help him.

Chad carried a folder in his hand. He opened it and handed me a picture of a kid, "You see this? His name was Grant Miller. He was fifteen. Grant was killed yesterday. You know why? Because he skimmed off the top." I didn't need Chad to explain any more than that. The photograph was a kid wearing blue jeans, a white t-shirt, and only one white tennis shoe. The other shoe was twenty feet away from the body as if he had run so fast that he had run right out of it. The kid had been shot in the back. It was a small caliber slug, because most of his face was still intact around the exit wound.

Mules carried a very precise weight of drugs, which was measured before they departed and measured again at delivery. If a carrier was short, then he needed to dig through the lint in his pocket to find the missing pieces.

Chad reached back into the folder and pulled out another picture of a bloody teenager. "She was Heather. That was last week. She was almost an adult." The photo showed Heather's body lying distorted on the ground, blood pooled next to her. Long auburn hair fanned out in the red liquid seeping into the asphalt beside her. Her hands lay at her sides. If the blood hadn't been there, she could have passed for someone sleeping.

I didn't know either of them. Fifteen – that was how old I was when Megan kept me from dying of exposure. She was dead the next day. The same job. The same risks. The same result. "Dammit, Chad." I shoved the photos back at him. "What do you want from me? I get it. It sucks. Kids are dying because of drugs. Kids die all the time. Stopping Johnny doesn't fix any of it. If he's out of the picture, someone else moves in."

Chad's hands gripped the folder, his knuckles white from the strain. He sounded like the kid I remembered when he asked, "What if we can save one? What if just one kid lives because you helped me put Johnny away? That one kid could grow up and make a difference. I'm not asking for much. I'm tired of burying kids. Just. . .help me."

I shook my head, my voice nearly unrecognizable when I whispered, "I can't. I've got too much to lose. I can't get out now even if I wanted to."

I started to put the car in gear when Chad's voice hung in the air. "Heather's funeral was two days ago." He rubbed his cheek with his knuckles. "She was a runaway. She grew up right here on the lower eastside of town. Her mom was working two jobs doing the best she could. She shouldn't have buried her daughter. I was there, Mark. I promised her mom that I'd find the guy who did this. If you won't help me bring Johnny down, tell me who did this."

"How would I know? I don't handle the mules anymore."

"She wasn't just a mule. She was a girl. She was seventeen. She took a little off the top. Someone killed her for it. Tell me who killed her."

Chad had lost it. He was coming apart at the seams. I recognized the look: it was the same feeling I had when I was helpless to help Megan. I needed to tread lightly, but a couple questions couldn't hurt. "Look, I can ask around. If I find anything out, I'll call you."

As if he didn't believe me, he leaned in through my window. "Her mom deserves justice. She needs peace. I just need a name. Somebody has to know something."

"I'll see what I can do. Johnny doesn't like this sort of thing, either. It's bad for business. I'll look into it."

I drove away, leaving Chad standing in the middle of the street gripping his folder. His words on replay in my head: *What if we can save one?* That wasn't some lofty goal. That was doable. Maybe I didn't like what I had become, but the idea that I could save one kid resonated from deep inside me. I couldn't save them all, but in my position, I could make changes to make sure no more Heathers, or Grants, or Megans died over less money than a pair of tennis shoes.

A plan started to form. If the mules carried a container that they couldn't access, none would be able to skim drugs off the top. Or better yet, most of them who tried to steal drugs didn't use it themselves; they traded the meth rocks for food, or money to go to the Goodwill. I could set something up, like a safe house, one that had food in the refrigerator, heat in the winter, and a toilet that flushed.

When I arrived at the dealership, I drove into the service entrance. A small SUV was waiting for me as my Mercedes was taken into the body shop. I noticed Johnny's Bentley was parked around the side of the building. After my meeting with Oscar, I felt like I needed to be sure Johnny and I were okay.

I went inside to find Johnny meeting with two men and a woman in his office. I didn't recognize any of them. The woman wore a fitted black suit and tall heels – someone who sat at a desk most days. Her face was slender, she wore her hair in an elegant twist, and from her posture, it looked like she was the one calling the shots. The men both wore gray suits and both blended into the background. I gave Johnny a wave through the glass wall. He held up a finger instructing me to wait, but pushed a button on his desk and turned his glass opaque.

Whoever he was talking to, he didn't want me to know. It wasn't like Johnny to keep much from me. When I was a lower level guy, everything was compartmentalized. Everyone on his crew operated on a "need to know" basis, but ever since I had taken over security on his estate – there was nothing he kept from me.

Who were those three? What didn't he want me to see? Since Oscar had told him about Davey, did he think I was keeping things from him? I took a seat in my office. It was kitty-cornered from Johnny's. It didn't allow for a direct field of view into his, but I'd be able to see when the glass was clear again.

My conversation with Chad kept playing in my head. He pulled me over to show me pictures of two dead kids. Johnny was a businessman. If Chad ever did put Johnny away, someone else would step in. Lew from Dallas had been to Johnny's estate once. He traveled with his own entourage. Lew was a lot like Johnny from the business aspect, but was nothing like Johnny when it came to people skills. One of Lew's guys didn't do a perimeter sweep fast enough; Lew slapped him in front of everyone. Lew's southern drawl was not something easily forgotten, "Son, you run around this house until I get tired. You stop before I get tired, and you'll be flying home in a pine box."

That guy ran full throttle for the first half hour, jogged for the next few laps, walked for a while then barely staggered while he circled Johnny's house over and over. Johnny would never treat any of his people that way. You could tell Lew ruled by threats and fear – Johnny wasn't like that. If Johnny were out of the picture and were replaced by someone like Lew. . .I shivered at the thought.

Somehow, subconsciously, I knew I was trying to justify my decision not to help Chad. But his latest request wasn't about bringing Johnny down. He was looking for someone in the organization who killed a mule. All the mules still reported to Kerry. I hadn't seen Kerry since the night I roughed up the dealer who split his lip several months ago.

I scrolled through the contacts on my phone. Before I looked into this, I needed to be sure Johnny and I were still okay. I set my phone on the desk and saw my fax machine had a list waiting for me. It was the VINs for the engines that would be coming in from Chihuahua next week. Five. Not bad. Having done this for over a month, I knew an identical fax was also setting on a fax machine at the assembly plant. If anyone were to stumble onto the piece of paper, there was no coversheet or words explaining what the numbers meant. As far as I knew, and as far as Johnny's IT guys knew, there was no way to intercept or decrypt a secure fax. This was the safest way to transmit data.

Johnny walked into my office as I was filing the latest list and shredding the one from the previous week. Johnny's voice had an edge to it. "Today was your day off. I wasn't expecting to see you today."

"Yeah, my fender caught a basketball earlier. The body shop is fixing it for me." Johnny stood just inside my doorway. He wasn't glaring and didn't look angry. If Oscar hadn't called him after I walked out, I wanted Johnny to know the two of us had talked. "I, uh, came here after I left Oscar."

Johnny's lips pursed together in two thin lines as his head bobbed slowly. Before he could accuse me of hiding things from him I stood up and closed the door. "I didn't tell you. I just found Dave a couple months ago. I thought he was dead."

He was a man of few words. "I don't like secrets." My reasons could have been infallible and it wouldn't have made a difference. In his mind I had deceived him. I didn't need for him to say it – I knew him inside and out.

The fact that Johnny didn't like secrets would have been laughable if he weren't two feet away and staring at me like I held the secret recipe for his favorite cannoli. "I wasn't thinking. Dave is great. I mean, he's twenty, he owns his own business – he's perfect. I didn't want to screw anything up for him."

Johnny took a seat and motioned for me to do the same. "You thought I would involve myself in your brother's life? That's why you didn't tell me?"

"Shit. I don't know what I was thinking. I thought he was dead. When I stumbled on him just a few hours from here – I didn't know what to do."

Johnny's gaze was stern. "I have to be able to trust you. I can't have someone, you, hiding things from me. I trusted you. I invited you into my home. You took care of my daughters. I kept nothing from you."

"I know, Johnny. I'm sorry. I was stupid."

"You ever wonder how a kid like yourself moves up in my organization so fast?"

Hundreds of times. I was the only one in his circle under forty. Even his mid-level bosses had all been around longer than I had. "Right place at the right time?"

He shook his head. "You don't let any of this go to your head." He poked me hard in the temple with his finger. "You are always where you say you are going to be - always. A couple weeks ago I wanted to run something by you, so I went to Lenny's – you weren't there. He didn't know where you were. I went to your apartment – no Mark. I called the Ops Center – they said you were gone for the day. You aren't in my clubs. You just vanish one day every week."

I didn't deny it. Here I had been so proud that I had no pattern when I went to see Davey, but my pattern was that I wasn't in Kansas City. Of course, Johnny would go looking for me. Before I met Davey, the only time I set foot out of Kansas City was when I was doing trades for Johnny. He put his hand on my knee in a reassuring way, "It turns out it's for a good reason. Oscar tells me you are visiting family every trip. Then I wonder why you would keep this from me."

"I was stupid."

"Yeah, you were stupid." He looked at me, studying me as if I were a complex equation. "You see, when you disappeared, I worried you might be meeting with the law. I questioned your loyalty."

I should have denied it. An innocent person would be screaming to high heaven at the accusation. I didn't. I stayed quiet for a full minute, weighing how much I could say without getting a bullet to my chest. "There's this cop. His name's Chad. We grew up in the same group home a couple hours east of here in Jefferson City. He stopped me today."

Johnny said nothing. He didn't look remotely surprised, either. His calm gave me the willies. "I wouldn't say we're friends, but I have fed him information different times. Nothing that would implicate you, but yeah, slime that I wanted rotting in jail, I nudged him in the right direction. He pulled me over today after I left Oscar. Chad told me two of our mules were killed in the last couple weeks."

This information wasn't what he was expecting. Johnny didn't flinch; he was waiting for me to say more. "He asked if I could look into who killed them. Chad isn't sure what I do in the organization, but he knows I've got a soft spot for the kids who move drugs around the city. Do you mind if I call Kerry and see what he knows?"

Johnny didn't answer my question. Instead he said, "You know your friend has been watching you for six months. That friend of yours has followed you to every remote dealership. He has enough surveillance to put you away for life. You still want to help him?"

Johnny didn't believe I had fed information to Chad. He believed Chad had done it on his own. But how would Johnny know what Chad has on me? Then Chad's words came back to me from four years ago, "*You'll never show up in any of my reports.*" Johnny had someone on the inside, but Chad had protected me all along. "Yeah, I do. I just want to find out what Kerry knows. If he doesn't know anything, I'll leave it alone."

"It's not our place to interfere with how the dealers deal with their employees."

I argued, "When the carriers worked for me – it was my place. No one, not one dealer laid a finger on the mules."

Johnny nodded. "I know. That was something I liked about you. You want to switch positions with Kerry?"

What was Johnny asking? Did I want to be demoted? He wouldn't let me step down, would he? Instead of taking Johnny's bait, I answered, "I don't like that kids are getting killed. Sure, some of them are bad news. But most of them are scared and surviving the only way they can. When I first moved here – that could have been me."

"You have an interesting perspective, one that I would be a fool to ignore. Go ahead and call Kerry. Find out what happened. Before you talk to your friend again, I want to know what Kerry tells you. Understood?"

"I will. Thanks, Johnny."

"Aren't you going to ask me about the three people in my office?"

"No. You'll tell me if I need to know who they are."

Johnny smiled, "I told you I don't like secrets; I don't hide things from you on purpose. I blocked the glass in my office because Felix was following you, and he didn't need to know who I was meeting with. The three do real estate acquisitions for me. If you see her again, her name is Ashley." He held his hand in the air as if he were making a phone call; the gesture was his way of reminding me to call Kerry. I didn't waste a second; grabbing my phone, I scrolled to Kerry's contact number.

He answered in the usual way. Acknowledging that he knew it was me on the line, but not saying my name. "Hey, Boss. Something must be wrong if you're calling."

"Yeah, a little. You got a minute to meet with me?"

"Sure. Spikes?"

Johnny owned a bar called Spikes Sports Bar that was just a few blocks from the dealership. "Perfect. I'll leave now."

I had spent a lot of time at Spikes. The bar tuned in every game broadcast. Twenty large screens hung along the walls, each able to display a different event. Kerry must have been at the bar when I called, because it took me less than ten minutes to arrive after we hung up, and Kerry was already at a table with a cold one in front of him when I walked through the door.

I took a seat beside him. Kerry was wearing one of his bright white shirts and a tie, just like always. I had offered Kerry my job when I took the promotion on Johnny's estate, but Kerry was happy where he was at, not interested in moving up. Given what had happened to Haden in Sioux Falls, Kerry had made a good choice. I liked him. Things ran smoothly most of the time; when issues arose, he didn't have a tendency to blame anyone else. He fixed whatever the problem was and moved on. Kerry cut to the chase. "What can I do for you, Boss?"

"You've had a lot of problems with deliveries lately?"

Kerry shook his head and blew out a breath slowly, "A few. Did Johnny get word of what happened to Grant yesterday?"

"Yeah. Heather last week, too." Technically, I hadn't gotten into the details on either with Johnny, but he told me I could ask questions about how two kids ended up dead.

"Shit. They both skimmed. They all know the rules. They get paid to move product from point A to point B. They take it – it's up to the dealer to figure out how they pay for the missing product."

"Two different dealers?"

Kerry shook his head. "No. Xavier both times."

Xavier moved almost twice as much as all the other dealers who bought from Johnny. He was seriously paranoid, a side-effect of having a long-term habit. When the mules reported to me, he was one of the reasons I implemented the rules that dealers were not to deal directly with any of the carriers. If the dealers had a problem, they brought the problem to me. "Did you go see Xavier and ask how much he was short?"

"No. He called me this morning. Told me if I couldn't get carriers I could trust, that he was going to go back to cooking his own." That was a hollow threat. It didn't matter if he intended to make good on it or not, the Mexicans' quality was high, and they sold theirs for less than the local guys could make it themselves.

"You got any reason to believe he's lying?"

"Other than he's crazy paranoid? I don't know if Grant shorted him, or maybe knocked on his door wrong. Grant was a good kid. He was young, did his deliveries on a bicycle." Kerry laughed, "Wore a helmet and everything."

The image of a kid delivering drugs on a bicycle wearing a safety helmet didn't make me laugh. It turned my stomach. "No more deliveries to Xavier."

"What? Hey, I'm all for taking care of the carriers, but Xavier moves a lot of product."

"It's not up for discussion. Xavier finds a new source. He doesn't like it, tell him he can meet with me."

Kerry sat up a little straighter in his chair. "Is Johnny going to be okay with this?"

"I'll tell him this is my solution. Johnny doesn't need police investigating two murders and having them tied back on him. Xavier's a loose cannon. It's not worth the money we make off of him if it means he sends us all to prison."

Kerry took a long slow drink, draining a quarter of his glass. His glass set hard on the table, Kerry stroking the glass absently with his thumb and middle finger. "If you are cutting Xavier off, it should come from you, not me. I'll deliver the message if you want me to, but he is going to be furious, and no telling what he'll do. Coming from you, it'll be a lot more clear that things aren't up for discussion."

He was right. Xavier had killed two kids in a week. I didn't know either of them, but word travelled fast. By shooting Heather last week, none of the carriers would have skimmed off of the top – the memory would be too fresh. Grant wouldn't have skimmed; there was no proof that Heather had, either. "When is his next delivery scheduled?"

"Xavier's volume has increased since he took out Romero a couple months ago. He gets a delivery the day after tomorrow, two hundred grams."

The dealers were forever fighting turf-wars among each other. Romero hadn't been dealing long, and I wasn't surprised that Xavier had scared him off. I did the math in my head: fifty-seven eight-balls. An eight ball was three and a half grams and sold for around two hundred dollars. If all his deliveries were the same, Xavier was pushing thirty thousand a week. I loosely paid attention to how much each dealer was going through. In a typical week we received twenty pounds, just over nine thousand grams. Xavier was responsible for almost ten percent of Johnny's product. Cutting him off was extreme, but we needed to send a message to the dealers, just the same as Xavier had tried to send a message to our carriers.

"You're right. I'll do the next delivery."

Kerry raised a brow. "Call Oscar. Have someone go with you. Xavier doesn't take surprises well."

CHAPTER 20

Friday Afternoon

Several hours later I lay in my bed staring at the ceiling. It was too early for sleep, but today had been borderline insane: all the way up to Lincoln, just to turn around and come back a couple hours later. Sneaking off with Libby, I had come close to telling her what I did. Thankfully she left me sitting in the park. If she had continued to press – I might have told her everything. What was it about Libby? I told her more about me than I had confessed to my own brother.

Oscar had discovered Davey and wanted me to know but didn't want to tell me outright. I was thankful to be looking at my ceiling – today could have gone so much worse. Things had turned out not just better than I had hoped, but better than I could have dreamed.

My gaze lowered from the ceiling to the light tropical color of my walls. My fingers absently smoothed over the finish of the four-poster bed. My comforter was soft and plush, easy to curl into. This was a room Libby would hate. I had glanced into her room once when I was visiting Davey and her bedroom door was ajar.

Clothes were haphazardly piled in an overflowing clothes hamper. A PlayStation controller set next to her nightstand along with rumbled bags of potato chips and a bowl that was empty except for a few lonely kernels of popcorn. A package of Oreo cookies was hiding under her bed next to a sock which had escaped her laundry basket. Her curtains were a deep green, her bedding a mismatched mix of colors and patterns, and a pile of pillows large enough to allow her to sleep standing up lay near her headboard.

I looked around my bedroom. Everything was in its place. The hues complimented each other in an airy, Caribbean way. Every time I walked into my bedroom, I could almost imagine the steel drums and flutes playing in the background. When I left Johnny's estate, someone had been responsible for relocating my furniture from the storage locker where it had been into my new penthouse apartment. Whoever had relocated my furniture must have decided I needed a decorator's touch because my previously vanilla apartment now had a touch of elegance everywhere I looked.

I wondered what Libby would say if she saw it. Would she question my sexual persuasion? Not that all gay guys had a gene for color coordination – I'd seen a few in Johnny's clubs who could have used a helping hand, but this place didn't scream, "Young available straight guy."

My phone was in my hand before I realized I was scrolling through contacts. My finger stopped on the image of Libby: her snow angel picture.

My chat with Libby had been less than twelve hours ago, but so much had happened, it felt like it had been days. I wanted to hear her voice. Stupid. I put the phone on my nightstand. "Out of sight, out of mind," wasn't that how the saying went? If I couldn't see the picture of her rosy cheeks against a fresh blanket of snow, then I'd stop thinking about her. *"You are good at the superficial, but if I wanted someone superficial, I'd be with Larry right now. When you are ready to let me in and let me meet the real Mark – then we can talk about something more."*

Her voice echoed in my head. Libby's words stung. Not out of maliciousness, but the truth was sharp. What was wrong with me? Twenty-two and I'd never had more than a second date with any girl. I wouldn't classify any of my outings with Libby as a date – but today was close. I couldn't understand why every time I started to relax – Libby's was the face that flashed in my head. It wasn't like she was even available. Davey's words echoed in my head about her fight with Larry. She might be available soon.

I picked my phone back up, her picture still the first contact displayed. Before I could come to my senses, I had dialed her. She answered sassily, "I knew you'd call."

"That's funny. I didn't. How was your walk home today?"

"Great. Dave said you stopped by to see him, but didn't stay long. That wasn't because of me, was it?"

"If I said yes, would you apologize for bailing on me at the park today?" If anything, my weird couple of hours with Libby made me want to spend more time up there, but she didn't need to know that.

She giggled and a warm glow washed over me. I loved her happy sounds. I found thoughts of her drifting to other happy sounds I could get her to make. Instead of saying something grossly inappropriate about her laughter, I answered, "No, nothing to do with you. I needed to get back to Kansas City – today was a quick trip because I had a little free time."

"Long drive just to spend a couple hours. What did you need to get back to Kansas City for? *Fast and Furious* reunion?"

"Funny. Nothing that exciting. There was an issue at work that I needed to clear up. Catastrophe averted and all that. What are you doing right now?"

"I'm wallowing in my grief."

Her voice didn't sound even fractionally sad. "Your grief? What're you talking about?"

"Larry and I split up." Sarcasm oozed when she added, "I'm broken up about it, can't you tell?"

My heart did a little double-beat. I needed to sound sincere. Purposely lowering my voice to keep any sort of excitement out of it, I asked, "Are you okay? What happened?"

"Nothing. Larry's always had this thing for one of the girls in the service department. The two of them went out last night. He called to tell me that he wanted to explore his options."

What a douche. Larry and I had worked together fine; we were friendly, but not friends. At least he didn't string Libby along while he was exploring his options. "That sucks. Are you okay?"

She laughed again. Damn, I wished I could record her laugh, loop it and pipe it directly to my brain – I could listen to it for hours. Her laughter did something to me. Libby's voice pulled me out of my psycho fantasy, "I'm fine. He's a nice guy, but I didn't have the heart to break up with him a second time. He was really sweet after my accident. I'm glad he took the initiative and did it for me." She paused for a second, then asked, "So what plans do you have for tomorrow?"

"Nothing. It should be a pretty slow day. You?"

"Tomorrow's my day off." As if hinting that it would be okay for me to come see her, she asked, "You think you'll make a trip back up this way any time soon?"

With Johnny and Oscar aware of Davey, there was no reason for me to sneak out of town to see him. Slow days I could just get in the car and head north. Tomorrow would be a slow day. I wouldn't meet with Xavier until Sunday. A comfortable feeling settled over me. "I'm sure I will, but I don't know when. Why, you miss me?"

There was no giggle in response. Had I misread her? Maybe she hadn't been flirting with me. Maybe she wasn't thinking of me the same way I thought of her. But everything she said earlier today led me to believe she was interested. Larry was out of the picture. There wasn't any reason we couldn't go on a real date – well, other than maybe she didn't want to. I looked to my phone to see if the call had dropped, but we were still connected. "Libby, are you there?"

"I'm here."

"You didn't answer me."

Her voice was quiet, barely audible. "How could I miss you? I still don't know who you are."

Ouch. She wasn't going to let this go. She couldn't possibly understand the implications of getting to know the real me. A small part of me knew this was one of those moments – a moment when I could say the wrong thing and the two of us would never hit this crossroad again, or I could say the right thing and the two of us could have the potential of something big. Her words turned over in my head.

The real me, not the person I was for Johnny, or the guy Kerry reported to, but the real me – I wasn't sure who that was. Maybe I would like that guy, too. "So come spend the day with me tomorrow and figure out who I am."

She didn't hesitate, "I thought today was your day off?"

"It was. Tomorrow's Saturday, I don't have anything pressing. I could show you around the city."

"You want me to drive to Kansas City? That's three hours away. You've seen what I drive: I'd get stuck half-way there."

She drove a Honda with more than 300,000 miles on it. The offer was hanging in the air before I could do anything to take it back. "What if I sent a car to pick you up?"

"You want to send a car? Are you nuts?"

"You just pointed out that I spent six hours in the car and was in Lincoln less than two. I'm not driving back up there to have you storm off and leave me in a park again. You want to get to know the real me, you come to my town."

"What would we do?"

A strange feeling erupted in my stomach. She was considering it. She wanted to come here. Possibilities for a day with Libby began sailing through me. The rock-climbing wall at the gym, go karts, mini-golf – anything competitive would be a day she'd enjoy. What I wanted to do didn't require us to leave my apartment – I quickly shoved that idea out of my head. "Be ready for a pick up at six a.m. You'll be here in time for breakfast tomorrow."

"You're serious? Six? Do I look like a rooster? How about a pickup at nine and I see you at lunch?"

"I know the best place in town for biscuits and gravy." She loved biscuits and gravy as much as a five year old likes balloons. "I'll send a car that you can sleep in. Be ready at six."

She didn't argue or try to come up with an excuse to turn me down. Instead she negotiated for a later pick up. "What about eight?"

"Fine, seven, but be ready." I hung up with Libby and called the limousine service Johnny used occasionally.

The car service wanted a credit card and wouldn't budge when I told them

I'd bring cash over tonight. I asked to talk to a manager, which did little good – the manager reiterated what the first lady had told me.

I did one of the things I despised. I'd rarely had to drop Johnny's name, but the mere whisper of it normally turned people on a one-eighty. "I'm an employee of Johnny Corozzo. He has an account with you. Can you use his account and let me drop by with the cash so you don't have to invoice him?"

The woman grew frustrated, evidenced in her nasally tone. "Not without authorization."

"Fine, who on the account can authorize a pick up for tomorrow morning in Lincoln, Nebraska?"

"I'm sorry, sir, we don't give out that information. In accordance with our policy, even with proper authorization we require twenty-four hours notice. A pick up tomorrow morning in Lincoln is out of the question."

Irritation began to take hold. Did she not hear me? I told her I worked for Johnny. I could just drive up to Lincoln. We could spend the day there. Davey would be off work. Candy wouldn't have school. It would be like all the other times: the four of us would find something to do. Did Libby really need to be in Kansas City to get to know me?

I started to dial Libby back to tell her she could sleep, then I stopped – I wanted her here. It was selfish on my part, but I wanted a day where I wasn't sharing her with Davey and Candy. I didn't want to be her pal, or just Davey's brother. I wanted to take her to the places I enjoyed. I wanted her to meet Lenny and sit in a dark corner of his bar, watching people like I had done a hundred times before. I wanted her to eat at Johnny's bistro and see her face when the first bite of filet minion melted in her mouth. I wanted to hit one of the little boutiques downtown, then take her dancing until she couldn't stand.

There was something about Libby. I knew her inside and out. I'd studied her without ever meaning to, but I couldn't anticipate her reactions the way I could for most people. She was a live wire. I loved the way her face lit up when she laughed. No one had ever told me they wanted to know me. Sure, people wanted to hang out with me, but no other person had ever demanded to meet the real Mark. The more her words replayed in my head, the more I wanted her to know me, at least, as much as I could show her.

It was after eight p.m. After our conversation earlier about trust and not hiding things from him, now seemed like the opportune time to spill my guts, again. Johnny answered my call on the second ring. "What's wrong?"

"Nothing. Sorry to call so late. Are you busy?"

Johnny let out a heavy sigh. "No. I'm at the bistro. There's no problem?"

"No. Everything's great." I felt like a kid. This could be a colossal mistake, but I was quickly running out of options. "So, you know how you told me you don't like secrets?"

Johnny didn't answer. He must have been waiting for me to drop a bomb of some sort. "There's this girl, her name's Libby. She lives in Lincoln. I tried to send a car service to pick her up and bring her here tomorrow, but I don't have a credit card. I knew you used a car service sometimes, so that's the one I called. I was hoping they would let me use your account, but the manager told me I wasn't authorized to use it. I know this is stupid, but I really wanted to show her around the city tomorrow." Everything had rushed out of me so quickly, I worried that I had not explained it right.

Johnny was thrilled, "A girl? I knew it! I told you it was just a matter of time."

"Yeah. You told me. I feel like a kid asking his dad for help to the prom, but could you call the limousine service and authorize me to use your account? I swear I'll pay for the whole thing."

"No." His answer was fast. My heart sunk; I worried I had just crossed a line I shouldn't have. Johnny waylaid this idea when he added, "Sending a car is impersonal. She isn't a client. You want to impress her, don't you?"

I thought sending a car was genius, and a very personal gesture – especially a limousine. Libby hadn't had a picture perfect upbringing, either, and I doubted she had ever ridden in one before. My first ride in one was after I started working for Johnny. "Well, yeah, I mean, she already knows me. . . I mean, she doesn't know everything about me. But every time I've seen her, it's been in Lincoln. I wanted to bring her here." Recognizing that I was sounding like a child, I clarified, "You're saying I should go pick her up?"

"Yes. But you do it in style. Hold on. Don't hang up."

Do it in style? Did he think I should ride up in the limousine to pick her up?

Johnny had set his phone down, but I could hear him barking instructions into another phone. He must have called to the Ops Center to have them coordinate the car. It was a full five minutes before he picked the phone up with me again. "You still there?"

"Yeah, I'm here."

"The flight there will be thirty minutes. That will impress her. Go to the hangar now. My pilot will meet you there. You show up at her door with some flowers and bring her back to the city in style."

His plane? All I wanted was his help with a car service. "Johnny, that's too much. She'll just ask a bunch of questions if I show up on your jet."

"Don't worry about her questions. It'll be a date she'll never forget. Go to the hangar. My pilot will be waiting for you."

CHAPTER 21

I had never argued with Johnny about anything; now didn't seem like the time to start. I imagined Libby's face when I showed up to bring her here. She hadn't been freaked out when I told her I used to be a car thief. I couldn't tell her what I did for Johnny, but I wanted her to see where I lived, to see as much of me as I could show her.

I did as instructed. When I arrived at Johnny's hangar, his pilot was doing the preflight checks. I could already hear the ribbing from Dave. He gave off a matchmaker vibe earlier today, and I'd never live this one down if things didn't work out between her and me. Instead of showing up on their doorstep, I opted for a close second. I pulled out my phone and sent Libby a text. "Plans have changed. Pack a bag and meet me at the airport in an hour."

Her response was immediate, "At the airport? What airport?"

"In Lincoln. See you in an hour. Taxiing, turning phone off."

After we landed, the pilot told me how to get into the terminal. It was a little tricky because the commercial terminal and private terminal shared a runway. I went into the private terminal where they gave me a swipe badge that allowed me to go into the commercial terminal building, which was already closed down for the night. Looking around, I didn't see Libby. It was a short flight, so she wouldn't have come here and left already. I pulled out my phone and sent another text, "I'm here. Where are you?"

I stood inside, my nerves a little worse for wear. The entire flight I thought about all the things that could go fantastically wrong with this plan. What if she were scared of flying? What if we had a fight? What if she found out what I did for Johnny? Or worse, what if she found out and told Davey? What if she hated doing the things I loved? What if she were downplaying the breakup with Larry and she was on the rebound, then ended up hating me a month from now? My nerves had me ready to call the whole thing off when her response popped in on my phone. "Impatient much? There in two minutes."

Candy's throaty Chevelle pulled up to the curb. Relief washed over me when I saw Davey hadn't tagged along with them. Libby climbed out of the passenger side, an overnight bag over her shoulder. She took in the dark terminal in front of her, then fished for her phone, I assumed to send me a text asking where I was.

I took a deep breath and released it slowly. Now or never. The sliding glass doors both opened as I eased toward them. Libby turned toward me – she looked amazing. She wore a red dress that hugged her thin frame. It was cut low in the front and high on the leg. She wore these silver heels that shimmered in the light from the streetlight above. I had heard it said before, but this was the first time I'd felt it – Libby literally took my breath away.

I walked out of the dark lobby to where Libby stood on the curb beside Candy's car. She wore a confused expression. "Um, it looks like all the flights are done for the night. Did you want to stay at our house and catch one tomorrow?"

I took her hand, still dumbstruck. "No, c'mon, our plane's waiting around back." I leaned down to the open door. "Thanks for bringing her, Candy."

"No problem. You two have fun. When are you coming back?"

"Libby has to work on Sunday, so I'll make sure she's back tomorrow night."

Libby offered, "I'll call when I know what time."

I lifted Libby's overnight bag off her shoulder, her eyes dancing in the moonlight as Candy pulled away. I led Libby a few hundred yards from the commercial terminal. The gate was locked with a warning saying, "Authorized personnel only." I swiped the badge I had received from the desk inside the private terminal, and the gate swung free for us to enter.

Libby's shoes clicked on the pavement, but besides her steps, the night was quiet. I didn't want for the quiet to turn awkward. I moved her bag to my left hand, wiped the sweat from my palm onto my pants, and took her hand with my right. She didn't flinch or pull away. She bumped her shoulder into mine and asked, "Where are we going?"

"You said you wanted to know the real Mark. I'm going to introduce the two of you."

Libby smiled, and damn, that was the smile that haunted me when I closed my eyes. I led her to the little jet. I motioned for her to climb the steps as I followed her into the cabin. Johnny's pilot folded the steps into the fuselage, and a few minutes later we were taxiing down the runway.

Libby cinched up her seatbelt and asked, "Are we seriously flying to Kansas City? What happened to the car?"

"That's a funny story. Turns out you can't just 'order' a car on a whim. You actually have to schedule a car twenty-four hours in advance. When I found out I couldn't get a limo to pick you up, I had to go with Plan B."

Libby looked around the inside of the jet. She sat directly across from me. She looked thrilled, probably a lot the same way I looked the first time I had gone for a ride in Johnny's jet. The cabin was small, with only four seats: the front two seats faced backward, the back two faced forward. We could see directly into the cockpit from the two backseats. The chairs were a lush tan leather, and unlike commercial planes with the tiny windows, the windows were larger and allowed for a view in all directions. She shook her head in disbelief, "Do I even want to know how you pulled this off?"

"Like I said, Plan B."

Once in Kansas City, my borrowed SUV waited for us at the terminal. "Another car?" she accused.

"Mine's in the shop. This one's a loaner. After you left me at the park today, a kid tried to pass his basketball to my car."

"You shouldn't have taken off so fast today. Dave could have fixed it for you."

"Yeah, he offered. I needed to get back to the city."

I waited for her question: asking me why I needed to return to the city. I had an answer prepared. I had planned to tell her that I needed to go over some sales figures with my boss, but she didn't ask. Instead she nearly bounded into the little SUV and threw me off-guard when she asked, "So, what are we going to do?"

My eyes took her in. I had planned on a quiet movie night in my apartment. I was even prepared to suck it up and watch a chick flick. But by the way she was dressed, she was ready for a night on the town.

"Looks like you're dressed for a club. I know the perfect place." The drive from Johnny's hangar to downtown was less than twenty minutes. It wasn't awkwardly silent, but there wasn't an enormous amount of conversation either. She commented on a building here and there, how much larger Kansas City was to drive through and how thoroughly impressed she was with Johnny's jet.

I pulled into the garage below my apartment building and left the SUV in my assigned parking spot. It was a Friday night, so there were a few clubs with decent music in the city. The club I went to a couple nights a week was close, and it was by far the best the city had to offer. The owner of the club was a friend of Johnny; she had been a Manhattan socialite who relocated after the economy crashed. She started over here after losing millions in real estate – only to have rebuilt her fortune a few short years later. Looking at Libby's outfit, she would fit in perfectly.

We emerged from the parking garage and walked toward the club's main entrance. The temperature had fallen, and I saw Libby clutching her arms tightly, trying to stay warm. Why did women never wear jackets? Although today had been a warm sunny day, April evenings were cool. I took off my jacket and draped it over Libby's shoulders. She clutched it tightly and shot me a grateful look.

The front door had a lineup of people waiting to get in. This happened every Friday and Saturday night. When the maximum occupancy for fire code was reached, no more could come in until others left – well, no more regular people.

I ignored the line and led Libby to the front door; the bouncer lifted the little red velvet barrier and allowed us to pass. "Evening, Boss."

Frustrated sounds came from the people waiting outside. I clapped his shoulder as we passed him, "It's shaping up to be a great one, thanks." I didn't wait in lines and neither would Libby.

The music was loud, drowning out the voices feebly trying to be heard in the building. I took Libby's hand a second time, and led her toward the steps to the second floor. Another bouncer stood at the bottom of the steps, his job to turn people away who didn't belong in the VIP area. He leaned closer to the wall to let us pass, and offered, "Good to see you, Mark. Shannon's tending bar upstairs now; I'll send Barry up to relieve her." I couldn't remember the bouncer's name, but I was impressed he remembered who my favorite bartender was.

I slid my jacket off of Libby and handed it to him. "That would be great. Can you have this put away?"

The bouncer took it and nodded, then turned his attention toward Libby. "If there's anything you need, Miss, just let me know. I'm Charles." Okay, so he was more of a concierge than a bouncer, a very large, beefy, neckless concierge.

She smiled, "Um, thanks." His offer likely surprised her as we passed and climbed the steps. Libby was a step behind me when she asked, "You have your own bartender?"

"No. Barry's just my favorite." She gave me the same look normally reserved for a spoiled child. Her stare made me defensive, "I didn't ask him to send Barry up. He offered." Libby shook her head in disbelief, but I didn't need to defend myself – I hadn't stomped my foot or held my breath. This was just a perk of being me. She was the one who said she wanted to meet the real Mark.

The music was much quieter upstairs. A neon "Eagle's Nest" sign hung on the wall in between large windows that looked down onto the multilevel dance floors below. I ordered two glasses of wine and returned to where she stood; her eyes were fixed on the dance floors below. She was still a few months shy of the legal drinking age, but she took the wine glass from me. After a couple sips she asked, "So, why go to a dance club if you aren't going to dance?"

"It's a better view up here. Figured I'd give you the bird's eye view before we hook and jab onto the floor."

Libby's eyes lit up. She sipped her wine and turned back toward the large viewing window. Without pulling her gaze away from the action below, she asked, "You get this kind of treatment everywhere?"

"Not everywhere." That was debatable. Places I frequented all treated me well. I was a creature of habit and didn't try new places just for the sake of trying them. My first trip here had been with Johnny and Oscar; so were several other trips. Johnny wasn't a dancer per se, but he liked the energy of the club. The nights I had come here with him, we spent the evening in the Eagle's Nest, not on the dance floors below.

We both drained our glasses, and Libby led me down the stairs and to the dance floor. She could dance, and not the typical white-girl dance of shuffling feet and clapping hands. When we first took to the floor, we were shoulder to shoulder with at least twenty others. By the third song, others had given us space as people backed up against the railings to get a better view of her.

Her red dress twirled as she spun into my awaiting arms. Her moves were both elegant and erotic: the arch of her neck, the grace with which she moved, the joy on her face, and the heat from her body each time she landed in my arms. It was easy to forget the hundreds of eyes leering at us, because I, too, only had eyes for Libby. The next hour flew by in a blur. Just after one a.m., she grabbed my bicep and leaned in to shout over the music, "I'm exhausted. Ready to get out of here?"

We weaved in and out of the wall-to-wall people, many of whom complimented her as she walked by. Charles was still standing his post and quickly retrieved my jacket from where he had stowed it earlier. I gestured toward a side door where yet another bouncer stood. He held the door for us to exit as the cool night air blanketed our wet skin.

I wrapped my arm around Libby, and hers effortlessly slid over my waist. It was a comfortable walk back to my apartment. The night sky was clear, stars twinkling above us over the city lights. Few cars were on the street this time of night, and the short walk to my place was too short. As I held the front door to my apartment building open, she commented, "I can still hear the music from the club. You live here?"

A greeting carried through the front door, "Good evening, Mr. Brewer." My building's doorman had effectively answered her question.

"Hi, Ted." I handed him the key to my SUV parked in the garage. "My car's in the shop, so I've got a loaner vehicle while mine's being repaired. I left an overnight bag in the backseat. Could you bring it up?"

"I'd be happy to, Mr. Brewer."

Libby looked at me like I had grown a third eye. I pointed her toward the elevator and looked over my shoulder at Ted, "Thanks."

We waited for the elevator. It was one of the old-fashioned ones with the metal needle that indicated the floor the car was on. The building had been an old department store in its past life, but had been converted to individual apartments a couple decades ago. Libby's face looked strange. I could usually read her pretty well, but I couldn't make out her expression this time. As the elevator doors opened, my curiosity got the better of me. "What's wrong?"

"Who lives like this?"

I chuckled at her. "Lots of buildings have doormen. It's a security thing."

"Right. And do you have stock in that club, or what? Everyone knew you."

I tried to dismiss it, pointing out her local celebrity-like status in Lincoln. "It's the same when we go into a bar in Lincoln. Everyone knows you wherever we go."

"Uh, that's not the same. Those are bars where I play pool."

"So. We were at a club that's close to my apartment. I'm a regular." The elevator deposited us on my floor; each floor only had four apartments. Mine was on the southeast corner of the building. I unlocked the door and allowed Libby to go in first. The entryway was dark, but my living room was positioned in the corner of the building and was lined with floor to ceiling windows. The Kansas City skyline shown through, washing the whole apartment in a soft glow.

Libby walked to the windows like a moth to a flame. I stood behind her as she watched my city below. Although I didn't want to interrupt the magic of this moment, I eased closer and gently wrapped both arms around her where she stood. Libby leaned back into me, sliding her head to the right of mine. We stood there motionless. This was one of those moments – one etching itself deep into my memory.

The perfume she wore was sweet and alluring, a fragrance I could get lost in. Her body was warm against mine. I nestled my cheek against hers; the suppleness of her skin invited me. I loved the way she felt in my arms. She looked out onto the city the way I had a million times before. Watching the city over her shoulder, it looked more beautiful than I had ever remembered. Part of the allure of my apartment building was being in the middle of Country Club Plaza with all the fountains and statues lining the place, but Libby fixated on neon lights stretching out for miles along the streets below.

A soft tap sounded at the door. I placed a kiss on her temple and released her from my grasp. Ted's smiling face was at the door: he exchanged her overnight bag for a healthy tip. When I turned back to where I had left Libby, she wasn't looking out the window. She was watching me. Her voice was low, but carried across the room. "Who are you?"

I was getting sick of that question. I pressed a button on the stereo and soft music filled the air. Grinning at her, I closed the distance between us. She stood there, head tilted up waiting for an answer. I stood only inches away from her, looking down into her beautiful blue eyes. My lips brushed hers lightly before I whispered, "The luckiest guy in the city." Libby threaded her fingers around the back of my head and pulled my mouth down onto hers.

I stepped into her, one hand around her shoulder and the other at the small of her back, pulling her equally hard against me. No distance separated us. Her lips opened and I greedily deepened our kiss, sliding my hand from her lower back onto her perfect ass. She responded by pressing hard against me. I wanted her – every inch of her. My fingers slid up to the zipper at the back of her dress, and eased it down.

The zipper was halfway down as I felt Libby's body stiffen. She didn't tell me to stop, but her eyes popped open as she stood rigid against me. My hunger for her was all encompassing – a primal need. There had never been another woman who set me ablaze this way. I had tried being a gentleman: opening doors, giving her my jacket, following her lead at the club – but my restraint was evaporating with each breath I took. My fingers returned to the zipper, sliding it down to her waist.

She took half a step back from me. "Where do you see this going?" Libby's words hung in the air.

Several inappropriate responses came to mind. None escaped me. I would have promised her anything in that moment. I wanted to climb inside her. I longed to feel the suppleness of her skin against mine. Cursing the distance she had put between us, I leaned forward pulling her against me once more. My lips moved from her mouth, to under her chin, and along the sensitive skin on her neck. Libby arched her neck, inviting me along the exposed skin from her shoulder to her chin. Goose bumps erupted on her flesh as my lips caressed her. Libby threaded her fingers through my hair as a soft gasp escaped her lips.

I pulled away slowly, hoping to see the same longing in her eyes that was coursing through me. Her eyes were closed, her dress still on, but rumpled loosely around her. She could have rolled her shoulders and let it fall to the floor – she didn't. I didn't want to pressure her, but I couldn't be Prince Charming. I didn't own a white horse. I needed her. When her eyes slowly opened, her lashes lifted and the look she gave me again sucked the air out of my lungs.

I glanced over my shoulder toward the open door to my bedroom in a wordless invitation. She looked but made no move toward it. The same question as before, "Where is this going, Mark?"

"As far as you let it go." My hands glided over the exposed skin on her back. I reached for the straps on her dress to help her slip it to the floor. She tugged at the back of my shirt still tucked into my trousers. I took her hint: unbuttoning the top few buttons and sliding the shirt over my head and depositing it onto the floor.

Her hands slid over my exposed chest. Everywhere she touched created tingles in their wake. Desire burned. Libby rested her head against my shoulder; her lips kissed me from my chest all the way to my jugular. A heavy sigh escaped me as the sensation caused me to grind my groin into her. My lips were just inches from her ear, "You are beautiful. I want you."

Her body tensed. She didn't answer. I had a guest room, but that's not where I wanted Libby. I pressed my groin against her a second time and erotic sensations rocketed through me. I was well past wanting her; my body needed her. I leaned closer to her ear, my teeth grazed her lobe, another heavy whisper escaped, "Say yes." I didn't care that I was begging, "Please, say yes."

Libby was never at a loss for words, but remained quiet. I parted the back of her dress wider, each of my hands slowly sliding the straps over her shoulders. I waited for her to tell me no, or roll her shoulders back to hold it in place – she didn't do either. I slid each of the straps the rest of the way off of her shoulders as her dress dropped to the floor.

Her bra and panties were black satin. Libby's beauty was all consuming. I kicked my shoes to the side, slid off my trousers and socks and stood in the dimly lit room wearing only my boxers and a love-struck look in my eye.

I put my palm to her chest. Her heart was racing in time with mine. "Say something, Libby." The heat from her body radiated to mine. I was drunk by the feel of her skin against me. My hands went to her shoulders, as my lips moved from her lips, along her neck, to her sternum and onto her stomach. I backed her onto the sofa and kneeled in front of her on the floor. My fingers caressed the skin along her ankles and then glided up her calves. I kissed her stomach, my tongue tasting her salty skin. Libby laid her head against the headrest and arched her back.

My hands slid to her waist, pulling her hips toward me where I kneeled on the floor. I breathed hot air against her panties, my fingers sliding just under the edge of the material. A pleasure filled groan escaped her lips – I had never been harder or more ready in my life. If she was going to put the brakes on, I needed her to do it soon.

Instead of yanking her panties off, I squeezed out the last bit of control I had and leaned back up to her ear. Her heart pounded hard against my chest, her breath erratic, her fingers clutched the skin of my biceps. Pleading for the permission I knew she wanted to give. "I need you. Tell me what you want, Sweetheart. I'll do it. I'll do anything."

Libby pressed both of her palms against my chest, wordlessly directing me off of her. I backed off – a feeling of dread washing over me. Libby stood up from the couch. Her dazzling smile from earlier was gone; her eyes were hooded and heavy with desire. I waited for her to shoot me down: to tell me this was too fast. Libby held her hand out and led me into my bedroom.

CHAPTER 22

I awoke to sun streaming through the window. Icicles all but formed on my nose; my feet felt like I should have rolled them in peanuts and called them drumsticks. My body lay in the fetal position while a sleeping Libby was on the other side of the bed bundled up in the comforter. My knuckles were white, desperately holding onto a tiny corner of the bedding not covering her.

I remembered her leading me into the bedroom and every pleasure-filled detail that followed. But waking up imitating an ice cube while she was toasty warm diminished a little luster from the previous evening. What was the etiquette when a woman stole all the covers in the night?

Libby was the first woman to spend the night in my apartment. I liked my space and had never invited another to stay. Women who wanted to encroach in my world had never been welcome – at least, until Libby. Another blanket was stored on the shelf in my closet; I could have stealthily eased out of the bed and retrieved it. I didn't.

I grabbed hold of the little triangle of the comforter barely covering my midsection and pulled hard. It unfurled leaving her body exposed. Libby awoke with a start when the cool air of the room rushed against her warm skin. In a sleepy stupor she attempted to pull the covers back over, but I held them in place. Feeling smug that I had taken back what was rightfully mine, I watched her struggle several times to cover back up.

Her eyes fluttered open. She took in the room and the fact that I was awake and was holding on to the still warm bedding. I waited for an apology. It didn't come. Libby's sleepy eyes narrowed, her fist doubled up into a little ball, and she punched me in the stomach. The shock not only took me by surprise but completely knocked the wind out of me. I let go of the comforter. She pulled hard and was fully snuggled back in before I realized what she had just done.

Gasping for the breath she had just knocked out of me, I accused, "You hit me!"

Her voice sounded angelic as she cinched the comforter tightly around her again. "No, I didn't. You're dreaming. Go back to sleep."

Aghast at her action, I was now wide-awake, not believing what she had just done. This was who I had been dreaming about? All those listless moments when I envisioned romantic moments: sweeping her off her feet, riding into the sunset, and at least twenty other cheesy scenarios. "I'm not dreaming – you just punched me."

Not at all concerned with her own behavior, she responded matter-of-factly. "You shouldn't have taken the covers." Her eyes closed again as her lips turned up in a sly grin, and she tried to nestle back to sleep. I slid to her, prying the comforter away far enough to slide my leg in between hers. I wasn't sure whether to wrestle her or snuggle into the warmth of her body. She kissed my neck, then whispered into my ear, "As long as you're awake, you could make breakfast."

Wrestling. Wrestling was exactly the right move. I shook my head. What kind of dating ritual was this? This is what I had been missing? "You're funny."

Her eyes fluttered open, "If we were at my house, I'd offer to make you breakfast." She yawned, "Didn't you promise me biscuits and gravy?" Her eyes closed as her hand poked out from below the comforter, and she pointed her finger toward the kitchen.

"I'm not making biscuits and gravy." A beautiful pout formed on her lips. That look would be the death of me, because the arrogance I felt just moments ago dissipated when I wanted to make her pout disappear. I started thinking through all the food in my cupboards and refrigerator. Sheepishly, I offered, "I could make eggs."

Her pout was replaced with a wide grin, "And French toast?"

I rolled onto my back and pulled her to me. She snuggled in, and I'm ashamed to admit it, I started to consider a trip to the grocery store for sausage to put in the gravy. Why did I have this insatiable urge to give into her whim? What the hell was wrong with me? I wasn't that guy – the one where a girl could snap her fingers and I'd start doing tricks. I hated that kind of guy.

Her voice more gravely than it had been, "I had a great time last night." She leaned into me and kissed my neck. "Thank you."

Break out the dog treats: I was ready to do tricks. "Yeah, you were pretty great, too."

She laid her palms across my chest and rested her head on them. "What are we doing today?"

"What do you want to do?"

"I already told you."

"Yeah, I remember. You want to get to know me. Aren't we past that?"

"Not hardly. The only thing I learned last night was that you have stamina on the dance floor. I'm going to grab a shower."

Thoroughly offended, "Stamina on the dance floor? No other stamina you were happy to learn about?"

She eased out of bed and stretched her arms high into the air. Libby blew me a kiss and closed the bathroom door behind her. What the hell kind of answer was that? Was she being coy? Did she want me to follow her? I needed a user manual for Libby.

Although the sun had shined brightly through the windows this morning, the day turned to overcast skies. I took Libby to the diner around the corner for biscuits and gravy, and to my delight, she agreed they were the best she had ever eaten.

After breakfast we went to the track. I had an old Oldsmobile that I kept in one of the storage garages there; it handled like a rocket. When Libby was behind the wheel, it felt more like a precision missile. I sat beside her while she drove. Turn four of her second circuit: I was sure the wheels were off the pavement. After beating my time around the track by more than four seconds, she pulled into the pit area, removed her helmet and said, "You need more practice. I'm not even warmed up, and I smoked you."

Nothing like being emasculated before ten a.m. If I'd have let her, she would have goaded me into hours of trying to beat her time, but reality was – she was better than I was. "C'mon, we've got other places to go." Libby jeered at me all the way to Lenny's bar. She had heard me talk about Lenny lots of times, so when I said I wanted to introduce her, she stopped gloating about her performance in my car. Lenny was in the office, buried behind a stack of papers. He looked up from his monitor when we came through the door. "This must be the lovely Libby. It's great to finally meet you."

I felt my cheeks blush. She held out a hand, but he gestured it away and gave her a hug. When he let go, he looked at me with a scathing expression, "You said she was pretty. . .but, damn, Mark." He looked back toward Libby, "What is someone like you doing with him?"

Libby came to my defense, "Easy, Romeo. I like hanging out with Mark. Do you know he took me to the track this morning and let me win?"

Lenny laughed, "Psha, I'm sure you beat him on your own merit. He keeps that old car in case Ms. Daisy needs a ride to her hair appointment."

Thoroughly offended, I cut in, "Enough you two. I've had about all the abuse I'm going to take today."

The two of them were fast friends. Lenny was one of my favorite people in the world. Watching him and Libby together stirred me – in a good way. Seeing the guy I idolized conspiratorially telling stories about me to the girl I obsessed about should have been mortifying. It wasn't. Libby was a hit – I knew Lenny would warm up to her as quickly as I had. A shipment of liquor arrived and Lenny needed to inventory it, so we left.

Libby and I walked along the quiet Saturday streets around the neighborhood. She asked, "You know what I want to do?"

"I wouldn't hazard a guess."

She rolled her eyes. "Let's go to Worlds of Fun."

"The theme park?"

"Is there another Worlds of Fun that I don't know about?"

It was an odd request, but I was learning never to be surprised by anything when I was with Libby. The theme park was open on weekends beginning in April, and as luck would have it, last weekend was its opening day. As we paid admission and walked through the gate, she went straight for the Mamba. It was one of the fastest, tallest roller coasters – not just at the park, but in the world. I hated roller coasters – I had only ridden one once as a child, and it hadn't been on my "to do" list as an adult. I hated the feeling of being out of control.

I survived the ride; however, my stomach was still a few hundred feet in the air, and the nausea felt like I'd be dragging it with me for the rest of the day. I started to make my way to a bench where I could allow my body to collect itself when Libby tugged me back toward the line to ride it a second time. I wasn't a fan, but her enthusiasm was euphoric, and by the time it was our turn again, I had forgotten how much I hated it the first time. As we exited the monstrosity for the second time, I put my foot down and told her a third ride was out of the question.

Libby found a vendor that sold turkey legs. She asked if I wanted one. My stomach was so queasy, the odor made me want to vomit. She bought one, and I swear she looked like a blonde Wilma Flintstone walking down the path gnawing on the disgusting thing.

Just as my stomach started to feel normal again, she was dragging me toward the Thunderhawk. I watched as a seemingly harmless gondola rocked to the right and then the left. When it looked as though it should have been slowing down, it started to go faster and higher, then did a complete circle, hanging high in the air, and the seats spun, hanging the riders upside down.

"You sure about this? Do you need to let your Brontosaurus leg settle first?"

She pushed me toward the line, depositing what was left of the turkey leg into the trash. I didn't want to ride, but I knew if I chose to keep my feet on the ground, she would never let me live it down. Instead, hanging upside down, I screamed like a little girl as Libby's laughter echoed over everyone else's. We rode two more roller coasters before a downpour stopped all the rides in the park. In that moment, I thought I should go to church tomorrow because there was a God in heaven who had listened to my prayers as I rode the grueling death traps she dragged me on.

Libby lived for adrenalin. The same way most people need air, water and food – she survived on thrills. I had never seen a face shine more brightly, a person laugh so loudly or scream with such delight the way she did while I was clenching every muscle in my body – praying that I could live through the next thirty seconds.

The downpour had soaked us to the bone, so by the time we were at the car, we were both shivering. Through clenched teeth she stuttered, "Th-th-that was awesome. You should get season passes."

"Never again. When today is over, I will never try to take you on a date again. You had me hanging upside down in mid-air, plummeting from hundreds of feet up, and twirling around like a jump rope. On what planet would this be considered a good time?"

Libby dismissed my tirade. "Seriously? That was nothing. I went to Six Flags last summer and did nothing but roller coasters for two solid days."

"You'll need to find a new playmate if you want to do that again. I'm out."

"I'd really like to go to Vegas. They have this roller coaster on the Stratosphere. You are supposed to be able to see all of Vegas from it."

I had been to Las Vegas. I had gambled, seen a couple shows, bet on a couple of games; I even watched a couple get married by an Elvis impersonator. I had also seen the roller coaster she was talking about; there was no amount of money in the world that would make me ride that – never.

"Okay, nutso, your turn is over. Now we go where I want to go." We went to Union Station. Outside of Lenny's bar, this was one of my favorite places to watch people. Tourists from everywhere showed up here. Accents and different languages hung in the air, architecture students with their sketch pads crouched in corners, classes full of kids rushed to the science exhibits – there was an energy here that lived nowhere else in the city. Beyond watching the people, Union Station housed my favorite restaurant – Pierponts.

The opulence of the detail in the architecture of the restaurant was only rivaled by the food. Intricate carvings hugged the wall around the bar. Eight glass shelves of liquor stood behind the glossy bar – the top shelves only reachable by an old wooden ladder, which precisely matched the wood of the bar and the tables. I swear, this was the bar where "top shelf" liquor earned its name. Enormous intricately carved pillars stretched to the twenty-foot tall ceilings; leather – real leather – booths were flanked by marble statues. Chandeliers hung between rectangular vaulted ceilings flanked by crown molding.

Libby watched me as I absorbed the ornate elegance chiseled into the room more than a hundred years ago. I loved coming here. If I had a favorite place on earth, this was it. The bartender saw Libby and me, still wet from the afternoon rain. Instead of waiting for us to come to him, he scurried toward us, "Good to see you, Mark. Jack and Coke?" I nodded, then he turned to Libby, "How about you, Miss?"

"I'm driving. Give him a double and I'll just have a Coke."

The bartender left to get our order when I argued, "You're not driving. I saw you on the track today, remember?"

She smirked, "Safety first. After all your screaming today, you've earned the drink. Besides, a drunk mind speaks a sober heart. The real Mark will rear his head if you have enough liquor."

"Always scheming. Just ask me whatever you want to know."

She leaned back in her chair, paying more attention to the carving along the crown molding than to me just a few feet away. "I'm not stupid."

"I never thought you were."

"Something tells me you don't sell cars for a living. Whatever you do, I'm not okay with it if it's illegal."

I had been waiting for this ever since I had picked her up last night. She saw my favorite places; she had seen more of me than I had probably shown Davey. Every minute with Libby was an adventure, albeit a crappy adventure at the theme park, but there was something about her. She was intoxicating, more so than any liquor I had ever had.

I didn't try to convince her that my job wasn't what defined me – that would be a lie.

We spent the rest of the day with significantly less adrenalin. Johnny's plane and pilot were waiting for us on schedule when we arrived at six p.m.

Conversation was strained at best after her comment at the restaurant. *"I'm not okay with what you do,"* played over and over in my head. When we were on the ground in Lincoln, she started for the steps. The pilot tapped me on the shoulder and pointed toward a storage cabinet behind the cockpit. "There's something for her in there."

When I opened it, a bouquet of flowers fell into my arms. Johnny – my detail guy. Libby had phoned Candy before we took off, and I could see her car waiting on the curb through the gaps in the fence. Something told me if I didn't stash the flowers, I might never live them down. I started to tuck them back in the cabinet when Libby turned from the bottom of the steps – her eyes lit up.

Dammit. I followed her down the steps and handed the flowers to her. Libby was brash and aggressive, she made me question my manliness, and the last twenty-four hours had been as much a struggle as a thrill. No matter how much I enjoyed being around her, she was never going to accept me. I should have pulled the steps back into the plane, turned my back and never looked back, but standing next to her – I didn't want to go.

I wondered if I could somehow quit Johnny, would there be a chance for us? She looked at me with those brilliant blue eyes, and I didn't want to be anywhere but next to her, at least, not until she opened her mouth. Libby's sweet voice said, "You weren't as creepy as I expected."

"Creepy?"

"Yeah. You've been wound so tight every time I've been around you – I was sure I'd get down to your place and you'd be a total freak-show."

I shook my head, not sure if I should be offended or thrilled that in her way she had just told me she was glad she had spent a day with me. "You have a way with words, Libby."

"I just gave you a compliment."

"No, you didn't. A compliment is something like: you have a nice car, or I like that shirt, or you're fun to be with. A compliment is not: you weren't as creepy as I expected."

Libby beamed. "Your car is excessive – no one needs to drive something that costs that much money. Your clothes are usually pretty lame, but today you looked okay. When you aren't screaming like a little girl or whining about me taking blankets, you can be charming. Better?"

Teetering on the profoundly offended, a laugh escaped me. "That's it. You are barred from divvying out compliments ever again. If you were to say something nice, at this point it'd give me a heart attack."

She leaned into me. Her faced nuzzled into the crook of my neck. "The truth is, I like you, sort of. But I don't want you getting a big head or anything."

After all the crap she had put me through, these were the words that made me want to dance around. I placed a kiss on the top of her head. "Wouldn't dream of it. I'll call you later." The constant replay of the words: *I'm not okay with what you do,* stopped in that instant. She had said she liked me.

After landing in Kansas City, I returned to my apartment. I called Libby initially just to let her know I'd made it back okay. She had just been here, so there shouldn't have been much for either of us to say, but we were on the phone until I could no longer keep my eyes open. It was a tough reconciliation. Every minute I spent with her she was brash, difficult, but beyond everything else – fun. When there was distance, she was sweet. I hung up and stared out into the city lights. Libby was someone I wanted around. I pulled the comforter up to my neck and remembered how I had woken up with nothing covering me.

A goofy grin spread wide at the memory of how she had punched me when I yanked the comforter off of her. Libby was more than I had bargained for, but I wouldn't have traded one second with her. I closed my eyes and let thoughts of her lull me into a comfortable sleep.

CHAPTER 23

Sunday morning I pushed thoughts of Libby out of my head. No matter how badly I wanted to lie there and take in her lingering scent from the pillow she had used, or reminisce about our day together – I couldn't. Today I was working. Kerry had told Xavier I would be delivering at ten a.m.

Carriers typically blended into the background. They looked like they belonged in the neighborhoods. I wouldn't blend in, but I didn't intend to make a habit out of delivering Johnny's drugs. Xavier would know something was up the moment he saw me. There were repercussions for murder; maybe not fair ones – no eye for an eye, but killing those kids would end his livelihood.

My jeans were a dark denim; I wore a white collared shirt and brown dress shoes. My face was cleanly shaven, my teeth a bright white, and I didn't smell of the streets.

I stopped by the dealership, picked up the package which had been assembled for Xavier, placed it in a duffle bag, and made my way to his place. Kerry had been adamant that I needed to bring someone with me. I had considered it, but knew I didn't need added muscle. No matter how pissed off Xavier was – taking that frustration out on me would be a death sentence. He understood the hierarchy in Johnny's organization – I was untouchable.

The little one story ranch house had been white sometime in its past. Chunks of paint were missing, garbage was piled up beside the house around overflowing green plastic garbage bins. Two cars in the backyard looked like they hadn't moved in years. The sidewalk leading up to his doorway was broken and uneven. A large stake protruded from the ground with an empty metal dog dish tipped upside-down beside it. Dirt surrounded the stake where the dog's chain had worn all the weeds down to bare earth.

Xavier answered the door. He smelled foul, as if he had been on a binge for days. His eyes were bloodshot; he wore a pair of saggy workout pants and a black t-shirt. When his eyes focused on me, he instantly took a half step back from the door. I lifted the duffle bag a couple inches from my side in a silent answer to his unasked question. Xavier held the door for me to enter.

The smell inside was overwhelming. A mix of stale air, cigarette smoke and wet dog permeated the air. A dog barked angrily behind a closed wooden door. The sound of claws shredding wood echoed through the little house as Xavier shouted, "Roy, lay down!" Two more scratches sounded, but the barking stopped and a frustrated whine came from behind the door.

I closed the front door behind me and did my best not to breathe through my nose. "Xavier, I'm concerned about what happened to two of my carriers."

"They shorted me! No one steals from me and gets away with it. Your thieving mules got what they deserved."

Xavier had no remorse, not that I had expected any. He was hyped up on something. My words shouldn't have elicited that strong of a response. I hadn't even told him he was cut off yet. My voice stayed even, "You feel strongly that they stole from you, and for that, I apologize."

A confidence washed over him. "You're here to make it right, aren't you, Mark? I always knew Johnny was a class act. Each one of them took a half ounce off the top."

"I brought your entire order. I weighed it twice myself. All of it is here."

"I trust you, Mark. I don't need to check it." He reached into his pocket and produced a rolled up wad of money. He held it out for me to see, then placed it hard on the wooden coffee table in front of him. "Here."

I picked it up, unrolled it and counted the money. He had given me nine thousand dollars. I pulled a thousand dollars out and handed it back to him. Xavier shot me a grateful smile. In his mind, someone owed him for the missing ounce. The two carriers' deaths were not a pay back. "We square, Mark. Tell Johnny I said thanks."

It was unlikely that even a half an ounce had come up missing, but I paid him for the "missing" ounce anyway. "That's not from Johnny. I paid you that thousand dollars out of my cut. Xavier, this is your last delivery."

"What you talkin' about? I been buying from Johnny for years."

"You have. You also killed two of our carriers in a week. If you believed they shorted you, you should have taken it up with Kerry. Pulling the trigger the second time effectively cut your supply. You will need to find a new source."

I turned toward the door, but Xavier grabbed my shoulder hard, "Hey, wait. You cut me off?"

"Yes. This is your last delivery." He searched my eyes as if checking my resolve. I made it more clear, "*I* cut you off."

The words sunk in. This wasn't something Kerry had asked for. Carriers hadn't refused to deliver. This was my choice. He had no recourse. Xavier's voice was urgent, "C'mon, Mark. I've been loyal to Johnny for longer than you've been with the organization."

"My decision's final." I pointed at the little black duffle bag at his feet. "That is your last delivery."

"Look, I get it. You're mad. I'm sorry."

He was apologizing for murdering two kids, not because he felt guilty for ending their lives but because he was being cut off. "I'm not angry. This is business. You are too much of a risk. The cops get wind of how those two died, they trace it right back to Johnny and me."

"The cops ain't gonna trace nothin'. I didn't do it here. I waited until they were a few blocks down the street. This is my neighborhood – no one's gonna tell the cops nothin'."

"Regardless. You need a new source. We won't be filling any more of your orders."

Xavier went from shocked to pissed in no more time than flicking a light switch. "Does Johnny know? If he knew, he would have sent muscle with you. You playing me, right?"

I turned toward the scum standing in front of me. He was the reason, him, that I had joined Johnny's organization to begin with. It was a bottom feeder like Xavier who had ended Megan for no reason. "It's my decision. It's been made."

I reached for the door handle when Xavier came up behind me and slammed the door shut. I refused to let a morsel of fear show. Libby's image flashed in my mind, and I pushed it away. When I did, Davey's smiling face flashed in my head. In that instant, I realized the reason I had never been frightened in these types of situations was I had nothing to live for – until now. I turned toward him, desperation showing on his face. "Look. Think it over. I make you a lot of money. So, I screwed up. I just told you I won't do it again. You can't cut me off."

"I just did."

I took the door handle a second time, wrenched it open, and stepped out onto the cement steps. Xavier sounded desperate, "Mark, hey, I got customers."

"That's not my problem."

I walked away. Xavier wasn't predictable. I hadn't expected for him to do anything stupid but was relieved when I climbed into the little SUV without a scratch. I eased away from the curb and drove slowly down the street. After I was several blocks away, I phoned Kerry, "It's done."

"What'd he say?"

"There wasn't anything to say. I told him it was my decision." I may have downplayed Xavier's anger, but it was irrelevant. "Put the word out to all the dealers. Let them know: no one lifts a finger against a carrier or they answer to me. Tell the carriers the same thing – they have issues with any dealers, they tell you. You get any complaints, I want to know about them."

"Got it, Boss." There was a hesitation before he added, "It's nice to have you back in the game."

I hung up with Kerry. I debated whether calling Chad would be the right thing to do or not. I had promised I would talk to Johnny before I told Chad anything. Although likely a huge mistake, I called Chad. I got his voicemail. "Hey, it's me. I dealt with the problem. There won't be any more problems with kids. The dealer has been cut off." I could have given Chad Xavier's name, but the last thing I needed was for Chad to use Xavier as a witness against Johnny and me.

CHAPTER 24

I dug my ringing phone out of my pocket ready to push whoever it was to voicemail, when the screen showed my favorite picture of Libby making that snow angel. It was mid-afternoon on Sunday. I had been thinking about her non-stop since last night. I stepped out of the Starbucks' line – wanting to hear her voice more than I wanted a cup of coffee. I could have pushed her to voicemail and called her in a few minutes, but it was Libby. I took a seat in one of the pretentious circular love seats and answered her call.

A high-pitched run-on of rapid-fire words shot at me. I wasn't sure if it was Libby, believing no one but a teenager meeting Thor could hit that octave. Thirty seconds into whatever she was screeching at me, I hadn't been able to make out a single word other than Dave and Candy. My body shifted forward, tension spreading through me as I thought the worst. An accident? She paused to take a breath and I cut in, "Libby, slow down. What's wrong?"

Her voice came down two full octaves, so it didn't sound like a banshee shaking hands with an electrical outlet, but her words were so fast I had to concentrate to understand. "Candy called me when I was at work this morning. Some guy from Kansas City called Dave and said he was a friend of yours. He wanted to plan a surprise birthday party for you and wanted for her and Dave to meet him. That was hours ago. I'm home now. They aren't here. They aren't answering their phones, either."

My birthday? I had just turned twenty-two a few months ago. "Who? Did they say where they were going?"

"No. That was the thing. Candy said Dave was weirded out by the call - he was sure your birthday was in December. Candy called me before they left to meet the guy."

"Candy said Dave was concerned about the call?"

"Candy called me at work, because whoever called Dave wasn't making much sense. The last thing she said before she hung up with me was that she wanted someone to know about this call. She said she had a weird feeling. I didn't think anything of it, but that was hours ago. What should I do?"

My first thought was of Johnny, then Oscar, but that didn't make sense. Both of them told me Davey was safer because they knew about him. I hadn't done anything to piss either of them off. Johnny wouldn't be mad about Xavier – cutting off Xavier was the right move.

Libby must have been running through all the worst possible scenarios, too. "Do you think that crazy Grey guy would have done something to them?" Of course, she thought of Grey. He had beaten her to within an inch of death and would have done the same thing to Candy if I hadn't inserted myself. I'd told Grey and Teddy both to leave Lincoln. Neither of them would have disregarded me.

I didn't know who had lured Dave away, but neither Grey nor Teddy would pull something like this. They might have been reckless and stupid, showmen trying to make names for themselves – Grey and Teddy were a lot of things, but neither had a death wish. Screwing with my brother would make that sort of wish a reality.

Libby's voice started to rise again. "She has to be okay. If she were in trouble, she would have called. I've had my phone on all day. She only called the one time. She hasn't called me back."

Something about the fear in Libby's voice wouldn't allow me to think straight. It wasn't like her to get this worked up about anything. Purposely keeping my voice calm, "Dave was right, my birthday's in December. He didn't try calling me. Let me call around down here and see if someone pulled a prank. I'll call you back as soon as I can."

I hung up on Libby then called Davey's cell phone – my call went straight to voicemail. I dialed Candy; hers, too, didn't ring through. This wasn't a conversation for a coffee shop. I went out to the little SUV and called Johnny. "Hey, it's me. You busy?"

"Ah, I was waiting for you to call. So, how was your day with the girl?"

I hadn't spoken with Johnny since Friday night. I had almost called him last night after returning from Lincoln, but I was high on Libby and didn't want to sound like an idiot. More than twelve hours later I was still consumed by thoughts of her. "It was. . .beyond great. Thanks again."

After the rabbit he had pulled out of his hat for me with his plane, I felt weird asking him if he knew anything about Davey. Johnny was the only person who could screw with my family and get away with it. Anyone else ballsy enough to try a move like that knew it would be as bad as if they had tried something with one of Johnny's daughters. Nothing was adding up.

"Something strange is going on. Someone called my brother today and wanted to meet him. The guy said he was from Kansas City. He had told my brother he wanted to plan a surprise birthday party for me." Johnny didn't say anything, so I explained, "My birthday is eight months away and no one has heard from him or his girlfriend in hours. This wasn't something you were planning, was it?"

"You're asking if I'm planning a birthday party for eight months from now for you?"

"No. . . I mean," a heavy sigh escaped me. The words tasted sour on my lips, "I don't know where my brother is. No one would screw with me unless they had your okay. . . you don't know what's going on, do you?"

"Why would I screw with you? What could you have done for me to want to get to you through your brother?"

An image of Chad holding the USB disc flashed in front of me. I pushed it away. If Johnny knew anything about me giving information to Chad, he would have confronted me with it. No, this wasn't Johnny.

A breath I hadn't realized I was holding released. "I didn't think so. Dammit. Something smells bad. No one down here knows about my brother except you and Oscar. If it wasn't someone from Kansas City, the only others that even know I have a brother are the two people I kicked out of Lincoln." He knew I was talking about Teddy and Grey without me saying their names. An idea bobbed to the surface: what if Larry knew I had spent yesterday with Libby? Would he try to pull something? I dismissed the idea. Candy and Davey would have recognized his voice.

"Come to my office. There are some things I need to share with you. I don't want to say them over the phone."

I didn't remember the drive to Johnny's estate. I was sure I had passed at least twenty signal lights, but I was driving on auto-pilot: my thoughts consumed with Davey. When I stood in Johnny's office, my nerves were frazzled: I wanted answers.

"You know what happened to Dave and Candy?"

Johnny's answer pulled me up short. "I can't be sure, but I believe the police may have them." He cleared his throat. His chair squeaked in pain as he adjusted his seat. His conclusion was without emotion, a matter-of-fact answer. "We may be in the midst of a police sting."

"What?! What are you talking about?"

His voice wasn't urgent or even slightly concerned. "I was going to tell you tomorrow, but you need to be prepared – they'll likely apprehend you first. The motor company received a subpoena today. Seems the police are interested in the new ownership of our franchise. They also wanted a listing of all engines coming out of Chihuahua, Mexico."

The same image of Chad weighed heavy on me. Ignoring the information on the subpoena, I asked, "You think the cops have Dave? What would they want Dave for?"

"The motor company is cooperating. Like any bureaucratic organization, they are delaying the information, but good corporate citizens that they are – eventually the prosecutor will get the information he has asked for. We have accepted our last special delivery from Chihuahua until things settle down." That was good news since I had effectively fired Johnny's highest volume dealer this morning.

"But why do you think that the cops have Dave?"

"You would never turn evidence on me. The police may try to convince you to help them by putting your brother somewhere they think I can't touch him. With the Patriot Act, they can detain anyone without cause on trumped up charges for a couple days."

Johnny's word choice made the hair on the back of my neck jump to attention. . . . *where they think I can't touch him.* Chad didn't know why I had backed out, but it wouldn't have been that hard to figure out. If Chad had me under surveillance like Johnny said, he'd know Davey was my brother. What kind of strings would he have had to pull to lock away Davey and Candy for their own safety? Johnny's explanation made sense, but if it were the cops, why would they come up with such a far-fetched story to get Davey to meet with them? Why wouldn't they just show up at their house and tell them the truth?

"So, what do I do now?"

"Relax, Mark. This happens from time to time. It's nothing to be alarmed about. My businesses have come under investigation from ATF, FBI, even the IRS. None have ever made a case. This will blow over. When it does, whoever has him will let your brother go." Johnny's even tone was impressive. Images of the two of us behind bars played in my head: him smoking a cigar playing a game of poker while I was in the background sucking up to a brick house of a man named Brutus. I shivered at the thought – I had no intention of living in a cage.

I left Johnny's house, feeling marginally better. If Davey were in custody, the police probably had told him all about me by now. He would know exactly what I was and what I did for Johnny. Even if they couldn't prove what they believed, they could tell Davey.

My heart sank. I didn't want to be his drug-dealer brother. I had just gotten him back – having him learn about what I did could ruin us. Davey had had just as tough a life as I had, yet he'd come out on top – he made something of his life. Shame washed over me.

I should have done exactly what I'd set out to do with Chad, or quit the moment I learned Davey was alive. Instead, I didn't do either, and now I really was a criminal. No one was forcing a gun to my head to help Johnny move all his drugs. That had been my choice. The fact that at this moment Davey could know the truth about me and might never want to see me again tore my heart.

I could have asked Johnny to get out, or to be demoted back to leaning on the bookies – instead I was living the life dealing with scum like Xavier. I wasn't disgusted by the lifestyle like I had been two years ago; instead I had borrowed Johnny's personal jet to impress Libby. I was more than stupid; I was a loser. I had become exactly what I set out to bring down.

When Davey found out how I was involved and who I worked for, how would I ever be able to look him in the eye again? A lump formed in my throat: I tried to swallow, but it wouldn't go anywhere. I could lose him, forever this time. I tried to force the blurred vision away. If this were going down like Johnny believed, there was nothing for me to do but wait. If I was to be the first one they arrested, I should make it easier on them, wait at my apartment. The sooner I was in custody, the sooner they'd let Davey get back to his life.

I drove home, took the elevator up to my apartment and called Libby. "No one I know is planning a party." Trying to offer her an explanation that might calm her, I said, "Those two go to the movies a lot. They're probably in a dark theater with their phones turned off. I tried calling them and both phones went straight to voicemail."

"But it's been so long. Why would they keep their phones off?"

A smile formed on my lips that she couldn't possibly see when I offered, "I turned mine off while you were here yesterday."

"What do you mean?"

"I mean I didn't want any disruptions while you were here. Mine was off from the time we got to Kansas City Friday night, until I got back last night. Dave's from the same gene pool; maybe he does the same thing when he wants some alone time with Candy."

She sounded a little less frightened. "Yeah, I guess they have done that before. I'm sorry. I still get a little paranoid about the attack, and then Candy's call had me seriously worried. You're probably right."

Libby said she didn't remember too much about Grey's attack. She didn't like to talk about it, but it was only a couple months ago, so I should have known that's what her fears had stemmed from. Something like that would make me jumpy, too. I wished I were with her right now. If Johnny were right, she wouldn't hear from Candy or Davey for a while – what would I come up with to calm her tomorrow night? Maybe Johnny would consider letting me hang out in Lincoln until I get arrested? He wouldn't want me around the dealership if the cops were planning to storm the place looking for me.

I'd ask about that later. For now, I wanted to savor the freedom I had. My head rested on the sofa, Libby's perfume still clinging to the cushion. "So did you have fun yesterday?"

"Yeah, like I said, when you don't scream like a little girl, you're sort of charming." The fear was tucked away and she was back to her typical abrasive-self. I would have been embarrassed if she could see the enormous smile she had just put on my face.

"What did I tell you about giving out compliments?"

"That I suck at it and shouldn't even bother."

I wondered if she had been thinking about me as much as I had about her. I didn't want to be that needy guy who would ultimately be a huge turn-off, but I needed to know if we were on the right track or if it was one-sided. It felt like we had seriously clicked, but she was so guarded all the time that it was hard to tell. Playfully, I asked, "Did I accomplish my mission? Do you feel like you know the real me now?"

"I know the you that you wanted me to see. The guy who is under all those layers of bullshit? No, I haven't seen him yet."

Her answer was not what I had expected. In typical Mark fashion, I deflected. "I'm pretty simple. Not nearly as complicated as you make me out to be."

"So where does the money come from?" Libby wasn't one to beat around the bush. Interesting word choice: Libby didn't ask where "my" money came from, she asked where "the" money came from. I wondered if she had made that distinction on purpose?

"I told you. I work in sales."

Unrelenting she asked, "What do you sell?"

"Pharmaceuticals."

"Legal or illegal?"

I knew Libby. Lying was not an option. Even one told in an effort to keep her comfortably in the dark was unforgivable. If I lied, I'd keep her for a few days until the police told her or until she caught me in the lie. If I told her the truth, I'd roll the dice on everything between us ending today. Relationships are like Band-Aids. If they aren't meant to be, you pull it off quickly and move on. I shook my head; at least I'd had one seriously awesome day with a girl I'd never forget. "They aren't FDA approved."

A long silence hung on the phone. She was waiting for me to explain it away, to tell her it wasn't as bad as it was. I didn't breathe – I knew what was coming. I said nothing. After listening to the silence on the line for what felt like forever, she finally said, "I didn't expect you to tell me the truth."

A smile formed. "If you prefer a lie, we could rewind, and I could give you a different answer."

Libby ignored my snarky remark. She didn't preach to me, or chastise me, or try to make me feel worse than I already did. Instead, she told me about her dad. "You know, my dad is where he is today because of alcohol. He can't hold a job for longer than a few weeks. It isn't his fault – not really. It's an addiction." I had never met her father. Davey told me much of what Libby had just confessed, so it wasn't a surprise. "You know the first time I ever hung a picture on the wall was when I came to live with Candy?"

I wasn't following, but I didn't want to interrupt. Her tone told me that what she was sharing was important. Then it hit me: her dad was an addict, and she blamed me, or at least people like me, for creating droves of addicts. I had seen it hundreds of times growing up, because the kids who were left behind in the wake of their parents' addictions were the same ones I had grown up with in foster care.

My voice lowered, readying myself for her deathblow. "I didn't know."

"Yeah, this one time we had a great apartment. I must have been about eight. Dad painted my room pink our first day there. It looked like cotton candy, and I loved it. He told me things were going to be different. He gave me a bunch of paint and said I could paint a mural on my bedroom wall because we were staying. I was so excited – I actually believed him."

She got quiet for a few seconds. I imagined Libby as an eight year old in a cotton candy pink room. When she spoke again, her voice sounded distant, "I painted an oak tree that stretched from the floor to the ceiling with a tire swing. Daises – tons of daisies lined the floor. I begged Dad to go back to the store to buy more yellow paint for a happy sun shining near the ceiling. The sky was a light blue, there were big fluffy white clouds, and I even had a stream with a happy fish jumping out of it. I painted that mural for two solid days."

I could picture it in my head. I would have given anything to see her painting. If I had had a room of my own at eight, I would have wanted to paint a happy world, too. Her voice turned icy, "We were living in his truck a month later."

"I'm sorry. I'm sure it was hard."

"Hard? You're sure it was hard? He wasn't there for me. Kids like Candy came to school and complained about having to clean the house or do the dishes, or when we were older and she didn't want to go on vacation with her sisters and parents – I used to get so. . .mad. I never knew where we were going to be living from one day to the next."

"You turned out okay. He must have done something right."

"No. He did everything wrong. Everything."

"Not everything. He didn't give you up." I couldn't believe those words had come out of me. I was six when Mom opened the front door and handed two plastic bags filled with clothes over to the stranger she called to take Davey and me away. Even at six I knew what was going on. She quit on us. She didn't try to hold down a job. She didn't do our laundry. Most of the time she didn't remember to feed us.

Libby was solemn. "No. He didn't. You know what we have in common? My mom didn't want me, either."

Libby had never once mentioned her mom. Not that she had been all that chatty about her dad before tonight, but I knew he was around. Because Libby never talked about her, I assumed her mother had died. "Tell me about her."

"There isn't much to tell. She had me when she was sixteen. Dad was a couple years older. She wanted to put me up for adoption. Dad said no. I saw her a couple times growing up. For all the crap he did wrong, he never stopped trying to do the right thing. Dad thought I'd be curious about her and wanted me to know who she was. She still lives around here, but. . ."

Libby trailed off, so I finished her sentence. "But you aren't interested."

"Yeah. You hear about all these babies who are given up for adoption because the parents do this real selfless thing and want a better home for their kids. That wasn't my mom. She just wanted to get on with her life. After I was born, she didn't want anything to do with me."

"Your dad doesn't sound so bad."

"He did the best he could. It was never good enough. I remember thinking when I was in middle school: how hard is it to get a job? I mean, I was in school eight hours a day. If he just worked while I was at school like everybody else's parents, we'd be fine."

"He must have worked some of the time."

"Yeah, long enough to buy booze and get a couple nights in a shitty motel. Or a month in an apartment. But it always ended the same – we would sneak out of wherever we were staying in the middle of the night and go stay in a homeless shelter for a while. I can't tell you how many times he promised me 'Never again.'"

I knew it was coming. What I did was a deal breaker for her. It made me feel good that she cared enough to tell me why, but it sort of made me want to make things up to her, too. Libby's voice shook when she said, "I don't think we should see each other. I know you aren't like my dad; I'd know if you were using. I can't be with someone who creates the same kind of addiction that destroyed my childhood. I'm sorry."

My voice didn't work. There were words ready to spill out, words explaining how I had started out with good intentions. Words telling her that I had given Chad everything he needed. Words that swore I would start over. None of those words came. "I get it."

"Do you?" She waited for me to respond. "I like you, Mark. But knowing what you do. . ."

I didn't want her to finish her sentence. I didn't want for her to tell me what I already knew. "It's okay. Not everyone can ride a white horse. If you ever need me. . .I'm here."

"Thanks."

Quiet hung between us, as if neither of us wanted to be the one to end it. She had already pulled the Band-Aid off; the two of us were over before we even started. I don't know what made me say it, maybe it was my way of letting her know I understood her decision, "You should paint a mural like that in your room now."

Strangely enough, while the silence hung between us, an image of her future flashed in my head. I could see the scene clear as day: Libby as a mom. If she ever had a daughter, they would paint a bedroom mural, they'd throw mud pies at boys, play football on neighborhood lawns, set off car alarms for fun, and. . . make snow angels. She would never be like our moms. The emptiness hit me – just because I could see each of those images clearly, I would never be able to see any of it in person.

"Libby?"

"Yeah."

"I'm glad I. . . I mean it was pretty great. . .you're out of my league. I'm glad you figured it out now."

"Mark, it's not that."

Swallowing every ounce of my pride, "It is that. One day you are going to find the right guy, one who'll be everything you need him to be. It doesn't matter how badly I want it, I'm not that guy – I'll never be who you deserve. Just, do me a favor. When I come up to see Dave – don't avoid me, okay?"

She didn't answer. This was the reason I had kept her at arm's distance before. If I ended up screwing her over, I didn't want things to be awkward with Davey. I wasn't sure how many days of freedom I had left. It seemed like a pipe-dream to hope we could go back to the way things were. "I promise I won't try to hang around you. If we can go back to just palling around when we're with Dave and Candy. . .I'd like that. You're a lot of fun."

"Sure. Hey, I'm going to try calling Candy again. Call if you hear anything."

Libby hung up. I lay on the couch. Her scent still lingered on the cushion. I'd lost her. It wasn't a fight or something stupid I'd done – I lost her because of who I was. Who was I kidding? I'd never really had a chance. There was a reason I'd never let a girl get close to me: I was stupid for thinking Libby was even a possibility.

CHAPTER 25

My phone rang Monday morning at one minute after seven. I looked at the screen on my phone to see who was calling; Libby's snow angel was stretched across the screen. I started to accept the call, but her rejection from last night was still fresh. I sent her call to voicemail. After two minutes my phone prompted me to let me know I had a voice message waiting. Davey and Candy were probably still gone. Libby might have changed her mind about me. Maybe she could ignore what I had told her last night.

I pressed play. Her high-pitched voice was back. "Mark, it's Libby. Candy and Dave still aren't home. I drove by Dave's garage and his truck's not there. Candy's car is here at the house. Neither of them is answering their phones. Have you heard from either of them? Please call me if you hear anything. I called Mr. Kravitz: he doesn't know where they are, either. If you think of anywhere they might have gone, call me. I'm just. . .I don't know what to do. Can you call me? Please?"

She was freaked the hell out, but something about the fact that she called me – that had to count for something. I leaned over to the pillow she had used Friday night and took a big whiff. The scent was faint, but her perfume still clung to it. I started to call Libby when my phone rang a second time. This time it was Kerry. It wasn't like him to call me this early. I wasn't known for being a morning person.

Remembering Johnny's conclusion last night: Kerry could be someone the cops had picked up by now. I needed to be careful what I said to him: other ears could be listening. I answered his call just before it went to voicemail. "Hey, what's up?"

"I'm downstairs with your doorman. I'm going to hand him the phone. Tell him you know me, so he'll let me come up."

After assuring the doorman that Kerry was an authorized visitor, he let him pass. A minute later Kerry stood at my door; I opened it for him to come in. "What, no coffee?"

Kerry had never been in my apartment before. He had dropped by different times, each time with a fresh coffee in his hand for me. Those times we met in the lobby, or if we had something to discuss, we took a walk around the block. I watched his eyes wander momentarily around my entryway. I opened the door wider to let him in, then closed it when he was inside. Kerry handed me a set of old keys. "I don't know why I'm doing this, but here."

I glanced at the keys in my hand. They weren't mine. "Okay, I'll bite. What are. . ." A little circular key ring was attached; it advertised "Bodies by Brewer." Those were Davey's keys! I didn't finish my question, instead grabbing Kerry by the collar of his shirt, "Where's Dave? Where'd you get these?"

Kerry's eyes opened wide. He tried to back out of my grasp. "Shit! Mark, let go!"

Yanking his collar harder, I pulled him back toward me. Kerry gasped for air. The doorman eight floors below probably heard me shout, "Where did you get these keys?!"

He forced the answer out through his constricted throat. "Xavier." My hand slacked and Kerry doubled over, sucking in air.

Xavier? How the hell did Xavier have Davey's keys? Why would he give them to Kerry? Johnny's theory last night no longer felt viable. No way was Xavier working with the cops. "What was Xavier doing with my brother's keys?"

He shook his head, let out a couple coughs and answered, "I don't know. I saw Xavier this morning when I stopped for a bagel. He was waiting on the sidewalk when I left the bagel shop. He handed me the keys, and told me I needed to give them to you. What the hell is going on?"

I didn't explain. I grabbed my wallet, phone, and keys and sprinted out the door leaving Kerry in my apartment. Johnny had it wrong. He was sure the cops had picked up Davey to safeguard him while a sting was going down – that wasn't it at all. Confronting Xavier on my own after yesterday was a bad idea. If Xavier was brazen enough to kidnap Davey and Candy and hunt down Kerry to pass the message, I could be busting into an ambush. After I was in my car with my wheels in motion, I called Johnny. "The police don't have my brother. Xavier does."

Johnny's voice was calm. "Xavier who?"

I couldn't say who Xavier was over the phone. Johnny didn't know who any of the dealers were; we purposely kept him isolated from the lower level drug dealings. "I'm on my way to your place. I need your help. Oscar's too."

As I approached Johnny's estate, I was halfway down the street when I blared two short blasts followed by two long blasts of the horn. That was our emergency signal that every security guard knew. The gate was wide open when my SUV turned into the driveway. The gate guard was radioing the roving patrol, letting them know a car had just blasted the emergency signal.

According to the SOP in the operations center, no one was supposed to use that signal unless Johnny or one of his girls was in danger. That wasn't the case, and I didn't care that I had just put every security guard on high alert by refusing to waste the fifteen seconds to get let in the normal way. I knew the roving patrol wouldn't recognize the little SUV I was driving; I rolled the windows down so they could see it was me behind the wheel before bullets started flying.

No one intercepted me as I jumped out of the SUV, sprinted up the path, and bounded through the front door of the operations center. Johnny and Oscar were both waiting for me. I told them who Xavier was and why I had cut him off yesterday, then showed them the keys Kerry had brought to me this morning. To drive the point home, I told both of them that Libby had called and confirmed that neither Davey nor Candy had come home last night. Johnny didn't wait for me to ask for his help: he stood up from his desk, looked Oscar squarely in the eye and barked, "We need to pay Xavier a visit. Let's go."

When I recommended to Johnny that we bring security from his estate, he waved off my suggestion. Trying to make him see reason, I offered, "They don't have to go in with us, but I want back-up close."

Johnny refused. "No. Security stays at the estate."

Johnny wouldn't yield, so I turned to Oscar. "Help me out here. Xavier is a wild card. We don't know what we're walking into."

Oscar angrily wagged his finger between Johnny and himself. "*We* take out the trash this time. Word hits the street about this, the message needs to be clear – family is off-limits. Johnny delivering this message in person ensures we don't have a repeat in the future. A second car will trail us, but they stay out of it unless we need them."

Xavier was unpredictable. He had murdered two kids in the last ten days. Only three of us confronting him were good odds if it was just Xavier. The vehicle with security would be just down the street if we needed them. Zane handed me a radio, "Use channel ten as a primary, four as a backup." Since I knew where Xavier lived, I drove one of Johnny's armored SUVs.

Johnny and Oscar may have built this enterprise together, but they had started it more than twenty years ago. Both had aged, neither was as quick on his feet, nor had either personally delivered a message like this the whole time I had worked for them. Xavier was angry with me and, from his perspective, maybe he felt he had nothing to lose. If that were the case, confronting him could be lethal.

I drove straight to his piece-of-shit house. I had gone alone yesterday; today the two men with me sent a clear message. If Xavier had my brother, he would never deal in this town again – not for anyone. We were a united front.

If Xavier did anything to Davey after he kidnapped him, Xavier's life would be over. Xavier hadn't just crossed a line with me; in our world he had crossed Johnny and Oscar the moment he made a move on Davey. Returning to the dilapidated little house, the only change was a snarling dog now stood guard hooked on a chain in the front yard. Davey's truck was nowhere in sight.

The SUV full of security from Johnny's estate parked down the street and around the corner. They were out of view from the little house, but could rush the door in less than two minutes if we needed them. I pressed the button on the radio, "Radio check, over."

Response from the other vehicle was quick, "Solid copy, over."

Pressing the button on the radio, I reminded them of the signal. "Roger. Two keys of the mike if we need you. Stay out of sight unless you hear the signal."

"Solid copy, Boss."

I clipped the radio to the back of my pants and nodded to Johnny. The brindle-colored pit bull chained in Xavier's front yard didn't seem to appreciate having three men approaching his door.

The dog took an angry stance, lowering its shoulders, its head parallel with its body, his ears pinned tightly to his head, readying himself to lunge. Sizing up the length of chain, he had more than enough slack to impede our entry into the house. The dog made me stop on the sidewalk, but did nothing to slow Oscar.

As the angry pit prepared to charge, Oscar turned directly at the animal, and shouted two words, "No. Sit!"

The dog paused, a low angry growl hung in the air as he considered his options. Oscar's voice boomed, drowning out all other neighborhood sounds. "Sit!"

The obedient dog's butt planted in the dirt. His ears were still pinned, but he no longer looked like he would charge us. Oscar reached inside the breast pocket of his suit jacket. I expected him to pull out a handgun; surprise registered when he tossed something to the dog and the animal caught it in mid-air. Oscar praised, "Good boy."

Not believing what I had just seen, "What the hell was that? A dog treat?"

Oscar's wrinkles set deeper on his face when he grinned. "A peanut butter cookie. They work on kids and dogs in any situation." He patted the breast pocket of his jacket.

My attention had been focused on Oscar and the dog; when I turned back to the front door, Johnny was already opening it. Two things struck me as strange: first, the door hadn't been locked. Second, Johnny hadn't bothered to knock. I couldn't imagine anyone in this neighborhood not locking their door, no matter how much of a criminal they were in their own right. For as long as I had known Johnny, no matter the situation, etiquette was everything.

I rushed up to the door, to try to enter before Johnny. When there was going to be trouble, the lower-level guy always entered first. If a bullet was shot, it was my body's job to catch it. Johnny pushed me against the open door, "No. Xavier needs to know I am offended. I go in first." Oscar, too, brushed past me and entered behind Johnny. My heart swelled. These two men wanted Xavier to know there would be no negotiation, there would be no easy way out – taking Davey hadn't been an action against just me, it was an assault on the Corozzo organization.

The message was received before my foot had even passed the threshold. Xavier's words dripped with fear. "Mr. Corozzo, Mr. DelFina, and Mr. Brewer, it's a pleasure to see you." The words were friendly enough, but his pitch was strained, and they spewed out in a frightened mess.

Johnny's answer was an angry growl, rivaling the pit-bull outside, "Where are they?"

Xavier's voice was still high pitched, "They're fine. Mr. Brewer here," gesturing toward me, "left me without a lot of options. It was important he know that there was more at stake than egos. This is my livelihood. People around here depend on me. I just wanted him to reconsider his decision."

Johnny took another step toward Xavier, not mincing a single word. "Where are they?"

Xavier cowered back a step. "They're safe. I swear I didn't touch them."

Oscar, for being as old as he was, surprised the shit out of me when he charged past Johnny straight for Xavier and shouted, "Listen, you little maggot. This isn't a social call. Get both of them out here now." Oscar's fist connected hard with Xavier's face. Standing just inside the door, it was as if I were processing the room in slow motion. Xavier's head absorbed the full force of Oscar's fist, his head wrenched to the side. Oscar stood feet away from Xavier, towering over him, readying to continue on the offense.

I thought of Johnny and Oscar as old men – that had been a mistake. I knew they hadn't gotten to where they were by congeniality, but I had never seen either so aggressive. Xavier staggered back two more steps, his expression as surprised as mine.

Oscar oversaw Johnny's clean-up crew, but I'd never seen him in action. He was quicker on his feet than I had given him credit for. His massive fist had delivered a blow worthy of a welter-weight knock out.

Xavier's hand cradled his quickly-swelling jaw. Something in his eyes changed. The submissive look was gone. His eyes narrowed. Xavier didn't address Oscar; his angry glare fell on Johnny, "Mark cut me off after his carriers shorted me. You're going to let him get away with this?" Xavier still holding his jaw with his left hand, pointed an accusatory finger toward me. "He cuts me off because of thieves who worked for him. I was just reminding the carriers what happens to thieves." He tried to play to Johnny's business sense, "I move more of your product than any three other dealers you have. It's bad for business to cut me off."

Johnny didn't mince words. "You killed two of *his* carriers. His carriers are *my* carriers. You shoot two of *my* employees and you think you get a pass? Mark took it easy on you. If he had brought this to my attention, there would have been more severe repercussions. I won't ask again, where are they?"

Xavier's eyebrows rose. He had tried to appeal to the business side of Johnny. What he didn't take into account was Johnny had more money than God. Nobody pulled a stunt like Xavier had, at least no one I had ever heard of – Johnny was full of rage. Johnny always kept a cool exterior, a poker player if ever there was one, but I saw the vein on his right temple pulsating. Fury ebbed just under the surface.

Xavier, too dense to comprehend just how livid Johnny was, took exactly the wrong approach. "That's it? I cap a couple thieves and I'm cut off? You think Fernando is going to be okay when you can't move his product? You need me."

Johnny's hands were balled into fists at his side. He stared directly into Xavier's eyes, fury no longer masked. I took a step back on instinct, glancing at Johnny, noting that his knuckles had turned white. Johnny's voice boomed in the tiny living room. "Fernando is a supplier. How I move his product and who I choose to move it is my business. I am not here to discuss your employment, I am here to pick up two of my family members." Johnny nodded at Oscar.

If it was not clear before, there was no ambiguity whatsoever. Xavier would be in just as much trouble as if he had kidnapped a family member of Johnny's. Xavier's hand dropped from his already swollen jaw. Johnny's threat sunk in as Xavier's answer came out slow and robotic, "So you won't reconsider our arrangement?"

Johnny's voice boomed. "No. Nothing's changed. We may let you live, but you have three seconds to get Mark's brother into this room."

For the first time, I looked around the inside of the little boxy house. The exterior of the house was rundown and dated; the inside looked just as neglected. The kitchen was in front of me; I could see it through an opening in the wall where a little countertop separated the two rooms. Behind me was the front door where we had entered. On my left were two doors; from the exterior of the house I knew one led to a single car garage. To my right, two closed doors stood together – possibly bedrooms. I could hear movement behind one of the closed doors to my right. Would Davey and Candy be here, or would he have tucked them away somewhere else?

I took a step toward the doors on my right. Xavier grabbed a cigar box from a coffee table and pulled out a handgun. His movement had been so quick I had nearly missed it, but instead of pointing the gun at me, it was aimed at Oscar.

I reasoned that Oscar had been the biggest threat to Xavier out of the three of us. Oscar had already hit him once. I froze initially then both of my hands reached into the air, even though the gun was not pointed at me. My eyes went to Johnny: he didn't so much as flinch while his hands remained at his side. I willed my hands to lower, to look strong like these other two men. I had a gun strapped to my ankle, but I was in no position to pull it without drawing attention to myself. The radio was clipped to the back of my pants – I slowly lowered my hands to reach for it when Oscar's shout startled me still.

Oscar's voice was menacing, "That was the last mistake you'll ever make." Oscar lunged forward, far too fast for a man of his age. Xavier's gun discharged, halting Oscar just inches away from him. Oscar tried to charge forward, but blood poured from his chest as he went to his knees. Johnny's posture stiffened as he watched Oscar roll onto his back on the floor. Johnny caught my eye and gave me a short nod. We both rushed Xavier from opposite directions. I keyed the microphone on the radio for help as I rushed forward, then dropped the radio to the floor as I launched myself at Xavier. Xavier fired a second time – Johnny went down in the same moment I connected with Xavier and knocked him to the floor. I wrestled with Xavier, trying to knock the gun free from his hand.

Xavier threw all of his weight at me and knocked me off balance. His foot connected with my stomach, knocking the wind out of me. I grabbed one of his legs, to try to keep him in close. He struggled to get away from me, kicking at my side but missing. I scrambled to get to my feet when I saw him aiming the gun directly at my chest.

The front door flew open. Xavier, still holding the gun, turned toward it. A third shot echoed in the little house. Xavier's body slumped to the floor beside me.

My hands shook. I looked at the scene, but had trouble understanding what I was looking at. It wasn't one of the men from our security team. Chad stood in the doorway, his gun still aimed in directly on Xavier's still body. Chad glanced around the room, took the five steps to where Xavier and I lay, and kicked the gun out of Xavier's hand. Security from our backup vehicle heard the gunshots and came running. They were in the little house shortly after Chad. Other uniformed police officers flowed in through the open door.

Chad kneeled beside me, "Were you shot? Mark, are you okay?"

I didn't have a scratch on me. I nodded that I was fine, and Chad offered his hand to help me to my feet. I ignored Chad's hand and scurried to Johnny on my hands and knees. Although blood still flowed from the wound in his head, Johnny was dead. I went to Oscar; his chest rose and fell rapidly, both hands holding the wound in his chest. Oscar tried to speak, but a sound similar to a deflating balloon came from his chest. He let go of his wound and grabbed my arm with bloody fingers. Oscar turned his head and coughed as bloody spit landed on the floor beside him. Digging his fingers into my arm, his raspy voice said, "Sister. . .have sistersss." Oscar's words trailed off.

Oscar was fading fast. He had told me about his brother in Cincinnati, but he hadn't mentioned a sister. "You want me to tell your sister something?"

His head shook marginally. His death grip on my arm didn't waver. "No.

You. . .have. . .sist. . ." More coughs, "Your. . .father. . ." He tried to suck in air through gritted teeth. I pushed both of my hands against his chest wound trying to stop the blood. "Not. . .Omaha." He looked at Johnny dead on the floor beside him and reached his hand out to try to touch his oldest friend. Oscar took one final raspy breath, his grip on my arm relaxed, and he died.

A sister? Oscar said we had a sister. Our dad was not in Omaha? My hands stayed on Oscar's chest, willing him to breathe again, willing him to finish what he had started to tell me. The next thing I knew Davey was lifting me off the floor. He was here. The whole time he was in this shitty little house. Candy was standing further away, leaning up against the wall near the door that had been closed. Her face looked pale, but not a visible mark showed on her. I couldn't understand what Chad was saying, but he was talking fast to several police officers near the entryway.

When did Davey come into the room? Did he hear what Oscar said? Had I imagined it or were Oscar's dying words an effort to tell me that Davey and I had a sister? I grabbed Davey's shoulder, "Did you hear what Oscar said?"

He shook his head, "No. I just saw you kneeling over him. He was a friend of yours: that's the guy who brought the Mustang up for a restore last week."

I had momentarily forgotten that Oscar had already met Davey. I looked into Davey's brown eyes. They were like looking into a mirror. How was I supposed to answer him? Oscar hadn't been a friend, not really. At least, before today I had never thought of him that way. Oscar was a necessary arm in Johnny's business. He was someone I respected, but if our roles were reversed, would I have attacked the man who kidnapped his brother? Would I have sacrificed my life for his or Johnny's? A tightness gripped my chest. I owed them each a debt I could never repay. "Yeah. He was a friend."

A uniformed police officer had directed Johnny's security team outside. Chad looked between Davey and me with the same wide look of disbelief on his face that everyone had when they saw the two of us together. When no question came, I offered, "Eerie, isn't it?" I gestured to Davey, "Chad, this is my brother Dave. Dave, this is a friend of mine. We grew up in the same group home."

It went without saying that Chad was the law, the badge on his belt and the uniforms taking instructions from him let that secret out. Davey narrowed his eyes, as if registering that whatever Xavier may have told him about me could be a lie. Chad must have seen the same look I did, because he leaned in close to Davey and said, "Mark has been instrumental in helping us crack down on the drugs in town. I'm sorry you were pulled into this." He turned to me, "I'll need to take statements from all of you, so stick around. Mark, your security team is waiting for you in the yard. Candy and Dave, would you two mind stepping outside with Officer Gatlin?"

The security detail from the estate looked shell-shocked. I left Davey long enough to give them instructions. "I'm going to need to give a statement. You four head back to the estate. Keep the girls away from the television. I don't want them hearing about this from anyone but me."

The rest of the day was a little bit of a blur. Chad had inferred to Davey that I was involved but on the good guy side. A female cop was sitting on the step outside with Candy, watching someone from Animal Control loading the pit-bull into the back of a truck. I pulled out my phone and sent a text to Libby. "They are ok. Can't talk now. C and D are safe."

I returned to where Davey stood by the front window. We watched through the open window as several police officers discussed the crime scene and someone with a camera took pictures. He turned to me, still not fully grasping what had happened. "All of this over us?"

I looked at Johnny's lifeless body still on the floor inside. I was conflicted. Part of me was angry. Annabelle and Anastasia needed him. Johnny had given his life for me. Oscar struggled to stay alive to tell me I had a sister. He didn't want to go to his grave with that secret. Why had these two men done this for me? Before I found Davey, I was doing everything in my power to send Johnny to prison, to shut down his operation.

Part of me felt the glimmer of hope that I could safely put all of this behind me. Chad didn't seem that anxious to arrest me: he had the perfect opportunity and hadn't done it. I didn't understand how this happened. "What happened? How did you end up at Xavier's place?"

"We got a call yesterday from," Davey pointed through the window to where Xavier's body lay lifeless on the floor, "him. He said he was planning a birthday party for you and wanted me to be involved. He said you talked about me all the time, and he wanted to meet me."

That didn't make sense. I had exactly one conversation with Xavier in the last month, and I had never mentioned Davey or, for that matter, anything personal. How had he found out about Davey? To my knowledge, only Johnny and Oscar knew about him. "Xavier and I weren't friends." More to myself than to Davey I asked, "How did he know about you?"

Dave looked furious. "There was another guy when we got here. Candy told me he was the same guy who attacked her and Libby and shot me in the arm a few months ago. It was Grey."

"Grey? Grey Blair told Xavier about you? He was here?"

Davey nodded. Grey had crossed the line. There wouldn't be a place anywhere in the country where Grey would be able to hide. He wouldn't have crossed me like this unless he believed I would never find out. Grey must have expected Xavier would kill me today.

"Before I stumbled across you and Candy, I was. . .helping the police. I didn't want for any of the people I was mixed up with to find out about you because I was worried they'd try to get to me through you." I took a second look at the carnage through the window. "I was right to be worried."

Davey didn't say anything. Trying to understand how all this had happened so quickly, I asked, "So you came down to help plan a birthday party? What happened when you got here?"

"It was obvious I'd been suckered. He separated us, tied up Candy, then threatened to kill her if I didn't handcuff myself to the bed. We got here yesterday afternoon, and had been in that bedroom the whole time. I had just broken the bed frame and was untying Candy when I heard people arguing in the other room. I almost shouted for help, but thought better of it and leaned into the door to try to hear what was being said. Then the shooting started."

"You were here for a long time. What all did Xavier tell you?"

Davey's expression looked conflicted. Candy, who I had nearly forgotten, was just feet away and answered for him. "He said a bunch of stuff. We got the feeling it had to do with drugs. Is that why you were in Lincoln when I first saw you?"

I nodded, remembering the night I first met Candy and Libby at Bank Shot.

Candy didn't know that I had been in Lincoln to meet with Libby's ex-boyfriend, Larry. I wanted to let that tidbit of information slip as a means to ensure the two of them didn't patch things up, but I kept it to myself. Davey found his voice, "So when you had a late night meeting, the first night you came to my garage with Candy, you left my place to go buy drugs?"

I nodded again. Davey looked disgusted, "All those times you came by for a few hours – you were buying drugs then, too?"

"No. Not all the times. Most of the times I just wanted to see you. It was hard to be gone from Kansas City for long without raising suspicion."

"So what are you? You're a drug dealer?"

I didn't want to be disrespectful to Johnny; he had made the ultimate sacrifice for me, but at my core that's what I had been – a drug dealer. Johnny was prepared to do anything necessary to save my brother, yet the two had never even met. I did things I'm not proud of, and I did them as Johnny's employee, but Johnny was much more than a drug dealer. I was finally in a situation where there would be no repercussions for the truth. "It's complicated. That's Johnny Corozzo. I worked for him. I helped him move drugs around the Midwest, but I fed the information to Chad, so he could bring him down."

Davey motioned to Chad still directing things from inside the house. "Your friend, he tried to get you to quit working for Johnny?"

Chad directed a photographer in the living room. A pained laugh escaped from me. "Not really. He's the one who talked me into taking the job." Davey got a strange look as if my words weren't processing. "Look, it's a long story. It would be better if I sat down and told you everything from the start. I never said I was perfect, but I did what I did for a good reason."

The beat-up little house was drawing a neighborhood crowd. Whispers initially, but voices were getting louder speculating on what had happened inside. The coroner's vehicle had arrived, and the driver was waiting for the go ahead to begin removing bodies. A uniformed police officer walked over and directed us to the back of a police cruiser just as a news van arrived. Davey, Candy and I were just climbing into the back seat when Chad jogged over. "Hey, Mark, I'll give you a ride. We can catch up with Candy and Dave at the station."

I handed Davey his keys that Kerry had given me. "Do you know where your truck is?"

Davey nodded, "He told that Grey guy that he was going to leave it in a parking lot. I've got an anti-theft system; the service dispatcher will tell me where it's parked."

I closed the door with Candy and Davey in the back seat and went to the car Chad stood by. It was an unmarked police car, and I took the passenger seat in front. Chad pulled away from the curb before he spoke. "I know you told me you were out, but I never took you off of my confidential informant list. As far as my bosses and everyone else knows, you were a plant we put in the organization."

I didn't know what to say. I wasn't going to be prosecuted? Johnny told me Chad had enough information to put me away for twenty to life. A million questions were whizzing through my head: how had he kept me a secret when Johnny obviously had someone on the inside with the police? How had Chad known we were at Xavier's place to begin with? Was there a sting, and what was going to happen to the salespeople from all the dealerships? Instead, I kept my curiosity at bay and said, "Thanks."

Chad turned to me and smiled. "I wanted to disrupt the drugs coming into Kansas City. I'd have to say mission accomplished. As far as everyone knows, you were helping me the whole time. I'd like for everyone to continue to believe that. But as of today, you no longer have that cover from me. If you keep doing what you're doing, you'll be behind bars by Christmas."

He was offering me the chance I wanted – the ability to start fresh. "How did you know Dave and Candy were at Xavier's?"

"I didn't. Word on the street was that you cut off Xavier's supply. It happened just a couple days after you and I had talked, then I got your voicemail telling me you had taken care of it. We had been watching Xavier for a while and knew he was moving a lot of product. After talking to you Friday, and learning you had cut him off on Sunday, I took a stab in the dark and hoped you'd cut him off because he was tied to Heather and Grant's murders. I was executing a search warrant for the weapon used in their shootings when we heard gun shots from the sidewalk."

"That was pretty good timing. A minute earlier and I may have been the one lying in blood. A minute later and I'm sure I would have been. I don't know how many guns Xavier had, but I'd bet that's the one he used on both of the kids."

We passed some old boarded up businesses along the city streets. Chad asked, "Dave's your brother. Is that why you backed off from collecting on Johnny?"

"I couldn't risk Dave."

"I get it. That makes me feel a lot better. I worried you'd decided to make a go of it as a full-blown criminal."

"Well, I am a criminal. But after today, I don't have to be." Those words felt good to say. Truth rang through them.

"What's next? Or do you think you'll change your mind and I'll be doing surveillance on you in a few months."

"No way. I'm out. Completely out." Maybe not completely out, I had one more illegal activity I intended to do. I wouldn't ask Oscar's boys to do the dirty work for me – I was going to find Grey myself.

CHAPTER 26

My trip to the police station was quick. In four hours' time I had given my statement, accepted congratulations from Chad's boss, and felt like a complete ass. I was grateful Chad stuck his neck out for me and made me out to be the hero, but I couldn't get over the fact that Johnny and Oscar were both dead. They would both still be alive if they hadn't have put my brother's life ahead of their own. I was responsible for both of their deaths.

Davey found me sitting on a hard plastic chair in a waiting room. "Candy and I are all done. We're going to head home. You want to ride back to Lincoln with us and take a breather for a couple days?"

I did. More than anything I wanted a break. I didn't want to face Johnny's circle or any of his employees. No way would the police be able to keep this under wraps, and it was only a matter of time before everyone learned I had gotten off free as a bird. Everyone would know I had been working with the cops. My life wouldn't be worth the shell casings from Xavier's house when word spread.

As badly as I wanted to go into hiding – I couldn't. Johnny's daughters were orphans; it was because of me that they no longer had a parent. I shook my head, "I'll be up in a few days. I need to take care of some things here first."

Davey's eyes lowered as he pressed his lips together. He turned to walk away, but I darted up from my chair and grabbed hold of him. My sudden onslaught of affection threw him off guard for a second, but he regained his balance and hugged me back. The only words I could get out were, "I'm sorry." Those words were true on so many levels. I was sorry Candy and Davey had been dragged into my world. I was sorry I had ever accepted Chad's offer to get in close to Johnny. I was sorry that I hadn't told Davey any of this before hand. But most of all, I was sorry Johnny and Oscar were dead.

Davey's arms pulled me tighter, "It's over, Mark. We're okay. We're both okay. Do what you need to do, but you can always come stay with us."

"Thanks. Call me when you get back." A police officer waited to give them a ride to Davey's truck. He put his arm around Candy, she waved goodbye but said nothing as the two made their way down the hall. I hoped that today wouldn't be the last day I'd ever see them.

I was confident that reports of what had happened had already spread wide all over the city. This wasn't the type of information that anyone could keep quiet. Once I was sure the police were done with me, I fished my cell out of my pocket and called the Ops Center. Zane answered, and I told him to send a car to pick me up at the police station. The backup security team had already retrieved Johnny's vehicle from Xavier's house. His voice was hollow when he asked, "Is it true?"

"Yeah. Johnny's dead. No one told the girls?"

"No. A state cop came by to give notification – we turned him away. We told the staff to keep the televisions off in the house. Mr. Brooks confiscated Anastasia's cell phone so she wouldn't hear it from anyone until we heard from you." Mr. Brooks was the head of security who took over after I left; he was the right man for the job: well-trained and not at all affiliated with Johnny's businesses.

"Good. Let Brooks know I'm on my way. I'll tell the girls."

The black SUV deposited me at Johnny's front door. The memory of my first time to the house assaulted me. It was Christmas Eve two years ago: Johnny had flown a bunch of us to New York City for dinner. He wouldn't let me go back to my lonely apartment and insisted I spend Christmas with his family.

I opened the door; the house was quiet – too quiet. The usual noise was gone: no dishes clanging in the kitchen, no music blaring from the pool, televisions in nearly every room were always on and today nothing. I walked into the sitting room to find Anastasia flipping through a magazine, looking irritated. Annabelle was coloring a picture full of pastels on a coffee table. Brooks stood tall in the doorway watching over both girls.

Of everyone who worked for Johnny, I was closest to the girls. I had lived on the estate, I had been there the last two Christmas mornings, and for every major holiday for the last two years; it was me who they saw their dad talking to late into the night. I cleared my throat. "Mr. Brooks, I've got it. Go inform the staff." He nodded; before he left the room, he reached into his back pocket and handed me Anastasia's phone. In a hushed voice he said, "She's been asking for it. I didn't want for her to hear anything before you got here."

Anastasia flipped her magazine onto the coffee table, which caused several of Annabelle's crayons to roll onto the floor. "If Dad went to the Caribbean without us again, I'm going to slice every suit in his closet into little strips and decorate his room for his return."

I took a seat on the couch next to her. "Annabelle, come up here for a second." She put her crayon down and climbed onto my lap. Anastasia must have sensed something was wrong because her demeanor changed: no longer the angry teenager.

I had gone over how to tell them several times on the way over. I remembered the stupid grief counselor who had come to deliver the news that Davey was dead. His words about Davey being in a better place and it being my responsibility to cherish Davey's memory hadn't helped me at all. I had wanted answers. I wanted to know what had happened to Davey. The putz didn't know, mainly because Davey wasn't dead and someone had made a huge mistake.

Remembering that empty feeling of having no answers, I wouldn't do the same thing to the girls. There would be no flowery words about Johnny being in a better place. "There's no good way to tell either of you this, so I'm just going to tell you. I want you to know that your dad did a really brave thing today."

Annabelle interrupted, her little eyes full of pride, "Dad says being brave isn't a choice. It is who we are."

I remembered Johnny telling Annabelle that when she was standing on the diving board last summer, too frightened to jump into the pool. Her swimming instructor had tried for nearly an hour to coax her into diving in; it was Johnny's subtle reminder that gave his daughter the confidence she needed. "That's right, 'Belle. He's one of the bravest men I have ever known." Annabelle smiled. Anastasia looked away, a single tear rolled down her cheek. She sensed what was coming.

Anastasia may not have known exactly what her dad did for a living, but she was nearly eighteen and was smart. I wrapped my arms around Annabelle and took Anastasia's hand. "Today I needed your dad's help. A bad man took my brother, and I wasn't brave enough to go confront him on my own. The man who kidnapped my brother shot your dad."

Anastasia yanked her hand away from mine. Annabelle's big brown eyes stared at me as her lower lip quivered. "I'm so sorry, girls, but your dad died. He loved you both very much."

Anastasia seethed anger. "Who shot him?"

"The man's name was Xavier. The police shot Xavier after he killed your dad and Uncle Oscar."

Annabelle clung to me as quiet sobs echoed against my chest. She refused to let go, but it was Anastasia who broke my heart. She didn't shed another tear, preferring to share only the tough exterior her father would have shown. One of Annabelle's nannies entered the room and tried to lift her off of me. Annabelle pushed her away, keeping her face buried in my neck.

Anastasia's voice was hard. "Can I have my phone back now?"

I understood Anastasia's response better than most. She wasn't callous or unfeeling, she grieved the loss of her father every bit as badly as Annabelle; she just didn't know how to show it. Rather than argue with her about her stupid phone, I offered, "You know when I came to live here, he told me he gave me a great honor by trusting me to protect his daughters. He didn't need to tell me that. I had met you both a couple Christmases ago. I knew it was an honor to look after both of you. He loved you both more than anything in the world."

Anastasia's posture softened as she leaned a little further into the couch we were sitting on. "He gave you your phone that Christmas. Do you remember? I'll never forget seeing your reaction, Anastasia. It was as if he had reached into your soul and found the one gift you would cherish more than any other. Then watching you glue all those crazy rhinestones and puffy pink paint to the phone's case that day – well, I was grateful to be here."

Annabelle, not to be outdone said, "You helped me put my kitty puzzle together, too."

I had dreaded that part of Christmas morning. Who would give an eight year old a 500-piece puzzle with five white kittens on it? "I remember. After we finished the puzzle and Anastasia called everyone she knew in the northern hemisphere, do you remember what we did?"

Both girls giggled. I knew they remembered the day as fondly as I did. "What, you don't remember?"

Anastasia smiled, her eyes glossed over, "Dad opened up a big box of Nerf guns, and we played teams chasing each other around the house. He dove into a snow drift in the back yard when Annabelle unloaded a full barrel of Nerf darts on him."

"I never thanked your dad for that day, or you girls. Did you know that was the best Christmas morning I've ever had?" Neither of the girls spoke. "You see you two both got the gifts you wanted that morning, but I got the gift I wanted, too. I grew up without a family, and I had forgotten why a family was so important until you two reminded me."

Anastasia sounded like a feminine Johnny when she stated, "You are family, Mark. Dad loved you, too." Guilt washed over me. Until this morning I never knew how much Johnny was willing to sacrifice for me. Looking in his daughter's eyes, I wished I had been the one to reach Xavier first.

Annabelle loosened her grip and turned her wide brown eyes on me again. "Why didn't you have a family?"

"I do, now. I found my brother a few months ago. When I told your dad that my brother was in trouble this morning, he wanted to help me. So did Uncle

Oscar." Surprised by the truth in my own words, "I wish I hadn't have asked for their help. I'm so sorry."

Anastasia asked, "He's really dead?" I nodded. Both girls were quiet for a long time. I rocked Annabelle on my lap while Anastasia stared across the room. Anastasia didn't look at me, but her voice sheepishly asked, "Can I call Mom?"

My heart lurched. In all the time I had known Johnny, the girl's mother never came up. I had always known Johnny to be a single parent. I assumed she had died, but I'd never asked. "Your mom?"

Anastasia's eyes darted to the floor as if she had said something wrong. "Yeah. She lives in Miami, or at least she used to. We haven't seen her in a long time. Would it be okay if I called her?"

I wondered if there was a reason I had never met their mother. There was nothing in the SOP about her, so I didn't know she existed. Absent any other idea on what to do, I nodded that Anastasia could call her.

Anastasia left the room and returned with a slip of paper. She handed it to me. "This was her number. I haven't called her in a long time." Her eyes darted to the floor again.

"Do you want me to call her?" Anastasia looked grateful at my offer and nodded. She and I had far more in common than I had ever realized. Not knowing the dynamics of their relationship, I could only guess that it might be as strained as the relationship I didn't have with my own mother.

I had found Mom's name and number in information after I ran away, but I had never dialed the number. I wasn't brave enough to take another rejection from her. I could only hope that the girl's mother wasn't as callous as mine had been. "What's her name?"

Anastasia answered, "Beverly. But everyone calls her Bev."

I dialed Beverly's number as both daughters watched me closely. Anastasia was hopeful, Annabelle's expression was. . .I wasn't sure: cautiously optimistic. A friendly voice answered the phone on the third ring. "Hello?"

"Hi, this is Mark Brewer in Kansas City. Is this Bev?"

"I'm afraid I don't know a Mark Brewer."

"That's right. You don't know me. I was calling on behalf of your daughters, Annabelle and Anastasia."

Bev squealed into the phone. "Oh my God, hi! Yes, this is Bev. How are they? Are they okay?"

A much better response than I had envisioned when Anastasia didn't want to dial for herself. "They're both okay. If it's okay with you, Anastasia would like to talk to you."

I heard the relief in the woman's voice. "Of course. Yes. Please put her on."

I handed Anastasia the phone. She looked at it for a long time, tears welled in her eyes but she didn't put the phone to her ear. I gently prodded, "Go ahead. It sounded like she was excited to hear from you." I mouthed the words to her, "Be brave."

Anastasia cradled the phone against her face, her hard voice was gone, "Mom?"

It wouldn't have been right to hang on every word, but I listened close enough to know in general what the two were talking about. The first several minutes was unabated joy on Anastasia's end of the conversation. The things you would expect: answers about school, boyfriends, her little sister; then the happiness in Anastasia's voice diminished as she got around to what had happened. "Mom, Dad was in an accident today." She told her mother that Johnny had been murdered. From the half of the conversation I could hear, it sounded like Bev wanted to fly up to Kansas City. I cut in and whispered, "Ask if she wants me to send the jet to pick her up."

Anastasia asked then nodded her mother's answer to me. They spoke for several more minutes before she handed the phone to her little sister. Annabelle was more clinical when speaking to her mom: no doubt she was answering a series of questions because her answers were several yeses, a couple noes, and a giggle. Annabelle handed the phone to me, and I made arrangements for Johnny's jet to retrieve her the same afternoon.

I strolled into Johnny's office. I had rarely been in this room alone, but had spent more hours than I could count with Johnny. Endless hours of strategy sessions, enterprise discussions, and stories from the old days echoed off the walls. I sat behind the desk, seated in Johnny's chair – something I had never done before. I phoned Johnny's attorney to tell him Johnny had been killed. Mr. Haberstein informed me that he was the executor of Johnny's estate. He would draw up the necessary papers for the businesses to continue to operate during probate.

Brooks tapped on the doorframe even though I had left the door open when I went inside. I looked up, "Yes?"

"Felix is at the gate." Brooks' expression was grim.

"Okay. What's wrong? He's on the access list."

"Mr. Brewer, he's pretty angry right now. He is on the list, but given his state of mind, I asked the guard to hold him in place until I spoke with you."

Word had spread – that was quicker than I had expected. If he was at the gate demanding to see me, that could mean only one thing – word was out that I was working for the cops.

"It's a tough time for all of us. Have him escorted to the Ops center. I'll meet him there. I don't want him frightening the girls any more than they already are."

"Roger. From what they called over the radio, it might be wise to give him a few minutes to cool down before you join him at the Ops Center."

I liked Brooks, and I took his advice. It was a full twenty minutes before I opened the door to the guesthouse where the Ops Center was located. I left Brooks with the girls with instructions that the televisions were to remain off. A triple homicide would be the lead story for days – the girls didn't need to hear any reporters' commentary on what had happened to their dad.

CHAPTER 27

I had just crossed the threshold of the door to the Ops Center when Felix shouted, "Is it true?!"

Not completely certain as to what he was asking, I provided the safest answer I could. "One of the lower level dealers shot Johnny and Oscar this morning. I was with them when it happened."

Accusatorily Felix said, "Why didn't I hear this from you?"

I was notifying everyone in order of their importance. Oscar's wife was to be my next call, but Felix had trumped her by making a scene at Johnny's front gate. Before I could answer as to why he heard about Johnny's death from someone other than me, he accused, "Pretty convenient, don't you think? Johnny and Oscar are both dead, so is the guy who shot them. Feels like a coup to me."

Until today I had wondered if there was something wrong with me. I never seemed to have the same emotions that everyone else felt. I worried that there was something seriously wrong with me because I was far more analytical than I was emotional. After breaking the news to Annabelle and Anastasia, talking to their mother who I didn't know existed, and delivering the news to Johnny's attorney, I learned that I did have normal emotions. Unfortunately, I was now emotionally drained. I didn't have the strength Johnny would have had in the same situation.

"No. I don't think it's convenient at all. Neither do his daughters. My brother wasn't too keen on being dragged into the mix, either. There is no coup and there is no jockeying for position. Go home, Felix."

"I've got a lot more experience than you. This is my town. I've worked for Johnny longer than you've been alive."

I had hoped to put this conversation off for a few days, but Felix wouldn't wait. If he was this ticked off, I could only imagine the other key people's reaction. "Fine. It's your town, Felix. Now grab a seat." I turned toward Zane who didn't want to be involved in this conversation. He was concentrating so hard on the monitors it looked like he was trying to validate each individual pixel in an effort to stay out of the conversation between Felix and me. "Pull up the recall roster, get Jorge, Spencer, Liam and Kerry on the phone. Tell them to get over here now."

Zane's fingers whizzed on his keyboard. He spoke quietly into his microphone. I sat down on another computer and pulled up the phone number of the one person I hoped never to speak to in person. There were plenty of layers in between us, but this wasn't something he could hear from anyone other than me. I asked the security team to step outside, so that only Felix and I were in the room. My shaky fingers dialed the phone as Felix sat watching.

"Fernando, it's Mark Brewer from Kansas City. We've got a problem."

His thick Mexican accent answered, "What kind of a problem?"

"Johnny was killed this morning. We've got a disruption in operations up here. I'm going to call Luis in Chihuahua to ask him to hold future shipments until we learn how much of our operation has been compromised. I wanted you to hear it from me."

"That's no' my problem."

"I know it's not. We won't be accepting any more shipments. The payments have been made for everything in the pipeline. What I'm saying is we are suspending all future orders until we can get things under control. I'm going to ask Luis to return your product to you. We aren't asking for a refund, I just don't want it shipped north until we get everything sorted out."

Fernando may have been a big time drug lord, but he was as much of a businessman as Johnny had been. Our willingness to pay for product that there was no guarantee we would ever receive was a show of good faith. Fernando asked, "How long do you need to sort things out?"

"We're not sure. A few weeks, maybe longer."

"Pass my condolences onto his family. I los' my brother Hector last year. He, too, was a great man. I will look for your call when things have been sorted out."

I hung up the phone and Felix tore into me. "Do you know what you just did? It has taken decades to get this set up! There is no reason to shut things down. Do you know what a disruption will do to the organization? You don't have the authority to make this change."

I stood up, walked to the door and let the security team know it was safe to come back into the Ops Center. Turning my attention to Felix, I responded, "I don't have the energy to deal with you right now. Sit quietly or I'll have you moved to another room."

"Moved to another room? Who do you think you're talking to? Maybe I should duck. Is a stray bullet going to find me today, too?"

Zane stood up from his chair readying for my order to have Felix moved elsewhere in the house. I shook my head, letting him know I wanted to keep my eye on Felix where he was. Jorge was the first to get to the meeting, his limp heavy on the sidewalk before he walked through the door. Spencer and Liam walked in together a few minutes behind Jorge, and Kerry was the last to arrive.

I cleared my throat, "I know it's a shock to all of us losing Johnny and Oscar today. I've been struggling with how to keep the organization together. I don't have many answers. What I learned today I wanted to share with all of you. Let's go into the conference room to discuss what I do know."

Felix made a disrespectful grunt and the other four looked at him in surprise. After we had relocated to a conference room adjacent to the Ops Center, I continued, "The police have more sophisticated surveillance than any of us had given them credit for. They seem most interested in the drug trade, and as a result, they have a great deal of intelligence on how and when we move drugs. Out of respect for Johnny and everything that he built, I plan to suspend all drug-related activities until after his funeral. This will give his family a chance to grieve without the potential media circus should the police choose to move forward with the intelligence they have gathered."

Spencer, Jorge, Liam and Kerry nodded their agreement; Felix continued to scowl like an insolent child. "I will be in contact with each of you, in person when possible, but there may be times I have to send messages to you to keep you all in the loop. Do any of you feel strongly about keeping operations going or dissolving any that could land us behind bars?"

Felix seethed, "Feeding information to the cops and now you're worried about us landing in prison?" All eyes around the room opened wide at his accusation. He didn't relent, "That's right. We know where their surveillance came from. Funny how Johnny and Oscar were both killed, and the dealer who shot them was aiming at you!"

Kerry's eyes had been resting on the floor, but he looked up to the group in response to Felix's accusation. "This wasn't Mark's fault. Xavier killed two of our carriers in less than two weeks. Mark found out and cut him off. Mark didn't tell me to deliver the message. Mark didn't even let another carrier make the last delivery; Mark took the last of Xavier's drugs to him and told him face-to-face that he was cut off."

Jorge and Spencer listened intently to Kerry. Liam had never attended a leadership meeting before, so he was paying as much attention to the others as he was to me. Felix silently fumed. Kerry adjusted his tie then looked squarely at Felix for his last remark to the group, "Oscar told all of us, Mark was next in line. I'll do whatever I'm told." Kerry's gaze shifted to me, "Mark, if you want to suspend drug operations, then we suspend drug operations."

Jorge had nothing to do with the drugs; he oversaw the bookies, loan sharks and set the numbers for every gambling transaction in the organization. Jorge concurred with Kerry, "Yeah, Oscar sent word that the organization's structure had changed months ago. Mark's next in line." He turned to me, "Whatever you need, Boss." I had "heard" I was number three, but this was the first conversation where I learned that Oscar had formally passed the word to everyone.

Liam hadn't been in the inner circle, but he had worked for Oscar for more than twenty years. He and I'd had very little interaction. In Oscar's absence, Liam needed to be involved in these types of discussions. His arms remained crossed over his chest. Liam asked cautiously, "So how did Oscar, Johnny and Xavier all get killed? Something doesn't add up. Why aren't you in jail?"

Before I could answer Liam, Felix shouted, "Exactly!! Not a scratch on him. He's walking around like he's calling the shots. He was in and out of the police station faster than most people get out for a traffic violation."

My phone rang. I looked at the picture on the screen and saw the image of Libby making a snow angel. If ever there was a bad time to accept a phone call, this was it. I wanted to hear her voice, but I pushed her to voicemail. I couldn't be distracted; I needed to be on my game.

"You're right Liam. Nothing added up for me either. Xavier shot Oscar, then Johnny. Xavier and I struggled, but he had the upper hand and was squeezing the trigger when the police came charging through the door. The police were executing a search warrant for the two kids' murders when they busted in the door after hearing shots. I'm not sure how I'm sitting here right now; believe me, I've never been a lucky guy."

I turned my attention to Felix rather than the entire group, "While I was at the police station, a junior cop let slip that they had our dealership operations under surveillance. If they are watching us, it would be stupid to continue until we know what we're up against. Johnny had this town wired, but with him dead, I'm not sure any of us could beat an indictment."

That was close enough to the truth to throw off suspicion; at least until I could get things sorted out. "For now, drug operations are suspended. Everything else is business as usual unless you hear from me. Understand?" Four heads nodded around the table. Felix leaned back in his chair, his arms crossed over his chest as he continued to glare my way. I wasn't going to win him over, so I might as well stop trying. I looked back at Jorge and Spencer, "If you need any muscle, let Liam know." Both men nodded their agreement. Promoting Liam needed to be done, but I struggled saying the words "organizational change."

I stood up from the gathering the way I had seen Johnny do thousands of times. When he stood, all discussion was over. As I took my second step away from the others, Felix said, "I've got some more product for you, Kerry. I'll have it delivered later today for distribution."

Felix was trying to undermine my authority – authority I didn't want, but his contempt for me had gone too far. Before I could turn to respond, Kerry answered, "Sorry, Felix. I forgot you're not as smart as you look. Suspended means: to discontinue. I won't be accepting any more deliveries unless Mark tells me to."

I didn't acknowledge either man, but Kerry had graduated from my "like" to my "trusted" list that second. I turned back to the group and said, "Liam, I need a word with you before you go."

Liam looked at me, then to Felix, and his eyes rested on me. Given the exchange between Felix and me, I'm sure he wondered if I planned to keep Felix in line using Liam's men. That wasn't what I wanted to talk to him about.

Liam was an average-looking guy: average height, receding hairline, slacks, loafers and a polo shirt. There was nothing about him that was remarkable; this was how Oscar had preferred his team look. Liam walked with me out of the little guesthouse toward the main house. We were well outside of anyone's earshot before I spoke, "Recall Grey Blair. Trump up a reason for him to be here. Don't tell him I want to see him."

"Grey's in town. He checked in with Oscar yesterday."

Liam was supremely loyal to Oscar. I wanted to kill Grey with my bare hands, but given everything else that was going on, I couldn't afford to get caught. "I couldn't say this in front of the others, but Grey is the reason Oscar's dead."

Liam stopped walking, his eyes wide as his posture straightened. "Grey killed Oscar?"

"No, Xavier pulled the trigger, but Grey's the one who set all of these events in motion. He knew his actions were putting Johnny and Oscar at risk. I want him dead. Today."

Liam didn't hesitate. "I'll clean this mess up myself. You have my word."

Without a moment's hesitation or a morsel of remorse, I continued walking straight to the main house to make the calls I had been making when Felix interrupted me and to wait for the girls' mother to arrive.

CHAPTER 28

Bev arrived early evening; one of the security guards met her at the hangar and brought her to the estate. Since I didn't know the girls had a mother, I wasn't too sure what to make of her absence from their lives. It was hard not to lump her into the same "abandonment" category reserved for my own mother. Brooks did some digging before her arrival, and we learned Johnny and Bev's divorce decree restricted her access to the girls. Johnny had been ruthless to anyone who crossed him. I couldn't imagine the strength Bev must have had to divorce Johnny eight years ago.

The moment the front door opened, before Bev could get more than a foot inside, Anastasia launched herself at her mom. Bev soaked her in the way a waffle soaks up syrup. Both ladies were high-pitched and excited. Bev was average height, slender, and sported a deep Miami tan. Anastasia had her nose and high cheekbones. Bev's hair was a light brown – the same color the girls' hair turned in the summer.

Annabelle stood up but stayed in the sitting room and held my hand, like I was her security blanket. I didn't encourage her to go see her mom, nor did I try to preclude it – I stood in place offering to be her anchor. Annabelle had lost the only parent she had ever known this morning, and that little girl could take as long as she needed.

Her big eyes watched Bev and Anastasia trying to make up for eight years apart in the first thirty seconds. Annabelle wore a pink nightgown and fuzzy white slippers. She had taken a position where she was partially hidden behind my body, carefully watching the stranger who had walked through the front door.

Bev's eyes looked past the marble columns separating the rooms and saw Annabelle watching her. She kissed Anastasia on the top of her head then walked slowly toward the sitting room where we were. Tears were in Bev's eyes when she reached into her handbag and pulled out the ugliest orange and yellow teddy bear I had ever seen. She held it out to Annabelle as the child slid further behind the safety of my leg. Bev pulled the bear back and looked at it, "I'm sorry, Annabelle, he missed you. I told him I was coming to see you, and he asked if he could come, too."

Annabelle said nothing, her eyes still wide. Bev wiped a tear off of her cheek, "He was your first teddy bear. You took your very first step trying to get him off of the table."

Anastasia offered, "I remember," Annabelle turned her attention away from Bev and looked at her sister. Anastasia smiled, "Belle, she's right. We were all in the living room. I had a bowl of ice cream; I was trying to get you to walk. I held a spoonful of ice cream out to you, to try to get you to walk to me. You ignored me and walked over to the table, reached up, and got your bear."

Annabelle looked back at the ugly bear. She held out her hand and Bev gently handed the tattered toy to her. Annabelle studied it for a minute, and then set it on the sofa beside where we stood. Bev was unfazed, "Where's Rocky?"

Annabelle's eyes lit up. Bev said, "I've missed Rocky almost as much as I have you two girls. Could I see him?" Annabelle let go of my hand and ran into her toy room. Annabelle had more options than Toys 'R Us; I couldn't have guessed which one Rocky was or even where it might have been stashed. Within two minutes Annabelle ran back into the room with a white stuffed ram I had never seen before.

Bev gleefully pulled a cord on the ram's belly and it said, "Rocky's going to knocky you into next week, if you don't go to sleep." Bev and Annabelle giggled. She pulled the cord a second time and the toy warned, "I'm Rocky the ram. Your job's to sleep like a lamb." As many times as I had been in Annabelle's play room, I had never seen Rocky – but from her giggles, Rocky was a cherished toy.

I stayed with the girls until I was sure Annabelle was comfortable with Bev. I knew they were going to be fine when Annabelle disappeared into her toy room and reemerged with a book, climbing onto Bev's lap and snuggling in to read it to her mom.

I returned to my apartment late. I took a seat on the sofa looking out onto the lights of the city. Just three nights ago I had been on the same sofa with Libby. I looked at the time: it was too late to call, but I dialed anyway. Libby's sleepy voice answered, "Mark?"

"Yeah. Are you sleeping?" I knew that she was. I wished for a lot of things today, but right now I wished that Libby were sitting on my couch looking at the city's lights with me.

"No, I'm baking a turkey. What else would I be doing at midnight?"

I lived for her snarky responses. "You want me to call you tomorrow?"

"Sure, maybe you could time it for when I'm in the shower, or better yet, while I'm leaving for work. No, I'm awake. Are you okay?"

What was the right answer? Davey and Candy were alive, but they wouldn't have been if Chad hadn't busted through Xavier's door when he did. Johnny was gone – how could I ever make it up to the girls? Oscar was dead and everyone in law enforcement thought I was the hero. I wasn't dead – yet. "I'm fine. I just got home."

A silence clung on the line. I didn't have a clue why I had called her, other than I wanted to hear her voice. She broke the quiet with, "Dave told me what happened. Why didn't you tell me any of that last night?"

I didn't know Xavier had kidnapped Davey and Candy. I didn't know I was still working for the police. Hell, I didn't know much of anything. "I couldn't tell anyone what I was doing." That wasn't true. I had believed I would be a criminal until someone put a bullet in my head. Nothing had changed since she and I spoke last night; I was still a criminal, and there was a real chance another criminal was going to end me – now more than ever.

"I wish you would have told me. I'm sorry I said the things I did to you last night." There was nothing to forgive because she hadn't gotten things wrong last night. Chad had just fabricated things today to make me look like the good guy. When I didn't answer, she offered, "Thursday is my day off. I was thinking I might drive down to see you Wednesday after I get off of work."

Felix's angry glare from this afternoon shot through my memory. Having her anywhere near Kansas City could be a huge mistake. "I'd like to see you, but this week sucks. I've got a lot of things I need to tie up down here. Maybe I'll come up there in a week or so."

Her voice sounded disappointed, although that could have just been wishful thinking on my part. "Right. Sorry, I forgot. Just let me know when you're coming up, and I'll move my schedule around so I'm off when you're here."

"I will. I better let you get some sleep. I'll call you tomorrow." I sat on my sofa long after I had hung up with Libby. I wished her perfume still clung to my sofa cushions. More than that, I wished there were a safe way for her to be here with me now. Until I was sure I wasn't a target by Felix and others in the city, I needed to make sure she kept a safe distance. Having her here Friday night had been reckless; I wouldn't make the same mistake any time soon.

I opened one of the windows in my apartment. My mind replayed every moment from the second Kerry had walked through my door this morning to the minute Chad had kicked Xavier's in. I wasn't sure how I was alive, nor was I at all confident that my reprieve from death was anything more than temporary. I lay there watching the city lights, wondering what I could have done differently, as the sounds of the city lulled me to sleep.

Sun streamed in from the windows. This wasn't the first night I had slept on the couch, but it was by far the worst sleep I had ever gotten. I looked at the time. Just twenty-four hours ago my biggest concern was that Libby didn't want anything to do with me. How had I been so self-absorbed?

I took a shower and went down to the garage. The little SUV waited in my parking place. I went to the estate to check on the girls. Bev, Anastasia and

Annabelle were eating breakfast when I walked through the door. Bev invited me to join them, but I declined and went into Johnny's office to try to sort through the businesses that I now felt responsible for.

I began piling papers in two areas with individual stacks in each area. One side of the room was legitimate, and the piles I formed on that side of the room were papers for the restaurant, sports arena, casino, sports bar, and several real estate ventures I hadn't been aware of. The other side of the room had stacks for bookies, loan sharks, prostitution, and drugs. The car dealership didn't seem to fit in either pile, so I left it in the middle of the room.

It took me two full days, but by Wednesday afternoon, I had sifted through every scrap of paper in his office. I had found a wall safe behind a picture on hinges, a floor safe under a Persian rug in front of his desk, a secret compartment behind a bookshelf and a flower vase with a false bottom. An envelope in Johnny's desk held a copy of my and Davey's birth certificates – no doubt left over from Oscar learning of my real identity and sharing that proof with Johnny. There may have been more hiding places, but those four places were the only I had found. The floor safe was full of old handwritten letters; from the postmarks the stash was more than twenty years old. I left those tucked away under the floor.

Confident that I had uncovered every hiding place for all of his records, I shut the light off in Johnny's office, and was pleased to see Bev, Annabelle and Anastasia watching the movie *Frozen* together in the media room with three large bowls of popcorn. Because Annabelle didn't remember her mother, I worried too much too soon could be even more traumatic – I was glad to be wrong. The four of us went to Johnny's wake together Wednesday night.

We were the first to arrive at the funeral parlor. Johnny's casket set at the front of the room, flanked by two enormous arrangements of white orchids and red roses. We had only just arrived when Annabelle tugged on my jacket; I squatted down to her level, as she whispered, "I need to see Daddy."

I looked at Bev, not sure if it was my place – she gave me a subtle nod. I led Annabelle to the casket, unsure what to expect. When we were just a few feet away, she squeezed my hand and said, "I brought something for Daddy. He needs it.'"

She was young. I stopped short, holding in place. Did she not understand death was forever? There was no coming back. Johnny would never need anything again. Annabelle dropped my hand, reached over her shoulder, and pulled her backpack off of her back. She unzipped the zipper and held it open for me to see inside. I wasn't sure what to make of it – it was her Nerf gun. "That's sweet, 'Belle, but I think he would want you to keep it."

"Nu-uh. He needs practice. One day I'm going to be in heaven with him and we're going to play again."

I swallowed a lump in my throat. I deposited the empty backpack on a chair, took her hand again, and led her to where her father lay. She placed the Nerf gun in the casket beside him. I couldn't say who all attended the wake. Each time I looked toward Johnny's casket, the memory of Johnny being chased by Annabelle on Christmas morning with a Nerf gun flashed in my head. My heart broke for Annabelle and Anastasia.

Johnny's funeral was at a large cathedral downtown Thursday morning. Reporters were stationed along the street, the story sensationalized on all the local networks – we hadn't had the televisions on at the house since Monday. Inside the cathedral, the area in front of the altar was lined with flower arrangements of every shape and size. I tried to take a seat near the door, but Anastasia saw me easing into a back pew. She stood up from where she was seated and waved me forward. Initially, I shrugged off her invitation; I didn't feel right sitting in the family row.

Annabelle saw me ignore her sister and stood up on the pew looking directly at me. Her little voice carried over all the low chatter, "Mark, c'mon, I saved you a seat." No matter how much guilt I carried, I couldn't deny her big brown eyes, even from fifty feet away.

Anastasia was on the end of the pew, Bev on her right, then Annabelle and me on her other side. I was to give one of the eulogies. When the priest invited me up to the lectern, I pulled a folded up piece of notebook paper out of my breast pocket and pressed the paper to get the creases out.

I cleared my throat as all eyes rested on me. "Looking around the room, Johnny Corozzo touched a lot of lives. Johnny was larger than life, but he wasn't all things to all people; he was something different to everyone who knew him. He was a savvy businessman, a dedicated father, and a man who redefined the meaning of family. Many of you thought you knew Johnny. Up until Monday morning, I thought I knew Johnny, too. It turns out, what I thought I knew about Johnny was wrong." The words poured out of me. Not the ones about the drug dealer I had dreamed of putting behind bars, but of the man who could never be replaced.

"I grew up in foster care. The word *family* was always in my vocabulary, but I didn't learn its true meaning until just this year." I stopped addressing the room as a whole and looked at the girls, "Annabelle, Anastasia, I pledge to you that I will always be the family you need me to be."

"Johnny's enemies would say he was ruthless – they'd be right. His family will say he was generous; they're right, too. Johnny's friends would say he was someone who could be counted on – right again. I think we can all agree that there was more to Johnny than what met the eye."

"As I look out over those who are here to bid Johnny good-bye, I know not all of you were able to attend the wake last night. Annabelle didn't say good-bye, she told her dad she was going to see him again and he needed to be ready. You see, Annabelle arrived at the wake carrying a large backpack."

My eyes darted to Annabelle who wasn't the least bit embarrassed as a smile beamed back at me. The first one I had seen her wear all day. Not a whisper sounded in the cathedral as everyone's eyes turned to little Annabelle. "She placed a toy in his casket last night. She said one day she's going to be in heaven with Johnny, and they'll play again. Annabelle didn't say good-bye, she told him to be ready for her when they were reunited. And, Johnny, if you're listening, you had better practice."

I didn't want to eulogize Johnny, and I wouldn't have honored the man any better than Annabelle did last night. She longed to play with her dad, who was only dead because of me. I couldn't continue. I motioned for Felix to come up to give his eulogy.

After Johnny was laid to rest, I had only an hour to get from the cemetery to Oscar's funeral. Thankfully, I hadn't been asked do give a eulogy for him. Oscar's widow knew I had been with him when he died. When she approached, I expected her to be angry or at least cold – she wasn't. She reached her arms up and hugged me, "I heard so much about you, Mark. I'm sorry we never met before today."

What had Oscar told her? Oscar was the one who knew more about me than anyone else because he had dug into my past. "I'm sorry for your loss, Mrs. DelFina. Oscar was a great man and my friend."

Her lips pursed together for a moment as she gathered her composure. "Oscar had his flaws, but I loved him for the last forty years. He told me you were the brightest person he had seen since Johnny was your age. He thought the world of you, and I'm glad you were with him in the end." Images of both my hands trying to cover his chest wound as he took his last raspy breath assailed me.

Given the fabrications that had been told during the last week by Chad, I thought one more little lie couldn't hurt. "It was you he thought of before he passed. He told me to tell you he loved you." Had he not have spent his dying breath telling me about a sister I had never met, I was sure he would have asked me to say those words to his wife.

Tears flowed down his widow's cheeks. She took me in a hug a second time and held on. A tall slender man with white hair walked toward us. Oscar's wife saw him as he approached and introduced us, "Mark, this is Cliff, Oscar's brother. Cliff, this is Mark Brewer. He was with Oscar when he passed."

Passed? That sounded like Oscar had surrendered to cancer, not that he had been murdered. Cliff nodded to me in a silent greeting. I nodded respectfully and said, "Oscar told me about you. You're a school teacher." Cliff nodded again, his expression grim. "He told me he wished he could have seen you more than twice a year." Cliff's lips pressed together in two thin lines, but his eyes glossed over as he took me in an embrace.

Although I was indebted to Oscar for what he had done, I didn't feel as tied to him as I had Johnny. Burying Oscar took a toll on me, but nothing like Johnny's funeral.

After both funerals were over, I returned to Johnny's estate and looked through the last of the documents in Johnny's office. I felt like I had a handle on everything, at least from a financial perspective and called Mr. Haberstein.

All day Friday and Saturday we sliced and diced Johnny's organization into two pieces – legitimate and illegal. The legitimate businesses were set up under a board of advisors. His daughters were named as owners and would take control of their inheritance once each was twenty-five. Until then it was set up as a trust with the board making all the decisions. The board members included Mr. Haberstein, Bev, and two retired CEOs – everyone but Bev had been selected by Johnny in his will; Mr. Haberstein added Bev at my request. When Mr. Haberstein looked at all the books from the illegal business ventures, his only guidance was: "Liquidate them."

This direction was both welcomed and frightening. Welcomed because in a few short weeks there would be no more organization for me to be a part of, and I would be in charge of my own destiny again. Frightening because the inevitable turf wars would erupt, and there was a good chance I would land squarely in someone's crosshairs.

CHAPTER 29

I found Jorge first. Based on Lenny's story that Jorge had, at some point in the past, wished to get away from the organization, I believed he would be the easiest to break the news to. Jorge's office was located by the service entrance in the casino; I had never been inside his office, but having been to the casino many times, I knew where to find it.

I knocked on his closed office door: no response echoed back at me. I knocked a second time: the only answer was more silence. I heard a heavy footstep walking down the cement hallway. I turned to find Jorge limping toward me. Jorge and I had never had a bad conversation; he had been supportive the night I called the leadership circle to Johnny's estate to break the news about the shooting. It was Jorge who told Felix I was number three in the organization, and he intended to follow my lead.

Jorge had a year-round deep tan and dark hair. He was always freshly shaven, or maybe he didn't have facial hair, but I had never seen him with a stubbly face. Jorge rarely smiled, but did not greet people with an angry look, either. He gave me a wave as he slowly made his way down the hall.

When he was ten feet away, he offered, "Wasn't sure when I'd be seeing you. Can't say it's a surprise that you're here." Jorge opened the door to his office, "C'mon in."

The décor in the casino was tasteful, but Jorge's office must have been where ugly fabric samples went to die. There was a crescent-shaped sofa in large red and yellow blocked colors. Next to the offending sofa were two chairs in the same block pattern, but in blue and green. A stainless-steel-looking box was set up between the three pieces of furniture as a coffee table with magazines on it. I didn't find a desk; instead the back of an easy chair was near a floor-to-ceiling window. A stack of papers lay on either side, and a laptop computer rested on the chair's seat. Nine large screen television sets lined the ceiling on the opposite wall from the easy chair: each of them tuned into a different station.

Jorge motioned for me to take a seat on the sofa. "So, what changes should we expect?"

"I met with Mr. Haberstein this weekend. His guidance was all illegal activities be shut down – immediately."

Jorge cocked his head to the side, "Immediately? We have a lot of customers who count on us. Are you planning to bring in a different bank roll to keep things going?" Jorge's question was a good one. Rather than subjecting our employees and customers to turf wars as a new organization came in, he was recommending bringing in a new boss and turning the organization over to him.

"I'm thinking more along the lines of dismantling the whole thing and letting whoever wants to come in have it. I want out and others may, too. A clean break is best for Johnny's family and the employees who want to start fresh."

"That's pretty risky. If we get a couple people fighting over things, it could get bloody."

"If we shut things down, none of Johnny's employees are obligated to work for anyone new." I hesitated for a minute, not sure how to phrase it without sounding disloyal to Johnny. "I heard there were guys on the team who were too scared to quit. By shutting down, anyone who wants out, is out."

Jorge watched me closely. He didn't speak up right away, but when he did, they were words I hadn't expected. "What happens if I shut Johnny's operation down and want to start up my own in his place?"

My lips cocked to the side, letting his question sink in. "The whole organization, or just the numbers and the sharks?"

He laughed hard, "Yeah, not interested in prostitutes or drugs – I'm just asking about what I'm already doing."

"We won't stand in your way." The "we" I referred to was what was left of Johnny's crew. It felt strange, but it was my responsibility to answer for the organization. To make sure it was clear, "If that's what you want to do, I'm all for it, but Johnny's business gets liquidated before you do anything on your own."

Jorge motioned for me to get off of the sofa. He lifted the center cushion on the sofa and started pulling out stacks of cash. Surprised that the cash wasn't locked up in a safe, I asked, "How much money is this?"

"Only three teams made the spread last weekend. Johnny cleaned up, so this is significantly more money than I typically have lying around. There are some outstanding notes, but those shouldn't be more than fifty thousand dollars. I'll collect those in the next couple days and get it to you."

I hadn't planned on Jorge handing over gobs of money; I sort of thought it would take some time. He handed me a black leather ledger. Everything was handwritten. As I examined the entries, Jorge must have believed I didn't trust him. "It's all there. Every penny."

As I read the ledger, it was very straightforward: name, date, bet, odds, result, owed, due and paid. Based on the outcome of the event, the final number was either in the owed or the due column. Once the person making the wager had either been paid, or paid what they owed to Jorge, an "X" was written in the paid column.

"I can see it's all there. So, once you liquidate Johnny, do you want to see about renting your office space from the casino, or do you think you'll move your operation somewhere else?"

Jorge gave me a subtle grin. "You think I could rent my office here?"

"It won't be up to me. There is a board of advisors who is overseeing all of the businesses that will be left intact; the casino is one of those businesses. No one is planning to shut down the casino, so it's a safe bet that if you requested to keep your office, they would accommodate your request."

Jorge offered, "I always liked you, Mark. I'm glad you are looking out for Annabelle and Anastasia. I think that's why Johnny wanted you in the spot you're in. Maybe he was a little bit psychic. He knew your heart wasn't in any of this, and if anything happened to him and Oscar – you'd do right by his family. Whatever you need from me, just say the word."

Looking at the big pile of money he had pulled out from inside his sofa, I said, "A big suitcase on wheels would be a good start."

I made a visit to Spencer next. Spencer oversaw all the escorts, the nicer way of saying prostitution operations. His office was in a converted hotel. As I approached the front door, a lady in a business suit ushered me back to Spencer's office. I gave Spencer the same talk I had given to Jorge. Spencer didn't immediately ask about taking over his aspect of Johnny's operation, but he did produce a similar ledger book. As I reviewed his ledger, Spencer opened up a wall safe, covertly tucked behind a floor-to-ceiling oil painting on hinges.

Spencer didn't have near the cash reserves that Jorge had, but it was still more than I could put in a briefcase. He put everything in a duffle bag.

I stopped at the Spikes and found Kerry at his favorite table. Kerry looked relieved to see me. "It's the unknown that scares everyone the most – at least they know things are going to be shut down. I can have the last of the product distributed tomorrow and have cash to you by Wednesday."

Liam, too, took the news in stride. After I delivered the news, he reached into his desk and pulled out a small white box with a red ribbon on it. "This may be the last time I see you, so, think of this as my gift to you." I opened the little box to find a single bullet casing made into a key chain. Not understanding the gift, he offered, "I would have had it engraved with Grey's name, but if the cops are breathing down your neck, I didn't want for you to get busted." Liam had followed my instructions, and I had no grief for Grey.

That left just Felix. I reluctantly went to the dealership, and to my complete displeasure, he was in his office. Based on the way he had tried to undermine my authority on Monday night, I needed to remind him of the pecking order.

I went to my office and called him on the phone. "I need to see you."

Irritation hung heavy in his voice, "I'm at my desk."

"Obviously, I just called you. Come to my office."

Felix hung up, and I expected him to come storming through my door – he didn't. Five minutes went by, then ten; after thirty minutes I had shredded every piece of paper in my office as well as Johnny's. Nothing remained, even the wall calendar was now in the trash can. I dialed Felix's number again, "Felix, come to my office."

"I'll stop by when I have time."

"No. You'll come over here now."

"Right. I'm on my way." He hung up again, I looked toward the door, but Felix never came in.

He was a complete jackass. I snickered at the idea that he was playing the same game that I was. It would be a force of wills, but as my underling, it wasn't my place to go hunt him down. I decided to go about this a little differently.

I scrawled a message on a piece of paper. It said, "I'll be at Spikes for 30 minutes. Mark"

I handed the piece of paper to the receptionist as I walked out and told her to deliver it to Felix. I found Kerry still sitting at his regular table when I arrived at the sports bar and took a seat next to him. No more than two minutes passed before Felix stomped up to the table – his face red and a scowl etched on his face.

"I don't have time for your childish behavior."

"Well, you won't have to put up with it for much longer. You won't be reporting to me after Wednesday this week."

Kerry's eyes grew wider. He knew just how sensitive Felix was about "reporting" to me, and I had just spelled out that Felix currently worked for me. Felix's eyes narrowed, "I don't report to you now, but I'll bring a cake anyway. Taking a full-time job with the police?"

I turned my back on him and faced Kerry. "You're sure you'll be fully liquidated by Wednesday?"

Felix took the open chair in between Kerry and me, as if not comprehending what I had just asked Kerry. "You're serious? We're liquidating the cartel operations?"

"I am liquidating cartel operations. You can help us or not, your choice."

Felix placed both his palms on the table and leaned in close to me. "The name placard by my door says General Manager. I call the shots at the dealership, so nothing is being liquidated. You told Fernando you were suspending operations until after Johnny's funeral. I'm going to turn him on again."

"As of 11:59 p.m. last night you were the General Manager of the dealership, but at midnight a board of advisors was put in place. All aspects of the dealership go through them now. They will decide if you stay on at the dealership, and if you do, what your title will be."

"All aspects?"

"I don't recommend you try to turn things back on with Fernando. These guys are going to be looking out for Annabelle and Anastasia. They won't look too kindly on you putting the girls' future in jeopardy."

"I didn't put the last twenty years into setting all of this up just to have you dissolve it on a whim."

I didn't attempt to mask my scowl, "Johnny paid you a lot of money to do exactly what you did. When he was in charge that was one thing; but he's not here to call the shots anymore. I am."

Felix glared, "Johnny was a great man. You may have snowed him, but you need to watch your back. One bullet is all it takes to remove you from your throne."

Kerry stood up from the table in a hurry, his eyes wide and his nostrils flared. "Felix, I'm going to pretend I didn't just hear that."

"Pretend all you like. You are all living in a fantasy land if you believe you can shut down Johnny's operations without repercussions." Felix moved his glare to me, "I could easily set up operations of my own. You couldn't stop me."

I nodded my agreement. "You could. In fact, you can do anything you want to do. I'll let the board know you have chosen to resign your position as general manager. Once Johnny's illegal businesses are shut down, you can do whatever you choose."

"I'll call Fernando tonight."

"By all means. Call him. Tell him you are going to go back to the old school way, because the dealership here in Kansas City is not accepting any more engines that require rework before they sell. The dealership is going to be legitimate sales, that's it."

Kerry still stood at the ready, his fists balled tightly at his sides. Felix was well past angry. "You are putting hundreds of people out of work."

"And in the process, keeping them out of prison."

Felix stood up. Under his breath, he warned, "Watch your back."

Kerry took his seat only after Felix left. "He's going to be a problem."

I agreed, but didn't want for Kerry to believe I was worried. A few more days and all of this would be behind me.

CHAPTER 30

Wednesday – nine days after Johnny's death

Money had always flowed in from the shady side, allowing Johnny to launder his own money through the bistro, sports complex, casino and cars. After the liquidation from Jorge, Spencer, and Kerry was complete, I wasn't sure how Johnny moved the money through his legitimate businesses. A few trusted guys from the security team helped me wheel four suitcases stuffed full of cash into the attorney's office Wednesday afternoon.

I assumed the attorney knew how to "clean" the money. He didn't want anything to do with them, at least nothing traceable. The lawyer took one of the suitcases, put it in the corner of his office, and told me, "Make the rest of that go away." I assumed the suitcase he kept was for his personal use – I didn't argue.

I could have easily put the three remaining suitcases in my car and retired to my own private island. That wasn't me. Instead, I called Jorge, Spencer, Liam and Kerry in for a quick meeting at the Ops Center. I asked for names of everyone who worked for them. Thanks to Felix, rumors were running rampant that I was working with the cops. Getting names from Jorge, Spencer and Liam was about as easy as shoving a frozen turkey through a straw when I first asked. I didn't press them when they said they'd need a few days to assemble a list.

Kerry had worked for me directly, so even with the rumors, he gave me a complete list of names while we all sat at the table. Each person whose name I had been given got a fat envelope full of cash Thursday morning with a slip of paper inside where I had scrawled the words: Severance from Johnny Corozzo.

I assumed a few of the people wouldn't understand the word, but they must have looked it up because by Thursday night I had people calling me to tell me they had also worked for Johnny. No one walked away a millionaire, but every single person who had been doing illegal jobs because they had no other options, now had options.

At first I wondered if Johnny could see what I was doing and might be unhappy that I was giving away his fortune, but I had a feeling that I knew Johnny better than most. Maybe I knew him better than people who had worked for him for decades. His last living act had been a selfless one and demonstrated how he viewed family, that we were all his. Deep down, I knew Johnny wanted his extended family taken care of, especially if he were no longer in the picture to protect them.

Everyone, including me, was waiting for the new turf wars to erupt as people vied for position when there was no longer a structure to adhere to. Lots of people who had worked prostitution, shake-downs, drugs and gambling took their envelopes and moved out of town. Others took theirs and established their own businesses. Regardless, whatever of their lives they devoted to Johnny for however long they did, I compensated them.

By Saturday night, Bev was planning to take both girls back to her home in Miami. Before they left, I told Anastasia she didn't have to leave if she didn't want to. Kansas City was her home, and I didn't want her to think she didn't have options. She was only a couple months away from her eighteenth birthday; I told her Johnny's lawyer could work some magic with the courts if she wanted to stay.

Anastasia said she wanted to go with her mom. Bev had made arrangements with the school for Anastasia to return for graduation – she had enough credits to graduate the previous semester so there were no issues with her picking up and leaving. It had never occurred to me while Johnny was alive that the girls had a mom they never saw, and I got the feeling Anastasia wanted to make up for lost time.

Chad and I had not been close when we were teenagers. We may have been roommates, but I had shut myself off from the rest of the world long before the day I saw Mom and ran away. The night I called Chad after finding Davey and told him I was done helping – he didn't give up on me. I don't know how many people he had lied to or how many reports he may have doctored along the way, but everyone believed I had fed him information until the day Johnny and Oscar were killed.

Chad had been the one to convince me to sacrifice my life for the greater good, if necessary, and in the end, he was the one to make sure not just I, but everyone who wanted their lives back, got them. There had been several trips to the police station between the Monday morning when Johnny was shot and the nearly two weeks later when everyone working the seedy side of the businesses got their severance envelopes. I had handed over the USB drive in my wallet; Chad was less interested in pursuing the low level guys. When I told him about the severances, he was rooting for them to take the money and start a new life as much as I was. Those who chose to continue doing what they were doing would stay on Chad's "watch" list.

Most of the follow-up interviews were with the federal authorities. It was a good thing we had shut down the illegal aspects of the dealership, because Alcohol, Tobacco and Firearms were knee deep in investigating the drug trade. ATF was very interested in how the drugs were moved and equally anxious to learn if other organizations were following suit. They knew things were coming out of Chihuahua, Mexico; but none expected our operation to be as sophisticated as it was. Drug cartels were known for ruthless behavior, forcing citizens to hide product in their cars and bodies to cross the border – ours had been a very clean operation.

Chad was present for every one of my interviews, even the ones which were technically out of his jurisdiction. His response was always the same no matter who wanted to talk to me, "Mark's my confidential informant; I can't have you blowing his cover. I'm using him for other activities, and I need his cover to stay intact." Felix went through almost as many interviews as I did since he was the General Manager, but in the end, he was never charged with anything, either.

Chad made sure I was safe. It was a full month before the official investigation into the Corozzo organization closed. It may have closed sooner if Chad had been calling all the shots, but the delays came from the FBI and ATF arguing over who had the authority to close the investigation. In the end, given that two murders had been committed, police had shot the perpetrator, and all were drug-related – ATF was the organization to close it down. FBI had red-flagged all of Johnny's legitimate businesses for tax evasion, but I had no knowledge of how any of those businesses worked; I let Johnny's lawyer and his accountants handle those subpoenas.

Chad knew significant changes were underway, but he never pressed me to divulge them. He did, on more than one occasion, remind me that any new illegal activities were on my own. I told him I had shut everything the IRS wasn't aware of down, but I think he was waiting to see if my claims were for real.

Chad invited me to his house for dinner six weeks after the shooting, which was two weeks after the Corrozo investigation was completed by all the three letter agencies involved. It struck me odd that we would do such a domestic activity, but I owed him, and I didn't have any reason not to go. When I arrived, a woman answered the door. My initial impression was that I had the wrong address. I started to mumble an apology and looked at the house number when she said, "Are you Mark?"

"Yeah, does Chad live here?"

"No, he lives at the police station, but he's my husband and this is where he does his laundry!" A smile stretched wide on my face. In all the conversations we had had, Chad never once mentioned being married. I didn't remember seeing him wear a ring, either. Maybe he was a little like me in that respect, preferring that others know as little about his personal life as possible.

She held the door for me, "I'm Mary Ann. Come in. Chad's in the kitchen." Mary Ann was petite, with a pretty face, big brown eyes and long straight dark hair. She wore blue jeans and a three quarter-length cotton t-shirt; her clothes led me to believe she was pretty laid back. I followed her to the kitchen where

Chad was chopping carrots on a cutting board.

"You made it!" No one had been that pleased to see me in a while, and I couldn't help but smile back at his enthusiasm. This was my first time seeing him like a regular guy. He wasn't trying to get me to bring down organized crime, or chastising me for stealing a football player's ride – he was cutting carrots.

Mary Ann offered, "It's great to finally meet you. Chad talks about you all the time."

What could he possibly have told her? I began to feel an uncomfortable vibe; new situations did that to me. I had attended dinner parties with Johnny for different occasions, but could never remember being invited to someone's house just for dinner. I had eaten dinner at Davey's house a few times, but that was different. A hush settled over the room for an uncomfortable second before I answered, "Wow, then I'm surprised you let me through the door."

Mary Ann reached down and pulled one of the sliced carrots from the cutting board and popped it into her mouth. "He said you're the reason for his promotion this week. I told him we should go out to dinner, but he insisted we were having you over. That's why he's cooking."

I wasn't sure what I was supposed to do. It was marginally awkward. "Promoted huh? I would have brought a bottle of wine." It hit me – I should have brought something anyway. If I'd known Chad was married, I would have grabbed some flowers for his wife – Lenny told me that's what you're supposed to do when you are invited over for dinner. When Chad invited me, I had this notion of pizza and beer in front of his television.

Mary Ann went to the refrigerator, "We've got one." She pulled out three glasses and poured one for each of us. "Why don't you two go chat. I'll finish up in here."

Chad beamed, "Don't have to tell me twice. C'mon Mark, she never lets me out of kitchen duties."

I followed Chad into the living room. It was nice. A blue sofa and matching loveseat were flanked by a recliner, all facing a fireplace with a television above it. The room was tight, but still welcoming. Pictures of the two of them were scattered around the room, a metal leafy wall decoration hung on either side of the television. He asked, "So how's everything going?"

"Fine. Things have quieted down. How about you? Congrats on the promotion."

"It's not really a promotion. I was just moved to major crimes. I'm getting the same pay, and the hours still suck."

Major crimes? As opposed to the parking tickets he'd been issuing the last four years? He had been involved in nothing but major crimes since I first saw him four years ago. "You never mentioned you were married. How long?"

"Almost two years." Chad glanced over his shoulder into the kitchen. "She bitches all the time about my job, but she hasn't gotten a speeding ticket in two years. I figure it's a good trade."

"So what does she know about me?"

"She knows we were in Hastings House together, that you saved my life. I told her about the night you tried to lift the Ferrari. She's asked about you from time to time – I told her you were helping me with a case."

"Does she know what I did?"

"No. At least nothing specific."

"What about Dave and Candy? Does she know you ran in guns blazing and saved them?"

"She knows about them and what Xavier did. She gets most of her information from the newspaper, though." He took a sip of wine and the whole image struck me funny. It was much more domestic than I would have imagined. "So, I wanted to ask, what's going on with Johnny's businesses? Word on the street is all over the place, no one knows what's going on."

"Is that why you invited me here?"

"Partly, but for the most part I just wanted to be able to talk to you. Since I'm a cop, if we went somewhere public, you would be forced to treat me like the enemy. Or there is always the question of who else is listening."

Fair enough. More than just Chad was curious about what had happened. I looked at Chad's face. There was so much I would have liked to tell him, but it wouldn't have been right. Enough people were getting fresh starts; I didn't want to speculate on how the new organization might emerge. "We dismantled the organization." Like I told you when I gave you the USB drive, there are a lot of people who got a fresh start this last month. So how'd you meet Mary Ann?"

The rest of the night went great. For two people who had lived, eaten, and breathed opposite sides of the law, we found some common ground. After dinner Chad took me out to his workshop where he built wooden furniture by hand. Each was a masterpiece, with intricate carvings adorning them. Looking at one particular coffee table made of oak, with hundreds of daisies carved into it – I asked, "How long did this take?"

He laughed, "The table itself, probably a week. Each daisy took about half an hour. I think I stopped after carving fifty of them."

Remembering what Libby had told me about painting a bunch of daisies on her wall as a little girl, I wanted this table. More than wanted, I needed this table. "Would you consider selling it?"

Chad cocked his head to the side, "You got a thing for flowers?"

"Maybe. I could ask you the same question. Who carves that many daisies just for aesthetics?"

Chad laughed. "You want it, I'll help load it into your car."

"I'll pay you for it."

Chad shook his head. "No. I'm not taking any money from you until it comes from an employer where you pay taxes."

For some reason this comment struck me funny. I was twenty-two, but all of my identification said I was a dead man in my forties. I wanted *my* identity. Tomorrow I would get my driver's license and begin living my own life. I accepted Chad's gift, and it fit perfectly into the trunk of my car.

CHAPTER 31

Johnny's businesses were no more, at least none of the ones I had helped him with. For the first time since I was fifteen years old, I became the real Mark Brewer, using my own birth certificate to get a driver's license, instead of borrowing the late Marcus Brewer's identity. Once I had my license, I requested a copy of my social security card. When it arrived I opened a bank account. Nothing that would cause suspicion, I only deposited nine thousand dollars. The bank gave me a check card, and a credit card with a five hundred dollar limit, small change for the life I had been living.

Libby's chiding about my Mercedes being too ostentatious somehow rang true. I had Lenny terminate the lease early and bought a Ford Escape. Something about that little SUV made me happy – like since I was ready to be a regular guy, it was ready to take me wherever I wanted to go.

I bought a modest house, nothing extravagant. It was a foreclosure, so the bank didn't seem to mind that I wanted to pay cash. It was eight years old in a neighborhood full of young families on the outskirts of the city. I had no idea what I would do with four bedrooms, but I reasoned that they would come in handy if Davey, Candy and Libby came to see me. Davey and I spoke at least every other day. He was pretty shaken up at first about what Xavier had done, but was finally over the shock. Candy was a different story. She had sworn off ever making another trip to Kansas City. Libby called me a couple times per week, but it didn't feel like the two of us would be picking up where we had left off any time soon. Too much deception in the beginning, I suppose.

The house wasn't a palace, the countertops weren't granite, the floors were just carpet, but it felt good to say I had a home. Chad's coffee table with daisies set in the living room holding my remotes. Each time I watched television and wanted to change the channel, the table was a pleasant reminder of my short time with Libby. I remembered once telling Johnny I wanted a big life now, and I had no desire for much of a future; everything had changed since then.

I was no longer forced into any kind of a career. The brother I had believed dead since I was a child was alive and well. The girl who was out of my league a month ago was still out of my league, but that didn't stop me from being hopeful that there may be a chance in the future.

I had gone through every scrap of paper in Oscar's office at the stadium. Since Oscar's records had nothing to do with finances and could only link Johnny and Oscar to extortion, intimidation and murder, I destroyed every piece of paper I found. If the police came through, they would find nothing more incriminating than signed sports memorabilia. While going through his office, there hadn't been even a post-it note about me, my father, or a sister. I had no doubt he had stumbled on more of my family, but there was nothing to substantiate or point me toward them.

My birth certificate stated my father's name was Mike Brewer. Years ago I had spent some time looking for him on the internet, but none seemed to be the right age. I was three when he walked out, so I barely remembered what he looked like except from photos Mom had and a few hazy memories.

I was more interested in finding him to satisfy curiosity when I had looked before. I didn't have some fabulous reunion scene in my head I wanted to play out. Truth be told, until Oscar's dying words spoke of a sister, I had never considered even trying to find him.

But unless I located Mike, trying to find a sister he had fathered would be like looking for a needle in a pile of needles. Oscar wasted his dying breath trying to tell me, so he must have thought it to be pretty important that I know.

Davey and I had discussed the possibility of a little sister. There was a good chance she was still a minor, so finding her on our own would be hard. His idea was to go to the Omaha high schools and look for female Brewers in yearbooks. That sounded lame, like an awful lot of work, and an unlikely way to find her. Instead, I told him that I planned to hire a private detective. I don't know what was holding me back, but I hadn't yet made the call.

Having terminated my lease at my apartment downtown, I stopped by to drop the keys with the doorman. Ted was on duty when I dropped by. I always got the feeling that Ted knew exactly what my profession was, but he had never asked questions when I was a resident in the building. Now that I was a former resident, he shook my hand, "It was my pleasure to have known you, Mr. Brewer."

Now that I was no longer a resident, being addressed as "Mr." felt wrong on several levels. I was ashamed that I had never taken the time to learn his last name to be able to pay him the same level of respect. "No formalities, Ted. I'm just Mark. Thanks for all you did for me." I handed him my last healthy tip.

Ted gave me a sly grin, "You know, I wasn't always a doorman. For twenty plus years I was law enforcement."

That surprised me. Cops all had a similar look about them; Ted didn't have that overt distrust of people I seemed to see in every law enforcement officer I had ever known. "No, I didn't know. What made you quit?"

"I didn't quit, I retired. Oscar liked people who lived in the gray area. I helped out when he needed me. He's the reason I took this job."

Ted's friendly demeanor came into question. Had I misread him all this time? Attempting to clarify what he had just said, I asked, "Oscar paid you to be my doorman?"

"No. Oscar pulled some strings to get me this job. He didn't know what to make of you when you first started working for Johnny. Oscar had me watching you like a hawk your first few months after you stopped working at Johnny's estate."

"When did he decide that he trusted me?"

Ted gestured to two chairs. "He thought you were too young. He thought Johnny had made a mistake moving you through the ranks so quickly." Ted winked at me conspiratorially, "Oscar was sure you were a police plant, but Johnny wouldn't listen." Ted's gray eyes bore hard into mine. "Oscar knew all about your pal Chad and that stunt with the Ferrari."

Ted's words brought me up short. Oscar knew about my deal with Chad? No, he couldn't possibly have known. If he did, Oscar would have killed me with his bare hands. There was no reason for Ted to tell me any of this, other than he wanted me to know. "Yeah, not my best night. Sounds like you knew Oscar pretty well. So, Oscar thought I was working for the cops?"

"No, he knew you were. He also knew you cared about Johnny and struggled with what was right and wrong." The wrinkles around Ted's eyes drew up when he said, "Oscar thought it was funny how you fed information to Chad so he could take down the people who crossed you. He told me about the drug dealer who killed your girlfriend."

Ted was talking about the dealer, Valentine, who had killed Megan. "So Oscar never trusted me?"

"I didn't say he didn't trust you. I said he had me watching you. I served on the force with Chad's father. Oscar and Chad's father were also very close."

Surprise wasn't the right word for the emotions that hit me. "Wait, that can't be right. Chad was just like me. He grew up in the same group home I did. His dad wasn't a cop. He didn't have parents."

"Chad's father was killed in the line of duty before Chad was born. His mother died less than a year later – suicide, I think. Karma's a funny thing. Had you been in cahoots with any other cop, Oscar would have destroyed you. Because you and Chad were working together, Oscar didn't have it in him to take you out or do anything that would affect Chad."

"Oscar knew the whole time? He told you everything?"

Ted clarified, "Oscar and I were friends. I still have a lot of friends on the force. We may have been on the opposite side of the law when we were younger, but after I retired, Oscar and I started comparing stories and learned we weren't as different as we had believed ourselves to be. I miss that guy."

That explained a lot. The whole time I was sure Johnny had plants in the police department, his biggest source of information had been my doorman. "Thanks, Ted." If Oscar had told anyone about finding my little sister, he may have told Ted. "One of the last things Oscar said to me before he died was that he had found my sister. I've turned his office upside down. Any idea where he might have kept any information about her? Or did he tell you anything?"

"No. Oscar didn't like to write anything down that was important. Maybe he was superstitious, maybe he just liked to be sure no one ever knew as much as he did. He committed that type of stuff to memory. If you went through his office and came up empty, I would bet there wouldn't be any paper record anywhere. He never mentioned anything about a sister; he did tell me he met your brother in Nebraska."

"Yeah, Dave. That freaked me out pretty good. Oscar didn't say anything to me directly, but he told my brother that I had referred him to his car restoration business. I didn't think anyone knew I had a brother, so Oscar's message made me want to crawl out of my skin."

Ted chuckled, "Oscar was always aces when it came to subtle messages. There's nothing those two wouldn't have done for you. I didn't know Johnny like I knew Oscar, but neither of them had a son; hell, Oscar didn't have any kids, and both of them came to think of you as their own."

A lump formed in my throat. "Yeah, they were great."

Ted looked at his watch, "I know you need to go, but I heard what you did with all of Johnny's employees. You could have easily pocketed every penny. Everyone on the street is talking about it." Ted put his hand on my shoulder, "Johnny would have been proud of you – so would Oscar. Good luck finding that little sister. If Oscar found her, she's out there."

"Thanks, Ted. Since you knew Chad's dad, would you mind if I brought him by sometime to meet you?"

"I'd like that very much. You know where to find me."

I left and headed back toward my new house in the suburbs. Stopped at a red light, I noticed a girl no more than sixteen leaning up against a building. I didn't need to ask her if she were a runaway; I recognized the look. She was hungry and scared, exactly the kind of kid monsters could exploit. She was another Megan. This city had too many Megans – too many kids who had been thrown away. If she met up with the wrong guy, she could be dead tomorrow.

I didn't want to go to college like Candy. I didn't want a business like Davey had. I didn't want a job just surviving like Libby. I didn't want to go back to boosting cars, and I swore I'd never do anything drug-related again. I wanted what I had wanted since the day Chad let me off of the grand theft auto charge: I wanted to make a difference.

The building behind the girl was run down with boards over a bunch of the windows: five stories of brick with mortar cracking and missing all over the place. The sign on the front said it was condemned and had a phone number to the city's urban development center.

Johnny's favorite mantra came to mind: "vision without execution is a hallucination. Stop hallucinating and execute your vision." I called the number.

The building had been an apparel factory at one time. The roof leaked, the boiler didn't work, the whole place needed to be rewired for today's electrical code, sprinklers needed to be installed, and no less than five hundred other items were required. It took a crew of forty men a full thirty days to right every wrong on the list, but five binders of paperwork later, Megan's House was born.

I had pocketed a generous severance like everyone else who worked for Johnny, but unlike everyone else, I had been stuffing pillows with cash for over two years, too. I wasn't sure how to pay for anything, because that much cash would catch the IRS's attention. I went back to Mr. Haberstein, told him what I was up to, and asked for his recommendation. He was happy to help me fill out the paperwork for Megan's House to become a 501(c), making it a non-profit organization and enabling it to accept cash donations. Once we were able to accept them, a very large donation arrived from an anonymous benefactor just in time to help pay for renovation costs.

It felt like things had gone full circle. Megan was the reason I had wanted to help Chad to begin with. I did things I hated trying to gather evidence to stop the drugs coming into Kansas City. In the end, Johnny had not only given his life to save mine, but it was money from his drugs that enabled Megan's House to open its doors.

When the doors finally opened, it was just a few months after Johnny's murder. We had three paid staff members and more than thirty volunteers. I wasn't sure how we would get the word to kids on the street, but one phone call to Kerry, and the kids began arriving in less than an hour. I had sort of imagined driving by abandoned houses and looking under overpasses at night, but Kerry proved much more effective. Most of the carriers or mules who worked for him previously had been runaways.

Megan's House may not have been perfect, but unlike the abandoned house I had shared with forty other runaways my first night in Kansas City, it had electricity, running water, heat in the winter, and air conditioning in the summer. We didn't serve fancy meals, but there was food in the kitchen for any who were hungry. The kids showed up with sleeping bags, but instead of laying them on the floors, they had cots to sleep on. A large screen stretched along a wall in a recreation room; it was surrounded by furniture and beanbags. We had a telephone the kids could use to call home.

We didn't offer counseling services, and we didn't judge. Everyone had a locker where their things were safe. Everyone had a drug test: if they passed, they could stay as long as they liked; if they failed, we sent them to a clinic. If they were looking for a job, they could use our address for job applications. If they wanted to get their GED, we did prep. classes every night from six to eight. We offered an anchor to kids who were blowing in the wind.

Before Megan's house, I never felt like I was part of a community. When businesses realized kids had a safe place to go, they offered to help. Before we opened our doors, a solar company installed panels on the roof at cost, so we cut our electric bill down to almost nothing. A home improvement store donated a bunch of dented appliances, three lawn mowers, four water hoses with car washing buckets and sponges, and ten snow shovels. It hadn't occurred to me at the time, but the owner of the store knew a safe place wasn't enough – he donated the tools for the kids to earn money during all four seasons, so they wouldn't turn to illegal avenues.

I watched kids come and go. Some stayed only a night or two; others stayed several weeks. I never knew how much of an impact Megan's house might have, but I liked to believe that I could save at least one kid. It seemed like my every waking minute was spent at Megan's House.

I talked to Libby a couple times per week on the phone, but things had never picked up where we had left them before Johnny died. Because I hated to leave the kids alone, Davey made far more trips to see me than I did him. He never said anything, but I guessed he knew Libby and I were in an awkward place, so he never pressed me to come up to Lincoln to see him. He tried to come down every other weekend.

A few weeks after Megan's House opened, a girl came in. Her eyes were huge, like she hadn't eaten a solid meal in weeks. I pointed her toward the kitchen. We weren't known for fine dining, but one whole pantry was filled with big jars of peanut butter and jelly. If anyone was hungry, there was always a sandwich for them in the kitchen no matter the time of day.

She didn't tell me her name. When the others tried to talk to her, she shied away from all of them. She sat at the table gingerly eating a sandwich. After her second one, she reached into her backpack and pulled out a sketchpad. I didn't think anything of it, but after twenty minutes she walked over to where I sat surrounded by kids telling me about their day.

She set her sketch face down in front of me and made her way back out the front door. I turned the paper over to find that it was a sketch of me wearing a long flowing robe with a halo over my head. The words "thank you" in elegant script were on the bottom of the page. I was nobody's angel – sure I gave out more peanut butter than JIF, but that didn't qualify me as an angel. The picture clouded my eyes – I knew I had made a difference, and beyond that I was making a difference every day.

I believed in Karma. I was sure my last life had been full of poor decisions. For all I knew, I probably had been a heinous serial murderer, because no matter what I touched before Megan's House always seemed to turn to shit. Finding Davey had been my first glimmer of hope my whole life. The fact that Karma had somehow decided to give me a second shot at life that day with Xavier wasn't lost on me. I wanted out, and, somehow, all the stars had aligned to make it possible. I tried to make up for any bad things I had done by making things better for a small community of kids without hope.

I left the sketch she had drawn on the table and bolted after her. The girl was halfway down the steps to the sidewalk when I caught up to her. "Hey, wait. You don't have to go. There are some cots inside. The girls have a whole floor to themselves. You'll be safe here."

She glanced over her shoulder toward the building, but shook her head.

"I liked your drawing. Can you paint?"

The girl cocked her head to the side considering my question. I clarified. "I've got a wall I've wanted a mural on since we opened this place. I've been waiting to find the right person to paint it. I'll buy the paint; I'll even pay you to do it."

Her voice was quiet – a little meek. "What kind of mural?"

I described to her the mural Libby told me about from her childhood. I don't know why I wanted to see it, but I had thought about it every day since she told me about it. The girl's name was Monica. She set to work that same day. Lots of other kids wanted to get involved. When it was done, the wall was more valuable to me than a Picasso would have been. It was exactly as Libby had described and I had imagined.

CHAPTER 32

A gruff-looking man wearing a red flannel shirt, faded blue jeans and cowboy boots stood at the door of my house. This was Billy, the private investigator I had hired to search for my little sister. He had called me earlier this morning to tell me he had information to deliver in person. This was the first time we had met in person – his contact information had been in Oscar's old paper rolodex. His gruff voice was all business, "Well, first, your daddy's name isn't Mike. That's what took so long. His name is Sebastian Brewer. He grew up in Omaha, son of Ray and Regina Brewer who still reside in Omaha."

I was getting tunnel vision. I asked this guy to find a sister; instead he found my father and grandparents. None of these three had been what I asked for. He continued, "I spoke to both Ray and Regina. Neither were aware Sebastian, or Mike as he likes to be called, fathered two sons. They requested DNA proof that you were indeed their family."

The private detective produced a cotton swab in a tube. "They have offered to pay for the test; if you choose to take the test, they are willing to contact me after the results prove positive."

"What the hell? I'm not looking to reconnect with them. I'm looking for a sister. Did you find anything on her?"

"Just her age. She's sixteen. There is no record of her in the Omaha school system, so without their cooperation I'm not optimistic. Look, I'm not going to tell you what to do, but I've hit a brick wall. Here is their address." He produced a written report and pointed at the third paragraph where Ray and Regina Brewer's address was listed. "If you want to find your sister, you are going to have to go through them."

A soft knock sounded at my door. I wasn't expecting anyone: I stood up and excused myself from Billy. The blue eyes and blonde hair standing at my front door stopped me short. "What are you doing here?"

"I was in the neighborhood."

Last night we had spoken on the phone. Libby said she wanted to plan a trip to Kansas City. She was still warming up to the idea of the two of us trying to reconnect. I hadn't pushed her for a date, and I certainly didn't expect for her to hop in her car this morning, either. "Really?"

"Can I come in?"

My hand holding the door open trembled. I hadn't seen her in four months. My memory hadn't done her justice. Libby stood in a pair of short jean shorts, leather sandals and this flowy white top. I swung the door open so she could pass. "Just give me a minute." I walked in to where Billy waited, grabbed the plastic tube and swiped the inside of my mouth with the swab, then sealed it back in the tube. "Send it off."

Billy tipped his head in a silent hello to Libby. "I'll be going. We should hear from the lab within two weeks." Billy let himself out. Libby took in the house, but didn't say much. She had spent the day with me in my apartment which had been meticulously decorated; most of this house was tan with contractor's off-white carpeting. It didn't have the "wow" factor, but I had put most of that behind me. Her gaze settled on the wooden coffee table covered with carved daisies.

Libby walked over to it, as her fingers smoothed over the hand carved flowers.

She looked up at me, "Is this new?"

"Yeah, a friend made it." Her stare disarmed me. Without intending to, I confessed, "It sort of reminded me of you."

Libby got a devilish smirk, and I knew I had said too much. Instead of giving me a hard time, she gushed, "It's beautiful." Her fingers continued to trace the flowers as she took another look around my living room. "It fits in here." I wasn't sure what Libby was trying to imply. Maybe that it wouldn't have fit well in my old apartment? Or did her words mean something more? That she fit in here? I was reading too much into it.

She stood up and said, "So, I was hoping to get a tour of Megan's House while I'm in town."

"Sure. I haven't been over there since last night. I'm due to go back. If I'm gone too long, they start swinging from the chandeliers. We could go now, then maybe catch a movie downtown."

The drive over was nice. Libby wore a new fragrance; different from the one she'd worn before. This one had more of a floral scent. I wanted to mention it, but felt strange. She had put the brakes on "us," and this was her first effort to see me since. I didn't want to say something stupid and have her drive away.

We pulled into my parking spot. Right after Megan's house opened, Libby asked me who Megan was. I'd told her the whole story, even the part about setting her murderer up on a drug charge and making sure he was safely tucked away in the penitentiary. As we climbed the steps to the front door, she asked, "Did you ever try to find out what Megan's last name was?"

"No. That was seven years ago."

She stood in front of the building. "I bet her family would like to know. If she made that big of an impact on you – someone misses her. They'd want to know that it's because of her that so many lost kids have a safe place to stay."

"I never really thought about it. Yeah, you're right. That Billy who was at the house when you showed up is the private investigator I hired to try to find our sister. If he finds her, maybe I'll see if he can find Megan's family. Whoever her family is, they should know what happened to her."

"Did he find your sister?"

"Sort of. She's a minor. It doesn't sound like she lives with our dad. Billy thinks our grandparents have custody. They wanted a DNA test before they'd even talk to me."

"That doesn't sound very grandparently." I opened the front door, and as expected, about thirty teenagers were piled around a big screen television. Some were on sofas, others were stretched out on the floor. Empty microwave popcorn wrappers lay on the floor.

Ignoring the kids and their inability to use a trashcan that was four feet away, I said, "I know. No one in my family has fit the mold so far, not sure why I would have expected anything different. How long are you down for?"

Libby didn't answer. I turned my attention away from the empty popcorn wrappers strewn on the floor, ignoring the impulse to pick them up, and saw Libby standing with her mouth open, staring at the mural Monica had painted. She said nothing, as if the mural pulled her toward it with an invisible rope.

Libby's fingers traced the lines of the oak tree, her eyes watering by the time they were at the tire swing, and tears slid down her face as her fingers rolled over the daisies. She said nothing, and with the tears now streaming, I was sure I had screwed up, big time. "I'm sorry. I forgot. Shit, Libby. The way you described it, I wanted these kids to have the same happy image when they came here. I didn't think what it would do to you to see it. Here," I tried to pull her away from the wall and back toward the front door, "let's go."

Both her hands were on the mural now. I felt like a complete jackass. This was something she had shared with me, not the whole world.

Libby let go of the wall and grabbed hold of me hard. Her voice squeezed all of her emotion into just two words, "It's beautiful."

I didn't know what to think. Was she pissed or happy? She said it was beautiful, so she liked it. This was a memory she had shared with me the day she told me she didn't want to see me again. I had taken that memory and had it painted on the wall for everyone to see.

I'd always been insensitive, a little obtuse, but I had never purposely hurt someone. The hurt in her eyes stripped me raw. I wanted to crawl into the sewer and make a home with the other rats.

The kids in the rec room had never seen Libby before, but a woman standing in the main lobby crying had them glued to our every word. I motioned for the kids to turn back around and give us whatever privacy the room offered. For the most part they did, all except Monica.

Monica had stayed for two full weeks. I didn't know her story, and it was just my luck, in this moment when I had totally screwed up what little chance I had with Libby, now would be the time Monica found something to say. Monica's raven-colored hair had hung stringy over her shoulders when she first came. She looked healthier; hair was always the first sign when a kid was bouncing back.

I motioned for Monica to go back where the other kids were, but she kept inching forward. Libby's hands were bunched around the material of my shirt, tears still flowing, not a peep out of her. Monica was only a few feet away, her eyes fixed on the floor and her shoulders slumped. I had nearly forgotten how quiet Monica's voice was – only having heard her speak a few times. Her eyes rose to Libby, "You don't like it?"

Libby's grip loosened, but she didn't let go, still anchored to my shirt. She drew her face back to look at Monica – Libby looked horrible. The skin around her eyes a blotchy red, eyeliner streaked from the tears, her voice gone. She answered Monica with a shake of her head.

Monica began to tear up, too, and I had no idea what to do. I knew Monica would bolt; that was her way of dealing with everything. I couldn't have her back on the street, not after she was finally beginning to come around. I pulled Libby to my chest and spoke to Monica, "It's beautiful. It's my favorite painting in the world. You know that. Can you take a seat with the other kids?" Monica's eyes met mine as if she were looking for a hint of deceit in my words – she didn't find any.

Monica ran her fingers through her hair and took a look at her masterpiece just a few feet away. "It needs rabbits." She pointed to the corner of the mural, "And over there, a slide would be nice." Libby didn't attempt to push away from me; she gripped me harder at Monica's suggestion. "He wanted me to paint this because he said this was a scene in his head he couldn't get out. I'm sorry you don't like it, but Mark stares at it all the time. It makes him happy."

Libby turned her head toward Monica, taking the girl in. She still didn't say a word to Monica. Monica looked back at the wall. "Can I show you something?"

Libby let go of me and nodded to Monica. Monica took Libby's hand and led her to the tree trunk. "Look at the highlights on the bark, only the highlights. Do you see it?"

I squinted as Libby's fingers traced the marks on the bark of the enormous oak. I had stared at the painting hundreds of times, consumed by the beauty, but I, too, was trying to see what Monica had put there. When I did, the message could have been a neon sign. In the bark that had been so seamlessly painted was a portrait within the rest of the mural. Monica had given me a gift I had never seen until she pointed it out. The words, "You are safe here" were camouflaged into the rest of the painting.

Libby answered Monica, her voice low, "I love it. It's beautiful. You are very talented."

Monica looked confused. "If you like it, why does it look like you hate it?"

Libby looked back at me when she answered, "That painting you made was the childhood I'd always hoped for. Seeing it on the wall took me by surprise. That's all."

Monica's sheepish smile faded, "If I've learned anything, it's that no one had the childhood they wanted. No one. Thanks to Mark, I'm not defined by the baggage I brought with me. He got me a job doing caricatures at a boutique in the park." She pointed toward the kids pretending to be focused on the television. "Allen got a job at the hardware store down the street. Misty's patched up stuff with her mom and is going home tonight on the bus."

Libby looked confused. Monica studied the wall, "I don't think this is a childhood you lost. I think this is our future: a bright sunny day, where clouds don't dump rain, and we can walk in a field of daisies."

Libby's hand slid to mine, and she gave it a gentle squeeze. Monica returned to the group of kids after sharing her profound words. I could still see hurt in Libby's eyes. Libby sniffed, and wiped the tears away, "So, let's say I really like it. I like the painting so much that I would like to see it every day. Got any job openings around here?"

My heart did a mini-flip in my chest. Was she kidding? "What kind of skills do you have? I was looking at adding a cooking class on Saturday nights. I could offer you a room full of kids who won't follow directions, three to four hours of prime date-night time down the drain, and as for the salary, a big fat nothing.

How's that sound?"

"Would you be here?"

Leaning forward, I confessed, "I'd be the one in the front row, burning the water."

"I'm in." Libby's eyes slowly closed as her lips found mine. It wasn't the promise of forever, or a sappy confession of love, but the door was finally open for more. My life was nothing like it had been when we had tested the waters four months ago and failed, but I wasn't that Mark anymore. She kept telling me she wanted to meet the real Mark. At the time I was worried if she peeled any of my layers back, she would learn there was nothing underneath – that I was a hollow person.

Having peeled my own layers back, I learned that there was something underneath. I wasn't perfect, but I was becoming more whole with every day that passed. I was sure Libby was still out of my league, but if she were willing to give me one more turn at bat, I wanted to take that swing.

NOTE FROM NANCY:

I hope you enjoyed *Fractured Karma*! This is the second book in my Brewer Brothers Series. The third book is *Shroud of Lies*. You met Dave in *His Frozen Heart* and Mark in *Fractured Karma*, the final book will unveil the *Shroud of Lies* that have been their lives up until this point.

I am an independent author, which means I do not have an agent, a publicist, or a publishing company backing me up. I DEPEND on word-of-mouth advertising. If you enjoyed *Fractured Karma*, it would mean the world to me for you to recommend it to a friend (or ten friends!).

Independent Authors live and die by reviews from readers. Before I became an author, I believed reviews were only written by professionals. I did not know that my opinion mattered. If you are in this category, PLEASE know that your opinion does matter!! If you could take a few minutes and write a review of Fractured Karma and post it to Amazon, I would be very grateful!! It doesn't have to be long, just a few words to tell others what you thought of it.

If you enjoyed my writing, I would love for you to check out my other books. If you enjoy Greek Mythology, my Touched Series is a modern take on the old fables. This series consists of four books; *Blood Debt* is the first and it is a free ebook. If you ever believed that certain people are supposed to be in your life and you have lived several lifetimes with them, my Destiny Series may be for you. *Meeting Destiny* is the first book in a three book series and is also available as a free ebook.

All of my books are available in print and audio.

Finally, if you would like to chat with me, here are the best places to find me:

My Author Page on Facebook:
https://facebook.com/NancyStraight.Author

My blog: http://www.NancyStraight.com

Twitter: https://twitter.com/NancyStraight

Goodreads: https://goodreads.com/NancyStraight

Email: NancyStraight@gmail.com

I read and respond to every message I receive. (Sometimes a day or two late, but I do respond to everyone who reaches out to me).
I hope to hear from you!

Happy Reading,
Nancy

www.ingramcontent.com/pod-product-compliance
Lightning Source LLC
Chambersburg PA
CBHW070639310726
48982CB00001B/339

* 9 7 8 0 6 9 2 6 6 0 7 7 5 *